CW00672131

# Brilliance of Hope

First published in Great Britain in 2021 by:

Carnelian Heart Publishing Ltd
Suite A
82 James Carter Road
Mildenhall
Suffolk
IP28 7DE
UK

www.carnelianheartpublishing.co.uk



Paperback ISBN 978-1-914287-07-7
Ebook ISBN 978-1-914287-09-1



Compiler and Editor:
Samantha Rumbidzai Vazhure

Assistant Editor:
Innocent Whande

Cover design & layout:
Carnelian Heart Publishing and Rebecca Covers

Internal design:
Typeset by Carnelian Heart Publishing Ltd
Layout and formatting by DanTs Media

**Acknowledgments**

I would like to express my heartfelt gratitude to the authors who contributed to this anthology. I believe each one of them is talented in a unique and extraordinary way.

To:

Tah
Rudo D M Manyere
Sibonginkosi Christabel Netha
Samuel Chamboko
Priscilla Nyahwa-Shumba
Tariro Ndoro
Brain Garusa
Tinashe Junias Chipenyu
Ivainashe Earnest Nyamutsamba
A K Mwanyekondo
James Wanangwa Kajumi Kuwali
Nobuhle N Nyoni
Flavian Farainashe Makovere
Lazarus Panashe Ivan Nyagwambo

Thank you for sharing my values, believing in my vision and entrusting your precious art to me.

I would also like to thank:

Innocent Whande who beta-read, proofread and helped to draft an overview of the short stories.

Daniel Mutendi of DanTs Media for the interior design of the book.

Rebecca covers for the beautiful cover design.

“Hope is the thing with feathers
That perches in the soul
And sings the tune without the words
And never stops - at all”

Emily Dickinson

## Editors' note

### *Introduction*

As part of my advocacy for the welfare of immigrants, I compiled and edited this anthology of short stories to provide a platform where a crucial element of Zimbabwean history could be recorded. This is also an opportunity for the contributors to amplify their voices globally.

This project, named "Diamond", is inspired by a gemstone known for its resilience under pressure, and its brilliance based on its ability to reflect light. When light enters a diamond, it is refracted by the diamond's internal angles, causing the sparkle diamonds are known for. This sparkle represents hope. When two or more diamonds are placed together, a superposition called entanglement, they vibrate at a low frequency only detectable by laser. Spiritually, a diamond represents clarity, promise and possibility. These characteristics of a diamond have been used as puns to name this anthology, **BRILLIANCE OF HOPE: Reflections, Refractions and Vibrations of the Zimbabwean dispersion.**

With contributing writers based in Australia, Dubai, South Africa, United Kingdom, United States and Zimbabwe, the fictional and autobiographical stories herein collectively reflect light on perspectives of the resilience and hope intrinsic to the Zimbabwean dispersion. I find it fascinating that the voices in this anthology not only complement one another, but they seem to complete each other's stories, with one picking up from where the other left, thereby magnifying the concept of universal oneness. In African philosophy, this is referred to as UBUNTU – I am, because you are. Together, the contributors are entangled in a common quandary and are vibrating the particulars of what it means to be displaced as first generation immigrants.

I am excited that I contributed to this anthology. For this reason, I asked Innocent Whande to assist me with proofreading and drafting an overview of each narrative. Innocent not only holds a master's degree in Creative Writing & Publishing, but he is a Zimbabwean based in the United Kingdom and has, like the contributing writers, experienced first-hand the joys and sorrows of being an immigrant. I am honoured and eternally grateful that he agreed to support me on this project.

Enjoy the book!

**by Samantha Rumbidzai Vazhure**

*An overview of the stories*

## Tah

**Elusive Dignity,** a well-written account that paints an authentic picture of the journey into the diaspora. Simba's experience shines light on the xenophobia and racism that Zimbabweans and other immigrants from across Africa face in South Africa. The young man is fortunate to have a friend, TC, who sets him up with a job as a waiter at the restaurant he works for. Simba holds his tongue even when subjected to abuse from colleagues and customers alike, because he has no papers. In true Zimbabwean spirit, he stays resilient and keeps his head down. His friendship with TC is the glue that holds them together through the trials and tribulations of being a foreigner in South Africa.

**Finding Her Voice** chronicles an enlightening perspective on the concerns of women in South Africa. The story starts off with a radio interview transcript before getting into the backstory of Mandy who faces a barrage of comments from drivers of the lift service she uses to commute. Upon telling her brother of her ordeal, she sets out to do a short animation, calling out men on their entitlement, and it goes viral on social media. The complicity of other women who enable harassment and normalise the gross behaviour of men is highlighted in Shannon, Mandy's cousin. A glimmer of hope through the harassment is Simbarashe, the only driver Mandy recalls treating her with dignity whenever she got a lift from him.

**Dawn** tells a heart-warming and inspiring story. Simba meets Mandy by chance at a park. They find familiarity through the struggles of being foreigners in South Africa. Mandy finds a sympathetic ear in Simba who validates her worries that she indeed was harassed and isn't overreacting.
After the writer takes you through the life of Simba seamlessly in Elusive Dignity, to Mandy's story in Finding her voice, he ends with the two characters connecting in Dawn. This is a tale about friendship, which promises to blossom into deeper intimacy.

## Rudo D M Manyere

**Kurauone** is an enthralling tale of unrequited love and a wasted life. Kurauone and Susu are former lovers reunited by the death of Kola, after many years of separation. Kola is Susu's brother and Kura's best friend. The captivating imagery of their reunion hooks the reader in, to the very last word. How fleeting time really is. Sparks of their love still linger and their bond is further moulded by the grief they are experiencing for the departed Kola. Will they pick up from where they left?

**3:15 AM,** a chilling story laced with several important life lessons - you do not need to compete with anyone in life, and you are enough as you are. A rivalry between cousins shows how much comparison can steal your joy and cultivate jealousy and resentment in families. A manifestation of guilt from an accident that led to her cousin's death makes the narrator experience her late cousin's ghost. A stern reminder that there is no escaping the past.

**Zadzisai** is a well-presented narrative of a desperate mother on a mission to be reunited with her daughter. It is the introduction to an upcoming novel, where a child pregnancy and family politics force Zadzisai's parents to give their daughter's new-born child up for adoption in fear of bringing shame on their family. The full story promises to be a page turner and a must-not-miss.

## Sibonginkosi Christabel Netha

**The Sky,** a beautifully crafted story about a romantic navigating young adulthood in the mean streets of Johannesburg. While going through mundane tasks in the butchery managed by his uncle, Bongani runs after a thief who has stolen a wallet. When he catches up with the thief, he has already been seized and is being beaten up. As Bongani retreats, he bumps into a familiar face. The scenes are vividly painted in a soothing poetic tone, keeping you hooked from the first to the last word, whilst highlighting pertinent problems that many immigrants will relate to.

**Finding Luba** tells a great story layered with societal issues and the effects of intergenerational family trauma. Maria's quest is to find her sister who ran away from home and to see her family reunited. After talking to her mother, she uncovers a dark family secret, one that once let out cannot be put back into the box. Her path leads to her father who had long abandoned his family for South Africa after finding out the truth.

**The Mouth of the Shark,** a heart-wrenching story uniquely written from the perspective of a child who moves to South Africa with her mother and brother, with her whole life in a backpack. Her mother works tirelessly to make ends meet. The young girl feels out of place at her new school, but makes friends who she can relate with and this ameliorates her anxiety. The theme of identity crisis is well explored in this forlorn piece that chronicles the fact that children too leave Zimbabwe with as much hope as the adults, only to find that the pastures are not necessarily greener; what the author portrays as an unappeasable hunger which is not for food.

## Samuel Chamboko

**Journey From Without**, a fantastic coming of age novelette that oozes the naivety of youth, layered with pertinent issues affecting Zimbabweans who leave for the diaspora. Three friends embark on a journey to South Africa with just the clothes on their backs and very little money, relying on the kindness of strangers on their journey to a better life. The writing style is very transportive and the scenery well captured through many lively characters and vivid descriptions of Karanga customs. The trials and tribulations of living in a foreign land are accurately illuminated, including the stern realisation that the grass is only ever greener after back breaking work.

**Mabvuku to Marylebone** is a captivating story of a young man who moves to the UK to help provide for his siblings and aging grandmother. He is taken advantage of by the relatives that help him to relocate before deciding to venture on his own. He juggles studying and work, because he must send money back home in compliance with black tax. A perfect illustration that burdens often shouldered by older siblings mean they end up living for others. This story showcases true Zimbabwean resolve - resilience and grit.

## Priscilla Shumba

**What Do They See?** is an excellent narrative about an immigrant coming to terms with and owning their piece of society. The story highlights how blacks typically blend into the background to avoid causing discomfort to others. The anecdote examines how black people often get seen for being black before being seen for who they are. This social reconnoitre explores the leitmotifs of representation and empowerment to occupy spaces without shying away. The intersectionality of being a black, African, Christian, feminist, mother is beautifully underlined in this piece.

**There's Nothing for You Here** is a heart-wrenching account depicting the loneliness and identity crisis often experienced by many immigrants living alone. Being homesick, but never being able to go back because there is nothing to go back to. Being misunderstood and feeling out of place in a foreign land. The story offers an insight into trials that come with displacement, such as untimely deportation of loved ones and the complexity of cross-border family relationships. Allusion and beautiful imagery run throughout the narrative, which ends on a hopeful note.

**We Were All Broken** aptly explores the inevitable break-up of families due to dispersion. The story is told through the perspectives of a father, mother and daughter in very touching internal monologues, highlighting what the family has lost through miscommunication. A declining economy back home and toxic masculinity within a patriarchal society all contribute to the tension which eventually results in the demise of a family unit.

## Tariro Ndoro

**Stasis**, a brilliant narrative depicting the plight of foreign black women in a dystopian future South Africa. Chiedza valiantly faces the trials of adulthood - feeling under pressure to progress swiftly, comply with black tax whilst putting on a brave face. Racism, sexism and harassment in the workplace are amongst her tribulations. The imagery and humour employed by the author make the distressing themes in the story more palatable. Chiedza's enlightenment at the end of the story is a breath of fresh air.

**La Duma 32/12**, a well presented allegory exploring the dissonance resulting from the quandary of living in South Africa as a foreigner. The death of a friend exacerbates the narrator's numbness - everything happening around her makes her feel conflicted about where she belongs. The piece is presented in unique form, like a dictionary in draft format, attempting to define what dissonance is for a Zimbabwean living in South Africa. Multiple "voices" are at play - the events on the ground, news headlines, social media posts, the author's own views - all are duly considered, to deliver a clear message - South Africa is an unsafe place to live. It ends with quite a miserable choice to have to make for the narrator – to stay in South Africa and risk death, or to go back to Zimbabwe and risk poverty.

**Abishai** tells an ingenious, perceptible tale of an expectant family whose father figure leaves the country for better opportunities, only for the deadbeat man to get lured into a long-term extramarital affair and return home with nothing but the clothes on his back. Not everyone is strong or committed enough to fulfil the purpose of dispersion, and we see that in Abishai when he sinks to the lowest depths. The man cannot even remember the name of his own daughter when he returns. We witness a stoic mother's fight for survival for her children through tough times. The story is expertly narrated and seasoned with just the right amount of humour to lighten the heavy subject matter addressed.

## Brain Garusa

**Kufakunesu**, a reflective tale confronting death and poverty in the declining Zimbabwean economy. An escape to a foreign land which is mishandled, leads to the untimely death of a young man with potential. Repetition is temperately employed as a rhetorical device to deepen the meaning of the message, increase memorability and enhance the rhythm of the narrative. The use of imagery and metaphors in this story will have you thinking, "what's in a name?" Was the name Kufakunesu (death is with us) just the narrator's excuse to live recklessly so that he could fulfil the prophecy he thought was embedded in his name? The freedom of being away from home results in a tragic end to the story.

**When Mother Cries**, a harrowing story of a grieving son who loses their mother to a gruesome ordeal. Being left with no one to rely on, he finds comfort in conversations with his late mother in dreams. The use of letters written from the mother's perspective and his replies are an excellent coping mechanism. A deep, sad and relatable story which not only confronts death, but manages to layer problematic societal issues aggravated by the dispersion.

### Tinashe Junias Chipenyu

**Restless Stalker** tells a delightfully complex tale, layered with pertinent issues affecting immigrants. The thriller-like opening to the story is gripping and vivid descriptions are used throughout the story. The themes of black tax and its challenges, the shame of failure to provide sustenance for your family back home, inertia and depression, amongst others, are creatively weaved into this narrative. The evolution of the main character, Munacho, is explored and his epiphany at the end is something many Africans are coming to terms with slowly, as they begin to realise that they may never return home.

**The Throes**, a heartrending account of Kudakwashe, a young soul who seems to be paying for her parents' mistakes. A well-presented example of what might happen when parents leave their children for better opportunities in the diaspora but fail to maintain an emotional connection with them. It is a story of abandonment – a child grows up with no one to turn to, struggles with mental health issues and ends up a victim of abuse.

**Different Shades of Brown**, a well presented chronicle merging the lives of three Zimbabwean women from completely different walks of life and the struggles they are facing in South Africa. We meet Laurah whose husband left her for a local South African woman and faces a tumultuous passage to picking herself up. Musawenkosi faces losing her job if her VISA is not renewed and she suffers various forms of discrimination at work. Anesu is an overworked, underpaid hairdresser. The three women eventually meet in a church led by a pastor with a dark side. The pockets of humour make this story an easy, enjoyable read.

### Ivainashe Earnest Nyamutsamba

**An Ode To My Aching Heart**, a heart-breaking story of a Zimbabwean woman who has resorted to selling her body to make ends meet in South Africa. She is taken in by a den mother who on the surface seems to care for her, but is only using her as an object to satisfy men. She gets infected with HIV while trying to make ends meet. A tragic end to a story of hope, delivered in an inimitable poetic style of writing.

**Yours Truly I Am Gone**, a touching account of some of the most bizarre stories we hear coming out of the diaspora. The abuse of men, hardships of staying with relatives that make you feel unwelcome, are some of the themes explored in this quirkily-written narrative. This story is a harrowing emotional thriller presented in an amalgam of soliloquies and turbulent streams of consciousness – the author's way of providing a more intimate portrayal of his subjects.

**A Passage Through the Tumultuous, Boisterous Sea** is autobiographical and heart wrenching – a story that many immigrants who have studied abroad will relate to. The narrative illuminates the mind of a student working on his future in a foreign land. The pressure of studying whilst destitute highlights the harsh reality that no one is coming to your rescue and only you can save yourself. The author invites you to take a peek inside his mind through employment of abstract internal monologue.

### A K Mwanyekondo

**The Interview** is a riveting, fast-paced read in dialogue format. The author's playfulness with form adds a layer of complexity to this story, for instance employing dashes in place of inverted commas to signal discourse between the characters – a style we witness throughout his stories in this anthology. Musa is a Zimbabwean doing well in Rwanda, to the frustration of his gateman Jon Paolo – a local who is shamed by his friends for being a foreigner's glorified door opener. Musa's life at home is strained, but the estrangement of his wife remains a mystery to him. Could the tragic end of this story be the missing piece to his puzzle?

**These Were the Voices** presents an abstract, heavily layered, multidimensional story about resilience and hope. Beautifully crafted poetic prose, laced with patterns through rhythm, imagery and metaphors throughout. Grace in part (i) is an illegal immigrant who endures a hellish job at a publishing house in Rwanda. Anesu Mufakose in part (ii), another illegal who left Zimbabwe due to push factors including the declining economy, political upheaval and drought, against his mother's wishes, only to find himself living in squalor in a home that feels like a coffin. He is overworked in a restaurant where he feels secluded. Holy, Grace's father whom we only meet once in part (iii) is a man who performed atrocities on his own daughter in the name of religion – deeds that shed some light on Grace's mental state. In the end, two of the characters, eking out a survival in a foreign land, are united (perhaps by fate) in a bizarre grand finale which one could only hope leads them to inner peace.

**Untitled,** a heart-shredding story that explores the life of a mixed-race woman torn apart by trauma - a trauma that doesn't have a name, but continues to crush her to a point where she is confronted by homelessness. There are many nameless things Martha has to endure, but with very little success, including being abandoned by her parents and everyone she is fond of. The plight of being foreign, feeling like she does not belong, not being accepted by her own (white) mother, suffering in silence and sticking to being a wallflower to avoid causing trouble. The themes of identity crisis, death, spirituality, loveless interracial relationships and hope, amongst others, are explored in a relatable plot. The author skilfully brings the diaspora back to Zimbabwe through Martha and weaves in some pertinent issues affecting Zimbabweans - the declining economy, corruption, to name but a few.

**James Wanangwa Kajumi Kuwali**

**The Republican** gives a mesmeric glimpse into the life experience of a black man in an upper class milieu - feeling out of place and treated like an outsider even when fully qualified to be there. The language employed is as opulent as the characters, with great use of poetic prose in some parts, quirkily laced with alliteration and assonance. Best of all, the wit throughout tones down the seriousness of the conflicts within this story. The themes of racism, unconscious biases, direct and indirect discrimination, the yearning to return home, are appositely explored by the author.

**Leaving Las Vegas** tells the story of a young government aide travelling abroad with the country's leadership. An unplanned detour amidst the frenetic pace of international diplomacy presents a moment of reckoning with demons, both personal and national. Humour and rich language build suspense towards a 'searing' end in this well thought out narrative.

**Nobuhle N Nyoni**

**Just Ask for Help!** is a touching autobiography detailing the relocation from Zimbabwe to South Africa to make a life for oneself. The trials that come with trying to do things alone, how a helping hand can spur you on and change your life for the better, are some of the messages in this story. It is harder to ask for help when you are away from home, for so many reasons – but mostly the fear of being mocked and judged. Because everyone seems to be competing against one another, people in the diaspora live in isolation a lot more than they do back home. A good read which carries important life lessons that many will relate to.

**What It Means to Be a Foreigner in South Africa** journals the hardships the author faces as a foreigner in South Africa. From the meagre pay to xenophobia, wishing she could go back home, but remaining in the dire situation across the border - because only suffering and heartache await in Zimbabwe. This is an authentically delivered account that paints a picture of what life is like for a lot of Zimbabweans in South Africa - distressing.

**It's Not Always the Final Destination** inspires learning the importance of being yourself and not living according to other people's standards. Showing yourself the love and attention you truly deserve ultimately starts with you. This is a great essay detailing how healing from childhood trauma can emancipate you mentally, emotionally, spiritually and financially. It is a piece that will hopefully help some readers to find it within themselves to seek that sort of freedom in different areas of their lives. Acknowledging one's troubled past is one thing that needs confronting in order for any progress to manifest for anybody who comes from a traumatised place.

### Flavian Farainashe Makovere

**Power** is an intriguing and thrilling story about a political asylum seeker. Pastor Mavhura, a former soldier in the liberation struggle is now seen as an enemy of the state because he is calling out their shortcomings. It gets him abducted and tortured to spill information on who is sponsoring his agenda. The collocation of dislocation to Mozambique during pre-colonial Zimbabwe vis-a-vis running away to South Africa in post-colonial Zimbabwe is an exceptional detail within a story where the intrinsic connection between politics and religion is well presented.

**Painted Feelings,** a beautifully written love story layered with relatable issues affecting Zimbabweans and other nationalities living in the diaspora. It highlights an evolution of Africans breaking through generational barriers - the use of therapy, for instance, is not usually considered worthwhile back home. Exploration of the Gukurahundi genocide is necessary and intriguing - an issue that continues to divide Zimbabweans. A shocking revelation presents a conflict that might make or break a young couple's relationship as they edge closer to their wedding.

**My Father's Shoes** explores in multiple layers the burdens of following in your parents' footsteps. The unfortunate dance with depression brings out superstitious views of bad spirits and their consequential power. This is a poetically presented tale of intergenerational trauma common in African families. The reluctance to address mental health issues, the habitual passing on of blame to things beyond our control. The imagery is exceptional and the story will resonate with many immigrants.

### Lazarus Panashe Ivan Nyagwambo

**Vessel for Misery** narrates a story about resilience. False promises of a scholarship lead to a life of hardship in Cyprus for Luke where he engages in back-breaking work for inadequate pay. The vivid imagery and detailed descriptions employed by the author allow the reader to travel with Luke through a rough day at and after work, and his thought processes in between. Many themes are fittingly explored – harassment at work, sexual assault of men, the economic crisis in Zimbabwe. In this heavy and overwhelming story, an "attack" ensues, but despite the trauma, Luke will get up tomorrow to face another day.

**This Game for Two** involves Prosper, a husband who goes abroad to search for greener pastures for his family, leaving his wife at the mercy of his mother and two sisters who feel entitled to his wealth. The turmoil of family politics as they rely on him as their breadwinner while disregarding his wife, is expressed through hilarious dialogue. The author addresses the serious themes of family separation resulting from the dispersion, the ever-suffocating tentacles of the patriarchy, with women being unkind to one another as a means to feed the system, amongst others. Emotions are tangible throughout, and a feasible shift at the end of this great story leaves the reader with a glimmer of hope.

**A Home Shaped Hole** is an autobiographical account exploring the reasons that might drive one to return home, having spent years abroad. Even after attaining a great education with employment opportunities on the horizon, the narrator opts to return home, because there is no place like it. This account, laced with humour in Zimbabwean expressions, is well-written and relatable. More importantly, the story could be viewed as a reminder to those struggling in the diaspora - that they could always go back home.

**Samantha Rumbidzai Vazhure**

**Barcode**, a captivating thriller highlighting the harsh truths of being an illegal immigrant in the UK. Living under his brother's roof, Kumbi is at the mercy of his demanding sister-in-law Benhilda who knit-picks at everything he does. A regular work trip leads to him spending time in a hell that is a detention centre where he experiences trauma while awaiting deportation. Upon arrival in Zimbabwe, he is met by an awkward greeting by his own children and wife. To make matters worse, his childhood best friend seems to have replaced him. Great use of imagery and vivid descriptions transport you to the scenes at hand.

**Tariro** is a wonderful piece of social commentary presented as a novelette. The urgency created by Tariro's dilemma invites the reader's curiosity to how it is resolved. Hardships and dilemmas alongside the themes of inequality, toxic religiosity, harassment and the bleakness of the patriarchal system, amongst others, are masterfully weaved into a well thought out narrative. The pacing of the story is aided by allocating each character a different day in the week, and through the resilience of Tariro as she takes each day as it comes. The diversity of characters seems to echo the message that we are living in a global village. Should we perhaps begin to feel at home wherever we are? This is a narrative which celebrates the brilliance of hope and aptly provides closure to this anthology.

***

As advocates for mental health we feel obliged to include a trigger warning for this anthology:

**Some stories in the collection contain themes of suicide, alcoholism & drug dependency, depression and abuse. If you are affected by the issues in these stories, please visit any of the following charity websites for help, or search in Google for similar charities local to your jurisdiction.**

Suicide - https://www.samaritans.org
Abuse, Anxiety, Bullying, Depression, Loneliness, Self-harm, suicide - https://giveusashout.org
Suicide and other mental health challenges - https://www.thecalmzone.net
Mental health issues - https://www.mind.org.uk

**By Innocent Whande and**
**Samantha Rumbidzai Vazhure**

# Table of Contents

## Tah

A curious, introverted husband and father born in Masvingo, Zimbabwe. Tah lived in Cape Town for 5 years but now lives in Harare, Zimbabwe. Writing was not a first love as he disliked everything literary, but it has become a passion and a conduit to share experiences, highlight, provoke thought, encourage discourse and hopefully connect audiences to a purposeful, fulfilling existence.

## Elusive dignity

I always believed and bragged that I would only travel outside my country for pleasure, and not for survival. Here I was though, about to board the cheapest bus from Harare to Cape Town to find work – any work I could find. Having abandoned my teaching career, I needed to find work urgently and pay back a local *mukorokoza,* the artisanal gold miner cum loan shark, the loan for my bus fare. I had to pay him back within three months or he would take my parents' livestock.

Motivated by the desire for more and better, I was not going to turn back and so I found my designated seat – sandwiched between a very loud man with a can of beer in hand and a woman with what I assumed to be a bag of cooked food judging by the aroma emanating from her direction. Just my luck! A prayer was offered by one of the passengers, more as tradition than conviction, and off we went.

I did not know much about South Africa except what I occasionally heard on the news and what the diasporans would narrate – mostly during Christmas when many of them came back home for the holidays. What stood out the most to me was the crime and xenophobia in their stories. Many from my community who had gone to find work in South Africa did menial jobs and that had always deflated the appeal of emigrating.

The diasporans and gold panners commanded the attention and awe of the young and the old alike. Such was the dire state of our community and nation in general, that professionals were reduced to poor peasants and those who had struck gold – both literally and figuratively, were like the *bourgeoisie.* Many underage girls in my community had become mothers while others were married off young to escape poverty. Education was no longer deemed essential and my accounting class of forty students had been reduced to ten. I did not blame them; at least not anymore, as I was headed for Egoli.

I had wondered if officially resigning was worth it, because the pension pay-outs were useless, but I figured there was nothing to lose, so I did. My parents had been retrenched from the mine they had worked for over twenty years, shortly after I had sat for A-Level examinations. The retrenchment forced my parents to expedite their retirement plan and move to the village home and rely on subsistence farming income and occasional livestock sales. The change in their fortunes and our nation's economic turmoil greatly affected my plans as well. With twelve points at A-level, I settled for a teaching qualification, planning to study further after raising some money. I berate myself for not thinking through all options and seeking out wider counsel.

My need for survival, and the burden of caring for my parents outweighed any fears of crime or the illegality of working without a valid visa. At least I had a passport, unlike many of my fellow passengers aboard the cheap bus. The corruption and bribery I witnessed at the Beitbridge border into South Africa was unbelievable. Earlier in my life, I would have judged it with disdain, but I was hopelessly desperate, and my moral fibre was tainted. I justified the means by the end I envisioned. I knew it was a dangerous road though because a violent armed robber, a drug lord or a sex offender could have justification for their choices.

The journey up to Johannesburg was long and sore, but it was just halfway to my destination. I wished I were disembarking in Johannesburg, but a former college roommate, colleague, and friend, who was my contact, was in Cape Town and that is where I was going. I did not really know anyone else. Several police officers asked for my identification on our Johannesburg lay over. I do not know if they were random or scheduled checks, but I was glad I had a valid passport. For others, fifty-rand notes became their passports to proceed. That was a lot of money, but a small price to pay for the prospect of economic sustenance I suppose. The aroma of deep-fried chicken that some passengers bought along the way was brutal, but a paltry diet of bananas had to sustain me. I had no idea what to expect on arrival, so I tried to keep a little extra money just in case.

Even though there was so much uncertainty in my novel travels, the lights and beautiful infrastructure of Mzansi offered some new hope and I dared to dream. At the same time, I was pained and filled with anger as to why a nation just next to us was doing so well when we were in such a deplorable state.

It was Sunday, the third day since leaving Harare, towards six o'clock in the morning; when a loud voice announced that the next stop was Belleville. That was my stop and my heart began to race. The winter rains steadily poured down as I got off the bus. Maybe, just maybe, the rains signified a new beginning. I found shelter and while I waited for my host to arrive, I took in everything going on around me. I heard different languages and observed different types of races and fashion flavours. I was indeed a long way away from home.

I was a bit shocked though, because I also observed people freely speaking on their cell phones and openly exchanging money. That was not what

I had pictured about Mzansi! I had my passport, money and my cell phone safely tucked in my socks to avoid being a victim of the much-publicised crime. I however, kept my wallet in my pocket with a ten rand and a twenty rand note. I had heard that criminals got violent if they did not find any valuables on a mark, so I kept the thirty rand for my would-be muggers. That was insanely messed up, but I needed to survive.

At around 7:30am I felt my phone vibrating against my ankle. Carefully, I took it, put it to my ear and covered it with my hoodie to avoid drawing attention to myself or my belongings. It was Tanaka Chuma, whom I referred to as TC. He told me to be alert as he was passing by in a taxi. I gathered my satchel and bag that had my possessions - toiletries, some clothes, a laptop, a journal, educational certificates, a Bible I had not read in a while - and I began to look out for TC.

"Simba! Simba! Simbarashe Shoko!" I could hear my name, but I could not see a taxi anywhere. TC called my phone again, "turn around, right across the road, I am waving at you."

I turned and saw a hand waving through the window of a commuter minibus. I ran across to avoid being rain soaked and boarded the minibus. "*Enkosi tata,*" (thank you “father”) said TC to the driver and off we went. I did not know if it was safe to talk or not, but I knew I did not want to be a victim of xenophobia, so I simply nodded and smiled. TC responded in kind. About five minutes later, TC spoke up again, "*ebus stop elandelayo.*" At that time, I could only make out ‘bus stop’, but later, I came to understand he had said “next bus stop”. A short while later, the vehicle stopped, and TC signalled for us to exit. He had paid for me already.

"I thought I heard you say taxi man."

"Yes," TC replied, "this is a taxi! Back home we call them Kombis, here, taxis."

"So, what are the typical meter taxis called?" I asked.

"Taxi still. Welcome to South Africa."

We shook hands, shared a two-second man hug, and exchanged pleasantries. I thought five rand was too much to pay for a taxi over a short distance, but I figured I was thinking like a Zimbabwean, in Zimbabwe, where five rand was not easy to come by.

TC looked good unlike many of us in Zimbabwe who had become scrawny. He had some dope sneakers on and very neat designer jeans. I wondered how much waiters earned to afford such luxuries. I was wearing a pair of tennis shoes and jeans that I had bought five years prior. Thankfully I had worn formal clothing to work, so my current clothes still had some life in them.

TC was working that day till after lunch. I could have used a warm bath and some sleep, but I had to wait for him in the mall before we could go to his home. What a magnificent mall it was! I was surprised that Sunday was business as usual, but not as shocked as I was about my blackness.

I know I am black, but I had never felt so black - surrounded by so many white people! I wondered if the few white people left in Zimbabwe felt so white among so many black people. From the time I was in preschool till grade six, the racial mix at my school was even. When I went to high school, the number of white classmates began to drop until they were countable. I was not sure if it had anything to do with the land redistribution program that had been implemented.

The mall was huge, and it had everything; I mean everything - a true one stop shop. I thought I had lived, but in that moment, I felt so small because I was exposed to a world I never knew. Back home, we would go to the city for business and groceries, but it still did not compare to this self-sufficient mall.

I was tired before I exhausted everything on display, so I found a men's lounge and sat there. With time, I learnt that the lounge was designed to cater for men while the ladies shopped. Heaven! I struggled to communicate with the security staff at some shops. They constituted the largest number of blacks in the mall. Unfortunately, they assumed I was Xhosa when I did not understand Xhosa at all. They therefore could not help me find a "parcel counter" to leave my satchel while I entered the stores.

It was later that TC informed me I could enter a store with my bag. We laughed at my *faux pas* and even though I knew there would be more, there was comfort in the anonymity that being in a new place afforded me. TC also informed me that the owner of the restaurant he worked for had opened a new branch and promoted him to be manager, to the displeasure of some of his colleagues. Some argued that the position needed an Afrikaans speaker, since they catered mostly to Afrikaans speakers, while others felt a South African should have been promoted. I was new to the dynamics of race and racism in South Africa, but I gathered TC's white colleagues were the former, while his black colleagues were the latter.

I was not sure I wanted to work in such an environment, but I was so certain of my priorities and motivations that when TC offered me a job as a waiter, I did not hesitate. I did not even know how much I would earn, but I was sure I could pay back the loan I took and would not be a burden to TC. The restaurant owner was around on that Sunday and I was introduced to him. When he asked when I would be starting work, TC said the following Monday.

TC lived about five kilometres from the mall, in a two-bedroom apartment. He occupied one bedroom, sharing the bathroom and kitchen, while a Congolese family of three, occupied the other spaces. That could not have been more uncomfortable for me because I grew up in a spacious four bedroom, two and half bathroom house on an acre of land; and my parents' village home had a three-bedroom house and two, two bedroom cottages.

TC's share of rent was enough to cover my Zimbabwean salary for three months! The landlords increased his rent by 30% to account for the extra head - my head - which he gladly paid. I never thought that at some point I would be a grown man needing another man to pay my bills.

TC had been in Cape Town for four years now and he had so many stories to tell. His first job involved picking oranges at a farm, then he did some construction work before taking advantage of the nearing 2010 soccer World Cup and moving to the hospitality sector. All the while he had lived in a wooden shack - the kind that used the bucket system as a bath and toilet. Whilst his accommodations had not been the best, his pocket was not so bad. Before I started work, TC helped me work out my potential earnings including tips and I drew up a working budget. I always thought it was lazy to want a tip for one's job - the arrogance of privilege and ignorance I guess - but here I was, a former private school student and qualified teacher, preparing to wait on tables.

The whole first week of my stay, TC acclimatised me to the lifestyle, cultural and racial dynamics of Cape Town. He bought me everything I needed in the new job, including a fake work visa just like the one he had. I struggled to accept all the generosity, but his argument was that I had done the same for him through college and that my family had accommodated and fed him for a whole year when we started teaching at the school in my village.

What followed was a week of training at my new workplace. I was 'as innocent as a dove but as wise as a serpent'. I kept my head down and did my job. I was not about to disrespect my friend or let my family down. Of course, there were a lot of embarrassing moments in training. I had never come across some of the foods on the menu; I dropped trays and broke crockery and glass.

One time a lady asked for the tab and I brought her bill, when she wanted the beverage Tab. I had a good laugh and so did she. Many asked me where I was from on account of my eloquence and manners and I wished they would offer me a job! Most times, it all ended with discussions about politics and how bad things were in Zimbabwe. Sadly, that was our reputation as a nation.

I did not know whether to be annoyed or amused by some who asked me if I knew John from Zimbabwe. Others asked, "Our maid, Rosemary, is from Zimbabwe. She has three kids there; do you know them?"

*Of course, I know every one of the thirteen million Zimbabweans!* The ignorance, both of clients and colleagues, was astounding - some of it arrogant, foolish, and demeaning. "Are there cars in Zimbabwe? Do you all live in mud huts?" I could not get over South African colleagues who thought they were better than me. With all their national wealth, I wondered why they were content with being waiters.

While I worked, I got to learn of the experiences of some Zimbabweans there. One guy narrated how his cousin had ghosted him when he arrived from Zimbabwe. He looked for a police station and was directed to a church that provided shelter. He stayed there until he got a job and could afford to rent a shack.

One week turned into two, two into three; weeks turned into months and so on. I was learning, gaining experience and confidence. More recruits were added, and I was no longer the newbie. Often, when I assumed a senior waiter was being generous by directing diners to the section I was working in, I realised I ended up serving crabby customers.

On a particular occasion, I and other waiters were at the restaurant entrance, greeting and seating customers. Suddenly, I was the only one left at the door without a clue as to what had happened. While I tried to process why my colleagues had disappeared, a black family of eight walked up. I followed the *ten steps of service* and went above and beyond. Explaining the menu to the family was a nightmare because they said my English was too deep. They were needy and I spent a good two hours there unable to serve anyone else. Their bill was 1494 rand and my tip was 6 rand! I comforted myself, *anticipate and be grateful for a tip, but do not expect it.*

I am afraid that experience fed the stereotype of black customers - that they were demanding, but cheap. As time passed, debt paid, sending money and groceries home, familiar with the system and learning to stay as far away from immigration police as possible, more and more black customers continued to come and I continued to serve them as I would Bill Gates.

As more time passed, as more customers came, as more tips were made, the more I noticed how certain colleagues always got the best sections, made the most money and did the least work. That was unfair, but I would not do anything to jeopardise my job. I did not even say anything when Zimbabweans were mocked and discriminated against. "This is South Africa," one lady of mixed race would always say, "if you do not like it here, go back to Mugabe. Except for you Simba, you are not like the rest." I do not know why I deserved the exception, but I did not want it and I would rage at such comments.

"Ask the Zimbabweans to do it; they did not travel all the way here for me to work for them," said a young white waiter, twenty years old, when given a task. What infuriated me the most was not the abuse but the response of my fellow Zimbabweans. Some giggled, while others simply said,"*hiiiiii, ende* Ruan *anowanza.* Gosh, Ruan is so nasty." I did not at all find any of it amusing, but what could I do? If I dared to take the legal route, I would expose my illegal stay.

Several times after I entered a store, a security guard or shop attendant tailed me. At first, I thought it was to serve me, but over time I realised that it was to monitor me. That was the stereotype of the black person. I knew the crime statistics and I too was wary of black people. Was I supposed to be okay with that treatment? I felt I constantly had to prove I was not a criminal. The presumption of my guilt rather than my innocence bugged me.

I saw myself being deported if I reported any abuse, and Zimbabwe was no better than when I left. Feeling powerless and helpless, and feeling I had no one to turn to for help, I began to pray again, if venting counts as praying.

No sooner had I started praying again did I face another demeaning experience. We had just been paid and TC and I were due to do some shopping. From work, I waited for him outside the strip mall close to where we now stayed. TC's boss had leased his one-bedroom apartment in an affluent neighbourhood, to us, for the same rental we paid our previous landlords! Talk about illegal *amakwerekwere,* as we were called, living well. I must have been there for ten minutes when I noticed two white men, likely in their thirties, step out of a car and approach me. They had vests branded 'Neighbourhood Watch'. They greeted me and enquired my business there. A lot went through my mind in that moment. I wanted to say it was none of their business and tell them off, but I was there illegally, and I could not afford to return home. So much for praying!

I took out the branded keys and ID tag to our apartment complex and informed them I was waiting for a friend. "Sorry man, we had a call that there was a suspicious man loitering."

I looked around and could see many people and many men in my vicinity, non-black of course. Just then, TC finally arrived, and we went into the supermarket. He told me that some time when he was taking a walk, he was asked if he belonged there. *The perks of living in a predominantly white suburb I suppose.*

We finished our shopping and when we got to our complex, the neighbourhood "watchmen" were at the gate as if to ensure we belonged where we were. The security officer at the gate greeted us by name as we swiped our entry cards. The gate opened and the two men drove off. If I did not feel discriminated against, I would have applauded them for their vigilance, but I do not think they would investigate a white man the way they did us.

I had had enough by that time. I had no rights and I had no dignity in this foreign land and neither did I have dignity in my motherland. TC and I sat in silence, staring at the TV while listening to our thoughts. Something had to change.

I went back to the first instance of racism I experienced. I did not even know I had been racially harassed. I led a white couple, probably in their seventies to a table. Before I could even introduce myself, the man demanded, in fluent English I realise now, "Get me a waiter who speaks Afrikaans." I went to a senior colleague of mixed race who spoke Afrikaans and relayed the request. My colleague enlightened me, "that *naaier* is racist! He means a white waiter."

*Why did we allow him entry then*, I wondered? I went to the manager on duty and told him. Gary, the restaurant owner happened to be there. He asked the manager, "Do you know the man? I do not want such filth in my restaurant!" Gary walked to the couple and after a few exchanges, they got up. I do not understand what the old man was saying in Afrikaans, but I knew he was cursing. "Do not come back, *klar*!" roared Gary.

In another instance, I brought a white man his breakfast, announcing that they were sunny side up eggs. "What is this?" he demanded. I calmly responded and he shouted, "What is wrong with you people? Why do you always get simple things wrong?"

"Dad, that is what you ordered! I am so sorry Simba, please do not pay attention to him," pleaded his daughter, who came to my defence.

I had thought "you people" meant waiters until he mentioned how the country was regressing since the leadership of a black president. Well, the lady tipped me 100 rand on a 78-rand bill, but it was not worth the dignity her father had taken from me.

As TC and I sat there mulling the erosion of our rights, wondering if we would ever live our dreams, and incredibly so, the news anchor announced that employed Zimbabweans who were illegally residing in South Africa would be getting work permits! We could not believe our ears! It is said that if something seems too good to be true, then it is likely untrue, but this felt like the break we had been hoping and praying for. Maybe with my experiences, I would finally be able to help fellow Zimbabweans find their voice. I sank back in my seat and closed my eyes. This time I did not vent but simply breathed a 'thank you'.

## Finding her voice

***Transcript of radio interview***

**Thabisa:** [00:05] Good afternoon Mandy and welcome to the Our World show.

**Mandy:** Good afternoon Thabisa; thank you for having me.

**Thabisa:** So, you are Zimbabwean, you've been in Cape Town for two years pursuing a doctoral degree in Educational Management and everything is going pretty normal; you then post a video on Facebook, addressing harassment…and in a two-week space, it's been shared and viewed three hundred thousand and two million times, respectively. Firstly, when did you realise it had gone viral?

**Mandy:** [00:33] Well, I pass as a typical social media lurker, mainly observing; not engaging, and preferring LinkedIn and Twitter. I can go months without checking my Facebook account. Anyway, my brother called a week ago asking if I had seen the reach of my video. I only have a little over five hundred friends on Facebook, so I thought he was kidding around. He insisted I check it out and that's when I realised.

**Thabisa:** Months without going on Facebook? We'll get to that if we have time. I'm sure what most people want to know is what happened; what made you make the video?

**Mandy:** [01:00] I'd have to say a lot of frustration, disappointment, exasperation and…

**Thabisa:** What exasperated you?

**Mandy:** Men! (chuckles) and women on a few occasions. I feel there are no safe spaces anywhere anymore; wherever I go, be it school, work, the mall, or even church, I feel piercing gazes undressing me and I sometimes feel threatened and vulnerable. Part of the reason I wear clothes is to be modest so having someone liberally undo that, and with entitlement too, is just demeaning. I am more than a body; I am more than a sex object.

**Thabisa:** Can you narrate one incident where you felt objectified?

**Mandy:** [01:30] There are so many, but I was quite infuriated with a driver of a ride hailing service I had requested. He looked older than my father, so I accorded him due respect and engaged with him as a father. At least until he asked if I had ever tasted (air quotes) a white man. That just…

**Thabisa:** Wait! Was it a white man?

**Mandy:** Yes.
**Thabisa:** *Haibo*! So, you are in his car and relating with him as a father figure and out of the blue asks if you have been…I'm assuming he meant sex?
**Mandy:** Out of the blue, no warning, and no invitation! I think we were talking about his daughters in Australia at that point. I thought I might have heard wrong, but he clarified and confirmed on my request, that he meant being physically intimate.
**Thabisa:** [02:00] What did you say? What did you do?
**Mandy:** Ordinarily, I might have simply ignored, but I was angry after the honour and courtesy I had extended to him as a father. I answered "no" – that I had never tried a white man.
**Thabisa:** You encouraged him? (shocked face)
**Mandy:** I set him up.
Thabisa: What do you mean?
**Mandy:** He then said that I had no idea what I was missing out on; to which I responded: "How do you know I am missing out? Have you tasted (air quotes) a white man yourself?"
(Laughter in the studio)
**Thabisa:** (laughing) O…M…G! That was mad! What did he say?
**Mandy:** I saw the short circuit head shake that Trevor Noah describes. It was the quietest, most unobtrusive journey home afterwards. (more laughter)
**Announcer:** [02:30] Ladies and gentlemen, this is Our World, with host Thabisa, and guest Mandy. We will take a short break and when we return, we will play Mandy's video that has gone viral. You can go to our Facebook page or YouTube channel to watch the interview live. You can hashtag #askMandy in the comments if you have questions and she will respond to some. You will also find a pinned comment with a link to her video.
[Break]
[animated video playing]

**Animated lady in video:** [03:05] If you think that I have a chic fashion sense; if you perceive me to be pretty, or brilliant, decorum informs me that I say, "thank you" and I might, depending on how familiar we are with each other. In a world devoid of equity and justice, a right might be mistaken for a privilege, and the normal might be mistaken for a favour. Thank you for acknowledging and appreciating my efforts, but should it impress me? I don't dress – intellectually, emotionally, spiritually, or physically - to seek validation or approval, and certainly not to attract flattery. I can't take credit for my looks – if they please you, may I suggest that you take a knee and thank the one who created me. You might say I'm arrogant, but I'd argue that I'm humble enough to deflect attention from me. I am not my body, but I am in my body; to therefore reduce me to the momentary pleasures that my body can provide, or to the mere object of your crude desires and fantasies is barbaric, demeaning and infuriating. May I suggest that you get a sex doll. My femininity is neither your conquest to subjugate nor is it the fuel for your vile lusts. May I suggest that you can it! To live in fear of your desires violating mine is coarse abuse; to denigrate my desires and use your physicality to impose yours on me is criminal and cowardly. You are weak if you do. To live and walk among humans feeling like a sheep among wolves is unacceptable. It is quite acceptable to notice a gorgeous somebody and not say anything and it is quite acceptable to let somebody be! Woo me if you must, but may I suggest that you not objectify me; romance me if you must, but I suggest that you be strong enough to accept rejection. If you have to use undue force or undue influence; if you have to intimidate [animated lady takes out a weedkiller and sprays it – fuuuuuuuuuuuuuuu]

**Thabisa:** [04:30] Welcome back Mandy; let's get right into it. Who made the animation? The sass and attitude of that lady is quite something. Are you dismissing compliments though?
**Mandy:** My brother created the animated character because I didn't want my face showing. Her tone represents someone fighting back and empowering themselves in the process. I'm not at all dismissing compliments, but flattery. It is so insincere and contrived to get something. Flattery really isn't about me but about the flatterer's intent.
**Thabisa:** Is it so wrong though for someone to shoot their shot?
**Mandy:** I don't see it in terms of wrong or right, but if you are going to step up to someone at least consider their potential perception. Will they think they are about to be robbed, conned, or kidnapped? They have to feel safe and not apprehensive; they have to know and feel they can reject you without fear of victimisation. Some shoot their shot for sport; whose prize is sex. Desiring physical intimacy is not a crime, but at least ensure the other party is also playing for that prize.
**Thabisa:** How can you know the other party is playing for the same prize?

**Mandy:** That's just it huh? We can't always know, and it then becomes vital to be courteous, respectful, and to make some darn effort.
**Thabisa:** Why didn't you want your face in the video? I must say that it took some doing to convince you to do this interview.
**Mandy:** I wanted to give voice to my feelings, thoughts, and convictions, while bringing awareness to all types of harassment that have been normalised. I didn't even know I was being gender and sexually harassed. I wanted to be a voice without being the face of it or drawing attention to myself. I believe every person has experiences and expressions unique only to them, which they can articulate with conviction if empowered with knowledge of their rights and the law. It would be an injustice for the injustices suffered by millions to be reduced to just my voice.
**Thabisa:** You said you didn't even know that you were being harassed; tell us how you realised it and how the feedback has been?
**Mandy:** It has been incredible! I still can't believe it. There have been thousands of messages of support from those who relate and conversations around abuse and harassment have been resuscitated, apparently. That's the positive. There has been a lot of blowback as well, name calling, verbal abuse, ridicule, and threats. At first, I regretted the video, but now, the negativity has shown how entrenched this attitude and behaviour is. I was ignorant and in denial too. Because it has been normalised, it is easy to roll with it. I felt I hadn't done anything to attract the unwanted attention and it was hard accepting that I was a victim – it made me feel useless and weak. A conversation with my brother – who made the animation – was the damascene moment for me. He defined harassment in a way that resonated with my experiences.
**Thabisa:** Your video challenged me Mandy because I realised, I was in some ways, by my beliefs and attitudes, enabling this culture. We all need to have this conversation. In closing, what's next?
**Mandy:** I'm just hoping the conversations will bring a cultural shift, justice for victims, protection, and empowerment to the vulnerable. No one should feel unsafe in their community, at work, school or in an electronic hail and ride vehicle.
[music playing] [07:30]

I felt so proud of Mandy as I watched the live feed of her interview on the Our World show. Seeing such a humble and level head on a beautiful, gifted soul is refreshing. I am not saying that just because she is my sister or because she referenced me multiple times in her interview, but Mandy has always been the epitome of measured, unassuming, and graceful. She has always been calm too, for the most part, because on a particular day, before she made her viral video, she was unusually anxious and psyching herself up; so much that one would think she was a gladiatrix before a fight at The Colosseum in ancient Rome. Far from that brute age though, it was the 21st century and disruptive innovative technologies were the order of the day. The advancements in technology and their accompanying conveniences, especially of her preferred ride-hailing service, amazed her! She could literally request a ride in the palm of her hand.

What had initially appealed the most to Mandy was the transparency, accountability, accessibility, and relative safety of the service – exactly what she had been yearning for. However, and disappointingly so, for some time, the celebrated convenience had become a dreadful prospect for her, and she wondered if the convenience was worth the discomfort.

All she wanted was a comfortable ride, but what she was getting was way more than what she wanted. She had especially come to loathe how the driver partners from her home country became all too unduly familiar on noticing her Zimbabwean name. At first, she somewhat put up with it because "hey, we are homies a long way from home," but she certainly did not believe it justified nor excused the unprofessionalism that sometimes ensued after establishing their common nationality.

On different occasions, different homie drivers had berated her for not leaving them a larger tip, when in truth, the service they had provided, warranted a refund. I cannot adjudge the most shockingly daring of her ride hailing experiences though. One driver had asked if he could make a quick stop to buy himself some food if she was not in a hurry; many had addressed her as "baby" among other terms in attempts of endearment; some had asked for her number and / or offered her a free ride as if to induce her to give "it" up; others had made references to her body filled with sexual innuendo, and one too many were so uncouth as to offer sexual healing if ever she "got lonely in a foreign land!" Now, I do not quite know the criteria that had been used to determine that she deserved a free ride, or that she was open to such gratuitous attention, but her code certainly did not welcome the prize.

Although Mandy was not naïve, she did believe in the best of people, but the boundary breaches prompted her to change her ride-hailing profile name from Mandy Maromo to Thando Ncube. At least that way she could claim to be a native South African to Zimbabwean drivers and vice versa. She had hoped the presumed language and cultural barriers would cut out the unpleasantries. Of course, there were a number of Zimbabwean drivers who were fluent in all languages spoken in Cape Town, so she resorted to plugging in earphones – even when she was not listening to anything - or calling me and talking for the duration of the trip. She could not fathom the liberalism adopted by her homies. If anything, Mandy had expected to feel safe with her "brothers."

Sadly, Mandy was devastated, yet relieved at the same time, to find out that the nationality of the driver partner was not the determining factor in her experiences. In the time she had been in Cape Town, she had been exposed to enough drivers across the diverse races and cultures to note that the discomfort she experienced was not perpetrated by Zimbabweans only.

Before I paint all of Mandy's experiences with the same brush with regards to the inappropriate informality, I have to admit that some of the driver partners in fact, offered, intellectually stimulating, thought provoking and culturally challenging engagements that she felt could help frame the structure, scope and vision of the organisation she intended to establish upon completing her studies. She had also felt that getting to know bits about how everyone she met got to where they were passed as application of anthropology, and gave her unique, first-hand information and insight into the different peoples and cultures, their challenges and their needs.

Mandy particularly remembered a driver named Simbarashe. Even though she tried not to judge or make assumptions, there were many, uniform attributes, and characteristics she had noticed in multiple driver partners – so much so that it made Simbarashe an exception. With the name Simbarashe, there was not even the slightest doubt in Mandy's mind that the uniquely eloquent driver partner was from Zimbabwe; neither did she doubt the authenticity of his manners. She was convinced they were not a fluke either because on all three occasions that he had driven her, he was consistent.

When the behaviour that Mandy encountered became too much to pass off as random, she brought it up with her cousin Shannon. Shannon had been in Cape Town for three years, and in South Africa for a total of eight years. They had finally put a date to when they would hang out for the first time, but Mandy could not wait till then, so she shared her experiences with Shannon in the hope of getting some much-needed counsel, assurance and wisdom to navigate her circumstances. Their conversation left Mandy feeling no more empowered or assured because Shannon had intimated that it was normal for a pretty lady like her to attract attention. She urged her to roll with it arguing that the men who offered favours, did so of their own volition and that it was within her rights to take advantage of the offers.

Shannon's counsel disappointed Mandy, but sadly, it did not surprise her. On the occasions that they had gone out or hung out together while they were both still in Zimbabwe, Shannon would bask in all the attention from men and respond with flirts of her own, to Mandy's bewilderment. She thought it was demeaning and could not comprehend how Shannon could misconstrue objectification as adulation. It was inconceivable to Mandy how any self-respecting woman could swell with pride at such blatant disrespect. Mandy recalled how Shannon seemed to have a different "friend" for whatever she wanted and how she was the family's concierge.

Their Kirstenbosch Botanical Garden catch up date was the first since Mandy had been in Cape Town. Shannon did not seem to have aged at all from the last time they were together. Her wardrobe was on point and she seemed to have doused herself in a perfume bottle as ever.

"I smelled you a mile away sis," kidded Mandy as they embraced for an eternity.

"You know how I do it Cody; impressions open doors," replied Shannon while showing off her manicured nails.

"Still calling me Cody?"

"You still live by a code do you not?"

After some pleasantries, multiple selfies, and giggles, the two ladies found a spot in the shade, spread their picnic blanket and began to talk.

"So, men problems?" Shannon asked, after a while.

"I would not say men problems per se, rather the sexual innuendo and shameless expression of lust. There are no safe spaces anymore. The other day I was ogled in a bathroom; you should have seen the way she winked at me!"

"You are in demand!" Shannon laughed, "Does it surprise you though, that men, and women apparently, find you attractive?"

"Not at all, but they do not have to express it to a total stranger, do they? It is just invasive."

"I personally have no qualms with someone appreciating me. I think it is bold and it is a huge turn on. We only live once Cody and I do not leave anything on the table. Frankly, that is how many get ahead in life."

"But nothing is for *mahala* sis."

"Well, you decide what you want in life and what you are willing to do to get it. I want a soft life. Remember Malvern who owned fuel stations back home?"

"Yes, he asked me out a number of times. He could not take a hint!"

"Well, why do you think I always had petrol even when the country was dry? He asked me to put in a good word and I used it to my advantage," boasted Shannon.

Mandy was thinking that what her cousin described was tantamount to moral decadence, grooming and pimping. Her heart sank and she felt sick on finding out that Shannon extorted favours from men on the promise of hooking them up with her. She wondered how a fellow woman could do that. She felt used, angry, confused, and disappointed; not just towards her cousin, but herself as well for being too trusting. It was then that she says she remembered my warning to not walk where Shannon walked.

Mandy's default defence mechanism was silence. She postulated that if she did not dignify foolishness with responses, then like a fire without air, it would die down. Her interactions were guided by the notion that *silence is the best response to a fool,* which was one of our father's favourite sayings. Well, it was our father's favourite saying in quotes only; in reality, he was quite the livewire and never backed down from an argument. Mandy believed that if she ignored, for example, the advances from thirsty men, any normal person would realise the encroachment and relent in shame. It seemed to Mandy though that humanity was running short on normalcy in that context, but she kept believing that at the core, everyone knew right from wrong.

That belief in humanity, knowing right from wrong, made the statistics of women abuse in South Africa a frightening read that troubled Mandy. The thought that there were people bent on doing harm to the innocent and defenceless was disturbing to her. She found it to be an inexcusable evil and though she did not want to live in fear, she had begun to wonder if she now needed a personal defence weapon – specifically pepper spray, just in case. The fact that she was contemplating getting a weapon deeply grieved her as it showed a deep brokenness in society. Mandy resolved to be careful and smart and that is why Shannon's confession represented a great betrayal.

Moments after her casual confession, Shannon received a call and excused herself. On returning, she told Mandy she wanted her to meet her boyfriend.

Shannon probed Mandy as they walked to the parking lot: "You have suddenly become too subdued even for your standard, what's up?"

"There is so much nature to take in sis," Mandy answered.

"Nature is not going anywhere darlin," Shannon said, oblivious to the implication of her confession. By then, Mandy was wondering how many men Shannon had betrothed her to.

Mandy was exasperated and she found it hard going to feign courtesy when she was introduced to Jean and his friend Dane. She was furious and did not care to hear how they had matched on a dating site and had been living it up since.

"Cody darling; we are going to the Sea Point. We will stroll the promenade and thereafter go to a pub to watch some rugby. You can keep Dane, the third wheel, company. Pun intended." Chuckling and turning to the two men leaning against a car, Shannon continued: "We call her Cody because she has set principles – a code – she religiously lives by."

Mandy could not avoid the sickening feeling that Shannon was again disregarding her and using her for her gain. "No thanks sis, I am going to take in some more sights then go prepare for school and work."

"Come on; let loose for once," Shannon persisted.

"No, you can go ahead. I'm alright." With every word Shannon uttered and every response Mandy suppressed, she could feel rage building within her.

"Can you just suck it up, so we have a good time? I thought after dating Terrence you would be a lot less uptight. Live a little."

Mandy had anticipated that Shannon would bring up the Terrence issue, but not as a weapon against her. She did not anticipate the well of tears rising at the mention of his name. She had struggled to forgive herself over what happened with Terrence. "For the record, I am leaving Shannon; what you are proposing is that I be irresponsible."

Shannon demanded - her voice getting louder: "So I am irresponsible? Please do not judge me Pastor holy! I am not the one who dated a married man."

Mild-mannered Mandy responded, "Why do you give yourself liberties to ridicule my convictions, but be so sensitive and defensive at the same time? I did not invite your boyfriends here; you babysit them." Shannon made everything a fight; she always had to win and have the last say. She lashed out: "Where were your precious convictions when you dated Terrence, Cody?"

"Pipe down, ladies?" interrupted Jean, sensing the conversation getting heated.

With rage, hurt and teary eyes, Mandy turned and started walking away. She could still hear Shannon yap, "She's such a spoiled killjoy. She was willing to give it up for a married man but wants to be self-righteous with us. She should wake up and grow up." Mandy kept walking until she got to an unoccupied bench, no calmer than she was when she turned her back on Shannon. She just wanted to be home in Zimbabwe surrounded by family and friends, but she was thousands of miles away. Wherever she turned, she saw strangers going about their business. No one knew her, or her pain, and that made her feel worse.

All she could do was go to her apartment - if she could summon the courage to request a ride. She wondered if a day could get any worse as she was not emotionally prepared for a potentially awkward trip. Seated on the bench, she took out her phone and dialled a number.

"Pretty lady…" I answered. With that, Mandy said she could feel the emotional excitement subsiding. She said she could sense the affection and genuineness in my voice, unlike Shannon's "darling" lavished on everyone she interacted with.

"Pretty lady wishes she had a pretty car right about now," Mandy responded.

"What happened to your outrageously ingenious ride hailing service? Do they pay you for advertising their brand?"

"I wish bro! Speaking of the ride hailing service, I need one right now, but I am dreading it." In that moment, Mandy narrated her ordeals to me.

I was enraged but all I could do was empathise with my beloved sister. I could only imagine the violation she felt. "It's not a crime to be beautiful; you are being harassed," I said.

"Harassment? No, why would anyone want to harass me? They do not know me. I think they simply do not know what they are doing, Tapiwa."

"And what does that principle of law say, sis? *Ignorantia juris non excusat.*"

"Fancy pants," Mandy quipped, "maybe you should not have dropped out of law school Gilbertus."

"Ignorance of law excuses no one Miss Taxi," I quipped back, "the longer you tolerate this, the longer you will be a victim of it."

"Victim?" Mandy mulled. She had begun to wonder if she did something; anything, to attract the unsolicited and uncomfortable attention.

She dressed modestly and was always prim in her conversations. What was she doing wrong? What was she not doing right?

"And it is not a taxi!"

"Fancy name and fancy app, but it is still a taxi."

"You are such a hater bro." I did my best to explain to my older sister that if the comments and passes were unwanted and unsolicited; that if they distressed her; that if she felt intimidated or uncomfortable; that if the advances were annoying and invasive; that if she felt tired and sometimes powerless, then she was a victim of sexual harassment and did nothing to deserve it – that it was not her fault.

Mandy had never thought it could happen to her, but I tried to help her understand some of the misconceptions that kept her in denial – misconceptions such as, harassment or abuse was no respecter of persons; that it knew no status, achievements, race or character. We spoke for close to an hour and it seemed to be just what Mandy needed to put the debacle with Shannon past her. She knew she had to do something about the powerlessness she felt. It was the 21st century, yes, with new innovations every other day, but some attitudes and behaviours were from the gladiators' era and needed reformation.

She now needed a ride home. With phone in hand, this was one of the times she was unusually anxious. Psyching herself up, she was getting ready to press '*request ride*'.

For all the talk of girl power, Mandy wished there were ladies in the ride-hailing service as she had never encountered any. She realised that her cringeworthy experiences had begun to inform her decisions and reflect in her habits. Whenever she needed service of any kind, whether in a bank, or supermarket, she would opt for elderly ladies to serve her, if available, despite the length of the queue.

Mandy also realised how presumptuous she had been to think that school and church – with presumed educated, refined, reformed persons, were safe spaces. She resolved to go through the articles that I had shared, research, email her ride hailing service provider and drive awareness.

As Mandy was about to request a ride home, she looked up and saw a familiar face seated on the bench across from her. What ensued was a debate within herself on whether she could go over. She convinced herself multiple times to go over, only to dissuade herself each time. He looked like he did not want company. She argued in her head that it would be intrusive, and she felt very nervous, so she got up to go to the parking lot. She walked about twenty metres before making a U-turn. She was still unconvinced and did not know what she was going to say, but she had walked the whole distance to him, and it was too late to turn back.

"Hi there Simba; Simbarashe. My name is Mandy – I have travelled in your car before. Of course, you have probably done thousands of trips and might not remember me. I am so sorry for intruding. Have a good day."

With that embarrassing monologue, Mandy was about to dash when Simbarashe, rising to his feet, gently responded: "Can I at least say hi, back?"

"My manners are failing me today," Mandy responded with minimal eye contact, "talk about first impressions."

"Technically, we are not meeting for the first time." Simbarashe answered.

"Touché." Said Mandy as she sat on the bench looking straight ahead. Simbarashe sat down too. Just then, Mandy's mind began to wander in overdrive. She wondered if he was there alone, so she quickly got up: "I did not mean to disturb you. Just thought to say hi."

"Thank you." Simbarashe responded, rising to his feet, again.

"Are you not working today?" Mandy enquired, to which Simbarashe responded, "I am. I drove a client here then decided to take a moment to relax. It is easy to be too busy to appreciate the beauty around us."

"Well said, I will use it some time."

"Royalties cometh to me."

Mandy smiled and asked, "What are the odds that if I request a ride on the app now, you will receive the request?"

"Right now, the odds would be zero because I switched off my mobile data connection," Replied Simbarashe.

"Bummer!" Exclaimed Mandy.

"I can still take you home if that is what you were asking."

"Thank you, but I prefer to pay."

"I prefer that you pay too. I meant that you can simply check the quoted fare for the trip, I take you home and you pay that amount."

"That works; thank you Simbarashe." Said Mandy as she sat down again. Sitting as well, Simbarashe responded, "You are welcome, Mandy."

## Dawn

He had observed many evocative sunsets, but none seemed as significant as the one that was setting over Cape Town. He had also observed just as many pleasantly refreshing sunrises. Was the sunset calling time on his decade-long stay? Was this the dawn of a new chapter?

Could he do more, and could he have done more? Should he have started a family of his own? The serene beauty of his surroundings seemed to filter all the noise and interference blocking the intuition of the deepest parts of himself. For the first time in a long time, he wished he had someone to share the charm of the scenery with, and possibly the depths of his being.

There was something about the botanical garden that oozed life. As he sat on a bench, he saw a familiar lady sitting on a bench across from him. He remembered carrying her in his car three times and engaging in a conversation on education, its importance, and its shortcomings. She seemed to be consumed by thoughts, and her phone, which she kept staring at. He knew better than to intrude and he knew better than to cross the line of professionalism with a client, so he continued to engage with his thoughts.

From where he sat, he could see his three-time client leaving, and he could not help a feeling of sadness that came over him. While he tried to process the strangeness of his feelings, he sensed someone in his space. Looking up, he perceived the embodiment of demureness and beauty. She was struggling to make eye contact and her words were rushed, but he was delighted she had not left when he had seen her leave.

"Hi there Simba; Simbarashe. My name is Mandy – I travelled in your car before – three times to be exact," explained the paragon of exquisiteness, seemingly to allay questions that Simbarashe potentially had in that moment, because he looked uninterested. Without getting a read on him and feeling stupid, she decided to save face, albeit twenty steps and nineteen words too late. "Of course, you have probably done thousands of trips and might not remember me. I am so sorry for intruding. I had just thought to say hi. Have a good day."

"Wait Cinderella, can I at least say hi back?" requested Simbarashe, quickly springing to his feet, realising that Mandy was about to dash. With that, she laughed and relaxed a little bit. In the short ensuing conversation, Mandy asked Simbarashe if he was working that day. After learning that he was, but had just taken some time out to take in nature, she enquired the odds – if she requested a ride in that moment - of her ride hailing request coming through to his phone and not another driver partner's. Simbarashe explained that his driver app was turned off. He however offered to drop Mandy home at the going fare and she gladly accepted. Thereafter, they sat on the same bench, some distance apart, but connecting, nonetheless.

"Cinderella huh?" Mandy amusedly broke the silence, "I suppose you are the charming prince."

"If being an only child counts, I suppose I am a prince. A very wise person said charm was deceptive and misleading so I will pass on that one," Simbarashe engaged.

"Charm is deceptive, and beauty is fleeting…" Mandy recited.

"The woman to be admired and praised…" Simbarashe joined in as the two turned their faces towards each other delightfully puzzled that they both knew the proverb. "Are you that woman?" he asked.

"I live to be," she answered, "but I would rather be admired by my husband, or husband to be. God knows I have had it with flattery and sexual harassment." That was the first admission by Mandy to being harassed, but the shock was that she had shared it with a relative stranger. *Why did I say that?* she cross examined herself in thought.

"You are engaged?" he enquired cautiously.

"Not yet; no, I am not at the moment. Not that I was at some moment or that I will be at a set moment. Of course, I will be at some point. Rather, I hope to be at some point. Not that it is looking hopeless, no. Argh!" and with that response, Mandy sheepishly kept quiet.

"I just thought of the game show *Crystal Maze,*" Simbarashe jumped in, "I think you are saying you are not engaged? I think you are saying that you are not dating either, so as to not jeopardise your chances, but clarifying that you are not desperate?"

"Thank you Simbarashe; I am relieved that you got it. Informed by the context of a number of experiences I have unfortunately had with some men, and a handful of women, I would prefer not to have to deal with flattery and fake compliments masking lust and lewdness. I am tired of having to hide, or dread requesting a ride out of fear of being accosted."

"I am sorry for what you have been through. Encountering perverts must be demeaning, and invasive. If I may ask, have you filed a complaint with the company?"

"Up to this point I had only vented to a couple of people, but I am definitely emailing them. I am sorry if it will affect your business."

In support, Simbarashe said, "A few unruly characters taint the image of all. That already affects the business and it is not right. I think you are making an about-time move, and no, you do not need my approval. If nothing is done, nothing changes."

The two sat in silence for a minute before agreeing it was time to leave. Walking to the parking space, Mandy asked if Simbarashe worked on Sundays. "No, I go to church, and rest."

"Is it? Where exactly?" asked Mandy. Simbarashe answered but expressed a desire to switch back to the one he went to when he was in Zimbabwe, which coincidentally, was the same church that she had gone to before the Terrence scandal. "If I may ask a personal question, Simbarashe; are you married?"

"Not yet; no, I am not at the moment," answered Simbarashe, "Not that I was at some point or that I will be at a set moment. Of course, I will eventually. Rather, I hope to be at some point. Not that it is looking hopeless, no."

"Touché," Mandy said and they both burst out laughing. Just as he had done on the three previous occasions that he had carried her, and just as he did with all his clients, Simbarashe opened the door for Mandy and checked all steps of service. "Which part of Cape Town do you stay Simbarashe?"

"About ten minutes' walk from your place actually." On a day she had learnt that her cousin extorted favours from men on the promise of hooking them up with her; on a day she had realised and accepted that she was a victim of sexual and gender harassment; on a day she had felt alone in a land far away from her motherland; on a day she wondered if she could ever escape the ghost of Terrence, Mandy's day was taking a turn for the better – or at least the day pertaining to her ride hailing blues.

Mandy asked if she could have Simbarashe's number and contact him if she needed to travel. He agreed and they exchanged numbers. He also advised her to check with him ahead of time in case he was out. "My name is Mandirwira Maromo by the way."

"Lovely to meet you Mandirwira; I am Simbarashe Shoko. Who is Thando Ncube though?"

Mandy immediately knew where the question was coming from, "O, that. I changed my ride hailing app profile name to Thando Ncube. Some drivers became too familiar with me after realising I was Zimbabwean, so I decided to go for an ambiguous name to avoid being bombarded with unwanted advances and generalisations."

"Tell me about generalisations," said Simbarashe.

"Sounds like there is a story there," probed Mandy.

Simbarashe obliged; he told Mandy how being black already had its prejudices – presumed guilty and not innocent; queried and despised. In fact, Simbarashe had been harassed multiple times while taking a walk because some fellow residents had been suspicious of a black man in that particular neighbourhood. Being black and Zimbabwean, working in the hospitality sector, was worse - being seen, but never heard, looked at as ornamental and not functional. When he worked as a waiter, he was immediately judged by the uniform he wore and the job title he carried. His thinking was never appreciated but conformity was encouraged. Simbarashe narrated how a restaurant manager had told him his name was a mouthful and that his name tag would read *Simon* instead. At that time, Simbarashe was an illegal immigrant and did not want any attention so he accepted, even though he did not understand how hard it would be to pronounce *Simba*, if *The Lion King* was globally celebrated.

"My perspective is that I am a businessperson providing a service and my personal brand has value. Unfortunately, I am often treated as a second-class human incapable of thought, knowledge, deduction or formulating solutions," explained Simbarashe. "Granted, there are those we mentioned who taint the image of many, but blanket statements are an injustice."

"I thought I had heard and seen it all, but with context and first-hand accounts of experiences, I appreciate the gravity of it all, more." Mandy responded with a heavy heart. "I have just realised that I understand issues like racism, harassment, abuse, welfare, rights, justice and injustice intellectually, but lacking context and empathy. I usually have statistics but, often they are of nameless and faceless people. I am so sorry if I have been demeaning and disrespectful; I am so sorry for our ignorance and arrogance. How have you coped?"

"Thank you, Mandy. It has been a hard and sometimes painful journey. A journey from ignorance and powerlessness to knowledge and rights empowerment; to knowing one's worth and value; to confidence and boldness to stand up for others in the predicament I was once in."

"How long did you go by the name Simon?"

"Only until I regularised my stay here, then I refused to pin a name tag that did not have my real name. Before that, I feared if I lost my job, with no viable options back home, I would be stuck in hopeless poverty."

"Did your manager simply accept your stand?"

"Not at all! He gave me an ultimatum to either pin it as it was or not come to work. Well, I did not put it on, but I still went to work. The internal protocols for a dismissal called for a hearing with a worker's representative and the company's legal representative. I had always avoided conflict up till that point, but I was looking forward to unmasking the foolishness of the manager, the oppression and vindictiveness. I was reinstated after the hearing, with apologies, and ever since then, I started wearing my name with pride. Funny thing is that I never liked the name Simbarashe because I felt it was too common, but when it was ridiculed, I fought for it. I still wish I had a different name, but I am proud of it and that is why I always introduce myself as Simbarashe, and not Simba, even though I am cool with it. You can say that I fought for the name I never wanted."

"I am truly challenged and inspired, Simbarashe. I feel quite proud of my full name, Mandirwira. If I did not know how to proceed with my own challenges, I know that I will at least fight, not just for me, but for the ones who need a voice."

That was the shortest journey home, ever, for Mandy. There was so much more to Simbarashe than he let on and she was intrigued. She wanted to know more and not just intellectually, but she was not getting ahead of herself. Terrence was the last person to dupe her.

Opening the door for Mandy to exit, Simbarashe asked if she went to church. Her response was that she was in-between churches. Bizarrely, Simbarashe produced his passport and showed it to her. He invited her to a church that was a walking distance from their respective homes, and she accepted. The two parted, each recalling the day's events and wondering if what seemed to be happening, was happening. Neither had enjoyed a fulfilling conversation in a while, but both wondered if maybe, it was a new dawn.

When Mandy settled, she did a Google search for Simbarashe Shoko. Quite a few of them came up in the search, so she tried Facebook. She came across the profile of a *Simba Shoko* that had Simbarashe's photo but there was very little personal information shared. She thought that either he was hiding something, or he was very private, and left it at that.

A few minutes away, Simbarashe was debating whether he should look up Mandirwira Maromo on social networking sites. At last, he decided to do so only after getting to know more about her in person, if he had the opportunity.

When Sunday came, Simbarashe found himself doing a little extra, but not too much, to look presentable and so was Mandy. Sunday best it was! They saw each other briefly before the service began but they did not sit together. The Pastor spoke on 'Rebuilding the Ruins' and it resonated with both Mandy and Simbarashe, but in different contexts. For Mandy, it was about letting go of the past and its failures, while embracing the new day with its opportunities. For Simbarashe however, it was the dilemma of whether it was time for him to return to Zimbabwe, which was in a sense, in ruins.

As was the custom in that church, first time attendees were given special mention and asked to remain behind for a few minutes after the service. Simbarashe was responsible for welcoming the first-time attendees, capturing their details, and enquiring if they had any specific requests. It was a bit odd because on that Sunday, Mandy was the only one there for the first time. She was quite appreciative of Simbarashe not presuming to know her. Partaking of a muffin and some juice, she listened to the passion in the voice and heart of the young man as he articulated the vision and the mission of the church. She responded with authenticity when he asked her to share a bit about herself, revealing that she was pursuing a doctoral degree in educational management and worked part time as a teaching assistant. In closing, Simbarashe gave her a word of encouragement, "The dream might seem too big and the challenges enormous; the past may seem impossible to get over, but each day presents an opportunity for a new beginning; the scars might be permanent but we can be all the wiser for them. You have a voice, use it. You will be fulfilled in purpose."

After the service, Simbarashe mentioned that he needed to submit a service report then he would walk her home. When he returned, she asked, "How did you go from a waiter to a driver? Thank you for inviting me to church by the way; I needed it."

"You are welcome Mandy. Well, a friend and I, with the help of an angel funder, saw an investment opportunity. We pulled our years of savings to buy cars and have them on the e-hailing platform. When I finished the degree I was doing – Psychology – of which I am a qualified Financial Accounting teacher, I decided to learn the business first-hand so I took one of the cars. I figured I could innovate something that better suited the Zimbabwean context, in the likely event that I returned."

"Interesting, very interesting. I had not been going to church because I went on dates with a church mate, to see if there could be more. His name is Terrence. I then found out he was married, with two kids, back in Zimbabwe. He presented himself as a single guy and I was told he had been in the church for years. The tag of being the girl who dated a married man was too much for me to handle at that time. I just thought I would let you know."

"Thank you for trusting me with such private information Mandy. I am so sorry; I do not really know what to say at the moment, but if I may digress a little, what do you intend on doing after school?"

"Return to Zimbabwe with all the knowledge, skills and failures, then try to create a curriculum that equips one for the real world. Ensuring that every child is equipped for life motivates me, and as I have learned from a wise someone, giving voice and empowering the vulnerable is something now in my heart."

With that response, Simbarashe felt he was indeed in a new dawn and that he had found someone to share his sunsets and sunrises with.

## Rudo D M Manyere

Rudo D M Manyere is a writer, booktuber, bookstagrammer, blogger and aspiring screenwriter. She has contributed to the 263 Africa Magazine and Afrobloggers.

Social Media Handles:

I.G: basicgirlreads
YouTube: Basic Girl Reads
Twitter: RudoManyere

## Kurauone

Waiting outside WHSmith next to a dilapidated structure that used to be a beauty salon, I see Adesua, Kola's sister, standing across the street. She is hard to miss, with her afro regally crowning her head. The olive-green pin-stripe blouse and the black pencil skirt trace every inch of her curvaceous body and make her look *almost* professional. However, if I am being honest, the print of her curvaceous hips takes me back to the yesteryears when the three of us roamed around the streets of Oxford after our service to the city, as cleaners at St Margaret's College. She has not seen me yet, so I am standing here and taking her in. She has aged, she has webs of wrinkles around her eyes and instead of the strides she used to rhythm her walk to, she now has the gait of a pensioner. The green handbag and black pumps with a green flower she is wearing give a youthful touch to her outfit. The earrings carved with the African continent, which I bought for her from this Zimbabwean lady who charged me sixty pounds because they had been handmade and crafted, shipped and "escaped" customs, all the way from Zakarinopisa in Masvingo, complimented the outfit. They still turned heads, the earrings, the nose, chin and back head of the continent holding on to the corners of each earring.

Even after thirty odd years since our liaison came to an end, she still makes my heart flutter under my chest. I examine my posture and choice of attire on the large windows of the bookshop. My beard seems to "connect" as the youth say. I stroke it and as much as I am aware, I am still surprised by how white it has become. I only turned sixty-three last week and even though the lines on my face portray wisdom beyond my years, I am still holding on to the intensity of my boyish charm. My tucked in striped shirt and suspended trousers now make me look ridiculous, as my big *bele* pokes out, stretching my suspenders to my sides. The overcoat which I am beginning to regret because the heat is giving me vertigo, drapes on my shoulders as if it has been hung on. I ignore the sensation and firm my feet which are sheltered by my only pair of formal shoes. I lean on the window and take a minute to collect myself. I am not going to let my anatomy fail me now, not today and especially not in the presence of Adesua. I shake the feeling off and lean on the window. I wave at Susu, that is the sobriquet I had given her. She is standing on the other side of the street obviously searching for my face in the crowd.

"Susu!" I shout her name walking towards her, but with the earphones plugged in her ears, she obviously cannot hear me. I get closer to her and tap her shoulder. The smile that spreads on her face gives me nostalgia, the curl of her lip that reveals her white, carefully arranged dentition is deja vu of how she expressed her joy when I told her I loved her. Her love language was words of affirmation, and I hope it still is. " Kura!" She pronounces the first part of my name in her strong Yoruba accent. The "*ra*" part comes out like the roar of a lion cub. I do not care; I love the way she says it. I have always loved it. She reaches out for me and I embrace her. She stands on her toes and as much as I am tempted to lift and spin her around like before, I know my back will fail me. I linger and take in the smell of her hair which masks my face. It smells familiar, like the hair conditioner one of my housemates, the Kenyan lady, uses for her hair. Kanto, Kanu or Kanyu, I do not remember. She takes a deep breath and pulls back. I look at her and she tries to look away. I touch her shoulder and keep my hand there; she sniffles and places her hand on top of mine.

"It was unexpected. Too soon, j-just like that he did not wake up shaa." My Susu says as she digs for a piece of tissue in her bag. I search my overcoat for my handkerchief and hand it over to her. I smile as a wave of nostalgia hits me again, how we used to argue as to whether the "word" s*haa* was a Nigerian or Zimbabwean colloquial. "I know, he was in great health and had so much to live for." I reply, reminiscing about Kola, her brother, my best friend and the glue between us, who last week had died in his sleep. We stand by the street for a few minutes, ignoring the shoulders that nudge us and the clamor that surrounds us. "Come." I whisper, reaching for her hand, "If we get on the bus now, we will get there before a lot of people arrive. We can catch up for old times' sake." She looks at me and forces a smile, I do the same. We walk through Cornmarket Street on to St. Aldates and wait at bus stop 4T. Bus number 5 to Blackbird Leys will take us to the Community Hall where mourners will congregate and discuss how to raise money to send Kola's body back to Nigeria.

We sit in our designated seats, for elderly and disabled people. I look at Susu and laugh. She looks at me, confused, pursing her lips. "Do you remember that day when we were coming from reporting, from uhm, ah Eaton House in Hounslow and we swore we would never be caught dead sitting in these seats because in our forties we would be out of this country and living in a villa in France?" I continue to laugh, with a mixture of glee and disappointment. Forty years ago, we both were undocumented immigrants, in love and invincible. The Zimbabwean government had failed dismally and in West Africa, Nigeria was facing the same situation. A multitude of us had run away looking for greener pastures. I remember the time I had left Zimbabwe; I had been a trillionaire and had marched at more than fifteen rallies by the age of eighteen. Kola and Adesua used to laugh at me when I told them, they could not believe that a whole nation once accommodated trillionaires, but no one was rich. They began to call me Mr Trilionare Sir. With their thick accents, the "sir" was pronounced as "sar".

"Ah, we were so young and naive. If only we had known life would take us here, I would have stayed in Nigeria and Kola would still be alive and I w..."

"And you would have never met me." I murmur, looking out the window, hurt. I understand where she is coming from, but I cannot imagine her thinking of a world where we never existed. Kura and Susu. Kurauone and Adesua. The Zimbabwean and Nigerian couple. The Shona and Yoruba duo. A concoction by the African gods deemed good and pleasant in a foreign land.

"Kura, you know what I mean. I just cannot believe I, we, wasted most of our lives hoping and praying for something that was not meant for us." My Susu is saying this looking down, she cannot say it straight to my face because she knows it is not entirely true. We did not waste time; our love was not a waste of time.

"Susu, I know what you mean, and you know what I mean too. It so happens over the last years, I have had time to think. Not being documented for over thirty years will do that to you." I am telling her this and my heart is drumming in my chest. I understand the timing might be off, insensitive even, but I do not want to die the way Kola did. He only got his papers six months ago after battling the Home Office for as long as I have. He died in his sleep from exhaustion. The marathon shifts he took working as a health care assistant also known as BBC - British Bum Cleaner - had caught up with him. You would think at sixty-three he would be getting ready to retire, but just a year from retirement that is when he started working full time as a "legal" person. Just like me, he had taken small jobs here and there, which was and still is illegal, but it was the only way to survive.

He is survived by two daughters. Oladayo who he last saw when he left Nigeria; she was only two years old and after forty years, she would see her father again, this time in a coffin. Adenike was the daughter he begot with Alina, the Romanian lady he had succeeded in getting pregnant but not her papers. He had proposed I take the same route, get a lady from the EU or even better, an English woman. Get her pregnant and stick around long enough until they include you on their papers, and just like that you are a British citizen. "*Gwam gwam*, just like that my broda you are in. This United Kingdom will be yours for the taking in Jesus' name!" he would say each time he tried to sway me into following his footsteps. I could not do it, I had Susu. She was the only one I wanted to be the mother of my future children and my only life partner. I would always remind him I was in love with his sister and would not disrespect her or myself like that.

"Kura, I like you, you are a fine man and I am grateful for the way you love my sister but my broda, love is only an illusion. Will love give you *paper*? Will love give you red passport? Eeh? You need to be wise, by all means necessary get your *paper* then worry about love later. Ok, even if you choose Adesua, how will you provide for *ha* eeh? Each day you are playing cops and robbers with the police and Home Office because you are working illegally. Is that life?" He would question me but never give me enough time to explain. Which was something that gnarled me about him, but I liked how practical he was. He was a man of action. The 007 amongst us who had a license to kill every obstacle in his own way. I had taken his advice once; we both ended up in prison and that was the last time I took his advice.

We had registered with an agency with fake ID's and documentation to get the jobs. The IDs almost looked original. Manish, the Indian guy from Cowley was behind the masterpieces, after the astounding recommendation from our fellow immigrant peers. I do not know how they noticed or if it was a routine check, but the day they called us for training, a SERCO van parked outside and four huge men came in and asked us to produce our IDs and scanned our fingerprints. Long story short, we were arrested together with four other women who were also using fake IDs. For two years, we shared a cell, not by choice but after my cellmate was released, the correctional officers at HM Prison Bullingdon where we were in remand before our transfer, put us in one cell. That chapter of our lives frayed and strengthened our friendship. After serving our sentences, we were sent to a detention centre awaiting our deportation. I will not lie, that place was worse than prison. Not knowing when you would get out was torturous and heartrending. I saw grown men, fit and able men, kill themselves in that place. It was like being caught between a rock and a hard place - living illegally in a country you would never be accepted or surviving in your own country where you were never certain where the next meal would come from. The former was more tantalising, but it had its own consequences. I too had begun flirting with suicide, on days when my immigration lawyer, funded by the government, would come, and advise me to leave and go back to my country because I had no further evidence. I would go back to my room and anticipate how long it would take for me to bleed out if I slit my wrists, clench my fists and stood under the shower. A bath would have been better, but that service is not available in detention centres. I know it was cowardice, but which other choice did I have? I had no family, no savings and no dignity left, only Susu. Susu was the one who kept me alive, gave me hope and gave me the will to live.

"You know, Adenike says she doesn't want to be called by her African name but prefers Denisa, her second name, because it is easier to pronounce." Susu ropes me back to reality as we pass Templar Square. I look at her and sigh, words have escaped me.

"Hhhmm, was Kola aware of this?" I engage in the conversation.

"Yes, he was. He was not very happy about it, but I told him what did he expect when she had no idea or had never been to Nigeria? She only knows of *oyibo* people as her friends and family."

"That is true. She has never been exposed to your culture."

"Well, now no one will *paster* her to use her Yoruba name now that he is gone."

"*Aika,* are you not the aunt? Do you not have a say?"

"*Tufiakwa,* God forbid! After what that *oyibo* woman said to me when she was at odds with my brother? No! They do not exist to me."

"Susu, you are better than this. Are you not the one who always said, our personal feelings about something do not give us permission to ignore God's feelings about it?"

"Nxaa, you know you ought to start calling me Adesua now." She is muttering this as we alight at Balfour Road. She knows I am right, but she will not admit it.

"But I love calling you that, you will always be my Susu. Even now as we are wrinkled up with aching backs, you are forever my Susu and y-."

"And I am a married woman. Remember Steve, he is still alive you know."

"Oh yes, him. Your husband. How is his rheumatism? You know, he never replied to me when I asked him how old he was when he wrote Leviticus. It still keeps me awake at night." I am jesting but I mean it. That man is and was still old even back then. He is only four years older than me but still, he wasn't and still is not good enough for my Sus-, for Adesua. If only I had been released sooner from that hellhole of a detention centre. If only I had not spent six years in that place, I could have married her, but she could not wait any longer. The Home Office had denied her appeal, she had nothing else to submit and she was at an impasse. I remember the night she called me, we had just finished our night prayers at the detention centre and I was on my way back to my room for a roll call. She sounded distant and absent-minded, we talked as usual about our day, our future and how strong our love was.

"I am getting married," she blurted out. At first, I thought she was teasing me, like the times she would say she was pregnant, then after a few minutes would say, “with blessings on blessings on blessings.” I was waiting for her to say that, but she went on to say she had met him online and he just wanted someone to be with and have children with - two maximum, she said. She had no choice, this was her only chance, so she took it.

I still had three more years in the detention centre when she decided to marry Steve. She would still send me money and write me letters, but I never replied, and I gave the money to those who were being deported to start a new life back in their homelands. I was not going to have another man take care of me. When I was released, I never tried to contact her, even though I would stalk her Facebook handle every night after my shift. It was Kola who had told me she had miscarried three times, but Steve had remained by her side because he had fallen in love with her. Who wouldn't? I did not like how he called her by her full name, Adesua, he was not creative or thoughtful at all. Although I am grateful, he did not tread towards Susu or Sue, at least Ade or Sua would have been inspiring.

"You are impossible, you know," she says laughing." He is a good man, a good husband."

"But do you love him, the way you loved me?"

"Kurauone, we are married. So, it means there is love there."

"In the words of Toni Morrison, your favourite writer, love is or is not, there is no thin or thick love. So, is it there or not?"

I know I must tread lightly, but I must know. Yesterday I finally got my papers. I found them on my doorstep after coming from work. They were in a large khaki envelope carefully sealed with a signed delivery sticker on it. My name was printed across the envelope in big bold letters: **MR KURAUONE NHAMO**. After forty-one years of waiting, they finally decided to grant me papers, but was it worth it if I had nothing to account for? Only a year from retirement and here I was trying to win the love of my life back. She is the real reason I have been keeping on and her reply will determine my future.

"We are moving. To France. Steve bought a villa in Lyon and we are retiring and moving there."

I feel like my soul has been punched out of my body. My ears are ringing and that vertigo feeling is coming back hard and fast. She is living our dream with another man, that man is living my life. I stop in my tracks and look at her, I can feel the brim of my eyes burning but I will not succumb to it. My dotage catches up with me as I balance myself on a pole on the side of the road. I do not look at her, but I laugh out loud looking at the community hall on the other side of the street. She looks at me confused and I look at her pitiful and ashamed of myself. So, this is how it ends? It is either death by work or death by heartbreak. At sixty-three years old, I am standing next to a woman I have loved and chosen over myself every time, but she is here choosing herself all over again. I look at her laughing, then cup her face in my hands. I lean towards her and without a doubt in my soul, I whisper in her ear.

"I am going back to Zimbabwe."

## 3:15 AM

I have been waking up at 3:15 am every day for the last five months, and each time my eyes open, I see her. I lie on my back and stare at the ceiling in the dark. I feel her glare, following me as I toss and turn. There is barking and growling outside my window, I think they are dogs, but I could be wrong. I tend to only hear them when she visits. She does not move but stares at me. She looks exactly the same as she did on that day back in 2002. It has been over 17 years since she died, but I can still hear her singing on our way to the river like it was yesterday. I have told Mama about how she has been visiting me, wearing the same clothes as that day, staring at me the same way she did as she took her last breath on that day, but I do not tell her the last part. Mama tells me it is because I miss her and she recalls how close and inseparable we were, but I remember it differently and I do not tell her.

I get up, put my bedside slippers on, a gift from Aunt Saru. I turn on my bedside lamp and I see her standing in front of me. I no longer freeze in terror or panic when I see her. We have become acquainted again. We do not talk, but our silence speaks volumes. I check the clock on my wall, 3:17 am, 3 more minutes until she leaves. I look at my phone, but I do not take it. The first time she visited me I tried to use my phone to call, but before I could even unlock it, I could not move and words would not escape my mouth. It happened again the following day when I tried to use it as a torch. I guess this is her way of telling me she needed my undivided attention. She was like that before she died, self-centred and commanded attention in every room she walked into. I shuffle to the door and pat my way in the dark to turn on the light as I head to the kitchen.

It is too late for wine and too early for coffee, so I put the kettle on and open the cupboard for a tea bag. There is no barking or growling. I take milk out of the refrigerator and open the bottle. I pour the last of the milk in my mug, hot water, a dash of honey then I put the teabag. The hairs at the back of my neck stand and that is how I know she has joined me in the kitchen. The usual flickering of lights and the flapping of the cupboard and drawers no longer shocks me. I am surprised that fear no longer suffocates me as before. She always takes longer to make her way downstairs. I think she will be giving herself a tour, taking a glimpse of what her life might have been like if she were still alive. I hear growling outside my kitchen window. I drag my feet to my kitchen bin and throw away the teabag. I sit on the kitchen chair and she sits opposite me. Her pale grey skin makes her look ghostly, but again, she is. I smile at her, but she vehemently stares back at me. She does not smile or flinch, just a straight line that is neither a smile nor a frown. That was how her lips looked too on the day she died.

My cousin Rukudzo and I were born a few months apart, and our mothers always bought us matching clothes. People used to think we were twins even though they said she was prettier and lighter than I was. She had big, upturned eyes, a carefully carved wide nose, full lips and smooth skin. I, on the other hand, did not possess her features of beauty, or what society deemed an acceptable standard. Even though my mother told me I was beautiful the way I was, I was always the *other.* Every school holiday, my parents, my older sister Sarudzai, named after Rukudzo's mother, and I would head down to Chivhu, in Njanja where we spent the holidays. There, we would meet Aunt Saru, Uncle Takura, Rukudzo and her little brother Kupakwashe. Gogo and Sekuru always enjoyed having us over, but I never enjoyed it. I always dreaded it. My grandparents always marvelled at how Rukudzo was already able to cook a big pot of sadza, enough for eight people at the age of ten. She would wash our grandparents' clothes at the river all by herself and was able to balance a 7.5-litre clay pot on her head. No one would pay attention to how I had come first in my class or how I was reading at Grade 7 level, even though I was in Grade 5. No one even acknowledged I was almost as tall as Sarudzai, who was 4 years older than me.

It was the last Sunday of the holiday. I remember it distinctively because we had come from church and Gogo had instructed Sarudzai to kill a chicken for dinner. The last Sunday was the only time my grandmother would have a chicken killed for food. She kept them for selling and to pay debts when push came to shove. Sekuru had given me his pair of trousers, shirt, and socks which he had worn for church and asked me to wash them for him before we left.

"I would love it if you washed these for me *muzukuru,"* he said as his adam's apple bobbed up and down his wrinkled throat. "You are a big girl now and I know you will manage these." he said, handing me the clothes. I loved how he saw me and acknowledged me. He could have asked Sarudzai or Rukudzo, but he asked me and that made me happy. I took the metal bucket which had accumulated a little rust, a small piece of Elangeni soap and made my way to the river which was not far from the house. I walked past Sarudzai and Kupa who were chasing the chicken around the yard to no avail. I remember laughing at Kupa who was running towards the kitchen when the chicken ended up chasing him. I walked down to the river, humming to myself. I was going to make Sekuru proud.

"Wait!" I heard Rukudzo shouting behind me. I ignored her and increased my pace.

"I know you can hear me. Wait!" She continued. I stopped in my tracks and waited for her to catch up. I had wanted to go alone so I could make Sekuru proud and show everyone that I could also wash clothes as good as Rukudzo, if not better. She caught up and stood next to me catching her breath. The red pendant on her necklace had moved to the back, she repositioned it and grinned at me.

"*Ko* why did you ignore me? Did you not hear me calling you?"

"No." I lied.

"Oh, *inga*. Maybe there is something wrong with your hearing because I was shouting loud enough for the whole village to hear."

"Well, maybe it wasn't as loud as you thought."

"Anyway, where are you going? You know we are not allowed to go down to the river without an adult accompanying us," she remarked, sizing me up and down. I was an inch taller than she and I knew it gnarled her that I was better than her at something.

"Sekuru said I was big enough to go by myself and wash his clothes." I said standing up taller, sticking my chest out, rubbing my stature in her face.

"*Kunyepa,* sekuru would never say that. You are lying. I will go and ask him," she said, threatening to run back home and ask.

"Go ask him," I replied, as I continued walking down to the river with the bucket under my arm. I did not hear any footsteps fading or approaching me, so I knew she was standing, digesting my words.

I was hoping she would go back home and leave me alone, but a moment later, I heard her walking behind me, singing to herself. She had the most beautiful voice I had ever heard, but I would never tell her that. Her head would grow too big and she would tell it to everyone who would listen. I ignored her and quickened my steps, but she picked up her pace, she was so close I could feel her breath when she sang. As I made my way to the *ruware,* the riverside dwala where we washed our clothes, Rukudzo hurried beside me and snatched the bucket out from under my arm. I tried to chase her but she was too quick for me and the ruware was very slippery.

"Give me back my bucket, Rukudzo! *Hunza kuno!*" I shouted after her as tears itched my eyes." Come back and give it to me, now!"

"Oh, don't be a cry baby. I am saving you. I don't want you to embarrass yourself *apa*." She retorted, taking out the clothes from the bucket.

"Rukudzo, give it back or I will beat you up!" I had never fought a day in my life, except playing the slap game with Sarudzai, which I never won, but that day I was willing to defend my honour. I was not going to let her win.

"*Eheeeeeeede*, you beat me?" She cackled and clapped her hands three times. She narrowed her eyes and looked at me as I stood a short distance from her. "Try me. Let us see if you will be able to talk when I finish with you." She said, taking off her shoes and tucking her yellow dress into her knickers. I was taller but not stronger and seeing that I was never going to overpower her, I decided to make use of the resources around me.

"Come and beat me," I said, holding a huge rock in my hand. If push came to shove, I was prepared to use it.

"*Zigwara,* you are such a coward. We both know I am better than you. Even your own sister said it too. You can't even defend yourself but need something else to defend you." She retorted looking me straight in the eye, but I did not flinch.

"You are lying, Sarudzai would never say that!" I shot back, trying not to cry.

"Oh really, so how do I know you don't know how to wash your own knickers yet? Huh, how would I know that? Tell me!" She jeered and laughed louder than her usual cackle. That set me off. Sarudzai knew I had been having a hard time washing my whites and she knew I was getting better. How could she betray me like this? I ran towards Rukudzo, not paying attention to the slippery rock and stood in front of her. Her toes were touching my shoes and I could feel her warm breath enveloping my nose.

"What? What are you going to do about it?" she asked, pushing me hard with her finger, but I did not budge.

"Give me the bucket," I said, standing my ground. I could feel the brim of my eyes itching, but I was not going to let her use my tears against me. I had to win this time.

"Take it, but rest assured you will have to go past me." She blocked me from the bucket. I leaned forward to grab the bucket and before I could grab the handle, a sharp pain spread on my cheek. I retreated my hand and held my cheek as Rukudzo pushed me and slapped my head. The tinnitus that followed confused me. I could not make sense of what was happening. By the time I came to my senses, Rukudzo had started washing Sekuru's clothes. I stood up and walked towards her. She had her back at me and was humming to herself. The nerve of her not turning her back and not being afraid of what I could have done to her annoyed me. Did she not think I was threatening enough?

"Rukudzo" I said, poking her shoulder. Seeing that I had been defeated, trying to fight her would end with me limping back home, so I opted for a civil approach. She stood up and as she was turning to face me, she slipped and fell into the river. She was on the shallow end and she tried to grab on to the rocks, but they were too slippery. She called out my name and I rushed to the riverbank. She grappled with the strong currents that were threatening to sweep her away. I held out my hand and when she was about to get a hold of it, I hesitated and pulled it back. She screamed my name and called for help as the water overpowered her. I stared at her as she wrestled with it. I waited for her to fight the water the same way she wanted to fight me. She had told me last holiday that she could swim, so I left her to her own devices.

She stared at me, the same stare she gives me when she visits. She gave in to the current and was swept away before I could reach out to grab her hand. I ran back to the house, shouting and screaming for help. It had just dawned on me that Rukudzo could not swim. Uncle Takura and my father ran towards me as I shouted for help. They came running towards me, but I could not speak. I only managed to point in the direction of the river. They ran towards the river and seeing how I kept looking to the east where the river flowed, Sekuru hobbled with his stick in that direction. By the time they found her, she was already dead, and her stomach was bloated, full of water. When they brought her home, Sekuru could not let me and Kupa near her, but I saw a glimpse of her face. Her blank stare pierced through my eyes and I have lived with that image in my head for the past 17 years. Even after we moved to London, I could still see her face when I closed my eyes, but it had begun to fade with every new face I saw every day. I guess her visiting me every day at 3:15 am, is a way of not wanting me to forget her.

I sip on my tea and stare at the clock. 3:21 am. the barking and the growling have stopped again. Silence. She is gone. I rinse my cup and carefully place it on the rack. I survey the kitchen to see if she is still around, but I am reassured of her absence by the flat hairs at the back of my neck. I make my way upstairs and get into my bed. I coil up, make myself comfortable and close my eyes, certain that tomorrow at 3:15 am, Rukudzo will pay me another visit.

## Zadzisai

The first thing Zadzisai did as soon as she sat in the *kombi* was to ask the conductor if he could drop her off on Green Lane, just before the Glen Lorne Shopping Centre. The conductor looked at her, sneered and continued shouting.

"Glen Lorne, Glen Lorne! Including those before Glen Lorne Shopping Centre." He ducked into the *kombi* and said to Zadzisai.

"*Eeeh* sister, did you hear that? We do pass by Green Lane, *kuvarungu*. If you tell me the address, I am sure I will know the occupants." She just smiled at him and shook her head. He grinned at her and she could see his three gold teeth at the back of his mouth. She could tell he had had *sadza nemuriwo* for lunch; the green residue between his front teeth gave it away.

It was a chilly Wednesday afternoon; the sky was overcast, and the August winds were beginning to introduce themselves. Zadzisai had been looking forward to this day for four years now. It was not her first babysitting gig, but she had been trying to get this exact job for six months now. Ever since she got back from England, she had been applying for this job and today she would finally meet the family whose life she would change. She sat between a man who reeked of garlic and could not stop coughing, and a lady who was speaking very loudly on her tablet, it looked as if she was holding a counter book to her ear as she shouted into the receiver.

"I sent the money via Ecocash Ba Nhamo, send Nhamo now *anotora*."

The garlic man would try to start a conversation with her here and there, but she had her earphones in and pretended to listen to music. Throughout the whole trip, she had her eyes on the conductor waiting for him to call for Green Lane. Zadzisai zoned out as she began to contemplate whether it was a good idea, or if it was worth the risk. She thought about how Dadirai, the only person who had stuck with her four years ago, had helped her get the passport and the visa.

The garlic man nudged her as the *kombi* came to a halt. "*Vekuvarungu*, Green Lane is that road there." The conductor said as he pointed at the road which was opposite the *kombi*.

"*Yaaah,* it's good you had 4 rands *yakakwana*. Or else I was going to marry you with someone." Zadzisai got off and thanked the conductor. He just nodded his head and banged the top of the *kombi* to signal the driver. As the *kombi* took off, she crossed the road and took out her phone. She began to look through her messages from Mrs. Warren to make sure she was in the right street. She put the address on Google Maps to make sure she would not get lost. It would take her 12 minutes to walk to the house.

The houses looked like the ones in Bicester Village in Oxford, the ones where you knew rich people lived. The air was clean and unpolluted, the birds sang a different tune from the ones from her neighbourhood. All the lawns were neatly manicured, and the houses were all more than two stories high. Zadzisai stopped briefly as a car passed by. She wished it was Mrs. Warren, but the driver was completely different from the picture she had.

Zadzie, you cannot go back now, she thought to herself as she walked. You have been waiting for this for four years now, you deserve to be happy. Yes, amai nababa do not approve and will not after what mukoma Tongai did. However, it is not your fault that he decided to run away with someone's husband, you cannot pay for his mistake. You deserve this, the way it happened was a mistake, but the result was not.

Zadzisai stood in front of the house at the address she had been given. It was not very different from the ones she had seen as she was walking, but the bronze gates had huge W's carved on them. The palm trees shielded the house, one could only see the Satellite Dish from outside.

*In two days' time you will be back in England Zadzie, just get it over with*, she convinced herself. She fixed her afro and as she was smoothing her dress, she spotted a clove of garlic. She took a deep breath, removed it and pressed the intercom.

"Hello, Mrs. Warren speaking, how can I help you?" A voice with a distinctive accent came from the intercom. "It's Zadzie, Mrs. Warren. The babysitter...how are you?" she said as she looked at the gate.

"Oh, darling, you made it. I was beginning to worry, but Owen told me you seem like a woman of your word. Let me buzz you in." She heard a soft buzz and the gates opened ajar; two brown dogs that looked like overgrown rats came running towards her.

"Gumdrop! Sheepy! No, get away from Zazi! Shuuu shuuu! Boys, where are your manners?" A blonde petite woman shouted from the balcony. She looked like one of those retired supermodels, you could only see her wrinkles when she smiled or grimaced. She came down the stairs and hugged Zadzie, looked at her and hugged her again.

"Wow, you are more beautiful than I thought. Is that your real hair?" she said as she reached to touch it. Zadzisai reached for her hand and shook it, directing away from her head. “Yes ma'am, it is my real hair. You have a very beautiful house," she said, moving a bit further from her.

“Oh, thank you, darling, please come inside. I need to show you around so that you are familiar with the place before you start on Friday. And please call me Victoria, ma'am makes me feel old. After all, forty-four is the new twenty!" Victoria laughed heartily as she led Zadzisai to the kitchen. As she followed Victoria, Zadzisai was looking for signs of the child she would be babysitting.

“Angelina, come down sweetheart. I need you to meet someone," Victoria shouted from the bottom of the stairs. Zadzisai's heart began to pound, and she could hardly breathe.

“How do you pronounce your name again, Zazie? Right? I always try to pronounce names correctly even though some of them are tongue twisters." she said as she poured herself a glass of wine and an Appletizer for Zadzisai.

“It's actually Zadzisai, but Zee will be fine". As Zadzisai was talking, Gumdrop and Sheepy came down the stairs and Angelina was behind them trying to catch up. The dogs disappeared into the lounge before Angelina could catch them.

Zadzisai gasped and held her mouth, “She looks just like him, she has her father's eyes." Her eyes became glassy. She stared at Angelina until she was in the kitchen standing next to Victoria. She wore a pink dress like hers but with a darker hue.

"Zee, what did you say? Oh, we adopted her four years ago, but a lot of people say she has Owen's eyes even though his are blue and hers are brown. I guess it's the shape they'll be referring to." Victoria exclaimed as she reached out to hug Angelina who was shyly staring at Zadzisai."

“Yes, I guess it's the shape that they will be talking about. You said she is four? How did you end up getting her?" Zadzisai tried to compose herself and act natural. Victoria looked at Zadzisai, smiled down at Angelina and asked her if she could go and find the dogs then she would introduce her to Zadzisai. Angelina ran towards the living room door and disappeared.

“Zazi, we haven't actually discussed or told Angelina about her adoption. We feel she is still young and even though she is black, and we are white, we see no colour difference because she is our baby. We got her from a family in Westgate after their daughter was impregnated at 17. They could not handle the embarrassment because unfortunately, their son ran away with someone's husband. It's a shame, the parents took the baby from their daughter and told her the baby was still borne. They sent her to England the last I heard, but they were very desperate. We received Angelina the day after she was born, on my 40th birthday," she said, as she reached for a tissue to dry the corner of her eyes. She took two sips of her wine and looked at Zadzisai.

"She is a real miracle, we could not have a child, so Owen and I opted for adoption and I do not regret it." Angelina came running back in with the dogs, she stood in front of Zadzisai and shook her hand.

"I am Angelina Warren, what is your name?" She smiled showing her toothless mouth to Zadzisai who laughed out loud, they all did.

"Mommy, I like her. Can we keep her?" She looked up to Victoria who smiled back at her daughter and said.

"Yes, we can keep her!"

As Victoria was walking Zadzisai out the door, she gave her an extra key and told her she could start the day after tomorrow, but she could come back the following day to get to know Angelina better whilst she ran errands. Victoria escorted Zadzi to the gate and hugged her tightly. Angelina walked behind Victoria and waved as the gate was closing.

As soon as Zadzisai arrived home, she called Dadirai.

"*Shaa,* I just met my daughter for the first time. She has Tapfumaneyi's eyes, she is beautiful Dadi. *Hiiii mwana wangu nhai!"* she began to cry.

"What are you planning on doing then Zee, are you still thinking of taking her to England? It is risky because this is kidnapping *ka.* Since Mugabe resigned *hakusisina* corruption so you might end up in prison. Chikurubhi straight before you make it to the airport."

"I am taking her Dadi, she is the only thing I have. You helped me with her passport and visa, all I need is her and *kuswera mangwana,* I am taking my daughter home. She is mine and she deserves to be with her real mother. They call her Angelina but before I gave birth to her I always called her Muneni. That is her name."

"*Hhhmmm* Zee you know I always support you, but think hard on this. I am not comfortable with this and I might end up losing my job at the Embassy if this blows over. Think about it, give it two days because *ndaakutotya,* I'm worried!" Dadi said to Zadzisai.

"Ok, I will think about it. I will take time, thank you Dadi. *Wakaita basa hako.* You gave me a chance to see the only thing worth risking my life for. Thank you."

"No worries Zee, but *chimbofunga* about it," Dadi suggested.

As soon as Zadzisai hung up the phone, she began to pack her bags and booked two one-way tickets to Heathrow Airport. She put her phone in water and began to plan for the next day, her trip back to Green Lane and straight to Heathrow with her daughter.

***

LOCATION: England, Manchester, 20:45.

Tapfumaneyi looked at the black velvet box and he put it back in his pocket, as he sat back in the restaurant chair and checked his phone. It was now ten minutes past his appointment with Gamuchirai. He peeped out the window of the restaurant, hoping to see her arrive at the restaurant. It was a snowy January evening and the streets were caked with snow. All one could see were the streetlights and those illuminating the restaurant entrances. He checked the time on his wristwatch and realised he did not mind her being late. He needed more time to brace himself for what was to be one of the most important decisions of his life. He stared out of the window again, his body suddenly rigid, skimming through the unfamiliar faces outside, trying to calm himself.

"Excuse me, Sir, are you ready to order?" the waitress asked, towering over him. She looked him in the eye waiting for a response, but he just shook his head and forced a smile. The waitress walked away, leaving him to his thoughts. He took out his phone to see if Gamu had contacted him, but he could not get past the wallpaper of him and Gamuchirai. He could not help but notice how happy she looked in the picture. It was from their last holiday in Tenerife, which she had demanded to go to for her birthday. She was all made up, her skin was sun-kissed, spirit free and he thought, as often as he did, what a beautiful woman she was. She wore a yellow summer dress like the colour of sand which complimented her complexion as she sat on his lap.

"You are lucky my guy, a woman like that is hard to come by. Educated, smart, ambitious and puts you first. What more can you ask for? She loves you man, if I were you, I would marry her before another *mandem* steps in." Takunda always reminded him every time they met up. He had come to understand that Takunda liked Gamu. The way he always insisted on them meeting up at his house rather than anywhere else, knowing fully well that Gamu usually worked from home, was the biggest clue. Takunda would sacrifice driving from Swindon to London for every match of the Premier League, to watch it at his house. He would always say it was because Tapfuma's

TV was bigger and Gamu always made snacks. He was right, however, Gamu was the woman of every sensible man's dream. She cooked for him every night, drew him a bath with special bath bombs she bought from *Lush* when he had had a bad day at work and most nights, she would stay up just to have her dinner with him. She knelt when she greeted her elders, and his aunt had commented on her manners when he went with her to Zimbabwe. She ticked all the boxes of the ideal woman. It made him feel pompous amongst other men, and he had what every other man was scouring for at the bottom of all barrels on dating sites, bars, and church. He understood this and he was aware that she loved him, but he did not feel the same way. Over the last year they had courted, he had tried all he could to inflict this feeling of infatuation that left him breathless but not wanting to be rescued. To him 'soulmate' was more of a myth or a once in a blue moon event which only happened once in a lifetime, if not at all. He had taken all the recommended steps of a gentleman in love, asking her to move in with him and had even started saving money for their children to show and prove to himself that he loved her, at least enough to see a future with her. He knew he was being unfair to her; she had given him everything he wanted and needed, but still, she would never be enough to completely give his heart to.

Tapfuma looked at his wristwatch again and began to get annoyed. He thought about how hard it was for people to keep time when all one had to do was be on time and be time conscious. One memory kept rewinding in his mind, he tried to eliminate it but the words "time conscious," had triggered him.

"Aaah Tapfu, you are too time conscious. I am not even that late shaa," Zadzisai would always say each time she made him wait. He always had a menacing look on his face and it annoyed him how she was never on time.

"Aaah no Zadzisai, I always tell you *kuti* being early is being on time and being on time is being late. It is not that late *kuita sei kwacho*? It's about principle." He would rant about and refuse to even look at her, but she always had a way to make him come around.

"*Sorry shewe,* I am very sorry. I promise to try and be principled like you. You are a very principled man huuuh. Please teach me how to be like you, *kurongeka kwakadai.*"

Tapfuma enjoyed Zadzi's sarcasm, but he mostly loved how easily she would change his mood, and he vowed never to tell her. He always ended up shaking his head with a chuckle, kissing her forehead.

"What can you not get away with?" Tapfuma would end up saying to Zadzi. He caught himself smiling, but he quickly dismissed the memory from his head and talked himself back to reality. He took a deep breath, sat back, and looked around the restaurant and was met with unfamiliar faces, except for the waitress.

It was an Indian restaurant that Takunda had recommended, and it came with good reviews too. It was named the most amorous and idyllic restaurant on Oxford Street. It was dimly cool, and the atmosphere was laced with the aroma of rich spices and conversation. He signalled the waitress and asked for a glass of water.

"She must be very special to have you wait for over an hour," the waitress said to Tapfumaneyi when she brought the water.

"Excuse me?" he asked, confused by her statement.

"You have been sitting here for over an hour, obviously waiting for someone because you keep looking at your watch," she said, smiling at him. He had not realised he had been sitting there for over an hour now, and Gamu had sent him a text eighteen minutes ago informing him about the snowstorm. He smiled and nodded at the waitress hoping for her to leave him to his thoughts. As soon as she left him, his mind wandered again. He began to question if marrying Gamu was right for him. He felt he was ready for marriage and a family at 26 years old. He knew what was expected of him at his age and reassured himself he was content and fulfilled by Gamu. Soon, he would be promoted to Sergeant from Police Officer. Tapfuma was financially stable, had investments and was paying up his mortgage on a three-bedroomed house with one and a half bathrooms. This time, he felt he was ready, and it was different from his first attempt to marry. Then, he was young and a student when he had to bring himself to plan for a future with a wife and child. He distinctly remembered the day Zadzisai came running to his house with tears in her eyes, terrified. The look on her face narrated everything and without question, he knew he wanted to be with her.

"Zadzisai, what happened? Is someone dead?" he asked as he stood from the tattered leather chair and walked towards the bed in his room.

"Tapfuma, what are we going to do? I told you to be careful, now *hona*?" Zadzisai began to wail louder. Tapfuma walked towards the door to check if anyone was near to hear their conversation. Mainini Rumbi had gone to *magrosa* with Tanaka, his cousin. He closed the door and began to console Zadzisai who now had her face in her palm, crying.

"Tapfumaneyi, *ndine nhumbu.* I am pregnant and I have no idea how I am going to tell my parents. You told me you were being careful. What are we going to do, because *handiskuda kuregedza kuchikoro*? I cannot stop going to school because of this. I told you to be careful and you agreed," she said, as she charged towards him and tried to punch him. He blocked her hands and pulled her close to hug her, then she began to sob again. He held on to her.

"Zee, it's ok. I am here, I am here." He towered over her, held her tightly, then led her to his chair and went out of the room.

Tapfumeyi came back with a glass of water and gave it to Zadzisai. At 21 years Tapfumaneyi was mature for his age. He had taken a year off school to work so he could support his aunt and cousin. After his parents had died when he was in primary school, Mainini Rumbi had taken him as her own son. She made sure he did not feel like an orphan and after Babamudiki Ngoni left, he became the man of the house. Mainini Rumbi unfailingly reiterated that there was nothing he could not do or solve; even his future was his to build.

Zadzie took a few sips of water then looked at him, searching his face for any sign of anger or remorse, but Tapfumaneyi looked at her and smiled. Confused and angry, Zadzisai sneered and as she stood up to bolt out of the room, Tapfumaneyi stood in front of her.

"Iwe Tapfumaneyi Mhodzi, you are smiling? It's not a laughing matter. My life is over, and it hasn't even started. I cannot keep it, where will I put it and in whose house? And in whose house, you know my father! *Maihwee zvangu*, my father! What am I goi... She began to cry again as it dawned on her that she had to inform her parents. Her war-vet father who still wore a red beret to commemorate his lost friends and right arm which he lost in the *Chimurenga* war. Tapfumaneyi sat and looked at her with hurt eyes, searching for her eyes.

"Zadzi, we will make this work. I am so sorry this has happened but please, let us think it through. I am smiling because I am happy the woman I love is carrying my child. I will take care of you both, I do not know how, but I will."

The next morning, Tapfumaneyi woke up to go to Zadzisai's house by himself. It was a warm Saturday morning in September and even though it was 9 in the morning, it felt like 12 in the afternoon. He had told Mainini Rumbi about the pregnancy the night before, and she had not taken it very well. He had explained himself and had promised to take care of Zadzisai and the baby. She had wanted to go with him, but he had told her it was better if he had gone by himself. He did not want her to be burdened by his situation and he knew he had disappointed her.

"*No Tapfuma,* you cannot go alone! *Hazvina hunhu*, do not act as if you come from an ill-mannered household. You already disrespected them by defiling their daughter, now you want to show up at their house by yourself like a grown man? If you do not want to go with me, go with Baba Netsai. You cannot go alone, no!" Baba Netsai was their neighbour who was the only father figure Tapfumaneyi had since his father passed away. As it was a Saturday, Tapfumanei went and told him everything, and after what seemed like a couple of hours, Baba Netsai talked briefly with Mainini Rumbi and they were off to Zadzisai's house.

"Babe, oh my gosh babe, I am so sorry. It's like people become dumb when driving in snow," Gamu said, as she walked towards Tapfuma and kissed him on his lips. He had not seen her as he was lost in his own thoughts and had to conjure his mind to the present moment. She stood opposite him with a wide grin on her face, searching his face for a response.

"It's ok," he said as he stood up to pull the chair for her. "I was just lost in my own thoughts. I was…how…ho... how are you? You look amazing...beautiful... you look great", he said as he sat opposite her, trying to compose himself. It dawned on him that he had not even rehearsed his proposal and had been reminiscing about Zadzie and the baby he was told was stillborn.

"Thank you. Baby, you do not look alright. We can go home, and I will make you something and draw you a bath? Oh, and we might watch The Help ag..."

"Will you marry me?" Tapfuma blurted it out without realising it. He had been caught up in his past, the thought of not having Zadzisai or no one at all scared him. He was as shocked as she was by what he had said. She looked at him with tears in her eyes and began to cry and laugh at the same time. Tapfuma wished he had not said it, he tried to take it back by trying to explain, but Gamu was already saying yes repeatedly, catching the attention of the other diners.

"What I meant to say was, I am grateful and glad you are part of my life bu..." before he could end his explanation, he was interrupted by the waiting staff who came with a dessert plate written 'congratulations' in chocolate, champagne and the waitress who had served him earlier began to sing a harmonised rendition of 'Marry me' by Bruno Mars.

Gamu was still crying tears of joy and she stood in front of him with her hand stretched out in front of him. He was very bemused; he did not even think of the black velvet box in his pocket.

"The ring, man. Show her you mean it." A man from the table behind him shouted as the waitress was singing. Everything was happening so fast; he was caught unaware when a bottle of champagne popped, and the waiter poured into the glasses on their table.

"Come on man, do not keep your lady waiting. Ask the question again...with a ring this time."

Seeing how he had no way out and Gamu was the best thing he had since moving to England, he knelt before her, took the ring from the box, and proposed. She said yes again, this time without tears, but glee on her face. As he stood up, Gamu hugged him tightly and he hugged her tighter. Assuring himself that this was the best decision, he kissed her deeply as their audience cheered them on.

This is the beginning of a new life and tomorrow is a new day, what could go wrong? Tapfuma thought to himself as he raised his glass and gulped it down together with his doubts and his past.

***

LOCATION: Great Manchester Police, The Next Morning 09:25

Tapfumaneyi sat at his desk and looked at the file. He picked it up then put it down again and put his head in his hands. Phones were ringing on every desk; the smell of coffee filled the office. He shuffled in his chair and picked up the phone, but he put it down again. He picked up the file again and as he was about to browse through it for the 12th time, Sergeant Major Finley came to his desk. He was a hefty man who took pride in his job. He was more of a legacy as his father and grandfather had all been part of British law enforcement. He always finished every sentence with "*love*". For a brawny man, he was very soft, and he always offered words of wisdom for everyone he saw at the office. Even when the criminals came in for questioning, he took a few minutes to sit down with them and talk to them about Jesus. Many convicts had complained about it, but he ended up being given a higher rank where he would have minimum contact with any of the criminals.

"Taps, did you get a chance to look at that file with the kidnapped child? I have Officer Bailey on the case with you. He is doing more research and has gone to the airport to find out when and how she made it back. Gosh, I cannot believe someone would travel all the way from here to Africa just to kidnap a kid and come back. And you know those immigration officers held her at the airport, but it was because of her passport, not the kid's. Poor little love, hope she is alright," he said, as he sat down opposite Tapfuma with a file in his hands.

Tapfumaneyi, still looking at the file, mouthed the child's name then looked at Sergeant Finley. He looked at the picture of the little girl in the pink tutu who had been reported missing 5 days ago in Zimbabwe. He could not explain how or why he was drawn to her, but he was. She was kidnapped by a young woman who was supposed to have been her nanny and supposedly her biological mother, the file stated.

"You know Taps, if I did not know any better, I would have thought that was your child. Look at those eyes! I do not want to come off as ignorant, thinking all black people look the same but..." he said, opening his eyes wider, gesturing for Tapfuma to look at the picture again.

"If I had a child, I think I would have known. And I'm not that type of bloke; I am old fashioned like that," he said, as he swung in his chair, trying to get his mind off the little girl.

"Oh yeah, you are old fashioned like that. Congrats mate, Taku told me the good news last night when he came on his night shift. Gamu is a good one, my Anne said the same when you came over with her last Easter."

"Thank you, sir, she really is special."

"Alright then, make it quick with the investigation mate, we have to make the arrest today. The parents of the girl contacted Interpol, so the case was given to us. Problem is that the parents of the little girl did not have a lot of info on the kidnapper. The mother was heart-rendered; she could hardly remember much, only the name Zazie. Are you familiar with that name? It is a Zimbabwean name." He said to Tapfuma. Tapfuma shook his head, he tried to ponder on the name. He presumed it could be a *Venda or Nyanja* name or another tribe other than Shona, within Zimbabwe.

"No sir, I am not familiar with the name," he said.

"Well, for all we know it could be a fake name. We got a number though, but it was registered to someone called ...Dhadhirai Moyo. Not sure if that name rings a bell, though I feel I am saying it wrong," he said, handing Tapfuma the file he had. He scanned through the file and recognised the name, Dadirai Moyo.

"Oh yes, that is a Shona name." He said, putting the file down.

"Well, better get it moving, we do not have much time. Those Southern buggers could not take it because they are swamped with similar cases. Better call your young bride to tell her you will be home late, because it is going to be a long day."

An officer came and called Sergeant Major Finley to the holding cell. There was a young man who had been arrested for selling marijuana and was asking if he could give his life to Jesus. He gestured to the officer that he was on his way.

"I do not know if it is the reefer talking or not, but I shall continue to pray for the young man. I hope it is not a scam to be let down easy," he said, walking towards the door. Tapfuma looked at the picture again and weighed up on why he felt drawn to her and could not stop repeating her name.

A few moments later, Officer Bailey came in delirious and almost out of breath and told Tapfuma they had found the woman's address and name.

"What is her name?" he asked, almost falling out of his chair.

"File is in the car mate, we need to go now. She is a flight risk." They both ran out of the office and headed for the police car. On the way, Tapfuma browsed through the files, ruffling through the pages to find the name of the kidnapper. And there it was highlighted in green: Zadzisai Justine Mwoyo. Tapfuma could hear his heartbeat loud in his ears. He was completely oblivious that they had been driving for over two hours. His mind ran through the course of his courtship with Zadzie, how old the little girl was and how she resembled him. There was white noise in his ears, and he could hardly hear Officer Bailey informing him they had arrived or the sirens of the other two police cars which also parked in front of the house.

"Sir, let us go. She might not be here." Officer Bailey said as he stepped out of the car drawing his gun. Tapfuma got out of the car and knocked on the door with four officers behind him with their guns pointing at the door.

After knocking twice, the door slowly opened and there was Zadzisai with tears in her eyes. She looked past Tapfuma without recognising him and focused on the officers who had their guns pointed at her.

*"Zee...Zadzi..."* Tapfuma whispered to himself but he could not bring himself to his emotions; he had to be professional.

"Are you Zadzisai Justine Mwoyo?" He asked with his head down staring at the file. She nodded then looked at the person asking her the question.

"Tapfu, is that you? Oh, my goodness, it's me. Tapfu it's our ba..." she said, opening the door wider for him to see Angelica who was standing behind her.

"Ma'am, you do not have to say anything. But it may harm your defence if you do not mention when questioned something..." he began to read her rights. Before he finished reading her rights, two officers stepped forward and handcuffed her, walking her to the police car. She began to cry saying it was a misunderstanding, she screamed Tapfumaneyi's name until they put her in the car and drove off.

"Sir, do you know her?" Officer Bailey queried as he stood next to Tapfuma, who was on one knee peeping inside the house. He looked up at Bailey and told him he used to know her, but not anymore. He opened the door wider and he saw Angelica, holding an Elmo puppet, eyes teary and scared. She stared at them both and stood still.

"I will go and call the Social Services and inform Sergeant Bailey," he said, as he walked away.

"Hey sweetheart, are you ok?" he said smiling at her. Angelina looked at him and asked where they had taken her "auntie."

"Can I go with her? I am scared, " she whimpered as tears trickled down her tears. Tapfuma walked towards her and picked her up, wiping her tears.

"Sweetie, you are safe with me ok. Someone will come and get you; they will take care of you. She stared right at him confused. Why can you not take me, you said I am safe with you."

Tapfuma simply smiled and walked out of the door with Angelica in his arms. Officer Bailey was on the phone and some of the neighbours were standing around the yard.

"I miss Auntie Zazie. " Angelica said as she played with her Elmo puppet in Tapfuma's arms.

"Me too," he whispered to himself and kissed her on the forehead.

***

*To be continued in an upcoming book...*

## Sibonginkosi Christabel Netha

Sibonginkosi Christabel Netha is a poet and a short story writer who was born in Chipinge, a small town bordering Zimbabwe and Mozambique. She has lived in Chipinge, Bulawayo (Zimbabwe) and Johannesburg (South Africa). Her writing is deeply inspired by her personal experiences of migration and struggles as a Zimbabwean girl child in the diaspora. In 2018 she was a finalist in the Africa Book Club short story competition for her entry, The Baby's mother. She also contributed three short stories to Turquoise Dreams – an anthology by Zimbabwean women. Sibonginkosi is passionate about social development and is a youth worker within the NGO sector.

# The Sky

I stood in front of the Park City Butchery and looked up. The old apartheid style buildings loomed above me, reminding me how small I was, and their cold grey exterior reminded me that I was an outsider. A foreigner. I looked up beyond the intimidating grey buildings that said I did not belong there, to the sky. It was a clear blue, and although I could not feel its warmth, I could see the sun as well. I took a deep breath and remembered what mama said to me the day I left Bulawayo.

*"The same sky that you see when you look up in Johannesburg, is the same sky that we will be looking at back here in Bulawayo. So, it does not matter how far from me you are, my son, you and I will always be looking at the same sky."*

I sighed at the memory of my mother, Uma Sithole. Oh! How I loved that woman! It had never occurred to me that I would ever have to go years without seeing her beautiful face. Those warm brown eyes that had often looked into mine every day for twenty-five years, the voice that was my alarm clock everyday as she shouted at me to get up and not be late for school. I swear sometimes I was sure she was not only waking me up, but the entire township's children as well. That same voice that was quite ruthless when I was being a disobedient son was the same one that sang soothing hymns for the church choir and connected the congregants of Believer's Miracle Church with the divine. I had long since outgrown my belief in a higher power at 15 years old, but I kept going to the church for my mother's singing and unlike most young people I actually enjoyed it when the church's cell group meetings were held at our house. I was not really a fan of the teachings, but I lived for the few minutes when our three-roomed matchbox house was filled with heavenly harmonies. The altos, sopranos, tenors and bass would flow into the smallest corners of our house, making it sing of a hope that had not been felt since 2008. Even the cynic in me had no choice but to believe when the gospel was packaged in the melodic notes of mother's velvety smooth voice.

"Hey *mfanami!* Why are you looking lost?" My Uncle Joseph's booming voice broke me out of my daydream. I struggled to collect myself as he fumbled with the keys to open the butchery.

"Erm, *liivukile malume?*" I cleared my throat and greeted him, hoping he would not make a thing about my daydreaming.

My uncle, Joseph Sithole was a practical man. He had moved to Johannesburg at the tender age of eighteen, landed at Park City butchery and found himself work as a cleaner. He scrubbed floors, washed knives and cleaned surfaces until the owner, Mr Abdul Yaseen promoted him to the till. He was now the manager of the takeaway section of the butchery that Mr. Yaseen had recently opened next door to the butchery and on some days, he was tasked with managing the butchery as well. Joseph had only gone back home a total of five times in all the twenty-two years he had lived in the city of gold and on the third time, he had married a girl from his father's village and moved to Johannesburg with her. They now had three children, Diligence, Patience and Perseverance. All-important virtues that had helped him build his life, he told me.

I looked up at the sky one last time before stepping through the door that Joseph had opened. The sky peeked out at me from between the buildings and I remembered that if I was under the sky that my mother was under back home, then I was not really far from home.

Nestled between Noord Taxi Rank and Park Station, Park City Butchery was one of the busiest places one could find themselves in Johannesburg. The sidewalk in front of the shop was always packed with busy pedestrians, always in a rush to go somewhere. Sometimes I thought they were not really in a rush, but just moved that way because of the pace of the city. From my place behind the counter of the deli, I could watch the pedestrians as they moved. I liked to play a game where I would guess whether they would come into the butchery and if they did, would they go to the freezers, the deli or the takeaway section? It kept my mind busy and made me forget about the stench of dead animals that surrounded me. It is worth mentioning that my appetite for meat had dwindled ever since I started working here. I would have been a full-on vegetarian had it not been for Malume Joseph's taunting and teasing.

"*Ah mfanami!* If you are ever going to be a man, you must learn to have an iron stomach! Heh? *Nxaa* man! I can't believe my sister raised a sissy!" He bellowed drunkenly one evening when I turned down the meat Aunty Selina, his wife, had put on my plate.

Ashamed, I explained that I would get used to it and have since made an effort to eat a little bit of it just to keep him quiet. Aunty Selina had started putting less of it on my plate too. What an angel she was.

I looked up from cutting cold meat to look at the passers-by in front of the store. The nearby primary schools had knocked off and the street in front of the store was filled with children, clad in many different uniforms and all shouting and laughing at the very top of their voices. I watched them in fascination as they moved past the shops on their way to the railway station, or maybe the taxi rank. Most of them were in various states of disarray, indicative of a long day of playing. Shirts were untucked, ties loosened, and the once neatly combed hair was now a mess. It was so odd to watch how downtown Johannesburg transformed from a cold unwelcoming fortress to a regular city, all because of a few children. I was sure it was all in my head, but I still could not deny that I liked Johannesburg better when she had noisy children nestled in her bosom.

Just as I was about to write a poem in my head about how children made Johannesburg seem less intimidating, there was a sudden burst of activity in front of the shop. Somebody screamed "*Sela!* Thief!" and a couple of the children had been pushed to the ground and were crying loudly. I saw a young man running and I immediately took off after him. It was not an easy task, due to the congested nature of downtown Johannesburg. The thief was shoving people and bins onto my way and I had to take care not to trip as I ran. He ran past the second entrance of the station and up the stairs that led to the taxi rank and I could feel myself getting winded as I followed him. Just as I was about to give up and turn back, I heard shouting from one of the caravans parked at the exit of the taxi rank. I looked up and saw that one of the taxi drivers had caught him and was about to serve a hefty punishment for his crime.

My eyes widened as the group of angry men circled him, yelling all sorts of different insults at him as they did so. Suddenly, I noticed just how small and skinny the thief was. He was a scrawny kid, probably a teenager, and his clothes seemed to hang loosely on his body, save for his distressed looking jeans which seemed too short for his legs. For a second he reminded me of myself when I first arrived, wearing Uncle Joseph's hand-me-downs.

"We are going to beat you, boy! You think it's okay to steal, *heh*?" One of the drivers shouted to the thief.

"Yeah! *Asimfundiseni isfundo!* Let us teach him a lesson!" Another one agreed with him and immediately delivered a resounding clap onto the thief's face. I flinched as it landed, making a sound so fierce it felt as though it landed on my own face. The taxi drivers became more aggressive after that first slap, shoving and swearing, raining random blows on the thief. I could not bear to watch the scene any longer, certain there was no way that the guy would make it out of there alive. This was not the first mob-justice scene I had ever witnessed and if the past were anything to go by, the thief would be lucky if he still had all his bones intact after this.

I decided that it was time I went back to work. I had left my counter at the deli unmanned and I was sure Uncle Joseph would not be impressed by my heroic antics if they cost me my job. Not to mention my chest was burning from all the running. I was never much of an athlete and now that the adrenaline had worn off, my body was reminding me of that fact. I had turned around to make my way down the steps when suddenly, someone bumped into my chest.

"Oh, I'm so sorry I did not see you there!" I said immediately. I looked down and noticed that it was a girl. A girl that I had seen before actually!

"It's alright, excuse me. I must go - YOU!" She was about to dismiss me hurriedly before she did a double take. Then her eyes widened in shock.

"Charmaine!" I said, surprised. We both were.

*It had been almost five years since our unexpected encounter at Beitbridge, almost halfway through a journey I had decided would be very unremarkable. Even the border post routine had proved to be less eventful than I had expected. After queuing for hours and getting my passport stamped on the South African side, the final stage in the entire process, I had walked back to the bus only to find that someone was sitting in my seat. They had their back turned to me and their nose pressed to the window so I cleared my throat to gain their attention. A young woman who looked roughly my age had turned to look at me and through the dim light of the bus I noticed how defined her cheekbones were, how smooth her warm chestnut skin was and how puffy her eyes were. I deduced that she had been crying and decided to sit on the seat next to the aisle instead of claiming my window seat. Confrontation was not my forte and I thought it better to avoid upsetting her further; she seemed to have already had a rough night. She, however, did not think so. Charmaine had boldly asked me why I had not confronted her about the seat and called it "bullshit" when I tried to brush it off.*

*"It is just a seat really. I don't mind," I said to her, taken aback by her barefaced audacity. She was not the timid creature I had assumed her to be.*

*"Bullshit! You feel sorry for me, don't you?" Again, her lack of shyness was unnerving. This girl was either very honest or socially inept. Her question had me cornered so I did the only thing I could.*

*"Why would I feel sorry for you?" I asked her, turning my head to the side slightly.*

*"Because you saw me crying." She answered simply. Not only was she audacious, but she was also honest.*

*"Actually, I didn't see you crying but I guessed that you might have been. And I did not confront you because I cannot handle confrontation. It makes me anxious," I told her honestly, emboldened by her own effrontery.*

*"What?" she said as she burst out laughing and although I thought my manly pride should have taken offense, I couldn't help but think of how beautiful the sound of her laughter was.*

*"Yes. I was afraid that you might argue or cause a scene and then it would have been a whole thing and…" I explained to the beautiful stranger while she laughed at me.*

*This proved to be an icebreaker and after we introduced ourselves, we spent the rest of the journey discussing everything from our favourite soccer teams (although, I was not as much of a fan as she seemed to be) to the people we had left behind back home. Charmaine was easily the most honest human being I had ever met. She seemed to be the kind of person who said exactly what was on her mind and meant it, which made her both intimidating and compelling at the same time. By the time our bus pulled into the Powerhouse bus station I had not only told her my deepest secrets and read her my favourite poems, but I had also made a silent vow to live as honestly and boldly as she did. I told myself that in this new chapter of my life I would never let myself get swept up in the pressure to pretend, as so many Zimbabweans who found themselves in Johannesburg did.*

Seeing her again made me realise just how far I had strayed from that path, starting with the fact that I had not called her all these years.

"Bongani!" she said as she threw her arms around me, a huge smile on her face.

"I- I'm fine. What. What are you doing here? Are you not supposed to be in Cape Town?" I was not expecting her to even shake my hand after what I did, much less hug me! I guess she was as forgiving as she was honest. Could this girl be any more perfect?

"Look, I ended up not going and it's a long story that I unfortunately do not have time to explain because my brother is getting beat up by a mob and at this very moment!" she said urgently, the words coming out of her mouth so quickly I could barely catch them all. I had, however, got the most important part. She had not gone to Cape Town; therefore, she would not know that I had not called the landline number she had given me that morning at Powerhouse. That explained her warm reception of me.

"So, the thief is your brother?" I said. There was a lot to take in here.

"He is not the *thief; his* name is Jacob, and he is supposed to be at school. And they are about to kill him!" she scolds me and pushes past me and starts marching towards the angry taxi drivers.

"Wait! You can't go there, that mob will kill you too!" I follow her, but I'm struggling to catch up.

"I don't care! We have to do something!" She shouted, stopping to look at me. I could see that she was prepared to fight and the determination clearly mapped on her face. There was obviously no way of stopping her now, so I just nodded and rushed to the mob with her.

We arrived just as they had knocked him to the ground, and someone kicked him in the ribs.

"Stop! Please!" Charmaine cried as she stepped into the middle of the crowd. The thief, her little brother, was lying on the ground, groaning and clutching his ribs. She kneeled to make sure he was alright.

"Please… don't hurt him," she said again to the crowd of taxi drivers that was starting to look annoyed at being interrupted.

"*Uyamazi lomfana?* Do you know this boy? Are you two thieves as well?" The leader of the gang growled out at us.

"Yes. She is his older sister. Please let him go." I said, trying my hand at bargaining. I had never been good at it and at that moment it felt as though my heart was going to jump out of my chest.

"But he is a thief!" the guy retorted. "He must be taught a lesson!"

"Yes, but he is only a boy. We will make sure it does not happen again, please. Please let him go." I begged.

"Fine." The man said reluctantly. "But he won't get this lucky next time you know."

"Thank you so much!" Charmaine gushed, and I felt relieved that the taxi drivers had not decided to beat us as well.

The crowd dispersed as we helped Jacob to his feet. He was not too badly injured and as soon as Charmaine made sure of that fact, she launched into a furious lecture, rapidly scolding the boy. The fact that he was taller than her by almost a foot did not seem to discourage her as she wagged her index finger at him.

That was Charmaine, unafraid of anything and anybody. Always ready to speak the truth when it was necessary. I smiled a little, although I felt sorry for the boy who was now being dragged away by the wrist. She seemed determined to discipline him very thoroughly. She turned to me before walking away.

"Bongani, thank you so much for your help. I must take him home now, but I will see you around. I live in Hillbrow now ...." She trailed off. Clearly there was a lot to catch up on, a lot had happened since we both stepped off that bus at Powerhouse station, but we did not really have the time to get into it all just then. She had to attend to the matter of her brother, and I had to rush back to the deli before Uncle Joseph became too angry.

"Don't mention it. Look, I work at the deli in Park City Butchery and my lunch break is at 2pm. Come by and see me when you get time alright?"

She nodded and then nudged Jacob who coughed out a "Thanks for saving my life," before they turned around and made their way out of the taxi rank. It was a mere formality because we both knew it was Charmaine who did that. Stubborn, determined, relentless Charmaine. Brave, beautiful Charmaine.

"Please don't wait another five years before coming to see me alright?" I shouted after her, although I doubted she could hear me.

I arrived at the deli to find Uncle Joseph fuming. The man was so angry I could literally see a cloud of thunder above his head.

"Where have you been, Bongani?" He roared the minute I stepped inside. "Do you think this is your uncle's shop where you can just give yourself a break when you feel like it?"

I felt like pointing out that my uncle was technically the manager, so he was not too far off the mark, but I knew he would not find it funny at all, so instead I offered him a sensible explanation.

"No *malume*, I ran after the thief that snatched the kid's wallet remember?" I said.

"Oh really? Where is this thief then? Did you catch him?" He inquired further and I could feel that I had walked into a trap.

"Uh, no." I gulped, "Some taxi drivers caught him at the rank. I arrived a little late."

"Oh, so you were not fast enough then." He continued with his cross-examination. Clearly, he was enjoying this.

"Tell me, Bongani, did you manage to at least get back the wallet he snatched?"

"No Uncle, I did not." I mumbled, looking around at the other employees who were trying hard to pretend they were not watching.

"No, you didn't! You stupid boy!" he thundered again, and I jumped. "You did not get the wallet because I have it right here!"

He waved the Ben 10 wallet at me before throwing it on the counter and I stared at it for a while, realising how stupid I had been.

"I didn't see, *malume*. I am so sorry. I thought..." I said, the words coming out fast and all muddled up.

The thief, Jacob, was probably new to this and was probably practicing snatching more valuable things hence why he had snatched a kid's wallet which probably had no more than a few coins and a train ticket if he was lucky. With this new information, my gallant attempt to catch the thief seemed useless and more importantly, reflected badly on my Uncle Joseph would now be known for having a stupid sissy nephew who wrote poetry and thought he was some sort of superhero. Of all the sins I had ever committed against Uncle Joseph, destroying the reputation he had worked so hard to build was probably the most unforgivable.

"It doesn't matter what you thought boy!" He bellowed, foaming at the corners of his mouth. "This is not one of your books and you are not stirring here to save the day okay?"

"Yes Uncle." I nodded sheepishly.

"Good, now get back to work! And the next time you decide to be Superman, remember to let me know so I can fire you!" he finished his tirade, threw an apron at me and then slammed the back door as he went to the storeroom.

I returned to my spot behind the counter sheepishly, almost regretting my actions. I could not be completely remorseful, however, because I was grateful to have seen Charmaine. In fact, I had half a mind to thank Jacob for his criminal antics because he was the cause of mine and Charmaine's unlikely encounter after five whole years! It was because of him that I was getting a second chance. As I worked at the deli, I could not help, but feel anticipation for the next few days.

Something inside me was excited and was telling me to get ready for a big shift in my life,

even as I repeated my monotonous routine the next morning. Arriving at the butchery, looking at the sky and reminiscing about my mother, I could not help, but ask myself if this was the story I would tell when people asked me how I met the love of my life. As I looked at the Johannesburg sky, the dreary grey sky that promised sunlight if only we would be patient, the same sky my mother would look up at back home in Bulawayo, the same sky my Charmaine would look up at just a few streets over in Hillbrow, I whispered a prayer to the knower of all our roads:

***Please do not wait another five years before bringing my Charmaine back to me.***

## Finding Luba

Maria came to the city of gold with the intention of finding her sister. Word back home was that Luba had been "eaten" by the city and as her only surviving sibling, she felt an immense sense of duty to get her back.

*I am not going to fail you, mama, Maria* thought as she walked through the turnstile at the University of Witwatersrand campus. If this were a regular situation, she would have been an excited first-year student, fidgeting in anticipation of what promised to be an amazing four years studying at a high-ranked university in South Africa, but this was not the case. All the anticipation and emotional energy she had was reserved for finding her sister, whom they had not seen or heard from in almost ten years.

The search for her older sister had her walking across the university campus in a foreign country looking for a man she had spent years trying to forget. A man who just woke up one morning and decided to turn his back on his wife and three children, one of whom was disabled, was not worth thinking about in her books. All the years of living as though one did not need a father at all had been undone in one afternoon, when Maria had sat by her paternal grandmother in her Esigodini home listening to her telling the story of why her grandmother, her mother's mother, disliked her father. Knowing this would help her understand why the man Maria loathed was the key to finding her sister and making her family whole again.

The answer to the question she had spent years trying to ignore had come tumbling out of her grandmother and Maria felt that she had no choice but to right the wrongs of the past.

*Why did her father leave them?*

The family had been quite shocked when Maria announced that she would be going to study in Johannesburg, because for as long as they had known her, she only had bad things to say about the city. To her, this city was neither the haven that her people viewed it to be nor the place of refuge it promised to be. In fact, when she and her siblings were younger and dreaming about what they would become, she had stubbornly refused to dream about crossing the Beitbridge border to South Africa and becoming *injiva,* the flashy South African returnees who brought home gifts and groceries for their families, as most of her siblings had done. She had been the only one who maintained that she would live in Zimbabwe for the rest of her life.

> "I am going to raise my children right here, close to my mother." 10-year old Maria would proclaim during these dreaming sessions. As they grew older and the situation deteriorated in the country, more of her siblings and cousins left for other countries, most of them relocating to Johannesburg for work or study opportunities. Maria, on the other hand, was adamant that living in the diaspora was not for her.
> "I am going to raise my children in Zimbabwe, close to my mother." 18-year-old Maria maintained when asked about the plans she had for her future.

It was quite a shock to her entire family when, during one of their frequent visits to her grandmother's homestead in Esigodini, Maria announced to her extended family that she would be applying to a university in South Africa. Her mother had simply smiled when the announcement was made, reserving her questions for later. She had always believed that her children should follow their dreams, so she did not want to express how much this decision grieved her. She had lost her husband and her firstborn daughter to that city and the thought of losing another member of her family made her anxious. But being the good mother she was, she understood that she could not stop her daughter from chasing her dreams. If she had decided to leave home, all she could do was offer her support.

Maria, who could sense her mother's anxiety and knew that it was not without good reason, sought to comfort her mother and assure her that she, unlike the last two members of their family, would not be gone forever.

> "It will just be for my first degree, don't worry. I will be back as soon as I complete it." She said to her mother softly whenever she caught her gazing at her with a pained look on her face. Although her mother wanted to believe her, the past disappointments would not let her.

***

Maria told herself she was a woman on a mission as she stood next to the massive white pillars of the Great Hall. The fact that this place was breath-taking was just an added benefit that she did not allow herself to indulge in.

But oh man! This place was amazing! Looking at the maps she was yet to memorise and the buildings she was yet to get lost in, she saw a promise of adventure in the place. It made her feel like excitement was looming just around the corner, and there was nothing she loved more than adventure. But still, she was not here to enjoy it, so she tried to push that feeling away.

Although her heart had been feeling like it would burst ever since she stepped off that bus and set foot in Park Station, she forced herself to focus on the serious business that brought her here. She guessed that this was the feeling that so many of her people felt when they arrived. This ambition-laden air with its undeniable ability to reach into a man's soul and make him reach out for heights whose existence he had not known before he set foot on this land. Maria imagined Johannesburg as a seductive temptress, her mountains like bejewelled breasts decked out in gaudy shopping malls and freeways. Weary travellers caught a glimpse of the "gold" within them and laid their lives down at her gaudy shrine to the gods of capitalism and never turned back. Such was her power. She imagined this was what happened to the trekkers when they found the first piece of gold in these mountains and she believed this was what happened to the fathers who left home and never came back in her community back home. Greedy Johannesburg had shown them a small piece of gold, then opened her mouth wide and swallowed them all.

So, no. She was not happy to be here and she would not be attending any of the fresher's bashes, *thank you very much*. She came here to save her family and get a world-class education while at it.

With one last longing look at the perfectly trimmed grassy field that was littered with excited students signing up for clubs and classes, she turned around and began walking towards the exit. It was time to find her father and save her family.

***

Alfred married Sbonokuhle, the only child of Thabisani and Maria Sibanda, in the year 1990, two years after their first child, Lubelihle was born. To say that the time leading up to their union was difficult would be a gross understatement. Impossible is what it was. Thabisani, a stubborn businessman and leader at the local community church, had a permanent frown that dominated his face almost as much as he dominated his family. He had been opposed to the relationship from the beginning and treated the romance between his daughter and mentee with grave hostility that left everyone in shock. After all, had he not taken Alfred under his wing when his parents, who had been close friends of his, passed on in an unfortunate car accident? Was Alfred Nyoni not an aspiring church leader himself, eager to learn all he could from such a respectable man as Luckson? When concerned friends and relatives inquired why Alfred was not an acceptable suitor for his daughter, Luckson simply replied that a man who could not control his bodily urges enough to wait until after the wedding, would never be able to lead a family.

"*He sneaks around with my daughter and then comes here expecting my blessing to marry her? Never!*" The man would roar with such violence that those who had asked cowered and resolved never to question him again.

He forbade Sbonokuhle from seeing Alfred for a year after Lubelihle was born and despite protests from other family members that what he was doing was a violation of their cultural beliefs, he would not meet with Alfred's uncles. His wife, a soft-spoken nurse, had urged their daughter to obey, with the promise that she would help the two lovers communicate secretly. In the meantime, they tried to wear him down every day, begging him to forgive his daughter for being promiscuous, to forgive his wife for raising a loose daughter, to forgive Alfred for disrespecting him and taking advantage of her and many other variations. Even the extended family tried to make him see reason, as aunts and uncles, grandparents and cousins all visited his home and negotiated with him to no avail.

Tired of her father's stubbornness, Sbonokuhle left her father's house on her daughter's first birthday when her father had gone out to a prayer meeting. Maria senior, having watched her daughter's misery for so long, helped her pack their things and when Alfred had arrived to pick them up, she kissed her granddaughter multiple times before handing her to her father. To her daughter she simply said, "*You are doing the right thing for your family, my daughter. Go very far from here.*"

Knowing the irreversible damage that this would cause in her family, she embraced her daughter and planted teary kisses before watching them go down the hill in Alfred's pale yellow Toyota Cressida. She was still weeping for her daughter whom she would never see again when her husband arrived home, and as he watched her sobbing on the floor in the empty room that had belonged to Sbonokuhle for eighteen years, all he could do was sit with her while she blew her nose into an old napkin that had belonged to her granddaughter.

"You have no idea what you have done, woman." Was all he said before they both stood up from the mattress and continued to live their life as always. Never to speak of Sbonokuhle, Alfred or Lubelihle ever again.

Their daughter got married a year later, in a Baptist church in Bulawayo, or so they heard. They were no longer on speaking terms with her and all her lobola negotiations were handled by a relative who lived in one of the townships in the city. An uncle on Maria senior' s side.

Thabisani was coming into the house to get some sugar for the *mageu*, fifteen years later, when the landline that stayed on the small table in the passage rang. On the other side of the phone was his daughter, and although he was trembling with emotion he quietly listened as she told him that Alfred had left her and the kids. Calmly, as though he had not prayed every night for another chance to hear his daughter's voice again, he asked for her address and said he and Maria senior would visit them soon. They were now living in Bulawayo, and, as it turned out, not too far from where Sbonokuhle lived. When he told this to his wife, she could not believe it.

"To think we could have walked past one of our grandchildren and not known it!" She exclaimed as her husband led her out of the field he had left her in when he went to fetch the sugar. From then on, Thabisani and Sbonokuhle resumed their relationship as though the past fifteen years had not happened. She now had three children: Luba, Maria junior and Thabisani junior. Thabisani went all out to make sure they never felt the gap of an absent father. He took it on himself to assist Sbonokuhle formalise her separation with Alfred and help her find a cheaper place to stay. Thabisani spent a lot of time with his grandchildren and was fiercely protective of them the way a father would.

It was only after he passed away that Maria learned of what took place before she was born. She had been helping her grandmother sort through a big suitcase of junk when she happened upon a copy of her parent's divorce papers. A little detail had stood out to her as she quickly scanned through the document.

"Gogo, why does it say here that khulu was a witness to mummy and daddy's marriage? I don't remember him being there at all." She had asked.

Her grandmother had quickly snatched the papers from her and said, "This is grown up business Maria!" With a disapproving frown on her face.

"I've already seen it, so please just tell me! Please gogo!" Maria pleaded, pushing away the other papers that were on her lap.

"It is too complicated for someone your age to understand. So continue sorting through those papers and do not ask any more questions." Her gogo said firmly, and Maria had no choice but to obey.

Later when they were drinking tea on the veranda, she told Maria the whole story, including how her mother had called them that afternoon in 2005, crying that she had messed up and now her children were going to suffer for it. Maria's *khulu* helped her mother with the divorce after Alfred left. He told the lawyers that he had witnessed the difficult marriage between Alfred and Sibonokuhle just to help make it easier for the divorce to be granted, even though he and Sibonokuhle had not been in contact for over ten years.

"But why did khulu hate my dad so much? Was he that embarrassed that mummy had a baby out of wedlock?" Maria wanted to know.

"That, *mtan'omtanam,* is something that I would have told you to ask your khulu himself, if he were still with us." She said with a wistful look on her face.

"For the many years we were married, your khulu never told me the reason behind it. All I can think of is that it perhaps has to do with his life on the mines." Maria senior said.

"The mines?" Maria junior asked, surprised. Clearly there was so much mystery around the man she thought she knew so well.

"Yes. Before I met your khulu he worked in the mines in Johannesburg for a few years. I do not know much about his life there except that while he was there, he met Alfred's father, Abednigo, and they were great friends even until the unfortunate accident that took him and his wife away."

Abednigo and your khulu were very close and even when they came back home, they spent a lot of time together. He knew when he met him that this was a friend he wanted to have in his life for the rest of his life. He said that life on the mines was very hard, but having Abednigo by his side made it all easier to bear. Their friendship seemed as though it would last forever until one fateful day, when Abednigo and your *khulu* met a beautiful girl at a tavern after a very long workday. She was new and had come from Lesotho to work for her aunt at the tavern. Abednigo fell in love with her on the spot and their days were spent thinking of ways to win her. Eventually, on the day that was supposed to be their last day in the mines, Abednigo walked into the tavern and proposed to her. She agreed and together with your grandfather they came to Zimbabwe. Abednigo was not from around here, but after witnessing the way your grandfather was fond of him, the community grew to accept him as one of us. He married his wife here and a few years later I married your khulu. They had Alfred almost right after, while we struggled to have a child for a while, until Sbonokuhle arrived. We all used to spend a lot of time together. When Abednigo and his wife passed on in that terrible accident, your khulu was inconsolable. Alfred was also very young and the church paid for him to attend the mission school over in Gwanda. When he came back as a young man, your khulu took him under his wing and taught him everything he knew. If you ask me, I will say he would have loved to have him as a son-in-law." Maria senior told her grand-daughter. Taking enough breaks to sip her tea while her Maria suffered from the suspense of it all.

"So what happened, Gogo? What problem did Khulu have with my dad?" Maria asked impatiently. This story had only filled her with more questions.

"That, I don't know, Maria. I am only telling you what I know, which is what I told your sister the last Christmas she was home." Her grandmother replied.

"Wait, you told Luba this? Why?" Maria's eyes widened.

"She said she had been having some terrible dreams, something about your brother, grandfather and father. She said they were becoming worse and she was struggling to focus at school."

"Is that why she has not come back home?"

"Perhaps. She said one of her schoolmates had a calling and suspected that she, too, was being called to become a *sangoma* and Luba did not want that."

"A *sangoma* gogo!" Maria exclaimed. "Luba would never! She has always been a staunch believer in that spiritual things are not real. She could not possibly have become a *sangoma*, could she?"

"I do not think so either. Your grandfather was still alive then, so I told him about Luba and he got angry that I had told her all this. He did not want to talk to her himself, so I sent her in the next best direction. Your father." Maria senior stood up after this last statement and her granddaughter realised that their conversation would end there.

*I must find dad,* she thought to herself as she cleared up the tea things and went into the kitchen to wash them.

Later that evening, as they all sat in her grandmother's sitting room eating millet pap with chicken, she announced that she actually wanted to go out of the country for university, maybe South Africa. Maria senior only nodded and silently requested that the heavens would keep her family from experiencing more pain.

***

The last time Maria saw her father was on the night of 13 April 2005 when he and Sbonokuhle sat the kids down in the living room to explain that they would be getting separated. For Maria's older sister, Luba, it was obvious that the separation would happen. Their parents' marriage had been strained and the fighting had been getting worse with each day. She accepted the news of separation with secret relief unlike 6year-old Maria, who worshipped Alfred and was confused that he was leaving. As she watched him pack up his things, she felt an unusually fierce emotion rise up from her core and engage her. She watched through teary eyes as Alfred explained that he would be moving out and would call the kids and arrange for them to visit him as soon as he was settled down and when he looked to the kids for a response, all she managed was a strangled "I don't care" before she ran off to her bedroom.

*I don't care.*

Those words had haunted Maria for weeks after that and when Alfred did not call, those weeks of guilt and shame turned into months for her. She had apologised to her mother and siblings, convinced her behaviour was what had chased him away. She had even written an apology letter to Alfred and begged her mother to send it to him. Her mother had taken it and promised to mail it to him on her way to work and Maria spent the next few weeks agonising over whether he would reply. Still, Alfred never got back to her and eventually Maria seemed to forget about it. She became one of the children who only lived with their mother and when people asked about her father, she simply shrugged and said, "I don't have a father."

Thirteen years later, those words rang in her mind again as she looked at the building that stood in front of her. She looked once again at the piece of paper in her hand to confirm that she was at the right address. She was.

*Inhale. Exhale.* She closed her eyes and practiced the technique that she had always used to get over her nerves at her tournaments. Her technique was interrupted by the sound of a siren that rang out from inside the building, and about a minute later the heavy brown doors swung open and what seemed like a thousand little school kids in green, grey and yellow uniforms piled out. The once quiet streets were now filled with the sound of the schoolchildren celebrating the end of the school day, screaming at the top of their lungs. She waited until the crowd thinned out before stepping into the building and walking to the reception. The receptionist was currently busy, answering phone calls and dealing with parents who had come to pick up their children, so it took him a while to attend to Maria. This gave her some time to calm down and by the time the receptionist directed her to her father's office she had practiced exactly what she was going to say.

She took one last deep breath and straightened her back before knocking on the white door that had the words *"Mr A Mulumba, Vice Principal"* written in gold lettering.

***

"It took a while for me to figure it out, but once I did it, it seemed so obvious. How had I not seen it before? It was practically written on the old man's face." Sbonokuhle said to Maria. The day after Maria announced where she was going for school, Sbonokuhle had come into her daughter's room and asked to speak to her.

The look on her face and the way she was nervously wringing her hands told Maria that this was about to be a very difficult discussion and now, after having heard the story of Abednego and Thabisani senior, she knew why her mother had always walked as though she were carrying all the rocks at Matopos on her shoulders. She too felt the same at this point. What her mother had just revealed to her was simply too much to wrap her head around.

"Your gogo doesn't know anything about this and honestly, I do not think it is our place to tell her." She said giving Maria a stern look that implicitly said this part was not up for discussion.

On other occasions Maria might have challenged this though with her modern ideas of transparency and openness in families and relationships, but what she had just heard was not something that she wanted to say out loud to anyone. Ever. She had known that there was something in her family. Something sinister and unsaid that seemed to throw her family into darkness and pain. But this? She had never in a million years thought this of her grandfather. Her eyes widened as her thoughts turned to her brother Thabisani.

"But Mummy, surely you don't think this is the reason for Thabisani…" she could not even finish the line. The thought of it just turned her insides upside down.

"No Maria, that is just superstition." Her mother said, again in her stern motherly voice. Maria nodded weakly. She wished her mother's voice had been more reassuring on that part. Maybe then she would have believed her, but now she had felt the fear that underlined her stern "mom voice" she knew that her mother too, was worried. Perhaps this was why she did not want to tell Gogo, because if Gogo knew she would not think twice about the issue. If Gogo knew she would definitely say it was because of the mishap and Thabisani junior, the boy her khulu had doted on in his elderly years, the boy who could have passed as their grandfather back in his youth, would be perceived in her different light. He would stop being their miracle boy and start being a curse, punishment for a transgression.

"I told you this because I know that you gave up your original plans in order to find Luba. I think Luba found your father and he told her."

"You think maybe she does not want to come back to us because she is disgusted by us?"

"Maybe. I do not know, but from experience I can tell you that carrying this secret by yourself cannot be easy. I do not think she is alright where she is."

"Gogo told me about the dreams, do you think they still haunt her even if she knows?"

"I don't know, my child. I don't know. I just do not want you to go there without full knowledge, like your sister.. Please promise me that you will come home to me?"

"I will ma, I will." Maria took her mother's hands and kissed them as she said this. There in that small bedroom with the morning sun pouring in from the sides of the curtains that were yet to be opened, they sealed a promise that filled Sbonokuhle with an unreasonable hope that everything would be alright, despite having had suffered so much pain already.

For Maria, this was the moment that came to her when she tried to remember the last time she saw her mother. Not the dinner they had two nights before she left, not the shopping trip they took to Botswana a week before she left and not even the hugs and kisses her mother had rained on her before she got on the bus at N1 Hotel. All of these were great, but that morning three months before she left had much more weight than the other goodbye moments ever would.

***

Looking into her father's face was like looking at Thabisani. The realisation hit Maria like a freight engine. It was like looking at a much older Thabisani, if Thabisani stopped smiling all the time and maybe drooled a little less. It made sense if you factored in the big secret and it was not at all strange that someone would look exactly like their father and grandfather.

She wondered what it would have been like if her father had been around when their khulu came back into their lives. It was impossible, she knew because her khulu would have never come back if Alfred had not left, but for the first time in her life, Maria thanked her lucky stars that her parents' marriage never worked out.

"You look like Thabisani." She said to her father as he gestured for her to sit. She still could not take her eyes off the man. She had refused to hug him and proffered a handshake when he opened his arms. She was not here to make up with *him.* If she could have found her sister without him she would have done it, but as it was, she had to see him and he was stirring in her some very uncomfortable feelings.

The abandonment she struggled with all those years. The anger at him for choosing to leave the family broken and in want of her father. She tried her best to push them down and remember that she had decided to forgive him after learning what happened from her mother. In her rational mind she knew that the situation was an uncomfortable one and the decision Alfred made was not something she should hold against him, but still, something primal inside her could not get over not having a father for all these years. The adult inside her knew the issue was bigger than all of them put together, but the eight-year-old in her still felt the hurt and confusion of it all. She wanted to put everything aside and address the issue that bothered her despite how selfish she thought it was. Deep down she felt as though she was ready to scream and claw at him until he told her that he loved her.

"I need your help finding Luba." She said calmly instead, ignoring the storm of emotions that was brewing beneath. Instead of a dramatic father and daughter reunion they would discuss the serious business that had brought her here. She was going to be calm here then call her mother and cry about it in her dorm room later.

"Why...why do you think I would know?" Alfred replied, peering at her uneasily. Now that she was over the initial shock, she realised he was fidgeting rather uneasily with one of the trinkets that sat on his big desk.

"Because mummy told me everything." She said simply and watched him. His face had become unreadable now, but he did not say anything.

"Luba was having bad dreams and after speaking to Gogo I think she came to you…and you told her the truth." She continued.

"She did." He responded slowly, as though trying to pick the best words to use in addressing the issue. "She wanted to know the truth and I told her. I never spoke to her again after that."

"So you did not bother to keep in contact with her even after she knew the truth? You didn't even care!" Maria felt the anger she had tried so hard to bury rising up along with her voice.

"It's not enough that you ran out on us like a coward when you found out. No. You also let your daughter wander around in a dangerous city haunted by the past without the protection of her father!" The words came out in a squeaky, high-pitched voice that was not her own and even as she said them, the rational adult part of her knew she would regret crossing this boundary, but she could not stop now. The words had been trapped inside of her for too long and it felt good to let some of them out, albeit disrespectful. So she did the only thing that a daughter who has not grown up with her father does once she comes face to face with him, or at least, what every daughter *wishes* to do.

"God! I should have known better than to trust a man who runs out on his family to show up when he is needed. All you know is to run and pretend things did not happen when in fact, they did. And you do not care who you hurt in the process too, do you? Because if you did, you would not have left us the way you did!" Maria shouted at her father.

She wanted to say so much more, but the fury was so fierce it blinded her and made her words stick to her throat so she had to end her tirade there. Breathing heavily, she slumped into her chair and threw her head into her hands as the tears finally streamed down her face.

Alfred, who had just sat there, frozen as his 21-year-old daughter confirmed the fears that had lived in his heart right next to his memories of the life he once lived with Sbonokuhle. That he had made a mistake and been selfish to leave them behind. He wanted to go over to her side of the big Vice-principal's desk, hold her in his arms and cry along with her for a relationship that they had lost due to his cowardice, but instead, he opened one of the drawers and handed her a box of tissues.

"I- I'm so sorry. I shouldn't have..." Maria tried to say in between sniffles and hiccups. She accepted the tissue that he handed her and blew her nose while Alfred watched in silence.

If this life they were living were a movie, or at least a well-spun fairy-tale by an optimistic storyteller, Alfred would have apologised profusely for his cowardice and selfishness. He would have offered to take his daughter out for ice-cream and ask about every little detail of her life since he left. He would walk out of his office with her hand in his and shout to the receptionist that he was going out to spend some overdue quality time with his daughter. She would be shocked that he, *solitary, always-alone Alfred*, had a daughter and probably gossip with the other staff during teatime that perhaps Mr Mulumba was not gay after all. Knowing this, he would smile smugly and walk out of the dreary building and into the sun with his lastborn and off would they go to find his other daughter and bring his family back together. Perhaps he would spend the rest of his life making up for abandoning them, he would suffer the difficult moments and weather the storms that were ahead of them, but it would all be worth it. He would never be alone again.

Unfortunately, this life they were living was neither a movie nor a fairy-tale. There was no straightforward path to happiness and the gold one often thought was to be found after digging for years would turn out to be nothing more than just a very shiny but useless rock. In this case there was no straightforward way to make things right in his family, so Alfred simply waited until Maria was done.

"It's alright. You are frustrated and tired." He said when he finally spoke.

"When I told Luba the reason why I left, she said that she understood and realised that she too, wanted to be away from it all so I should not try to contact her. We made a pact not to look for each other because we both understood how difficult it would be to see the family," he spoke slowly again and regarded Maria with interest after each sentence, as though expecting her to explode again. Maria only nodded her head.

"I broke that pact four years ago, when your mother called to tell me that the old man had passed on and begged me to find Luba. I told her I would not get involved, but after she told me that she too, now knew, I promised her I would think about it. I looked for Luba but my search was fruitless until she contacted me herself, telling me she had heard that I had been looking for her. She was not happy, but after I told her of your khulu's passing on she gave me a card and said I should only contact her if there is a death in the family."

Maria's eyes widened as she realised that she had indeed come to the right place. She had to have that card and she did not care whether Alfred agreed or not. To hell with their ridiculous pact! She was going to find her sister, even if she had to go to jail for stealing a card first.

"I have spent years trying to forget about our family and the situation we all find ourselves in. The only thing I have managed to gain is an extreme loneliness. It is a loneliness that has no relief, like a gaping hole that will not close, because it knows there is something that should be there and will not compromise. I know that you have felt it too because of me and maybe you feel it even now." He said, looking intently at his daughter, knowing he now had the opportunity to stop some of the misery.

He opened a drawer, took out his wallet and out of it he took out a small white business card. It had become a little tattered from all the times he had taken it out and dialled the number that was on it before chickening out. As he handed the card to Maria, he knew she would do what he could not do. She would actually press the dial button after typing out the numbers and she would face the monster he had cowered from, head-on. She had something that he did not have, alongside her fear. Something he had seen only in Sbonokuhle that day she ran away from her father's house. Something he had heard in her voice the day she called and told him that on his deathbed, Thabisani senior had told her that Alfred Mulumba, the man she had married and borne kids for, was his illegitimate son.

## The mouth of the shark

I am late for school today, later than I usually am. I feel embarrassed at the thought of walking into class so late and I wish I could turn back. Everyone will already be in their seats and they will be looking at me. At my grey slacks that stop way too far above my ankles and do not hug my curves the way most girls' slacks do. I do not even have curves and they will see that; and the fact that one of my school shoes is torn - you can see a bit of the white socks I am wearing peeping out. And my hair, it is not done up in a sleek ponytail or bun. Everything about me is so wrong. All wrong. I do not want to stand in front of my classmates and have them see this. I should have been early then I could have snuck into class and sat down without anybody seeing me. Maybe then they would not have seen all the things that are wrong with me and maybe I too, could pretend that these things do not exist.

I just wish I could get away with not going to school, but if I go back home mummy will find me there when she gets back from the night-shift at the hospital and I will have to explain why I did not go to school if I am not sick. I am not even coughing a little, so I cannot convince her that I have the flu. She will shout that school fees are expensive, and she is tired, because she is working very hard to make sure I get an education. She will shout that we came to South Africa so that we might have a better future, not so that we can be lazy. I cannot tell her that I do not want to go to school because of my uniform or that last week, a white girl in my class offered me her old pair of school shoes. She is already so tired, always. So I will go to school even if I do not feel like it. I will smile when the other girls talk about my appearance and when the white girl offers me her shoes again I will say "Thank you Melanie, but my mother will take me to the shop to buy a new pair today. She just has not had the time, you see," and walk away.

At breaktime I sit with my friends Buhle and Yolanda on the bleachers and eat my polony sandwiches. The bread tastes dry in my mouth and the polony slices are very very thin, but at least I have juice to wash it down. The taste of the polony reminds me of the morning I arrived in South Africa. We went into a spaza shop to buy bread before we went home to drink tea. All mine and my little brother's stuff was in a backpack. It is funny to think I moved to a whole new country with just a backpack full of stuff. All my other stuff was left at my grandparents' house in Bulawayo. I look at my backpack now, filled to the brim with books, pens and other stationery. I would need more than a backpack if I were to move countries now.

"What do you think you would need if you were ever to move to a new country?" I ask Buhle and Yolanda.

"Uhm…depends on where I would be going." Yolanda replies.

"Yeah! Like how when you are going to Durban you have to pack a bikini and sunscreen because you will be going to the beach." Buhle adds to Yolanda's answer.

I nod, but deep down I feel as though they did not really answer my question. Maybe it is because they are South Africans and they do not ever think of moving to a new country, or so mummy says. They have everything they need at home. I really cannot blame them. If I could have everything I want in Zimbabwe I would have stayed there, but as a Zimbabwean life is always better somewhere else. Home is the mouth of a shark, as Warsan Shire puts it, so I must constantly think of going somewhere better. I left my home, my baby photos, my father and my grandparents behind because South Africa is supposed to be somewhere better but, even here, I feel the shark slowly breathing on my neck, reminding me that I do not belong, so my heart will always be set on a better place. I will continue to make up stories for future-me the way I do for the characters in my Paper-doll game. Stories where I have long hair, cheese sandwiches and pants that hug my curves. I must admit that I get tired sometimes. My mother is tired too because the shark breathes down her neck on her way to work and back, reminding her that it will get all of us if she does get work. We have already jumped one border for goodness' sake! What more do we need to do for the shark to leave us alone?

When we were still in Bulawayo, my older brother, my little brother and I were sitting in my grandparents' kitchen one day, hungry and thinking about all the good things we wanted to do once we got to South Africa. My older brother said one day we would all remember that conversation and laugh about it over a cup of juice. He said it almost like a promise and I remember it like a prayer. Even now, I really hope it will still happen, although we have been in this country for almost four years, and the only juice mummy buys is for school, and we are not allowed to drink it at home. One day, she will not be tired and we will drink juice at home, then I will remind everyone about that conversation so we can laugh. I will probably cry because a little bit of my dream will have come true.

I do not think a lot about home, especially when I am at school. I make up a new story for myself when I am with my schoolmates. Nobody ever asks me, but if they were to ask, I would tell them that I was born at Coronation Hospital, that my mother is Zulu and my father Xhosa and that I grew up with my mother's surname. I do not have specific reasons for picking these details, but just the thought of having a new story, one that is different from my actual story is comforting. It makes me feel better than it would to explain that I came here in a Quantum minibus, then a lorry at the border post and then an old bus, running away from a shark. I cannot tell them that my mother has worked and worked and worked, all so that the shark does not devour my family.

Perhaps the most difficult part of this story, the part I do not like the most, is that I am no longer the girl who left Zimbabwe. How do I explain to South Africans that I left not only photos, my father and my mother in Bulawayo, but my last name as well? The girl who made it out of the shark's mouth, Memory Ndlovu, is not the same as the girl who left. Memory Mleya left at the mercy of the shark with all her clothes and photos and stuff. Memory Mleya made it out with only a backpack and a lot of confusion.

It seems to me that we gave up a lot of things, all of us, in hopes of leaving the hunger behind only to find that there is a hunger much worse than the one of food. On most days, I find that I am hungry for something I cannot quite describe. I am hungry for intangible things like being seen, known and loved. Things that I cannot go into a store and ask for or ask mummy to buy for me. I sit with my school friends and find myself drifting away, as though I am not right there next to them. I try to imagine a different scenario, a better one. One where I do not worry about the sound of my voice being too loud, or My Zimbabwean accent slipping through my teeth when I speak. I imagine being in a place where what I am is the norm. So I wonder if maybe, in our attempt to escape the shark of poverty and hunger, we accidentally let it swallow us whole.

## Samuel Chamboko

Sam is a husband and father. By day he works in finance and is involved in farming. Growing in the dusty streets of Mucheke, Masvingo, like most people of his generation he had a balanced upbringing which involved attending a multi-racial school in town and school holidays spent at his family's rural home herding cattle with other boys of his age. The result was an exposure to two worlds, seemingly apart which had to be reconciled somehow. He has worked and lived in Zimbabwe, South Africa and the United Kingdom, including other shorter professional stints in East Africa. Writing helps him to escape the trauma of working daily with lifeless numbers.

"My contributions in this anthology are dedicated to my friend and original *Mjubheki*, Luke Mavirimidze (Luka Murinda). Rest in peace Ngwenya. *Ri takalela zvitu zwahashu.*"

# Journey from without

The bloody heat! The heat makes it impossible even to think at times. The dry hot wind does not make it any better. Even in the shade, he could feel sweat trickling down his brow. They still had quite a distance to go to get to the highway where they could finally get 'taxis' to Johannesburg. The thought of Johannesburg and all that it could offer, did Pedzisai Ndhlera's head in. All the stories he had heard from the older boys from his village were difficult to believe, as some of the things they talked about were a far cry from his humble upbringing in the semi-arid Maranda area, deep in Mwenezi district. Mwenezi is one of the poorest districts in Zimbabwe, and is located in the southeastern part of the country. It is there where he had been born and raised on *sadza rembunga* and the highly nutritious, *masondhla,* mopane worms. He had never travelled more than 100km from the place he was born. Most of the journeys he had embarked on were either by ox-drawn cart or by foot, to the grinding mill, clinic or to take cattle to better pastures during the dry season. His first journey in an automobile was on a school sports trip, when he was 14. Barefoot and with oversize football jerseys borrowed from the local secondary, their school bowed out in the first round of the tournament.

This particular journey had started more than a year ago. It started when Bhudh' Ranga, Pedzi's older brother, had suggested that Pedzi join him in South Africa, so they could both work and buy more cattle for the family. In these parts, if you worked for a year and could not buy even half a calf, you were considered a failure. If you were married, then your relatives blamed your wife who would be accused of spending too much on cooking oil and flour, making *vetkoeks, magwinya or zvifuturamvana,* every morning. If you were single, it was pinned on the fact that you were not married. You needed a woman to calm you down and give you a sense of direction. So Bhudh' thought Pedzi had come of age and like all young men should venture into the world to seek his fortune. Mhai, their mother, was not pleased by this suggestion. Not only did she think that Pedzi was too young, but she was also worried about who would help her with the chores and the work in the fields, growing *mhunga.* Bhudh' had assured her that he would pay for *mukomana,* a male helper, to assist with the cattle and the *mhunga* fields. Mhai was not convinced and hoped to buy time by insisting that Pedzi only move to Johannesburg *gore rinovuya,* next year. Reluctantly Bhudh' agreed, although he moaned that he had promised his *murungu* another pair of hands at the small warehouse where he worked in the booming Midrand Industrial area. Bhudh' had then said he would leave with Pedzi after the Christmas holidays, the following year.

Pedzi's mind had been made up about wanting to go *kuJoni*, the collective all-encompassing name for any part of South Africa, from Musina to Cape Town, from Tshipise to Cofimvaba, Phalaborwa to Port Nolloth. To Zimbabweans, it's all *kuJoni*. It had been on his mind since the day he dropped out of school on the first day of form one. School had never been a priority anyway. Primary school attendance had been punctuated by periodic spells of absenteeism due to a plethora of reasons. Chief among the reasons for bunking school was attending to the *mhunga* crop in the fields during the rainy season.

"Growing *mhunga* is a lot of work you know," Mhai always used to say.

There is the preparation of the land, sowing, weeding and looking out for the birds when the cobs were near maturation. Then came the harvest, *kucheka nekupura,* and finally it was ready to sell to *maHarare* who came to buy bulk *mhunga* for their chicken projects in Budiriro, Dzivarasekwa and other high-density suburbs. Mhai could not manage on her own, so she would coerce Pedzi to miss school for a couple of days. Pedzi on his own accord would also decide to miss school and spend his days in the nearby forest herding cattle with the other boys who no longer had the burden of going to school. They would spend their days eating *nhunguru, nhengeni* and wild honey, *monga*. Occasionally if a cow went to the pasture with its calf, they would milk directly into their mouths. In most households, this was a cardinal sin punishable by a major league spanking. The boys would get caught out by the dribble of milk on their shirts or skin which left a fatty stain, the result of a misdirected squirt as they tried to keep the cow calm while at the same time pressing its milk pregnant udders. Pedzi would threaten any of the other school going children who so much as entertained the thought of ratting on him for bunking school. His dropping out of school is the story of legends. On the first day of high school, Pedzi was late for school and by the time he got there all the form ones had already been allocated classrooms. Because of his height, the teacher on duty who was standing at the gate directed him to the form threes where a screening test was being written. Pedzi was immediately ushered in and given the test question paper. For someone who had spent 10 years in primary school, repeating various grades, and who had left barely able to read and write, this experience was hellish. After two hours Pedzi walked out of the classroom, never to be seen again within a 200m radius of a school. He spent the rest of his day setting traps for *mbeva,* wild mice, in the fields close to his village.

He spent the next 5 years working the land with his mother and looking after their cattle. Then December of *gore rinovuya,* had finally come, and on cue, Bhudh' and most of the village *njivas* had made a beeline for the village. Arriving with boxes and bags full of groceries, liquor, electronics and empty 20 litre containers known as *magumbure* or *zvigubhu*. Economic exiles of different ages could not fathom the thought of spending *Kisimusi* in faraway lands. For many this was an opportunity to come to the village to thank their ancestors for their good fortune, by slaughtering goats, sheep or cattle and performing rituals. For others it was just an opportunity to come and show off a new wife, radio or vehicle. The village for those few days was a hive of activity. In preparation of this influx, the village *machembere,* old ladies, would brew the most potent *mapfunde* beer to quench the thirst of those coming from *masango*. Even the shops at the local business centre made sure they were well stocked with bread, cooking oil, flour, soft drinks, and other 'special' food types which were only eaten during the festive season. Every shop had huge speakers outside on their verandah and would blast the latest music from both Zimbabwe and South Africa to accommodate the diverse tastes in music. Pedzi and his friends would spend Christmas day participating in dancing competitions at the local business centre. Runesu, from across the river, was always taking away the top prize every year. Word was going around in herd-boy circles that Runesu had *muti* that his grandmother, Mbuya vaHwicho, prepared for him. This last Christmas was a blur as Pedzi could not contain the excitement of finally moving *kuJoni* to make his own money and buy clothes so that girls could take notice of him. He hoped that he would also finally cavort in the meaty thighs of a nameless woman. Stories were abound of how loose the girls in *Joni* were, unlike the stingy ones from the village. They were so stingy, they couldn't even afford to look your way when you cat-whistled at them.

The time for Bhudh' to leave was fast approaching. Mhai called a family meeting to address Bhudh' and Pedzi's imminent departure. Unbeknown to him, Mhai had other plans. During the family meeting Mhai made an impassioned appeal to Bhudh', requesting that he leave money for Pedzi to follow after they had finished the harvest, *kucheka*. Mhai's reason for this request was because she had failed to find *mukomana* to replace Pedzi. Most of the local households were hanging on to their available labour and could not afford to let go even a single pair of hands. It was agreed that Pedzi would follow as soon as he finished *kucheka*. Bhudh' left R1000, which was enough to get Pedzi to *Joni*. It was enough for him to bribe the soldiers at the border fence close to Dite and then to pay *maguma-guma* to facilitate movement through the forest to the N1 taxi pick up spot. This is where taxis destined for Gauteng picked up illegals, and made the six-hour trip at night, making the first drop outside Bosman Station in Pretoria and then final destination was Power House, in the Johannesburg CBD. These drops had to be made before dawn to avoid the police. A few days later, Bhudh' bade farewell and reassured Pedzi that they would be reunited in a few months. Pedzi would spend the next two and half months working assiduously in the *mhunga* fields. As soon as the *mhunga* was ready for *kucheka*, Pedzi would wake up every day at three in the morning and make his way to the fields to start harvesting. By the time Mhai and the rest of the family joined him just after dawn, Pedzi would have a substantial heap of *mhunga*. The better part of the morning would be spent in the fields, only taking breaks to drink *mahewu* that Mhai had prepared the previous night. Knock off time was normally just before noon. They would all then trek home with Muchaneta and Davidzo, Pedzi's younger sisters going via the borehole to collect water for domestic use. Then came the agonising wait for lunch. This whole routine was about to end when the accident involving Kuda happened.

Kuda was Pedzi's nephew, born of his late sister Putsai. Kuda was now old enough to go *kumbudzi*, to herd goats after school, with other village boys of his age. One afternoon when Godhi, one of Kuda's friends, came running to the fields where Pedzi and the family were harvesting *mhunga*. Without even giving Mhai a chance to ask why he was running so hard, Godhi blurted out breathlessly that Kuda had fallen from a *munyii* tree and he could not move. Pedzi dropped everything and ran in the direction of the *munyii* tree close to old man Mhanga's field. The young boy was wailing and clearly in excruciating pain. Pedzi proceeded to the local business centre to find Mathuthu, the local hustler, who owned an ex-Jap Toyota Granvia, that occasionally plied the route between Maranda turn off and Maranda Business Centre, popularly known as *paNumber One*. Nobody really knows why it is called *paNumber One*. Mathuthu wanted money. The only money between Mhai and Pedzi was the R1,000 Bhudh' had left for Pedzi to use on his trip to Joni. It was a no-brainer, Mhai told Mathuthu that she had money at home and they were off in no time, Mathuthu R1,000 to the good. They went straight to Matibi Mission hospital, run by the Catholic Church, where Kuda was immediately sent to theatre to have surgery on the leg. It was then decided that Mhai would stay with Kuda while Pedzi and Mathuthu returned home. It would be two weeks before Mhai and Kuda were discharged from hospital and returned home, courtesy of the generosity of the nuns who covered their transport costs. Kuda's leg was in a cast. As soon as Mhai returned, Pedzi saw this as his opportunity to leave. While Mhai was at Matibi Mission hospital with Kuda, Pedzi had unsuccessfully tried to call Bhudh' to inform him of the unfortunate incident, but Bhudh''s number was unreachable. Because most households had finished harvesting, a few of the other village boys were also making their way to *Joni*. Pedzi joined a group with Talkmore and Vengai. Among the three of them, they had no money, or at least so they thought. Their plan was to walk or hitchhike to Nottingham Estate, *kwaTshivhala*, a citrus growing farm on the banks of the Limpopo River. The place is called *kwaTshivhala*, which is short for *Tshivhalamakhulu,* pronounced *chi-va-ra-ma-ku-ru*, meaning he who counts in thousands, a reference to wealthy owners of the establishment. The plan was to work for two months *kwaTshivhala*, to raise bus fare to Johannesburg.

Their journey began early on a Wednesday morning. Wednesday was a good day to travel because it was *chisi*, the compulsory midweek day when no one was allowed to go to the fields. If you were found working in the fields on Wednesday, you were fined a goat by the village head, *Sabhuku*. Wednesday was a popular day for villagers to do their admin. There were folks going to collect their pensions in Masvingo, those going to get birth certificates for children, medication and those with itchy bums, the ones who couldn't spend a few weeks without leaving the village, for no apparent reason. During the busy season, there was never a good enough reason to miss a day of working in the fields, well maybe with the exception of one's own death. Even then, there would be mutterings from disgruntled neighbours from your *raini*, because they had to stop working to come and pay their last respects, a day or two of work lost. You could hardly afford to die during the rainy season. The three young boys were at the local business centre just before dawn, *mashambazhou*, the time when elephants bathe. There were already a few other commuters before them and in no time, a decent crowd was waiting for the first vehicle to come and pick them up. After almost 40 minutes of waiting, they could hear the humming of a vehicle engine in the distance. Vengai quickly declared that it was Mathuthu's Toyota Granvia. Mai Tawanda disputed saying she had heard Mathuthu's granvia leaving *kuma three*, well before dawn. They eventually caught sight of the grey-brown Toyota Granvia approaching the *mukamba* tree which was the official bus stop. Vengai could hardly shut up, telling everyone who cared to listen how he could tell the sounds of different vehicles that plied that route, even in his sleep. Mathuthu's Granvia only had space for two people who were going to Masvingo, *stret*. The boys had to be patient. Within a few minutes though, there was a convoy of trucks of traders who moved around the district selling their wares at cattle markets popularly known as *showa* or *mariketi*. When villagers liquidated their animals at *mariketi*, they then used the money to purchase anything and everything from these traders. It was the village's version of walking out of a bank into a big department store. The boys were able to jump onto one of them and were dropped at Maranda turnoff on the Masvingo-Beitbridge Highway.

The boys immediately crossed the road and waited for cross border haulage trucks, *magonyeti*, which were destined for South Africa, via the Beitbridge Border post. They wanted to be dropped off as close as possible to Beitbridge and then they could make their way to *kwaTshivhala*, 46km west of Beitbridge town. This journey, they reckoned could be made on foot, and Talkmore assured his two comrades that it was possible. This was Talkmore's second attempt at going *kuJoni*. The first had ended 18 months earlier, when he was arrested just outside Musina. This time round, Talkmore was better prepared and as the veteran of this excursion, he had to show leadership. For two hours, all the trucks that stopped could not help them because they had no money. Most truck drivers on this route supplemented their income by picking passengers and cargo on the route. They had no time to help sweat drenched, firewood-smoke smelling young boys. The fact that they were three was also suspicious as they could easily be highway robbers, preying on long distance drivers. Out of the blue Talkmore pulled out a R50 note and offered to buy his two friends a loaf of bread and the popular energy drink *Dragon*. When they heard what Talkmore had, the other two suggested that they only buy bread and share one 500ml can of *Dragon* so that they save and possibly have some money to buy more bread in the evening, wherever they would find themselves. They settled on the loaf and one *dragon*. It was now approaching noon and their luck was not getting any better. As they despaired sitting in the shade of a *mupani* tree, a few metres from the highway, a truck that transports cattle from the villages to the abattoirs in Masvingo, stopped. This truck's engine was overheating and the driver quickly jumped out as soon as the truck stopped to head to the radiator opening at the front of the vehicle. A few moments later he was back in his cab, fumbling for this five litre container of water. He went back to the front of the vehicle, opened the radiator, and poured water into it. There was a big gush as the overheating engine expelled the water. The rank touts, *mahwindi*, on the other side of the road started shouting to the driver, "*mira ipore*", advising him to wait for the engine to cool down before pouring any more water. The driver took heed, but by then his container was nearly empty. Vengai saw an opportunity and quickly offered the driver to go down to the river and collect water for the vehicle, while the engine cooled. The driver agreed. The three boys were soon on their way to Mwenezi river which is half a mile away from where the truck had stopped. Forty minutes later they were back, and the driver poured water into the radiator. Talkmore then told the driver their story.

"*Vakuru*, we would like to go to the border."

"But I am only going as far as Capfuce. I can drop you off before the toll gate, if that's okay?"

"*Munenge mati pusha,* but we have no money."

"It's fine, you have helped me a great deal. Jump in, *handei!*"

Capfuce is a village about 30km from the border. Talkmore told the others that they could walk from Capfuce to Lutumba and put up for the night at Lutumba. The following day, they would then make their journey on foot to Nottingham Estate, *kwaTshivhala*. They jumped into the back of the truck and were soon on their way. The smell of cow dung hardly deterred them, they were herd boys after all. As they approached the tollgate at Capfuce, the driver stopped the vehicle and dropped them off. Lutumba Business Centre is a further six km up down the road, towards Beitbridge. The boys commenced their trek, walking along the highway. Even as the sun was setting, the heat in this part of the world was unforgiving. Their next challenge was water. They were all thirsty and parched due to dehydration. It took another two odd kilometres before they found a dry riverbed. Finding a dry riverbed was a eureka moment, for any herdsmen. They soon began digging the riverbed with their bare hands and in no time, they hit the wet sand and water started filling up the hole, *mufuku*. They found a dry shell of a *gwakwa* fruit, which they used as a cup to drink and quench their parched throats. Bear Grylls could learn a thing or two from these fellows. They rested for a few minutes and were on their way. As the sun was approaching the western horizon, they could hear the raucous sounds from the music being played at the business centre. Lutumba is a small, but vibrant business centre, some 20km north of Beitbridge on the Masvingo highway. It became a popular stop over place as long distance drivers avoided criminal elements in the border town. It was also a transit point for border jumpers who had the choice of different exit points. Some would choose to go east via Chikwarakwara, some via Nottingham Estate, two of the popular exit points. There were however many other exit points along the river which depended on the water levels of the river.

As the sun kissed the hills in the distance beyond, the boys reached Lutumba. It was a hive of activity as vendors, commuters, shopkeepers and other random villagers went about their business. The boys were very excited to have reached this milestone in their journey. They rested outside one of the shops that had no speakers playing loud music. At least here they could hear each other when they conversed. As the adrenaline subsided, hunger pangs kicked in. They asked if there was anywhere where they could buy some *sadza*, and they were directed to Mai Mobi's kitchen. Mai Mobi's kitchen was a rudimentary sit down 'restaurant' serving *sadza,* and usually goat stew, from dawn to midnight. They made their way via a very dark alley and found themselves behind one of the shops. Talkmore approached the lady in a denim apron who had runny eyes and was battling to keep the 3-legged pot of *sadza* on the fire and inquired.

"How much is one plate of *sadza nenyama*?"

"R20, should I dish three plates?"

"No, just one will do, we do not have enough money."

"Okay, the meat is almost finished though."

"No problem, put more gravy as compensation, we are hungry for sadza."

"No, problem. By the way, are you from Maranda? You speak *Chipfumbi*."

"Yes!"

"Oh, my mother is a *MaNgwenya,* she is a daughter of the Maranda people, from your area."

"Nice to meet you, *muzukuru.*"

They were soon devouring the mountain of sadza, sweat streaming down their brows. They were famished, and this meal would at least enable them to sleep better and have energy to walk the remainder of their journey. After their supper, they went to one of the few shops that was still open. It turned out to be a bottle-store, an off licence of sorts. A few patrons were hanging out outside their shop, with bottles of warmish beer dangling from their palms. Before long, one of the patrons realised the three were new in the area.

"Where are you boys going?"

"*KwaTshivhala.*"

"Wait here and I will give you directions for a short-cut."

He then went on to direct them to *KwaTshivhala* using a 'shortcut' that passed through the villages avoiding the highway. He advised them to hang around the bottle store until it closed and he would show them a safe place where they could put up for the night, when all the other patrons had gone. Just before midnight the music died down and there was an eerie quietness as a cool breeze began blowing. The bottle store patron took them to a semi-finished house on the outskirts of the business centre and showed them into a small room with no doors, windows or roof. He assured them they would be safe and he left. The boys huddled together and were soon snoring away in awkward sleeping positions. At about the ass-crack of dawn, Vengai woke up his two friends and they started off. They walked as directed by the patron, whose directing skills turned out to be impeccable. He had told them that if they left at dawn, they would be at *Tshivhala* just before workers knocked off. Indeed they arrived just before 1530hrs. At the gate, the guards asked what they wanted, and they told them that they were looking for work. Much to their surprise they were told they were in luck as it was the beginning of orange picking season and they could be employed as casual labourers for the rest of the season. The boys were so thrilled they even forgot to ask how much they would get paid. They were directed to the compound where there were large rooms housing casual labourers who had also come to work during the orange picking season. Men had their own lodgings and women were housed separately. They were introduced to the supervisor of the casual labourers who took down their names and showed them where they would put up. He also arranged food rations of mealie meal, cooking oil, salt and *matemba*. The rations were supposed to last them two weeks. If they ran out before the two weeks, they would have to sort themselves out, they were told.

The next morning, the hard work started. By 0500hrs, they were at the entrance of the orange tree fields. Their names were ticked off the attendance register and they were given sacks to put the oranges they were picking. Each worker had a daily target based on the weight of oranges picked. Each time your sack was full, you would come to the unloading bay and get your oranges weighed and the weight written against your name. When the cumulative total hit the target you were free to continue or to go home and rest. Working extra also meant additional income. The boys figured this out quite early on. They worked hard and managed to make decent earnings in their first month. They were tempted to quit, but counselled each other that they needed enough money to live on before they got jobs in *Joni*. They also needed money to buy mobile phones so that they could call their relatives when they got *kuJoni*. In Pedzi's case, he needed to track down Bhudh', whose mobile phone still remained unreachable.

After the second month's pay, they were confident that they had saved enough to continue with their journey. During their stay, they had also made friends with *guma-gumas* or *magweja*, who helped people to cross the river and ensured safe passage to R572 which connected them to Musina. In Musina, they would be able to get transport to Johannesburg. One of the workers at the farm introduced them to a trader who used to come and sell his stock on the farm. He offered to go and buy them mobile phones so that they would be reachable when they crossed into South Africa. They contributed to the purchase of one phone and handed over the money to the trader. A week passed with the trader not returning and the boys' patience was wearing thin. They decided to proceed without the mobile phone. On the night of their departure, Talkmore broke the news to the rest of the crew that he would not be joining them. It turns out Talkmore had decided that he didn't want to work too far from home, so that he could regularly go back to see his mother. Pedzi and Vengai decided that Talkmore's personal choices were not going to hold back their life journey.

They gathered their few earthly possessions and were soon joining a group of other border jumpers who had been transported from Beitbridge under the cover of darkness. They crossed the dry riverbed and then walked toward the fence on the South African side, their *guma-guma* leading a long line of men and women in single file. They soon met members of the SANDF who were on border patrol, the *guma-guma* greeted the officers with an air of familiarity. He then did the needful, which was handing them a few notes of South African Rands. The soldiers advised them to rest before getting to the R572 as there were police officers patrolling the area for illegal migrants. The police would demand even bigger 'passage fees'. *Guma-guma* immediately relayed this message to the transporter. The transporter agreed to pick up the 'clients' just after 0500hrs at the usual pick up point. The walk to the pick-up point was long and punctuated by numerous stops as *Guma-guma* made sure that everything was safe. At around 0330hrs they arrived at the 'usual pick up point' and they could finally rest as they waited for transport. Smack on the nose at 0500hrs, the transporter arrived and asked everyone to quickly board so that they could take advantage of the change in shift as police officers went home, leaving some checkpoints unmanned for a few hours before the next shift began. As the sun rose in the east, the transporter pushed his Toyota Quantum overloaded with illegals through the gears, making his way to the drop off point in the heart of Musina's dusty long distance taxi rank. In Musina, the illegals could blend in while making arrangements to proceed to their final destinations.

Pedzi and Vengai disembarked from the Toyota Quantum van and started wandering aimlessly, a bit dazed by the heat and sunlight after their ride in the van which had no windows, for obvious reasons. This van was ordinarily used to carry cargo, not to transport human beings, but who cared. While the crowds were beginning to build up on the streets of Musina the two boys had an opportunity to caucus. They realised that their money was not enough to buy a phone, and pay for transport to Johannesburg and rent lodgings while they tried to look for their relatives or find employment. Talkmore had spoken about the Venda area around Thouyandou being a potential area to look for work, a sort of dipping a toe. The boys decided to go to Venda instead, it was closer and they would be able to work and save for their trip to the *City of Gold*. They waited for the Indian run shops in downtown Musina to open and they bought a cheap mobile phone. Vengai, who was more literate than Pedzi concluded the transaction, also asked the Indian shop owner where they could buy a sim card. He was directed to a vendor who was loitering on the street. They bought a 'registered sim' and loaded it with airtime with the help of the vendor. They tried Bhudh's number but it was not going through. Vengai tried his maternal uncle, Malume's number, but it was also not going through. The boys decided they were safer leaving Musina, as they could easily be arrested and deported back home like what had happened to Talkmore 18 months earlier. They asked the vendor where they could get transport to Venda, and they were directed to the taxi rank. There they boarded a taxi to Thouyandou. They planned to get off somewhere before the town, in a farming or communal land where they could look for work. After over an hour in the taxi, the vehicle stopped at Tshilamba, a one horse *dorpie*, in Limpopo Province, 30km from Thohoyandou. The boys dropped off. They started wandering around the area trying to orientate themselves and acclimatise to their new surroundings. Tshilamba is a town teeming with migrants, mostly those who are afraid to go to the bigger towns like Makhado, Polokwane, Pretoria and Johannesburg. Within a few minutes they had found a quiet spot where they sat and mapped out their next move. A car guard at the nearby shop called out to them. He asked if they were looking for work, and they responded affirmatively.

Vengai's hotch-potch TshiVenda was coming in handy. He had learnt the language while staying with his mother's family in Zezani, as a small boy. The car guard told them that a local white farmer occasionally picked up casual labourers from a spot up the road. However, it was too late, they would have to wait until the next day. The challenge of looking for a place to sleep now faced them. They asked the car guard who directed them to disused Eskom electricity sub-station. It had a door but no windows, for one night this would suffice. They decided that they wouldn't want to be seen going in there during daylight so they found a Spar Supermarket where they bought *pap,* South Africa's version of *sadza,* and chicken stew from the deli. They could also afford a two litre imitation soft drink, which they shared. They didn't realise that the two plastic 'sticks', straws the cashier gave them were to help them share the cool drink. They threw the straws away as soon as they were out of sight of the Supermarket. They found a quiet street near the post office where they sat and ate what would be their supper. The long wait for darkness started. At dusk they scrambled to the disused substation. On the way, they found cardboard boxes to use as bedding. It had been a long day and before they knew it, they were both out cold.

The next morning they woke up and limbered casually to the spot where they had been told farmers came to look for casual labour. They had no luck. This routine continued for seven days, with no luck. As they were about to re-work their strategy, they were approached by a local black gentleman. He introduced himself as VhoMulaudzi. He needed help on his piece of land, however he could not pay the boys in cash but would provide full board for them for as long as they wanted. The boys took a few minutes to confer and decided to take up the offer. They would be saving on food money and would have a much safer place to sleep. They drove to VhoMulaudzi's home. They were greeted on arrival by Mme aRhudzani, VhoMulaudzi's wife. She was a typical Venda woman, dressed in bright yellow and blue cotton print traditional attire, with the face marks on her cheeks, as was customary. VhoMulaudzi showed the boys the room they would use as their lodgings. The boys immediately asked for a bathroom so that they could wash their bodies after a week of just wiping the crust off their eyes. VhoMulaudzi immediately instructed that they be given 20 litre containers and soap so that they could clean up before joining the rest of the family for supper. After cleaning up, they joined the family in a large open area between the kitchen where Mme aRhudzani cooked and the western style house where the family had their bedrooms. They were formally introduced as the help, but they were treated as family. They ate with everyone, and just like the other Mulaudzi children, they had their own room, albeit a shared one.

This period at VhoMulaudzi's home gave them an opportunity to rethink their strategy clearly while not worrying about their physical wellbeing. All their meals were catered for and they had a roof over their heads. They stayed with VhoMulaudzi for a month and they became quite popular with both the family and their neighbours. They were polite and always willing to help. They made a few friends with people in the area, including with the local Pakistani spaza shop owner, Abdul. Abdul introduced them to the bread delivery truck driver, Doubt, who was also from Zimbabwe. After meeting Doubt a number of times and helping him unload bread into Abdul's spaza shop, they became buddies. Vengai explained to Doubt their predicament. Doubt offered to give them a lift to a farming area near Polokwane where they could get jobs picking tomatoes, or harvesting potatoes. On the agreed day, the boys bade the Mulaudzi's farewell. Mme Rhudzani even prepared some *atchar*, pickled mangoes and chillies, for the boys to take with them. Doubt took the boys and dropped them off at Modjadjiskloof. From there they took taxis to Tzaneen, a fruit farming area, which produces over 40% of fruits consumed in South Africa. Abdul had phoned one of his cousins, who also ran a shop in Tzaneen to look out for the two boys. With Vengai conversing in broken English they called Mohammed, Abdul's cousin, who directed them to his shop. He offered them a place to sleep in the shop where they would also double up as security. Pedzi and Vengai, however, would have to feed themselves. The boys were grateful for the offer. They would spend their days looking for spots where they could be picked up for 'piece jobs' by local farmers.

On day three they got their first gig helping Hennie, a local fruit trader, to load fruits from his storeroom into a truck destined for Mozambique. Hennie was so impressed by their work ethic and shy demeanour, that he referred them to his brother-in-law Jappie, who was a local tomato farmer. Jappie employed the two boys as tomato graders in his huge shed where tractors were constantly coming in and out with loads of tomatoes harvested from the fields. Their job was to check that the tomatoes going into the packing bays were plum and juicy, and healthy tomatoes were categorised according to their size. A Mozambican guy by the name of Antonio was their mentor. He kindly showed them what was required and off they went, grading tomatoes. Antonio also showed them their lodgings in the compound. The boys worked from 0530hrs until 1430hrs. They would knock off and go to the compound to rest and recuperate. They soon met some of their colleagues in the compound and started making friends. They became very popular with the women folk who worked on the farm because of their shyness and boyish looks.

Koketso, a young Pedi single mother from Mankweng, took a liking to Vengai because he could converse in some English with Jappie, the farm owner. She could hardly hide her excitement every time she walked past Vengai or when they bumped into each other at the communal water tap. Josphat, the Malawian machine operator, began nudging and teasing Vengai about Koketso. Even Pedzi noticed the electricity when Koketso met the two of them anywhere on the farm. Pedzi and Josphat encouraged Vengai to pursue her. It took Vengai a few weeks to gather enough courage to speak to Koketso about his intentions. Like a well raised African village girl, Koketso did not immediately agree to date Vengai, she took a few days to make up her mind. She met Pedzi at the tap.

"Pedzi, go and tell Vengai that I said it's ok."

"It's ok, what Koketso?"

"You are too young for these things Pedzi. Anyway, tell him to come to my room tonight."

"Tonight?"

"Yes, tonight."

Pedzi, like the dutiful friend, relayed the message to Vengai. The boys could hardly contain their excitement. Finally one of them had a chance of getting laid, or would they? They argued.

"Why is she inviting you at night? She wants you to do it to her Vengai."

"What if she just wants to talk?"

"She could have come to talk to you outside the shed during tea break."

"She wants it!"

"You have to give it to her properly, otherwise she will never give it to you again. She will know you are an amateur, a small boy. You should have no trouble, she is not a virgin anyway, *imvana*, she has a child already."

The stingy village girls never gave them herd-boys a second look. They were interested in the *njivas* from Joburg, or the young teachers who were posted at the local schools. And here was Vengai, facing what would probably be his sexual debut, unsure even how to wear a condom. After work, they gathered at Josphat's room to discuss how things would potentially go down with Koketso later that evening. They explored all the angles, and the three decided that Vengai should go prepared, with a packet of condoms, just in case Koketso decided to treat him to the sweetness of her loins. They went through their usual evening routine, which included taking a bath in the communal washrooms and preparing their supper. After dinner of *sadza* and tinned pilchards, Vengai bade Pedzi farewell.

That evening, Pedzi went to Josphat's room and spent a few hours hanging out with him, killing time while he waited for Vengai. Vengai did not return. Josphat and Pedzi concluded that Vengai was spending the night at Koketso's and they retired for the evening. At around 0200hrs, Vengai made his way to the room he shared with Pedzi. Pedzi woke up to find out what had happened.

"We were just talking."

"Up to now?"

"Yes, we just talked."

What a *fucking* anti-climax! All that fretting and they just talked? It became Vengai's routine every evening to go and spend half the night at Koketso's then come back to their room after midnight or even later. Still, he was reporting to the two friends that they were just talking. Koketso, on the other hand, decided to approach Pedzi.

"Hey wena Pedzi, does your friend not like me?"

"What do you mean? He has been coming to your room every night."

"Does he know how to handle a woman? Or am I not attractive enough?"

"Oh, you mean *thaaaat*? I am sure he is shy."

"Tell him to try, he might be pleasantly surprised," Koketso said, walking away.

Pedzi explained his encounter with Koketso and from there, the boys prepared for Vengai's first run out. That evening, Vengai made his way to Koketso's. That night he did not return, Pedzi only saw him in the morning as the siren for the start of work sounded. Vengai nodded to Pedzi and Pedzi knew it had gone down. From that day on, Koketso offered to cook for the boys, so she would prepare food in the evening and the three of them would eat together before Pedzi retreated to their bachelor quarters, while Vengai was entreated to carnal pleasures. Vengai could hardly believe his good fortune, every night as he pumped vigorously, between Koketso's golden yellow thighs. It was heaven.

The boys were enjoying their work on the farm, but they had not forgotten that the final destination was, after all, the City of Gold, Johannesburg. They would sometimes day-dream, imagining what *'Jo-beg'* was like. Would they find their relatives? Would they find employment in a big factory, where they got paid every Friday and would spend the weekend, buying two litre *ko-kora*, and *braai*-ed meat at the *tshisanyama*? Buying jeans and nice *tenes* shoes? Mobile phones with WhatsApp so that they could *wapura* all their friends back in the village. *Joni*, they imagined, was a place of infinite opportunities. They would be able to earn ten times what Jappie was paying them on the farm. They had to go. Pedzi reminded Vengai that there were even more beautiful girls in *Joni*, girls whose shit did not smell, girls who washed their curvaceous bodies in milk, and smeared their skin with butter. Girls with skin as smooth as an egg. Not like Koketso, whose hands were rough like a *dhaka-boy's* hands. Vengai shot at Pedzi with the corner of his lazy eye and looked away. The boys worked at the farm for six months. Because they were saving to go *kuJoni*, they turned down Jappie's monthly offer to take all employees into Tzaneen town for shopping, once a month on payday. They were saving. They lived off the food rations and free board provided on the farm. Vengai, however, was not telling Pedzi that every month Koketso was asking him for money to send home because her child had been kicked out of creche for non-payment of fees, or her grandmother had been taken ill, or that their dog had eaten the neighbour's chicken. Every month, there was some sort of emergency. Vengai did not have the courage to tell his friend. He continued as if everything was normal. By a stroke of luck, Vengai had finally managed to make contact with Malume.

"Malume, *ndi*Vengai."

"*Hawu* Vengi, *uripi mchana*?"

"In Tzaneen Malume. I came a few months ago and have been trying your number."

"Apologies *mzaya, ndanga ndakagwevewa*, I was in prison." Vengai posed no further questions to Malume. He was just glad to have finally made contact. Malume encouraged him to come to Joni, for better prospects.

After month six, the boys agreed that the time for them to move on had come. Armed with their savings, entry level Ztel mobile phones and basic *SePedi*, they were ready. They sneaked out on a Saturday night and made their way to Tzaneen, where they got taxis to Polokwane. From Polokwane they were told they would get taxis to Bosman Station or if they were lucky to Park

Station in Johannesburg. Vengai then contacted Malume, to inform him of their imminent arrival. Malume advised them to drop off at Bosman and take taxis to Centurion. He would wait for them at Centurion. Pedzi and Vengai did as instructed. They dropped off at Bosman Station, a place that paints a good picture of the social and economic divide that exists in the rainbow nation. On one side was the bus and taxi rank, sooty and filthy from the fumes of the buses and engine oil leaks. A hundred metres away was the fresh out the box, Pretoria Gautrain station, with its well-dressed security guards, with manicured military type haircuts. They kept all the riff-raff as far away as possible from its middle class clientele, most of them mildly of a nervous disposition, afraid of being mugged around the precinct.

The boys had never seen so many cars. They could hardly believe what they were seeing. They could not say anything though, as they could be identified easily by *tsotsis*, as Johnny-come-latelys. They soon dropped off at Centurion and tried calling Malume, but his number was not going through. They agreed to give him a few more minutes, as he could still be on his way. An hour later, there was still no sign of Malume and still his number was unreachable. Just as they were about to give up and make other plans, the shrill of the tiny Ztel handset disturbed their mangled trains of thoughts. It was Malume.

"The battery had died, *mchana*. My *sola* was stolen last week, so I couldn't charge the phone last night."

"It's ok Malume, *tasvika*. We are here at Centurion."

"Ok, can you see the big KFC sign at the end of the station?"

"Yebo, Malume."

"Let's meet there, *neh*."

They met Malume at KFC, who bought them '*streetwise two*' to welcome them to the place of Gold. They soon were on a taxi to *Spreit*, where Malume had his 'house'. They dropped off at a dusty drop off point, which marked the beginning of what seemed like an unending arrangement of shacks made from different materials. Some were made from corrugated iron, some plastic and cardboard, some had windows, some had two doors, some with satellite dishes, others had carports in front of them. There were even double storey shacks. They made their way to Malume's 'house'. A humble, single storey shack, with one window. Inside, it was divided into a cooking area, a dining cum lounge and the 'bedroom' in the far corner. The floor was a coloured plastic sheet, so thin, that you could feel the uneven ground beneath it. Malume welcomed them and encouraged them to feel free. In Pedzi and Vengai's minds, they were wondering what the sleeping arrangement was going to be. They had seen hung in the right side of the bedroom, what looked like a woman's panty and bra. Also, the way the room was so organised was clearly the handiwork of the fairer sex. They had hardly settled down on the brown sofa, when a voluptuous, *yellow-bone* woman with a well-formed drearier and comparatively small buxom, burst into the room greeting them in *isiXhosa*.

"Molweni!"

"Yebo!"

Malume introduced her as Zandi, his wife. Malume could see the shock on Vengai's face. Vengai knew Malume's wife, NaDumisani, was back in their village near Zezani. So who was this woman Malume was calling his wife? Malume quickly diffused the awkwardly tense situation by offering to show the boys where they would sleep. They got out of the shack and Malume started laughing at Vengai.

"*Mchana*, this is Joburg!"

"*Hawu,* Malume?"

"How can I call myself a man if I have no woman to sleep with every night?"

"But does Zandi know that you are married back home?"

"What for? Maybe she has a husband back in Mthatha. This is Joburg *mchana*, you do what you have to do to get ahead."

"Yes, Malume."

"Also remember, what happens in Joburg, stays in Joburg. Don't go off running your mouth when you go back home. We are all men here."

Malume led them to a shack a few hundred metres from his own. There they met Sipho. Sipho was going to be their *maStanda*, the landlord. He introduced the boys to Sipho, who then proceeded to open the shack to show them what would become their new home. It was made of shiny corrugated zinc sheets, it had no window and the floor was bare ground, with no covering. Malume then told the boys that they had to pay Sipho R400 rent for the month. Vengai asked Pedzi to pay, on the understanding that he would square him later. Pedzi paid and Malume said they would go to the other side of the settlement nicknamed *Marabastad*, after the famous downtown complex west of Pretoria CBD, that sells cheap Chinese products. They went to *Marabastad* and bought a black plastic sheet to use to cover the floor, and two single bed size foam mattresses to sleep on. They were sorted. Malume ensured that they were comfortable and then said for the first week as they were settling, they would be welcome to come and eat at his house, in the evenings. He would ensure that Zandi cooked enough food for the four of them. Malume and the boys then spent the rest of the afternoon *chilling* at the local tavern, listening to Malume's pointers about how to look for work in the big metropoli. Malume advised them that they should never tell any potential employer that there was any type of work that they could not do. Here in Jozi, they were Jack-of-all-trades. In the evening as they retired to their lodgings, Pedzi asked Vengai for his R200 portion of the rent.

"Baba ndine R50 chete."

"What happened to the rest of the money we were saving?"

"*Eish mudhara!*"

"*Wakadhliwa na*Koketso? *Unofa uri rombe mpfanha uchichengeta vana vemahure!*"

"Who are you calling a whore?"

"*Shamwari*, I am not going to take care of you so that you take care of single mothers and their kids, I want my money as soon as you get a job."

The very next day, the real journey started. The boys started 'marketing' at the nearby Builders Warehouse, a national chain store that sells building materials. They had been told by Malume to 'market' themselves as painters. Painting was the easiest thing to do. Other trades, they would learn on the job. For the first three weeks, the boys hardly got anything, the competition was stiff. There were a lot of other young men who spoke better English than them, who always seemed to get the jobs. Then there was the issue of potential employers who already had their people. They would come to the pick-up spot to look for specific people, by name. Three weeks of trudging up and down was becoming quite depressing. Vengai was struggling to come to terms with their new situation. He was thinking of his life in Tzaneen with Koketso. A big part of his worry was that his money had run out before they got any work. Asking Pedzi was a non-starter since he had already let his feelings known about him spending money on Koketso. Malume on the other hand had mentioned, in not so many words, that "out here it's each man for himself". Relying on Malume was also quite tricky because of the influence Zandi had on Malume. Malume could not spend a single rand without Zandi's approval. The purse strings seemed to be attached to Zandi's inner thigh. Vengai was in a fix.

Getting a job was not easy, the boys would occasionally get 'piece jobs' here and there, nothing permanent. During this time Pedzi was constantly trying Bhudh's number but to no avail. He hoped that if he could at least get in touch with his brother then his fortunes might change. Unexpectedly on a hot Tuesday morning, Pedzi saw a Hyundai H1 truck pull up at the usual 'marketing' point. Pedzi looked at the driver, a black guy, who seemed quite familiar. The driver also noticed him and shouted.

"Ndhlera!"

"*Mukoma*!"

"What are you doing here?"

Pedzi realised that it was Bhudh's friend Nhamo. He ran to the driver's door and greeted Nhamo.

"Does Ranga know that you are here?"

"No, I tried to call him on his number but *haipindi*, it's unavailable."

"Oh, he changed numbers when he lost his phone. Here, take his new number."

Nhamo informed Pedzi that Bhudh' was staying in Tembisa, a vast township, bordering Johannesburg, Midrand, Centurion and the City of Ekhurhuleni. They bade each other farewell and Nhamo went on his way. After buying R5 airtime Pedzi dialled Bhudh's number and it rang. The relief that ran through Pedzi's body when a familiar voice on the other end said 'hello' was indescribable.

On the Saturday morning, Pedzi woke up and informed Vengai that he would be visiting his brother in Tembisa. Two taxi rides later, Pedzi arrived at the place where Bhudh' was waiting for him. Bhudh' greeted Pedzi with a manly half hug, a shoulder bump to be exact. They went to Bhudh's backroom lodging where Bhudh' had prepared sadza and beef mixed with *rape*, a typical township meal, also known as *imomo*, meaning everything in one pot. As they ate, in between morsels of *sadza*, Pedzi answered Bhudh''s questions about people in the village. Pedzi then got an opportunity to narrate to Bhudh' what had happened on his journey so far. He also told Bhudh' about the struggle of *basa*, employment. Bhudh' answered.

"*Haisi nyaya*, that's a minor issue. I will speak to my boss on Monday and let you know."

The rest of the afternoon was spent visiting Bhudh's friends in the township and in the evening they then went to the popular braai spot in Tembisa aptly named, Busy Corner. Pedzi spent the rest of the weekend with Bhudh' and on Sunday evening returned to the shack that he shared with Vengai. On the other side, Bhudh' found an opportunity to talk to Jason, his boss, about his brother's predicament. Bhudh' had worked for Jason for over four years, having started off doing 'gardening services' at Jason's house. Now he worked for Jason's online business, as warehouse supervisor. He was effectively Jason's right-hand man on the warehouse floor. Jason listened to Bhudh' and advised him that he would want to try Pedzi at his father-in-law's company. They needed a cleaner. He said he would speak to his father-in-law that evening and revert to Bhudh' the following day. From here, everything happened very fast and in no time, Pedzi started his new job. He also had to move out of the shack he shared with Vengai and moved in with Bhudh'. Vengai took the opportunity to return to Tzaneen to be with Koketso. He was never heard from, ever.

Pedzi started his cleaning job at *Meneer* Botha's vegetable processing company. *Meneer* is Afrikaans for Mister. He was lucky, he only cleaned the offices and not the factory where vegetables were cut and processed into pallets, ready for the supermarket shelves. All Pedzi had to do was make sure that all the offices were cleaned before the bosses rocked up for work. Occasionally, *Meneer* would ask him to bring water or make tea for visitors, when *Ausi*, the tea lady, called in sick. *Meneer* soon discovered that Pedzi was such a conscientious worker and decided to give him a gardening services contract at his residence, every Saturday morning. *Medem*, *Meneer's* wife, would supervise him. He worked there Saturday mornings and had the rest of the day off.

What Pedzi liked about this gig was that *Medem* paid him at the end of his shift, so every weekend, Pedzi was always relatively liquid. He became quite popular with his neighbours for being the go-to-guy on Monday mornings, if they needed to borrow bus-fare for the week. This, however, did not go down well with the local *matshonisa*, loan sharks, who felt that Pedzi was encroaching into his turf. Bhudh' gave Pedzi basic financial education, how to save, how to send money home and the rest. After the first year, Pedzi had managed to buy two heifers and 4 goats back in the village. The following year, Bhudh' was asked by Jason to move to Cape Town for a year as they set up their new warehouse to cater for the Western Cape market. Bhudh' explained to Pedzi that he would be away and that Pedzi should be responsible. For the first two months, everything went well for Pedzi, as he held down his two jobs. *Medem* was so impressed by him that she wanted him to get a driver's licence so that he could double up as the cleaner and driver for the family. Pedzi continued helping his neighbours with soft loans, until MaKhumalo, the lady who worked as a domestic for a wealthy Jewish family in Morningside, borrowed R500 from him. After two months of following up the debt, with no success, one day MaKhumalo pitched up at Pedzi's just after 1900hrs. Pedzi was quite taken aback since he felt she had been avoiding him. MaKhumalo quickly declared that she would be unable to return the cash. However, she was willing to return the favour in *kind.* Pedzi was shocked. It was such an awkward moment. To quickly rid the awkwardness, Pedzi told MaKhumalo that he would think about it. The next day, Pedzi discussed the issue with Bra T-boz, the factory supervisor at work. Bra T-boz, a thorough-bred *Panstula*, township hippie, from Atteridgeville west of Pretoria, told him that he had two options, to write-off the money, since MaKhumalo could not repay the loan or to *'hit it and call it even'*. Pedzi was nervous about the second option. He was inexperienced and wondered if he would be able to *extract* full value from that option.

The next day, he called MaKhumalo and told her he had decided to take her up on her offer. She said she would pass by his place after work and discuss the finer details. During his trip home, he convinced himself that MaKhumalo was not bad looking after all. She was of medium built, ample C-cup bra size and wide lucious hips. She didn't look too old either, maybe she was in her mid-thirties. He started wondering what she looked like underneath the long skirts. The big question though was whether he should present to her his non-existent sexual *resume*. MaKhumalo made her way to Pedzi's just after 1930hrs. She seemed to be in a good mood. She was a straight talking woman. She started by teasing Pedzi about him being inexperienced. She put him at ease by saying that she would teach him how it's done, and boy did the young man get his *tuition fees'* worth. As with all things, Pedzi was a quick learner and soon he and MaKhumalo were doing it *on the regular*. MaKhumalo started opening up to Pedzi that she was divorced and had 2 children back in Eshowe, near Richards Bay. She had also not been with a man since her ex-husband left her 10 years prior. MaKhumalo had a voracious sexual appetite, but it was matched by Pedzi's youthful energy. Soon enough, the whole street knew they were an item. The news reached Bhudh' in Cape Town who called Pedzi and told him to stay away from 'old *magogo's*'. Pedzi was not having any of it. How could he live without the warmth of MaKhumalo's smooth copper coloured thick thighs and wide hips? He would die before giving up MaKhumalo. News of their romance reached MaKhumalo's ex-husband. In Zulu culture, there is no such thing as divorce. MaKhumalo's ex tracked her down and found Pedzi in MaKhumalo's bed, with nothing on but a pair of boxers. He tried to attack Pedzi with a knife, but Pedzi took advantage of the fact that he was drunk and knocked the knife out of his hand. He made for the door and disappeared into the darkness. He found himself knocking at Nhamo's door, at some ungodly hour, only clad in his underwear. He thought going to his own place would be risky as the ex-husband could follow him. Luckily MaKhumalo made a report to the police and her ex-husband was arrested. She then went to court to apply for a restraining order, which was granted. The two love birds were soon back at it.

This was only the beginning of Pedzi's misfortunes, a few weeks later, he was mugged on his way from work. He was beaten to a pulp and left for dead. He only survived because a police car on patrol saw him lying by the side of the road and took him to hospital. He spent two weeks in hospital and when he came out, he started putting his life together again. Word on the streets claimed that the local *Matshonisa* had a hand in the attack. Pedzi and MaKhumalo moved to a different section of the township. Bhudh' called again to register his disapproval of Pedzi's relationship with a woman old enough to be his mother. Pedzi was intent on continuing the relationship with MaKhumalo. She treated him well and was a mature and well-grounded woman. MaKhumalo had helped him get asylum papers, which in turn allowed him and MaKhumalo to get married at Home Affairs, giving Pedzi a semblance of legality. He was now able to apply for a driver's licence and be formally appointed *Medem's* official driver.

The acquisition of a driver's licence was initially hampered by Pedzi's inability to comprehend the reading material for the oral learner driver's test. He failed three times until MaKhumalo introduced him to her cousin Ntando. Ntando took Pedzi to the testing centre in Parys. Parys is a small town on the border of the Free State and North West provinces, along the Vaal River. There, because it is a relatively quiet testing centre, Ntando was able to 'facilitate' the learners' licence, in exchange for R1,500. In the greater scheme of things, this was a worthwhile investment. After a few months they were back with R3,000 for the actual driver's licence and Pedzi was set. At work, *Meneer* immediately 'transferred' him to be the driver for his household, reporting to *Medem*. Pedzi's main duties involved running errands for *Medem*, like picking up groceries at the supermarket, taking the family pets to the vet and other mundane activities that *Medem* couldn't be bothered to attend to. Occasionally, he was also palmed off to one of the Medem's grown up children to run their errands, mainly school runs, or picking up out of town visitors from the airport. Besides the occasional communication breakdown with *Medem* due to his poor grasp of the English language, Pedzi found working with Medem very pleasant. Also with the 'lateral transfer' and promotion had come a bump in his pay packet.

For Pedzi, life was sweet. He had a good job, he could afford to take care of himself and send Mhai money home every month, via Mukuru. He had also sent Mhai money to buy two more heifers on his behalf. He was now saving to buy building material for construction of his corrugated iron roofed house, *imba yemazen'e*, back in the village. This would be a first on the homestead, something that even Bhudh' had failed to do. In Pedzi's mind, he was even going to electrify using solar panels and second hand deep cycle batteries stolen from mobile phone networks base stations, which had a ready market across the northern border.

The day the journey effectively ended was a balmy Saturday morning, MaKhumalo and Pedzi decided to go shopping. It was month-end and like most workers, in formal employment, they went to the local mall to withdraw some cash and replenish their domestic provisions. Pedzi's memory goes a bit fuzzy when it comes to the events of this fateful journey. Their first stop naturally was the bank. Everything seemed every bit ordinary, until unannounced four men in balaclavas, armed with automatic rifles, entered the banking section of the mall. They rounded up everyone who was standing in the queue outside the banking hall and ordered everyone in. One of them then ordered everyone to lie down while they asked the bank tellers to empty the tills. He was also shouting for the bank manager to lead them to the vault where cash was stored. This was when some idiot who wanted to be a hero cost two people their lives. As two of the robbers went into the vault with the chief cashier, two of them kept watch at the entrance of the banking hall. One of them kept walking in and out of the banking hall, making sure everyone was following instructions. The would-be hero tried to make a run for it, thereby startling the robber who was keeping guard at the entrance. The robber reacted by opening fire at the crowd of people lying face down on the floor of the banking hall. In the melee, Pedzi felt what initially felt like a sting on his back, which was followed by a trickle of a warm sticky fluid. Pedzi reached for his side with his left hand, when he looked at his fingers, they were soaked in crimson red, it was there that he knew he had been shot. What followed thereafter he does not remember.

The bullet had severed Pedzi's spinal cord. Unable to walk or help himself, Bhudh' was left with no option but to put Pedzi on a cross border taxi, *Malaitsha*, instructing him to go and drop off Pedzi at their village in Maranda.

As they turned into the bumpy gravel road, from the Beitbridge-Masvingo highway, Pedzi's mind raced to the day they had helped the truck driver whose vehicle was overheating. The hope and optimism of that day had now been overtaken by the pain, despair and utter hopelessness of facing the reality that at 19 years of age, he potentially, would never walk again. The journey had ended where it began. A journey from without.

## Mabvuku to Marylebone

Air Zimbabwe flight UM725 touched down at Gatwick Airport's south terminal at exactly 0630hrs on a chilly spring morning. Tichaona Zhuwao held his brand new green passport tightly as the plane taxied close to the terminal building. The relief of finally landing on *terra firma* after ten hours floating somewhere in the atmosphere was quickly overtaken by the anxiety of whether the Immigration Officials would buy his story that he was in the United Kingdom to study. Farai, the know-it-all from his street in Mabvuku had pointed out that the college that Mainini Jenny, his maternal aunt, had enrolled him in, was an obscure college used by West Africans to gain entry into the United Kingdom. Mainini had organized all the paperwork and sent it to Mai Mugadzaweta's work email. Mai Mugadzweta was the only person in their social circle with a properly functioning email address and access to a printer at work. She worked for the global giant Unilever, so they were one of the first companies to start using email. She had printed all the necessary papers and put them in a plastic folder for Ticha. As the cabin crew member's voice came on the in-cabin intercom system, "Welcome to London Gatwick…" Ticha's legs nearly gave away as he tried to stand up to collect his carry-on luggage, or rather a satchel with half his worldly possessions. He quickly steadied himself as he straightened up into the airplane's aisle.

Moments after disembarking the aircraft, Ticha stood before an immigration official, with an accent that he could barely make out. After one too many "I beg your pardons", the official resorted to slowly mouthing every word, but still the thick Scouse accent, Ticha would learn later, was still difficult to decipher.

"What-is-the-purpose-of-your-visit?" Oh, finally Ticha got it.

"I am here to study Computer Science at Grosvenor College, here is my offer letter and…"

The official didn't wait, he quickly grabbed the folder out of Ticha's hand and ruffled through the wads of pages. *Mainini* had advised Mai Mugadzaweta to print everything she had sent, which included bank statements for sponsor, letters confirming that the sponsor would take care of Ticha's accommodation until he moved into student digs at the beginning of the academic year in September, his parents' death certificates, letters from his pastor confirming that he was an orphan, his child immunization card and a lot of other unnecessary documents.

"Too many documents will confuse the immigration guys and they will allow you in. They are not very good at reading those ones!" Mainini's voice had squealed over the neighbour's telephone. Mainini had to communicate by making calls at the neighbours', Mai Tambu's house. Mai Tambu was the only one with a fixed telephone during a time when mobile phones were still a novelty, the good old mid 90's. The official continued to flip through the pages, and after what seemed like eternity, he asked Ticha to step aside, and explained that they needed to verify a few things before allowing him in. Another official soon came and took him to a small office behind the immigration booths. They asked him to sit and wait as they made a few phone calls. After almost an hour, two officials came back with his passport and plastic folder, they sat down and advised him that he had been granted entry into the United Kingdom on a visitor's visa, and that he should apply for a study visa within 6 months. They went on talking for a good five minutes about the terms and conditions of his visa, but Ticha did not assimilate a single word of that monologue. The last thing he remembered being told was that he could collect his luggage and be on his way.

After collecting his luggage, Ticha pulled out the piece of paper with directions from his pocket. Mainini could not come out to meet him at Gatwick because her paperwork was not in order. She had paid James, her colleague, to 'arrange' paperwork for Ticha's move to the UK. James and his cousin Sarah had Caribbean roots. Their parents were of the Windrush generation and had managed to regularize their stay in the UK. James and Sarah were now British citizens by virtue of having been born in the UK. James was a hustler. He could arrange anything. He had managed to sort out all the papers required by Ticha, for a fee of course, and was due a bonus payment if Ticha made it through. Now Ticha had made it and was trying to make sense of the travel instructions that Mainini had sent, which had been printed again, courtesy of Mai Mugadzaweta's generosity. He needed to get to a place called St. Pancras Station where he would board his train to Leicester, where Mainini was based. He almost forgot to find a public phone to call Mainini to tell her of his good fortune, he was in. As he walked out of the terminal building, he found a public phone. He quickly dialled Mainini's number which was on the piece of paper with the travel instructions. It barely rang, and he heard Mainini's voice on the other side, "Hello, *ndiTicha mainini*". There was a scream from the other side, he could hardly tell her that he was in, she knew. Mainini then gathered herself and told Ticha to follow the instructions. She added that when he got to St. Pancras he should call again to tell her what time his train would be arriving in Leicester. Mainini re-emphasised that Ticha should only ask for help from policemen at the stations, who would gladly assist him. They rang off and Ticha made his way to the railway station at Gatwick. It was clearly marked and the fact that the medium of communication was English, made it easy for him to find his way. In no time he was on the Southern train to London Victoria. At Victoria Station, he would change to the London underground's Victoria line to King's Cross St Pancras Station. On arrival at St Pancras Station, he bought his ticket to Leicester. The train was leaving in 45 minutes, so he had time to call Mainini and inform her of his expected time of arrival.

The journey to Leicester was a blur. Ticha's thoughts were racing, imagining how life would be in this country. Would he easily find a job so that he could send money to his siblings for food, school fees and other things that they required? Would he be able to study and get a degree like his late mother would have wanted? Ticha had been orphaned at the age of 15, when his mother succumbed to breast cancer. He had never really known his father, but family gossip whispers were that his father was from Malawi. He got his mother pregnant during the late 70's and moved to South Africa with his white employers in 1980 when Zimbabwe gained Independence. Ticha's mother went on to get married. However, she left Ticha in the care of her mother, Gogo Zhuwao in Mabvuku. Gogo was the nearest thing to God that Ticha knew. She cared for him in a way that only grandmothers know how. Throughout his childhood, Gogo always made sure that they had enough of everything. His mother would occasionally pay them a visit with his siblings, but Ticha was so comfortable that he never saw any need to ask to move in with his mother and her new family. Gogo was his everything. She and the late Sekuru Zhuwao had made a life in the township when they moved in, in the mid 1960's. Sekuru Zhuwao, who was of Mozambican origin, had met Gogo, a rural girl from Musami when he worked for Jesuit priests at St. Paul's Mission School. Sekuru had been raised by the missionaries after his father had died while also working for the Jesuit priests at Makumbi Mission near Domboshava. Fr. Christopher had promised Sekuru's father that he would ensure that his son was taken care of. The priests took the then young Sekuru Zhuwao to St Paul's where he went to school up to Standard 4. Sekuru then asked the priests if he could join the staff at the mission, as he was finding school very difficult. He was placed in the mission's carpentry workshop, where he served his apprenticeship under Brother Luke, an Irish missionary of the Society of Jesus, who was a hard task master, stickler for detail and a perfectionist. The thorough training provided by Brother Luke moulded Sekuru into a consummate artisan. When Brother Luke retired and returned to the Republic of Ireland, there was only one candidate to take over the running of the workshop. During this time, Sekuru met Gogo, a young village girl whose parents were devout Catholics. They had hoped that Gogo would join the nuns at the mission and become a 'sister'. After Sekuru noticed Gogo, these hopes were put into serious jeopardy as Sekuru made his intentions known that he wanted to marry Gogo. Their wedding was legendary, the older folks around St Paul's Musami Mission still talk about '*muchato waZhuwao*' to this day.

Their first born son, Sekuru Martin, was born at St Pauls and named Martin de Porres, after the Peruvian lay brother of the Dominican order, who was canonized in 1962 by Pope John XXIII, to become St. Martin de Porres. Sekuru fell out with the Mission authorities over an order from an outside customer who wanted school furniture made. Sekuru had negotiated a sweet deal, but the authorities were refusing to give him a 'bonsella' for his effort. In frustration, Sekuru uprooted his family and moved to the fairly newly established suburb of Mabvuku. Gogo, who had qualified as a teacher, thanks to the generosity of the Jesuits, also found a teaching position at Donnybrook Primary School. Because of his skills, it did not take long for Sekuru to find a job at a furniture making factory in the Msasa Industrial area. His new employers realised that Sekuru was not only a skilled artisan, but a leader of men. He quickly rose through the ranks and became workshop supervisor, something some of his colleagues attributed to his foreign roots. During that time, migrants from Malawi, Mozambique and Zambia were feared because of their association with *muti*. The promotion came with a decent pay packet and soon Sekuru and Gogo were well respected people within the community of Mabvuku. Soon enough Sekuru set up his own workshop at Kamunhu Shopping Centre. He manufactured sofas, coffins, kitchen units, room dividers, *madisplay* and other bespoke wooden paraphernalia. It became a successful business, relative to the circumstances that black people were living in during the time. Sekuru soon had a staff complement of four semi-qualified carpenters and three apprentices, an office, a personal assistant cum bookkeeper cum receptionist, accompanying a fully equipped workshop. The money was flowing in and Sekuru soon opened a general dealer shop and bottle store. He built a beautiful 4 bedroom house for the family in New Mabvuku. Sekuru and Gogo sent all their children to mission schools around the country and this afforded them a good education. Ticha's mother, Amai, was a disappointment when she fell pregnant soon after sitting for her O'levels and could only proceed with her education after she had finished nursing Ticha. She made amends by qualifying as a nurse and specializing in midwifery. After Amai got married, she moved to Gweru with her new husband, where they bought a house and started a family. Ticha's stepfather was then tragically killed in a car accident when Ticha was 12, and Amai was diagnosed with breast cancer a year later. As she battled with cancer treatment, her husband's family kicked her and her children out of the house she and her husband had bought.

Amai and her younger children came back to Mabvuku where the cancer and the heartbreak of losing her house was too much for Amai. She passed on, leaving Ticha and his two siblings in the care of Sekuru and Gogo, who were now in the twilight of their lives. Gogo had retired from the teaching profession and Sekuru was struggling to run the business. He would eventually hand it over to a distant relative with the promise of monthly payments, as consideration for the purchase of the going concern, lock, stock and barrel. He only got paid three instalments before the stories started. Two years after Amai's death Sekuru passed on, succumbing to a heart attack. As the Zezuru saying goes, "*munhu anoenda nezvinhu zvake*, a person goes with his worldly possessions." After Sekuru's demise, Gogo struggled to maintain the lifestyle that Sekuru had provided. However, she did not want to show her grandchildren that she was under any strain. She continued to shower them with love, care and affection. When Mainini moved to the UK, she decided that Ticha should follow as soon as he finished his A' Levels so that he could help Gogo to look after his siblings. The day had come and Ticha was finally on his way to Leicester to start a new life.

Ticha's mind was wandering as the train pulled into Leicester Station, its first stop on the way to Sheffield. The train still had to make stops at Derby and Chesterfield before getting to Sheffield. As the announcement came through the coach speakers, Ticha was jolted back to reality. He quickly gathered his luggage and prepared to disembark. Mainini was there at the entrance waiting for him; she hugged him, soaking him in tears of joy and disbelief. Mainini and Ba'mnini had moved to the UK a few years prior when Ba'mnini had lost his job at the mine, due to ESAP. They had come to the UK under the guise of wanting to study, but they had found the sterling made in the care work industry or *rese rese* too sweet to resist. Their study visas had expired and now they were living illegally in the UK. Mainini was so happy to see Ticha, she could not believe all her efforts had actually been fruitful. They bundled Ticha's luggage into the car, a red Vauxhall Nova, and they were on their way home. When they got home, Mainini sat down with Ticha and asked after everyone at home, with Ticha responding '*Vanofara vese*', they were all in good health. Mainini then went on to say, "You are in luck *mwanangu*, I have already secured work for you through the agency that I am working for. They are looking for male care workers who are able to be live-in carers for terminally ill clients."

Mainini had arranged papers to enable Ticha to work as a carer, certificates proving that he had basic first aid training and was experienced in caring for terminally ill patients. She explained to Ticha that he would be staying with the client, meaning that he would be saving on accommodation costs and he would soon be able to send Gogo some money to help with school fees, medical bills and food for the family in Mabvuku. Mainini then got on the phone to call the agency to confirm the address of the client where Ticha was supposed to go. She wrote the details on a piece of paper and then rang off. She prepared some food for Ticha while they discussed the type of work that Ticha was going to do. She said she would take him to the client and do some basic orientation. After they had eaten, Mainini took Ticha to the shops and bought him some warm clothes and a mobile phone so that he could be reachable. By the time they got home, Ticha's cousins were back from school and they were happy to meet their older cousin for the first time.

Everything was happening so fast, Ticha never got the chance to ask how much or when he would be getting paid. Deep down, he assured himself that Mainini had taken care of everything and would inform him in due course. They arrived at Mr. Clarke's residence where they were met by Mr. Clarke's daughter, Fiona, and his out-going carer Dave. Dave was moving back to Inverness, Scotland to be with his ailing mother, who had recently been diagnosed with stage four stomach cancer. Mr. Clarke was an 80 year old WW2 veteran. He served in the 3rd Infantry Division, in France, Belgium and The Netherlands. He was now suffering from dementia and his family had resisted the option of putting him in a care-home, opting for him to be cared for in the comfort of the home he had shared with his late wife, Diane, for over 40 years. Dave showed Ticha around, and handed over the list of things that needed to be done for Mr. Clarke and the medicines he needed to take and the times. After the handover, takeover process was done, Ticha's shift started in earnest.

It took Ticha a few days to adjust to the job, and for the client, Mr. Clarke to adjust to having a new carer, a black person for that matter. Ticha's work was relatively simple. Mr. Clarke was still in a position to do a lot of things for himself, he just needed to be reminded. The critical issue was making sure he did not go out of the property unaccompanied, as it was feared that he would probably not remember how to come back home and end up in a lot of bother. At night, Ticha had to make sure that all doors leading out of the house were secured and locked. It took a few weeks for Ticha to gather courage to ask Mainini about his remuneration. Mainini then informed him that he was on minimum wage, but was being paid in Mainini's bank account since he had not yet regularised his stay by applying for a study visa. Out of the blue, Mainini then informed him that for the next few months, she would also be deducting the cost of the expenses she had incurred in trying to get Ticha into the UK. This included the cost of the air ticket, travel, James the fixer, settling in finances she had advanced him, the cost of applying for the student visa and an admin cost, for good measure. It then dawned on him that a huge part of the motivation for Mainini was so that Ticha could start looking after his siblings and remove the burden from her. He had not expected that Mainini would try to recoup all the costs she had incurred. After all, Mainini was the *Sarapavana*, the guardian of her sister's children. That night, Ticha felt the loneliness of orphanhood that he had never felt in all his life. He had lived a sheltered life, with Amai, Sekuru and Gogo. Now he was in the real hard and cruel world. He had to man up very fast.

For five months, Mainini only gave Ticha £100 as pocket money, while she repaid herself and sorted out Ticha's student visa. It was sort of a blessing in disguise as this gave Ticha time to plan and research the things he wanted to do in the UK. The overwhelming ambition was that he wanted to study and get a good job, a professional job, a job where he would work in an office, not this job of looking after rich old people like they are young children. He counted himself lucky that Mr. Clarke was still able to go to the toilet and clean himself up. He could not fathom the thought of having to clean up another adult human being's backside. He vowed to himself that he would pull himself by his bootstraps and achieve his goals. Ticha decided that he wanted to study law. He had three years to raise money for Law School while doing these menial care work jobs.

Mainini helped Ticha to sort out his student visa, using the papers from the shady IT college in South London. The visa meant that Ticha had three years to work to raise his fees and also to support Gogo and his siblings back home. When the visa came out, he went to Barclays Bank and opened a student account. He was legal now. Mainini told him that she had informed the people at the agency to start paying Ticha into his own bank account. This did not happen. As it turned out, Mainini was working as a sub-agent of the agency. For every hour of work by Ticha, she had a cut, hence her reluctance to allow the agency to pay Ticha directly. This only came to light after two years, when Mr. Clarke died in his sleep and Ticha had to move to another client. After discovering this, Ticha decided that he would look for work in other parts of the country so that he could totally wean himself from Mainini's apron strings.

At the same time, Ticha had made a few friends in the Zimbabwean Community in Leicester. He had formed a strong friendship with Nhlanhla, a much older man from Kezi, in Matebeleland. Nhlanhla had been in the UK for more than five years. He had been a civil servant back in Zimbabwe, working for the Ministry of Local government, as an Assistant District Administrator in Shurugwi District, in the Midlands Province. His wife was the first to up and leave when she couldn't find work after studying a secretarial course at Kwekwe Polytechnic College. She moved to the UK and raised enough money for Nhlanhla and the children to join her. When Nhlanhla came, it was then decided that his wife enrol for the government funded nursing degree. This was the easiest and fastest way to get into a well-paid job in the NHS. While she was studying, Nhlanhla was working in the care industry, paying the bills. She was now in her final year and hopefully when she finished, it would free up resources to allow Nhlanhla to enrol for the nursing degree as well. As Ticha was researching which university to apply for his law degree, Nhlanhla advised him to rather go for the nursing degree which was fully funded by the government and then when he was a qualified nurse, he could then enrol for a law degree with the University of London's distance learning programme. Nhlanhla's idea seemed easier, but nursing was never on Ticha's radar. Why should he study something that he was not interested in? Ticha reached out to Ba'mnini, a reserved man who minded his own business, the type that only spoke when spoken to. He would never render unsolicited advice. Ba'mnini had adopted the Brit attitude of 'just get on with it'. He never complained about the long hours he put in, about how he hardly had any quality time with his wife and children due to their conflicting work schedules. He just did what he needed to do. He was mainly concerned about building a house on the residential stand they had bought in Bindura, his hometown. He was working so hard to put funds together to start the construction. It seemed though that every time he had raised enough, Mainini always came up with another emergency that depleted the 'construction fund' budget. Ba'mnini still entertained the thoughts of one day retiring and returning to Bindura to live peacefully in his twilight years. Ba'mnini's advice to Ticha was very concise, 'be careful that you do not live life through other people's fears'. Ticha got the message. He applied and was accepted to study at the University of Bristol. Bristol is a city near the Welsh border in the South West of the United Kingdom, and a 2 hour drive from Leicester. Far enough from Mainini's clutches.

A few months before university opened, Ticha moved to Bristol to try and settle in before University commenced. He was lucky to find a job and decent lodgings in Southville, a 30 minute train ride to the University's law school. Ticha worked and made all the necessary preparations for University. While he had taken the plunge to enrol for law school, according to his calculations, his savings could only pay for one and a half years of law school and living costs. He was now hoping that he would be able to get a weekend job to supplement his savings and be able to send Gogo some money for food and school fees for his siblings. University opened and Ticha immersed himself into his studies. He knew he could not afford to fail as his budget had no allowance to pay for repeated courses. His cohort in law school was cosmopolitan, a lot of international students, most of them a bit younger than him. He made friends with the middle eastern students from the Emirates. These were young men who came from oil rich families in the Middle East. Most of them did not have a care in the world, and they viewed this sojourn as a period to party and enjoy life away from their ultra-religious and conservative families. Ticha was studious. He became a favourite of the Emirati gang as he would provide them with notes from lectures they missed, and he gave them extra tutorials whenever they had tests coming up. They also became a source of income for Ticha as he 'helped' them with assignments and to prepare for tests. In return they would show their appreciation in the form of cash. In the second semester, Ticha managed to hustle a security job, where he worked evenings only. During the day Ticha ended lectures at the university and in the evening he worked as a security guard. Ticha's work was manning the control centre of security cameras at a Bristol Shopping Quarter, a mall in the Bristol City centre. He worked there four nights a week and had specifically asked his supervisor to only schedule him on the night shift, as he was a student. The job allowed Ticha to work on his assignments and study, on quiet midweek evenings. On the weekends it was different as the mall was busier and there were a lot of security related incidents that needed to be reported. Still, this job gave Ticha some extra income to cover his rent and board and also to send money to his grandmother back in Mabvuku.

While working at the Mall one evening, Ticha met Salif, a Kenyan from the port city of Mombasa. Salif was also working as a security guard at the mall. He had come to the United Kingdom to study social work. He had only managed to complete one year of study before he dropped out and joined the scores of illegal workers in the care industry. He was staying in a sub-let council flat, with eight other African brothers and sisters. The flat had two bedrooms, one which was previously the sitting room, now converted into a bedroom. One bedroom was for the ladies and the other one for the men. They had worked out a sleeping roaster, since each bedroom only had two beds. Others slept during the day, if they worked night shift and others had their turn at night. No one cooked at this flat, these folks lived on takeaway food, mainly curries from the nearby Indian fast food joints. If your work schedule changed without prior notice, and it was not your turn to sleep, you would spend the night sleeping in the kitchen where a chair was available for such eventualities. The main rule was when you wake up in the morning or evening, you had to remove your bed linen and pack it away, to make way for the next person, whose turn it was to sleep. Salif and Ticha struck up a friendship. They would talk about their respective countries, engaging in long political discussions about how colonialism had fucked up African countries. On some days, their talk was motivational. They became each other's support structure far away from home. They would cover shifts for each other in case one had an emergency or was not feeling well. Salif became his brother from another mother.

Academically Ticha was finding the courses in Law of Tort and Criminal Law very fascinating. He still had time to help out his Emirati friends and do well in his studies. He did so well in his studies that in his second year, the University offered him a bursary to cover more than 80% of his tuition fees. It was also the year that Gogo fell ill. Gogo fell while tending to her small backyard garden and needed a hip operation. As Ticha was 'now in the UK', he was expected to contribute to Gogo's medical expenses, which included the cost of hip replacement surgery and subsequent rehabilitation at St. Giles. Ticha had to dig into his savings. No one was going to understand that he was a student and that the money he had tucked away was for his studies, when Gogo's health situation was desperate. With the university bursary, Ticha was thinking that he would be able at least to pay part of his final year's fees, but even the 20% that the bursary was not covering was now a difficult target to meet. The stress that this caused Ticha also impacted on his studies, meaning that there was no chance of getting other merit-based financial relief. By the end of his second year, Ticha owed the university part of his tuition fees for that year, and had no money to enable him to enroll for his final year. Again, he turned to Ba'mnini who had become his mentor and advisor of sorts. In his usual calm manner, Ba'mnini advised him to take a year off his studies and find some work, then proceed when he had raised enough to clear off the debt and pay for his final year of law school. Ticha had no choice but to defer his studies.

In the year Ticha deferred his studies, he went back to the care industry and found another live-in client. Live-in jobs were better because they saved him on the cost of food and accommodation. It turned out though, to be a client from hell. His client was Raj Patel, a 30 year old man of Indian descent. Raj had been involved in a road traffic accident, which had left him with no use of his limbs from the neck downwards. Unlike most families of Asian descent who ran small retail businesses, Raj's brothers and sister were professionals and had moved out of Bristol to work in London, Munich and other parts of the world. Raj lived with his mother in the family home and she could not take care of him on her own, since she was now old and could not manage. Raj had still not come to terms with the extent of his injury, even after years of counselling. He still felt very frustrated by his lack of independence. These frustrations manifested in tirades of verbal volleys to anyone including Ticha and his mother, who were his primary care givers. Mrs. Patel spent most of her time in the kitchen making meals for both Raj and Ticha. Unlike living with Mr. Clarke, Ticha found living in the Patel's household was a bit different. He had to sleep in the same room as Raj to make sure he was alright because Raj was totally dependent on his caregiver. Raj did not allow Ticha to have his meals at the same time as him and his mother. Ticha was only allowed to eat after everyone else had eaten, because he was the help. Raj did not allow him to take personal calls during work hours. Whenever he had messed himself, Raj wanted Ticha to attend to him immediately, meaning he would have to stop everything else that he was doing. It was the insults that really got to Ticha, but he would quickly gather himself and remind himself that this was his only way of getting out of such situations in the future. Mrs. Patel felt sorry for Ticha and would come to his rescue when she felt Raj had completely crossed the line. As the academic year approached, Ticha registered with the University and paid his fees. A week before the opening of University in September, Ticha moved out of the Patels' and found himself a student digs close to campus. Salif arranged a job with the security company and Ticha was back doing the evening shifts. The plan was to work only in the first semester and then stop and focus on finishing his final year courses, in the last semester. The final year research project required a lot of work.

The academic year started and Ticha noticed that there were a few familiar faces from his original cohort, a few of the Emirati gang. One of the lecturers who was now taking them for Trusts law, recognised Ticha from before. She asked him to become a tutor for one of her first year classes. This was a shot in the arm for Ticha. Extra income. Ticha focused on his studies. He could see the light at the end of the tunnel. He took a keen interest in Banking Law, and his project was related to the banking industry. This would be of great help when he finished his degree and he had to look for a job. A legal firm, specialising in niche venture capital transactions and other complex financial transactions. Most of the firm's clients were based in the City, the financial square mile, the UK's answer to Wall Street, gave him his first job as a trainee solicitor. He was studying for the Legal Practice Course. The firm was generous enough to pay for his studies. Every day as he got off the tube at Marylebone station, for the short walk to his firm's offices on Knox Street, a stone's throw from Old Marylebone Town Hall, he could not believe how privileged he was to be working for a top law firm in one of the most sought after areas of posh West London. He had managed to get a flat to share in Holborn and every morning he took the Central Line to Oxford Circus before connecting onto the Bakerloo line to Marylebone. He shared the flat with an American investment banking trainee, who worked for Citibank.

Ticha's family life had stabilised with Gogo's recovery, his brother who came after him had decided to join the priesthood and was now training at the Jesuit novitiate in Lusaka, Zambia. He wanted to become a Jesuit priest. His youngest brother, Malvin, was in his final year of high school and wanted to go and study architecture at the Wits University, in Johannesburg, South Africa. Ticha was preparing financially to send his brother there and was putting aside all the money he could. He even entertained the thought of taking a second job to supplement his modest income as a trainee solicitor, however, the employment contract with the law firm did not allow him to take up other gainful employment elsewhere. Ticha's hard work at the firm did not go unnoticed, because at the end of the year he got a performance bonus, over and above his 13th cheque. With this, he paid for Malvin's tuition and accommodation fees at Wits. At the back of his mind he thought about his experiences getting an education in a foreign land and promised himself that his brother would not go through the same. He had missed out on parties at university because he had a job to go to or was too tired, and just needed to sleep. He had even missed out on the vibrant campus dating scene because he had no money to spend on dates and nights out with a girlfriend. Now that he had paid his brother's fees and would be able to take care of Gogo from his monthly income, he was now able to live a little. His American house mate introduced him to his social circle which included bankers and young American expatriates.

Malvin's first year at Wits University was generally uneventful, from Ticha's perspective. There was the odd request for money here and there, but nothing much to talk about. In his second year though, Malvin asked Ticha if he could move out of the University's official residences and find accommodation in private digs, around Braamfontein. Braamfontein, the area where Wits is situated, is on the border of the Johannesburg CBD and Hillbrow. A former predominantly Jewish suburb, now known for harbouring some of Gauteng's most dangerous criminals and drug dealers. Malvin and his housemate became popular with throwing the best student parties at their digs. With that, they attracted the attention of drug dealers and soon their house became the go-to place for students wanting to experiment with recreational drugs. Malvin soon joined his friends in the partaking of drugs and was soon hooked. He began to struggle to balance the pressure of his academic pursuits and hustling for his next fix. He sold his phone, textbooks, computer, clothes, actually anything that could be ascribed a commercial value. Drugs nearly cost him his life when he was attacked by a drug dealer who he owed money and could not pay back. His housemates managed to contact Ticha. Ticha arranged for one of his old school friends, Benford, who was now based in Johannesburg to go to the hospital where Malvin was admitted and assess his condition. By the time Benford got there, Malvin had already had an operation performed to stop internal bleeding. Malvin had suffered a ruptured spleen. The doctors assured Benford that Malvin would recover. In the meantime Ticha arranged for Malvin to move back to Mabvuku, to convalesce. After he was released from hospital Malvin was sent back to Mabvuku to stay with Gogo.

Malvin's subsequent recovery brought with it unforeseen problems for Gogo. As soon as he could get around independently, Malvin started looking for drugs and in the process started stealing from Gogo to fund his habit. Gogo soon discovered what was going on and tried to talk to Malvin, but to no avail. Malvin would disappear from the house, for days on end. It was during one of his sojourns that Gogo got a visit from the police on a Saturday morning. Malvin had been involved in a house breaking incident in Greendale and was being detained at Rhodesville police station. Gogo could not take it anymore and collapsed. That is when the call came in from Mabvuku to Marylebone, Gogo had passed and Malvin had been arrested for housebreaking.

## Priscilla Shumba

Priscilla Shumba is a wife and mother of two beautiful children. As a child, she dreamt of becoming a journalist, but never found interest in politics, news, or sports and with little encouragement soon gave up on that idea. She remembers being told by her professor that her writing was decent, but if she ever wanted to make any real money, she should try her hand at something else. She studied Women's Studies at the University of Massachusetts Boston and later pursued an MBA at Midlands States University. She is passionate about entrepreneurship and faith. These themes are central to her blog and podcast, Reinventing Perspectives; and her most recent book, The Christian Entrepreneur's Toolkit. Writing is her happy place.

## What do they see?

Am I wrong to want to be seen? Not because I think I'm important. I'm not. Not in a show-offy kind of way. I'm not a fan of attention. Not in a *being famous* way. The lights of the stage life would most likely cause me to break out in a sweat.

Sweat dripping down my face while people gaze at me is my nightmare. Frozen on a stage, not sure if I should wipe my face with my hand or try to wipe it with my t-shirt. My hand is not an option, because I still have to find somewhere to wipe my hand. If I use my t-shirt, how do I stop people from seeing more than they paid for? So, I do nothing. I stand there sweating my face off, pretending nothing is happening, and hoping to disappear when I stand on the illusion of a floor tile the magician uses to make his assistant disappear. I am not built for the spotlight. I work best in the background, helping those who want to sparkle, shine.

I have already lost my train of thought.

Oh yes, I just want to be seen as a person. Like any other person. I can't even say this out loud. The audacity to want to be an equal is frowned upon. The politically correct police will have you put away, dark skinned woman, for being deranged. No one likes a trouble-causer, so let it be our secret.

I don't want people to say I am looking for special treatment, because I am not. I don't want to ruffle any feathers. You see, my stating the obvious leaves others exposed and I don't want to make anyone feel naked in my presence. Not to mention that I wouldn't know where to look. It's best to avoid this matter. It leads to all kinds of awkwardness for everyone. In my attempts to save us both from the attacks of the enemy, I sweep the carefully crafted weapons that demean and criminalise the black body under the rug. Deep down I know that I am creating an arsenal that if found by the enemy will surely lead to the annihilation of humanity. Today it is the dark-skinned that are a problem. Tomorrow it is you. Hatred is a fuel that keeps being renewed by dismissal. I know it's dangerous territory, but what's the alternative? Should I always carry the injustice, just to not let others feel bad?

All I want is to be seen in the same way as anyone else.

Some will accuse me of being dramatic. Perhaps I am a little. Wouldn't you be if you were not visible to the human eye. Or if you were like a mime, using gestures to communicate your pain and having passers-by pay you attention for long enough to determine that you must not have very many options to be doing what you do. The first step is to be seen. To be heard is a luxury. Being visible doesn't mean having attention. It just means no one will bump into you unless that is their intention. That's all I want, for people to stop bumping into me.

I am no drama queen; in fact, I love the feeling of being one person in an ocean of people. That's why I love the city. I move around often unnoticed. It feels good to be part of the movement of the ocean. To be moving with all of creation. It feels like peace. There's no greater existence than to live at peace with all men. Moving with the flow and not against it. I don't want to cause any trouble.

Tell me...

What do they see when they watch me? From their enthusiasm, I gather that they see something rare. From their disdain, I gather that they see something they loathe. From their indifference, I gather they see nothing. Which is best? I do not know.

What I do know is that my black-ness always goes before me. It enters a room before me. It speaks even before I open my mouth. I know this because it is received or rejected before I am. At times I am oblivious of it being one step ahead of me. At times I feel it because although it's only one step, it seems to take up a lot of room, leaving me with a small space to fit myself into. Other times I must admit I enjoy that it goes before me. It makes me stand out. It seems to say to me, "All attention is good attention, right?" Better to be remembered than to be forgettable, I reply to her. In business you must be remembered, that's what networking is all about, right? Always stand out. Somehow, I know that this is just pep talk. The words of a star coach to a team member who needs that extra encouragement to perform. Is it a performance though? I wonder. If it is, I hope it is worth the being as much as it is worth the viewing.

I scan the room for those who look like comrades, but even they have abandoned the mission. Do they not know what I know? Maybe I am the one who doesn't understand that times have changed. But have they?

We don't need to argue over the phrase Black Lives Matter comrades. Yes, we all know, all lives matter. It's not about the words, it's about the truth behind the words. When one has done all, they can get the attention of the bear, all that is left is to risk one's life by poking the bear. Our words are not meant to injure. Only to rouse one from their sleep. Let's face it, everyone sees all the other lives.

I turn on the news. Nothing new in the news. Only the lives worth saving hit the headlines. Conflict should only be ended when the victims' matter, or the motive is perverted by the glitter of resources. It's the same old story. Nothing has changed.

I just want to be in line with everyone else and not in the shadows. People make up stories about people who lurk in the shadows. It's not a kind place for a person to live. I hear a voice whisper into my soul, "Come into the light. There is warmth here." I just want to stand in line with all of humanity. To be seen.

This takes me back to the cold mornings at Victoria High School. Standing in line, waiting for my name to be called out in roll call. I never realised that the act of yelling "Present!" was a rare opportunity. I can't go back in time. I must be found present in places where my name is not on the list.

When my name is not called and I am left sticking out like the last child left in a pick of teams, I must justify my presence. Before they beat me to it I quickly state that I am not here because my skin is dark, and I am not a token for those who need to feel they are doing something to right the wrongs of the past. I am here because I represent the same thing as all who have been selected. The potential to grow. Even as I say this, I know it is not true. The woman in me must fight the blackness in me which together must bow down to the presence of Christ in me.

I juggle it all. The feminist is me says I deserve to be here. I stand in allegiance with all who choose to push women empowerment to the front of every agenda. The dark skin on my body says I deserve to be here. Representation matters to little black boys and girls everywhere. The heart of this dark-skinned woman loves Jesus and bows down in recognition of the grace of God. I am humbled because His favour allows me to stand in places where I have no business being. I look around and wonder, how did I get here? The truth is, the Owner let me in. Divine privilege has ushered me in. How then, can I avoid the looks of being allowed to jump the line by the owner of the party? I chuckle at the thought.

Where anger could take hold of me, love now overwhelms. In prayer I fight for people to see people.

But why must anyone have to fight? I now understand the meaning of pilgrimage deep in my bones. I reminisce on what it means to return to one's home, even though I must be honest and admit that even the home feels less like home as time passes. The familiar has a way of creating comfort in discomfort. Is this why the Israelites continued to look back at slavery in Egypt as a better alternative than the journey to freedom? The journey to freedom is not for every heart. It requires a spine and back bone that frankly most of us lack. I know, because the journey looks too difficult for me, and I'd like to think I am only part of a big community that longs for the promised land but isn't willing to fight for their territory.

Where is the promised land? Can it be found here on earth? Will I ever arrive? What if I pack up and decide to go immediately in search of this land where all people are people? This journey I cannot take alone. Even lions that move alone will get taken out in the jungle. But what if none will go with me? It's too heavy for any person to carry alone. I will form the resistance of one and hope to identify my comrades along the way.

For this reason alone, I will gladly allow my black-ness to make an entrance. Fluffed up afro and African beads in case my ancestry is questionable, giving me a sense of being rooted. I know the beads are from my local department store, far from being authentic. Who needs authenticity to spark conversation? All that matters is the planting of a flag. The same way David Livingstone discovered the Smoke that Thunders, I have discovered the land our ancestors were brought to. Being rooted in a distant soil, I walk like a flag being blown along by a strong wind. Announcing my heritage even when not asked. One day I will be a part of this newly discovered land, even if just for a moment.

Perhaps I have stayed in my own head for too long. My thoughts have been harassed by experiences I wish not to revisit. I have to ramble around issues to avoid being caught up in ugliness. Surely, you can understand this.

I claim my place as a citizen of the world. All who are born have a right to walk the earth and feel at home. Who told you this was your land? If my God created the whole world, the heavens, and the earth, and what lies beneath; then a child of God should run across the lands with abandon. It is only for a time, a short time.

When my son and daughter make loud noises in a public place, I no longer shush them. I used to feel that they were being a disturbance in a quiet and calm society, causing people to look at them but not see them. I was misguided. Who were they disturbing by being children? If loudness is within them, then let it be released. If great laughter bubbles up within, then let it overflow. We are only here for a short time. Run across the lands. Dance upon the rocks. Now, I let them play as loud as children play. When people stare, I smile on the inside. Everyone has to come out of the shadows some time.

"Take up space my children." I whisper to myself, "This is your home."

## There's nothing for you here

The last words whispered into the phone, "There's nothing for you here."

"Yes." I reply in acknowledgment of what has been said. "I have to go now. I will call again next week. Goodbye." This is our routine.

As I hang up, I wonder if those words hurt my mother as much as they hurt me. To have nothing waiting for me in my home. I now understand deep in my soul why people keep pets. I never used to understand the crazy animal love, but now I do. It's a basic human need to have something waiting for you when you go home. To open the door and be greeted with welcome and excitement. Although I still have no intention of ever getting a dog or cat or bird or anything else that needs to be taken care of, I now appreciate the role of man's best friend. It's not that a person loves their pet, as much as it is that the pet allows the person to feel loved.

I know being dramatic about things doesn't help me in any way, but I have to be about this. How can the Motherland have nothing for her children? I see her, a big brown woman with big hips and big arms that embrace softly and warmly. She has to be calling out to her children to come home. Is she not?

Surely the Dark Continent has a place for its dark children. Where else can a dark child like me be called with welcome and excitement?

I cannot believe there is nothing for me in the soil because if I do, then I have accepted that I am a wanderer with no place to call home.

Homeless?

No. I cannot accept that.

As the sorrowful thought makes its way to my heart, I am Immediately reminded of the words of my Saviour. "The son of man has no place to rest his head." Now who am I to desire a home on this earth? ...But I do.

I whisper to the skies, "Lord, how then do I find peace on this earth?"

The annoying ringing of my alarm drawing me out of my closet space. Our phone calls often need to be followed by some time in the closet. The mother-daughter relationship is one of creation's complexities. The conversations we enjoy can sometimes continue long after I hang up. I need them to end, so I can be present.

The alarm gets louder. It's almost as though it's warning me to stop going down the rabbit hole with my thoughts. On most days I stay clear of all rabbit holes, but on this day, I really want to see where this conversation will take me. But it's time to go to work.

I have set up numerous alarms as reminders to hurry up, as part of a great effort to not always be late to everything. It has hardly made a difference in my punctuality, but it gives me a sense of comfort to be trying to move away from what my African friends and I call "African time."

Funny enough, I never felt late for anything during my African life. The rhythm of Mama Africa just synced with mine, and I synced with hers.

Work is always the same. I feel like a performer being constantly watched and making every effort to please the audience. Sometimes the audience will cheer and sometimes they will throw rotten tomatoes. 'It's the price of showbiz' I chuckle, while seated in my cubicle. Finding the fun in the mundane has made my imagination come alive. I just have to be careful to separate showbiz from reality.

I imagine this must be the very reason Oprah Winfrey makes her own lunch, to separate OPRAH from Oprah.

When you live alone like I do, you have to be extra careful in managing your thoughts. That little saying, 'the walls begin to speak to you' holds some truth if you allow the walls to be heard. I look forward to nights out with friends and my weekly call home. Even though I can predict the conversation word for word, I still like to hear the voices of my loved ones.

Christmas is in the air! I can smell it, and I can't wait to taste it. Irene and her husband, Ranga have invited me for Christmas brunch. She is an amazing cook. She always serves passion on a plate and I appreciate the way they have taken me in as their family.

Before I leave the house, I take a long hard look at myself in my wall mirror. "You look good." I whisper. I don't know why I whisper, no one else is here but me. Still, I don't want anyone listening in on my private chatter. Off to Christmas brunch I go. As I drive over to Irene's, I remember how it was only on Christmas day that my grandmother would make her famous scones for us. I enjoy reminiscing about my beloveds that have since moved on to higher ground, especially my grandmother. She was all woman; strong, loud, and loving. She was well known for her cooking in our community. My grandfather took great pride in being a man who only ate good food. As children we loved everything she made. My taste buds have since become more sophisticated, and I realise that it was never about the scones, but the sharing of love. This was the one day we had to wear new clothes. It was something special. Memorable.

That's strange!

Maybe I'm the first one to arrive. Early for a change maybe? I have come bearing gifts and don't want to have to parade them in front of everyone else, so this is good. I can quickly hand them over to Irene.

"Knock, knock!" I shout as I ring the bell. Irene and I enjoy being a little over the top. It makes us feel very Zimbabwean. Perhaps, she can't hear me with all the cooking. "Knock, knock!" I say a little louder with a girlish laugh.

I can't smell anything. It doesn't look like there's anyone here. Did I get the time wrong? I quickly check my messages. No. I'm right on time. Maybe they left me a note. Let me look around.

I notice the neighbour waving for me to come to her door. Suddenly, my heart begins to race. What happened? Did something happen to Irene? Or maybe Ranga? Or both of them?

Did they fight? That Ranga has a bit of a temper.

Or maybe someone broke in and did them harm. That neighbourhood is suspect. I don't know why they chose to stay there.

Maybe they were in an accident. I told Irene to stop letting Ranga drive after he drinks.

I can feel the blood draining out of my face.

"They got picked up two nights ago by the immigration police. It was terrible. I can't believe they do that to such good people. They were not causing any trouble." Cathy says in her British accent.

My heart sinks, no longer racing, it's now just faintly beating.

It's worse than I imagined. They're gone for good.

To be honest, I don't know if I'm sadder that Irene is being deported or that I have nowhere to go for Christmas. Both realities crush my spirit.

I rush back into the car to call my mother and tell her what Cathy told me.

"They were picked up like animals. They didn't even have time to take their belongings. Treated like criminals and yet all they have done is be law abiding and tax paying. There are worse people in this country. Why don't they arrest and deport any of them? It's our green passport I tell you. I know it is. Holding them in prison among real criminals. Can you believe that?"

I am screaming into the handset at this point.

I don't give my mother a chance to respond.

"Irene went to pick her friend from the airport who was coming from Zim, and she didn't know that the immigration police were surveilling number plates. They picked up that she was undocumented from her number plate. Her kindness is what caused all of this. She's too kind, that Irene. What will I do now? They are my only family here. Where will I go?"

I forget the need to breathe.

"I'm hurt, Mama. I don't have anywhere to go for Christmas. I will be all alone now!" My mother replies, "You will make other friends." Silence follows.

Here it comes, that whisper, "There is nothing here for you."

And I reply with a convincing lie, "I know."

We say "Goodbye" at the same time, as if we both felt the falsehood of the moment and immediately needed to hide from it.

I slouch in the driver's seat of my car.

I understand she does not intend to be cold or hurtful, but her words of encouragement are consistently salty. I just poured out my heart about how difficult life has become in the diaspora and all I got were marching orders.

Don't look back. Keep marching soldier, because there's nothing for you back home. What's so bad about looking back? I immediately see Lot's wife turning back to look at her beloved home with longing, and in an instant transforming into a pillar of salt. Chills run down my spine.

Yes, I must stop looking back. But what if I can't?

I have to stop this. How can one be content while always longing for a past that no longer exists? Everything is different now, they say. You wouldn't like it at all, they say. How fortunate you are to be where you are, they imagine.

And here I am, just trying to find a place to rest my head.

I better drive home before the neighbours get suspicious of my presence. The drive home feels long and exhausting.

What if there's nothing here for me too? Where then will I find my place? Does it exist? A place where there will be something for me.

I've made up my mind! I am going back to the arms of my mother. There is something there for me! The land has a place for me. I have prepared my monologue in time for my weekly call. I have an answer ready for every one of my mother's objections.

Soon after my mother says, "there's nothing here for you." I ambush her!

"Are you not something?" A family, grandparents, aunts, uncles, cousins, and friends. You don't understand me at all. I long for the streets filled with the sounds of our mothers' tongues. It sure felt like something special to me. Now all I do is spend my days following the news headlines, tweets, Instagram posts, and latest music to get a taste of my home. It's giving me anxiety, Mama. I'm tired of living this way.

"Carve out a new life," my mother says.

It's easier said than done. "Growing heartfelt friendships is not as easy as the movies make it out to be Mama. The people are ice cold."

She bombards me with a list of facts. Did she know I was going to make my case today? After her display of evidence and carefully curated statistics I reply, "Yes, I need the job." It feels like I have lost. This is the end.

"Okay. I know. Goodbye Mama."

I hang up the phone confused as to what just happened. Has my well thought out case fallen apart over a three-minute phone call? My mother should have been a lawyer. She has the mind for arguments.

I told her how cold the people are, and she accused me of being the one who is cold. Am I the one who is cold? Mama Africa doesn't have cold children. Her warmth radiates in her children. I have to change this! If my world reflects me, then I have a lot of work to do.

Where do I begin? I know! Maybe I'll finally take up my co-worker's offer to join the team for coffee.

## We Were All Broken

He waved goodbye and said, "See you soon." But he never returned. I can never forget the way he raced towards the boarding queue, almost knocking people in his path over. We would have missed his flight if we had just delayed by a few more minutes. Perhaps he would have never left. Like a martyr on a mission higher than his own understanding, my father agreed to lay down his life for his family.

We missed him terribly at first, but after a while life moved on without him. Our relationship that was once full of smiles, laughter, and close embraces, soon became merely transactional. At first, we deeply appreciated his providing for us, but at some point, we just expected the money. It was our wage for being his family. Are we not the reason he went abroad?

I know it was wrong to turn him into an ATM. At times I sensed the sadness in his voice and tried hard to strike a cheerful phone conversation, but somehow it always felt manufactured. Everything is broken. We were not the same people we had been standing at the airport ten years ago, embracing as if our lives depended on it. I remember my heart feeling torn and weeping beyond what I could control. In many ways I think I mourned the death of our relationship before it died. I wonder if Daddy did the same.

Sometimes I wonder how he lives where he is. I have heard rumours that he has another family. Could it be true? I cannot picture Daddy smiling and laughing with another. Surely, he reserved those moments for only his true family. Whoever they are, they can't love him like we do. That I know for sure.

***

I remember that day too my daughter. I still hear you wailing as I ran toward the boarding section. I never imagined my first time on a plane would be surrounded by such heartbreaking sadness. "I will be back soon." I whispered beneath my breath as I rushed to terminal 2. Did I know I was lying? Was I lying just to hold back the tears of losing the family of my youth? I was going to provide for this family no matter what it cost me. With tear filled eyes I nodded at the airhostess. Have I not kept my promise?

I could no longer stand the silence, and the long stares of your mother as she recounted the last of the money we had. It was as if she thought I didn't realise how little it was. I knew it well my daughter. She deserved better.

How could I have taken this beautiful young woman as my wife only to watch her waste away under my care? Her skin once glowed. Her smile once sparkled. Her laugh once electrified a room. I looked for that young woman in her sorrowful face. Where did she go? I could not bear the thought of being the one that had chased her out of this woman. If I called her back would she return? What kind of man would destroy a perfect gift? I dreaded the days your grandfather would bring us food from his harvest. As grateful as I was, I was more embarrassed. It was not merely the pride in me, my daughter, that chased me far away from you. That I assure you. I felt ashamed, yes deep in my spirit I could not get up, I questioned my very worth. That's why I did what I did. Good men provide. I had to leave to find my goodness. Even the bible tells us my daughter, a good man leaves an inheritance for his children's children. I feel your sadness too.

***

It is this man that I hardly know who buys me these beautiful clothes and fancy things. I woke up in a sweat the other day when for a moment I forgot his name. What kind of wicked woman am I becoming who forgets the name of her true love? I shall make every effort to recall all the moments we shared. As I look through our old and torn pictures, I try to make out what your facial expressions meant. Do you still laugh when you are nervous, my husband? My mother warned me about men who laugh when they are nervous. She was convinced you were a man without a backbone. For a little while she was proven right. Those days were hard. After you lost your job, I could hardly look at you without boiling with anger inside. How were we going to look after this family with no means? Today, I am ashamed of the cold wind I blew that chased you into the skies never to return home. Forgive me dear husband. I wonder if it is true that you have found another to love. I would ask you if I didn't fear the truth. What does it matter now? The skies will always separate us. You have found a new life and left me holding the place of a life that will never be filled.

***

My dear wife, this was never my plan. You know this. We came up with this plan together. Things have never been smooth sailing for me. I encouraged myself when the days got long and the nights got restless, that this was the only way. When tears welled up in my eyes, and pain crept into my body I rebuked it like a man does to his enemy. "Who are you to tell me enough is enough?" I screamed in silence as I got ready to go back to work. I live in between jobs you see, the more I work, the more I can be a good man and earn your approval.

Were your father still alive, I am certain he would be proud. I look at the photos of you and our daughter and am proud of the way your skin glows. You are as beautiful as the first day I met you. Older, a little sadder, but oh so beautiful my true love. My friends used to ask me how I got so lucky. I still have no answer for them.

Cheer up! This is all going to be worth it. This dream plays on loop in my tired mind. It's all that keeps me going. I dread waking up from this dream every morning. One day I will be the King of my castle. I will visit all my old friends and tell them tales of all I have encountered on this journey. They will welcome me into their homes because I have returned to take up my Kingdom. My wife and my daughter will cherish me for the sacrifices I have made to provide them the luxuries I only see in photos. Their joy is my joy, and my happiness remains set aside for an appointed time.

I am breaking my back for their happiness. They will understand this for sure and consider me a hero. I am a hero. I speak to my wife on the phone, she sounds sad but how can a woman who has everything be sad? I wonder to myself. Can anyone please this woman? When she waved me this way, it was clear that she could no longer stand the sight of me. The hardships we faced had created loathing in her heart. A man who could not provide. She would have never said these words to my face, but I heard her talk about men like me with her friends. Never mentioning my name, but always checking to see if I was within earshot. I could no longer hold my head up. The shame I carried was too heavy for me. Yet now she sounds sad. I am a man who provides now.

Do you not wear the finest clothes? While others cry about the economy, I have held you up above their cries. Don't listen to the rumours. You are my real family. That's all that matters. I will return my love, and we will be like that family we used to admire. You remember the ones who had that big house at the end of Silundika drive. That will be us. Just hold on.

In the early days, I always used to remind her of our dream when we were dating every time she asked of my return. She has since stopped asking. Our phone conversations have become cold and distant, like an enforced obligation to the master who pays the wages. The desire to connect and talk all night like new lovers with bright dreams to share with each other is now just a distant memory. Our telephone meetings are to discuss our daughter and projects. I scribble their budget on my hand before saying goodbye.

It's always more money. It's never enough. Will it ever be enough? I thought I could buy your happiness my wife, but I failed to meet the price. I thought I had broken my back for you, my wife and daughter, but now I realise that we were all broken and there will be no repair.

## Tariro Ndoro

Tariro Ndoro holds an MA in Creative Writing from Rhodes University. Her debut poetry collection, *Agringada: Like a Gringa, Like a Foreigner* (Modjaji Books, 2019) was the recipient of the NAMA Award for Outstanding Poetry Book. Her poetry, short fiction, and creative nonfiction have appeared in a wide range of national and international literary magazines and anthologies including *Afreada*, *Cyphers*, *Fireside Quarterly*, *Moving On and Other Zimbabwean Stories*, *Oxford Poetry* and *SAND Literary Journal*. Her short stories have been longlisted for the Writivism Short Story Award, the NOMMO Award, and the Black Letter Media Short Story Award. Tariro was shortlisted for the 2018 Babishai Niwe Poetry Prize, the DALRO Poetry Prize and the Intwasa Short Story Prize. Tariro has made appearances at Pa Gya! Literary Festival, Page Poetry Alive, Paza Sauti, Off the Wall Poetry, and Wordfest.

## Stasis

***Today 4:15 am***

When Chiedza startled from her dream, her mobile device told her that it was 4am, 19 degrees out and partly cloudy. She'd programmed it to tell her that. Sean was not beside her, so she scrambled out of bed and strode straight to her fridge in the open plan bedsitter.

Damn that Sean, she thought as she pushed cartons of fruit, veg and lactose free "healthy" snacks to reach the thing she needed most – a 500-gram tub of double chocolate ice cream. Wielding a tablespoon, Chiedza sat cross legged like a five-year-old on her only sofa and stared at her silent TV that was set to Al Jazeera while chomping on ice cream like it was her only salvation.

Chiedza had dreamt of high school again. Somehow her dream-self had landed in 2006 and she was back at Regina Mundi School except she didn't know where any of her classes were and no one knew her name. She'd last had that dream after she was retrenched from Mazibuko & Associates and now… now it was because Sean was leaving, and she didn't know what to do. She knew he was already half gone because of the way he smiled less brightly, called less often and most importantly because VeriSoft® had called to tell her that her Manic Pixie Dreamboat Experience™ contract was coming to a close and she wasn't nearly ready to be on her own again.

"Ms. Macheke, our Manic Pixie Dreamboat Experience ™ typically lasts ninety days. After such a period, the recipient is expected to have amassed enough joy and independence to walk forth into a fulfilling life with a real-life partner, or even alone," Tumi from VeriSoft® customer services had explained the previous day, like Chiedza didn't know. "Of course, for a fee, we allow customers to extend this service, but our records show that you have already extended this service twice. We will have to terminate your contract within three working days."

Tumi had terminated her call after telling Chiedza to enjoy the rest of her day. "Who could enjoy their day after that?" Chiedza had huffed into the deadline. She wasn't ready for her life with Sean to be over. First, she hadn't quit her job at van der Merwe & Bosch yet. Second, the idea of having to troll bars, book clubs and churches for someone to be co-dependent with didn't hold much appeal. Besides, there were creeps and rapists out there. Chiedza shuddered, then dug deeper into the tub of ice cream.

***

When her alarm blared half an hour later, she'd fallen asleep on the couch with one hand in the ice cream tub. The television showed images of a downtown bombing with paramedics rushing everywhere. She shut the images off and hustled into the shower, emerging from her building 30 minutes later as a blinding blur of high heels and a monochrome outfit, complete with an overflowing purse and travel mug. After the Zimbabwean sun, Johannesburg felt as though it was constantly set to autumn especially since the tall buildings crowded out whatever sunlight there was, so that even on days when the sun was bright, Chiedza's skin always puckered into goosebumps. Chiedza remembered the exact day she'd first started collecting manic dream boys.

***Last year***

Chiedza huffed into a narrow seat just as the Gautrain began to pull away from Marlboro Station. Even though it was a Wednesday, everything screamed Manic Monday:

1) She'd tripped and broken the heel of one shoe and couldn't go back home for a fresh one because of her status. As the token black hire at van der Merwe and Bosch, Chiedza could *never* be late for work.
2) She'd spilt coffee on her white blouse and the man who sat across from her on the train stared unrepentantly at her now transparent chest.
3) Her mother had sent a voice note about Cousin Tanya needing help with school fees and the claws of financial anxiety had reached out from within and squeezed at her heart so that she'd hardly slept through the night.

Tired before the day began, Chiedza plugged in her air pods and her daily motivational medley flooded into her ears, giving her enough oomph for nine hours and nothing more. The train glided in the direction of Park Station and unlike old train models, the suspension belied the speed at which they were travelling. Halfway through the motivational mash up, an advert interrupted Chiedza's thought.

"Are you tired of running around all day, but never escaping the same old rut? Is your love life at a standstill? Do you work at a job that is steadily sucking you dry?"

That was exactly how she felt, chewed up, sucked dry and spat out. Chiedza giggled as she thought of the AA batteries her grandmother used for her portable radio in rural Midlands. The way she'd chew at them and lay them in the sun to "charge" when their power waned. She'd always get a few more hours out of them alright, but the batteries themselves would look like they'd survived a war. Chiedza figured that's what a portrait of her soul would resemble.

"Well, HMCorp® has the solution for you!" The chirpy voice continued, "for a nominal fee each month we are offering the Manic Pixie Dreamboat Experience™ – a bubbly and holistic life partner all wrapped up in one attractive racially ambiguous and gender appropriate partner to help *you* actualise your best self."

Chiedza had heard the advert before and swiftly ignored it. In fact, she'd laughed at it, declaring that anyone who'd waste money on *that* was probably sad. But today she was sad, and The Algorithm had probably picked up on it. The Algorithm picked up on everything – heart rates, sleep patterns, hormone levels. Just the day before, van der Merwe's son had been promoted ahead of her after dropping some of his case files onto her already overflowing desk and she'd had to clap politely over the champagne and hors devours van der Merwe senior had ordered during lunch hour.

For a week now, Chiedza had been wearing the newly decreed green armband that immigrants were now required to wear in public spaces. Apart from the humiliation of it, the subvert shunning she'd experienced made it harder to hold her head high. For a second, Chiedza wondered if all the versions of herself in the multiverse were this downtrodden and whether a Manic Pixie Dream Boy would be so bad.

"My name is Mandla," the advert continued, "and a year ago, HMCorp® hooked me up with a manic pixie dream girl. I was struggling to cope with the demands at the tax firm where I worked and deep down, I knew I really wanted to pursue my music career."

Chiedza cut the advert off and searched for HMCorp on her mobile device. Hadn't the motivational speakers always told her to find her 'own happy'? One had to effect change before one *experienced* change. Besides, Chiedza wanted to see colour in her life again. Only happy people saw in colour nowadays, something about a gene mutation that happened in the 60s so that the eyes' rods and cones could only be activated if a person had enough dopamine and oxytocin in their brain. By the time the train pulled into Park Station, Chiedza had filled in her preferences and hobbies and by the time she disembarked, she'd paid the deposit for the Manic Pixie Dreamboat Experience™.

***Today***

Chiedza was not late, but when she marched into the offices of Gert van der Merwe and Jaco Bosch, attorneys at law, other junior associates were already knee deep in depositions and the messengers already had court summons and divorce papers to deliver.

"Morning, Chi. Senior would like to see you when you're ready," Louisa said.

Immediately, a coldness that had nothing to do with her ice cream binge settled into Chiedza's stomach. Being called up to Gert Senior's office was like going to the headmaster's office back in school. A quiet dread threatened Chiedza. She knew for a fact, did she not, that as a woman of foreign descent she ticked several BEE boxes and her hire probably had more to do with affirmative action than her CV. Her salary had been several times lower than Gert Junior's even before his promotion and he'd been hired three years after her.

Chiedza felt herself stalling, floundering. The Sean experience hadn't changed things for her and neither had the Xolani experience before it or the Charlie experience that had started it all. Chiedza was fast running out of companies that would supply her with a Manic Pixie Dreamboat Experience™ and fast running out of money with which to keep the habit. Her vision blurred at the edges, black and white encroaching into her newfound colour.

Chiedza looked at the drafts section of the email app on her mobile device. Two emails sat there – one was her resignation letter. I*f Senior is set to fire me, wouldn't it be better if I resigned*, Chiedza thought. But resigning to what? Who the hell would take care of her grandmother in Silobela and where would Cousin Tanya get school fees and even the tiny bedsitter she lived in needed rent? The pressures piled on her till an ache hit the left side of her chest.

Right, Chiedza thought, take it easy. She sank into her workstation and did a centring exercise the way Sean had taught her, breathing in, holding her breath then letting it out slowly. He was worth his weight in gold, that one. After whipping a mirror out of her purse and giving herself a look over, Chiedza went to face the fire.

"Chiedza, is it? Come in, come in," Gert Senior called out impatiently when she knocked on his door. She felt small in her crisp white shirt and black pencil skirt, but it would have to do. The universe hadn't warned her that she'd have a meeting with the boss today. She wondered if The Algorithm had known about it and how much she'd have to pay for access for such information in the future.

"Ms. Macheke," Senior began, after they'd shared "good mornings" and Chiedza had sat opposite him in a lower chair, "you've been with us for six years now and your work with us has been promising. We've had a few setbacks with you, but I suppose you'll do."

Do for what, Chiedza thought. Looking at the file Senior was rifling through and wondering what sort of things it said about her. She knew for a fact that the file would have something about her being hired in 2014 after passing her bar exam and working briefly at Mazibuko and Partners, a firm Jaco Bosche had sneered at during her interview. She suspected her curriculum vitae was in there too and it would say something about her obtaining her law degree from the University of Cape Town. There may even be a complaint from Helen Theron, the managing partner, but there'd be a lot too that wasn't there.

The thin file that Gert Senior toyed with probably said nothing about the hours his own son had spent distracting her from her own cases because he needed his hand held. The file probably said nothing about the clients who'd touched her in ways they shouldn't, and how Helene Theron had refused to file her harassment claims because she thought Chiedza had been lying. The suffocation of having to compete with Lerato and Themba for cases and promotions because outside of the messengers and support staff it was just them and they had no real seat at the table; and since the government had ordered immigrants to wear the green armbands, it had also been legal to fire foreigners with no due process.

Chiedza sighed.

"As I said, Ms. Macheke, you'll do. The bloody government is tying our damn hands again." Although Senior spoke in English there was no denying the heavy Afrikaans accents that lay beneath it, especially when he was flustered, and nothing flustered Gert van der Merwe like affirmative action. "It wasn't enough to have BEE or BBEE or whatever. Now there's a new B4E5 track for affirmative action. As you know we'll have to make Themba one of the partners here, so there's two of them with Ashraf Naidoo. I'll give you Themba's workload. This makes you a senior associate and you get Themba's old office and salary. Congratulations, Ms Macheke."

Senior didn't look happy to be congratulating Chiedza, but she kept that information to herself.

"Of course, I'll ask you to keep this information to yourself for now. We'll have an office celebration for you and Themba on Friday with champagne and snacks." This time, Gert Senior deigned to smile but it only touched his lips and thus looked menacing.

Chiedza swallowed.

Senior stared at her.

Someone in the office laughed.

"Well, I'm quite speechless, sir. Thank you," Chiedza said, robotically.

"Good, you may go. Speak to Themba about the cases and shut the door on your way out."

***

Chiedza boarded the train home and clutched her purse close to her chest. She put the box in the seat next to the window.

"Your anger is the part of you that loves you," Sean had said to her before, "it's the part that gets outrages when people mess with you, that won't let you get pushed into a corner."

She hadn't understood. She'd ignored it and filed it under all the pithy quotes Chiedza suspected he stole from inspiration books but now that Chiedza was angry. Chiedza *understood.* For years, she'd let the stress of the office, Helene's rage, and Senior's condescension slip into her and take up residence in her soul. For no reason at all she spent at least ten minutes of her lunch break sitting in the bathroom and trying not to weep. When her family video called on Sunday evenings, she did everything in her power to force a smile because how would they feel if they knew their needs were forcing her into the miserable life of swallowing the rage every day?

"You must let go of your comfort space; it protects you from the darkness, but it also blocks the light out. You need to let the colour in to escape the grey."

That she'd understood, but she'd been too scared to change it and now change was crowding in from every direction. All she'd felt as Themba had explained all the intricacies of his caseload was that she couldn't hide anymore. Van der Merwe and Bosch kept her from living on the street, but it was also making her crazy slowly. She opened the email app on her mobile device and looked at the resignation letter she'd first drafted a year ago and let her thumb hover over the "delete" button.

Just then, a young couple deposited themselves in the seats across from her. The man wore a loose-fitting grey suit and the woman looked like a paint store had vomited all over her. Her hair was dyed pink and she was singing some happy song from the nineties – the time before happiness broke. Chiedza wondered if the constant bags under her eyes matched the man's. She wondered if he also used work as an excuse to miss all his friend's weddings and his never ending expenses as an excuse to live in an apartment he hated and for not opening the interior design business he'd dreamt of since he was nine years old.

"Are you ready to start a new business? The Bright Foundation offers bespoke business solutions for small to medium enterprises," an advert interrupted her music. Chiedza wondered how her mobile device knew she was ready for her next big thing. And immediately she looked up the Bright Foundation. As the train glided westward, Chiedza cancelled her Manic Pixie Dreamboat Experience™ and signed up for Bright Life online workshops. To experience change, one always had to effect change.

When the couple across from her stood to leave at Rosebank Station, the man dropped his wallet and Chiedza picked the fallen item up. She grabbed the man's attention by tapping his shoulder.

"Thank you," he said, and she felt tired just by looking at his defeated posture.

"You're welcome," she said, "and when the time is right, you'll know. It won't be so hard."

The man frowned at first but nodded wearily when he realised what she meant. As she watched him walk toward the waiting doors, Chiedza realised she had changed. Despite the claw of anxiety that sometimes touched her heart, she wasn't as tired or defeated as she'd been a year ago. Chiedza took her seat and looked out the window as the train resumed its journey. The city had never looked more colourful and for no reason at all, Chiedza laughed. The algorithm always knew.

## La Duma 32/12

**dissonance** – ***noun*** a lack of harmony.

**1.**

I don't cry at the funeral – not when I look at the solitary coffin, the three candles or when I watch Justin's family huddled together in the front pew. I do not believe he is gone. Not without seeing his face. The burial is uneventful, not the blazing sun of cremations or the sleet drizzle of funerals in movies; but a few words, a few prayers and then the men are shovelling dirt on top of his coffin. Karabo cries. Silently.

**2.**

He is buried on the same day as South Africa faces off England in the Rugby World Cup final. The whole country is watching the game from taverns and sports bars and there we are, five girls sitting in a VW Polo after a funeral straining to watch a rugby match from one phone. Francine's phone has the best internet connection, so she streams it. Not that anyone's driving, but I'm sitting shotgun and can't see a damn thing.

*- Can Rumbi see?*

*- No, the angle's bad, do you want to crack your seat, Rumbi?*

*- No thanks.*

I do not need to push the seat back to hear the ref's whistle or the screaming fans when Mapimpi tries… or Kolbe. At some stage, the game ends and the commentator screams that it was over a while ago – the last try was icing on a cake.

-We needed the win.

-Yes, things have been bad, *shem*, so much bad energy. At least we have something to celebrate now.

There is to be a luncheon at the airport, right before Lerato and Noluthando fly back to their jobs and families – for old times' sake. And so, that is where we go, to OR Tambo. The girls' eyes still glued onto rugby highlights playing on an iPhone and my eyes glued to the windowpane. People pour out onto the streets dressed in Springbok green and yellow, and we're in the freaking East Rand; which means people in the street, people at the corner store, loud

families cheering each other on and cars blaring their horns like it's a wedding procession – this is what national pride looks like.
But then again, *we* needed the win.

**3.**
-Play it again, let's see the highlights.
Someone presses rewind on the video and there is the last try again, the last whistle and the sounds of fans rushing onto the field at Yokohama stadium and…
- They're not lifting Cyril up, like they did Thabo and Madiba! (laughter)
…and suddenly the wind just knocks right out of my chest and for the next five seconds I'm not quite tethered to the universe. I didn't cry at the funeral. Now it's all about to burst right through me like a broken dam wall, except I'm riding shotgun in Francine's car and they're talking about the Webb Ellis Cup and tears would make it awkward. I wouldn't just be grieving Justin.

**4.**
*We* won.
Two words.
Innocuous.
Five years ago, they may not have mattered, I believed in the Rainbow Project. I was one of them. A sister from a different tribe, a Zimbabwean tribe. Then I decided to answer the call of philanthropy, go back home, make something of a broken nation but between the shouts of non-coups and unemployment that didn't work out right.

**5.**
*We needed the win.*
There will be headlines and this time they'll be good. A month ago, all press was negative:
**A Nigerian Man Kills A Taxi Driver**
**The Taxi Drivers' Association of Pretoria have Called a General Strike**
**Taxi Drivers Looting Foreign Owned Shops**
**South African Shop Owners Caught in Crossfire**
A month ago, I lived near Hillbrow and it was my mother who offered money for an air ticket out of Dodge "just in case," as if she wasn't the one who told me never to come back home when I left the country. Thus, my love for

Zimbabwe is a boomerang affair. I can't decide which side of the Limpopo my feet should stay on. Caught in the middle and one day the tension will tear me apart.

**6.**

*We needed the win.*

There is a list.

David Dento. Thomas Evans. Brian Mujati. Munyaradzi Kotaro. David Pocock. Tendai Mtawarira. *Our* boys. Someone on Twitter says we should be proud of all our boys, the ones who played under different flags, that one day the Lord will shine down on us and people will stop leaving the country, but PRIDE is the last thing I feel.

**7.**

*Morena boloka Sechaba sa heso. O fedise dintwa le mastwenyeho*. Lord protect our Land and end all the suffering and strife.

He sang it with gusto, the South African anthem. Like it was his own. The Beast. Like he wasn't playing for *their* side. Perhaps he was right to do so. This land has been kinder to him perhaps, than the Motherland was to either of us. Before 1994, we all sang it, the whole continent: *Nkosi sikekeli iAfrica*. It was ours, but now in freedom we bear arms against each other.

*We needed the win.*

**2 Zimbabweans were reported dead.**

**170 are to be repatriated.**

**The rest cannot afford to go home ~~to hunger~~.**

*We needed the win*

**The South African Government should guarantee the safety of foreign nationals.**

**Foreigners should go back to their countries.**

**Foreign nationals are stealing our jobs ~~and our women~~.**

**I don't care if a white man takes my job, the foreigners must go.**

**You are in our thoughts and prayers.**

**8.**

- We needed the win

- So true, so many bad things have been happening this year.
It is the 2nd of November 2019. Cyril Ramaphosa has become the third South African president to hold the Web Ellis Cup. He shook Prince Harry's hand after the game was called. Prince Harry attended alone as his wife Meghan was pregnant with their first son. A month before that, a different Megan had been murdered in South Africa, then an Uyinene had gone missing…

*We needed the win*

…then an Eastern Cape man killed his wife and his children, and a female boxer was killed by her boyfriend. And the list grew longer and longer. I knew one of the victims. A week after the femicide, the xenophobia began.

"This week has really shown me how difficult it is to be a black Zimbabwean woman living in South Africa" – Panashe Chigumadzi (Twitter).

**9.**
OR International buzzes just as much as the streets of Reiger Park – everyone now and then, a *Shosholoza!* a *Go Bokke!* We settle for Mugg and Bean. Between the ordering of lunch and the "how've you beens?" I think about the weight of four years. How living in a functional country is all the difference between four years of a healthy salary, a good diet and planning a wedding. I'm exactly where I've started.
- So, how've *you* been Rumbi?
- ~~I've spent the past two months wanting to jump off a high-rise building.~~
- ~~I didn't cry at the funeral.~~
- ~~A score of 32 – 12 doesn't bring back the dead~~
- ~~La duma doesn't erase my panic attacks.~~
- I'm good, hey. You know, the usual.

**10.**
The black majority was not happy with the reckonings of CODESA. The white minority threatened to go to Australia. "We're going to the dogs," they said. Madiba was the first president of a democratic South Africa to hoist the Web Ellis Cup. He needed the win.

**11.**

Alone, in the evening, I remove my black skirt and black jersey. I hear *vuvuzelas* from a bar across the street. I didn't cry at the funeral. We needed the win. I will never be a part of that 'we'; maybe amongst my friends, but not when I'm facing the business end of an angry knobkerrie. The same streets that were filled with Afrophobic looters carry whistling crowds in green and gold. My body is a site of fear and I am both fearful and isolated on whichever side of the Limpopo I find myself on.

**12.**

Rumbi buries a friend. Rumbi listens to a rugby match. Rumbi breaks down, alone and in the dark.
*la duma!*
*We needed the win.*

## Abishai

Unlike the rest of his compatriots who, at least, pretended to be returning home to "rebuild the nation" when the GNU was formed in 2009, Abishai Moyo had no such pretensions. It is safe to say that rebuilding the nation was not high on his list of priorities.

Neither was he being obedient to those South Africans who told him, "go back to your country, kwerekwere!" He was neither sent away by visions of necklaced people nor by the bad reports he saw on the 7pm news each night on ETV.

What caused Abishai Moyo to spend R800 on a Harare bound CityLiner with nothing but a duffel bag full of broken promises and shattered dreams was a broken relationship and an expired job contract.

Unlike his compatriots who travelled with great suitcases of new clothes and groceries to impress their relatives with, Abishai left South Africa poorer than he had entered it, if at all it is possible to believe that one can sink lower than bribing a *gonyeti* driver to let one ride at the back of the 18-wheeler amongst the cargo. At least when he entered South Africa, he had hope, however valueless it had felt to him and however empty it had made his stomach.

Even now, his stomach was empty – he didn't have much over and above the R800, such that whenever the bus stopped at different ports and the woman sitting next to him bought a KFC boxmaster and wings, he willed himself to dream instead of the sadza and hearty beef stew his wife would have waiting for him when he returned.

She was a good wife and save for the fact that he'd abandoned her for close to six years, he still believed he could salvage something there. Ahh, he dreamed of the reunion when the CityLiner flew past Messina and Louis Trichardt – he dreamt of Aretha and her good cooking and Takudzwa, his boy and the girl… What was his daughter's name again? He couldn't remember.

What Abishai did remember was that things had deteriorated too quickly with Rachel. If he'd known Rachel had been picking fights with him for the sake of picking fights, he wouldn't have looked at her cell phone when she'd gone out for her girl's night *Chesa Nyama*. Maybe then he wouldn't have read the texts from the new boyfriend, "Mr. Sandton" who drove a BMW and lived in

Sandton. The suitor's real name was Joseph Kgwasi, but Abishai was a petty man and being petty he gave his opponent a nickname.

"Is this all the girl's nights you've been going to?" he yelled at Rachel, when she got home drunk and stumbling.

She laughed the laugh of the wasted.

"Answer me, I said is this what you've been doing all this time? Meeting with this J Kgwasi behind my back when I'm the one who's paying for your weave and heels?"

"Oh please, *wena* you can't even afford the weave I'm wearing."

She had the gall to hiccup after saying this.

If he'd known that Rachel was a liberated woman, he wouldn't have pushed her, but Abishai had never been known for his brains. Besides, having been married to Aretha for seven years before he went to find his Egoli dream, he'd fully expected Rachel to get down on her knees and beg for forgiveness.

"Sorry *kani*, Ba'Takudzwa," Aretha would have said. He would have yelled some more just to get steam off his chest and afterwards she'd serve him a good supper and do everything in her power to iron out all the tension. She'd even apologise whenever the girl *what's her name?* cried.

Yet Rachel was a Liberated Woman. Even in her inebriated state she remembered to be offended by his violence. She threw a heavy based frying pan in the direction of Abishai's head. It might have done serious damage to his skull; except she was bad at throwing and it was only the pan handle that got him in his mouth and left the trail of a split lip and a broken tooth. Rachel had the good sense to run to a neighbouring flat after that.

Abishai had thought nothing of it when she hadn't returned all night, he'd got wasted and had fallen asleep on top of the blankets with his day clothes still on. It was in this hungover state that Mr. Sandton's friends had come for him with sticks and heavy boots and taught him a thing or two about domestic violence. Rachel collected her clothes whilst Mr. Sandton stood and watched over Abishai's crumpled form. Abishai never heard from Rachel again.

His neighbours had looked at him with "*ag*, shame" eyes when he finally emerged two days later and they may have felt even sorrier for him if they'd known his boss had replaced him with a Mozambican when he'd shown up for work on Tuesday with bruises all over his body.

"You Zimbabweans are all the same – you have a steady job then now you want to go fighting at the shebeens on weekends and you think I'll still have a place for you? Well, we do serious work here, you want to act funny and I'll replace you."

Abishai's "please, *baases*" never made a difference.

"Don't please *baas* me today. You could have called in sick yesterday, but today you want to 'please *baas*' me. Go say please to your father. Anyway, I've already given Lance a job. I can't fire him just because you now decide you want your job, *mos*."

The site manager dismissed Abishai by turning back to his cigarette and his cell phone conversation. If he'd been a South African citizen, Abishai might have gone to the CCMA but it was no good. If he hadn't been an undocumented immigrant, he might have thrown a punch at the balding coloured man, but he considered three things: although he'd be grateful for a free ride home he knew he'd get jail time before his deportation so he couldn't push it, his right hand was already giving him trouble so he couldn't win a fight and he was tired.

By the time Abishai had got a taxi back to Yeoville, news of why he got his face beat in had done the rounds and instead of the "*ag*, shame" eyes that had made him feel uncomfortable earlier, he got hostile eyes from the women hanging their laundry on lines and looks of superiority from the groups of men hanging out at street corners. No matter how hard he looked, he couldn't find a job to hold onto, and after months and months of sketchy work and sketchier pay he remembered that he had a family in Zimbabwe.

***

If we were to follow the laws of karma or justice, dear reader, we would invent a rich philanthropist and urge them to gift Mrs. Aretha Moyo and her children a new house and a new car. We might even create a reality in which Mrs. Moyo receives news that her long lost husband was shot to death by some gangster in Hillbrow, leaving her free to marry a kind man who understands the meaning of 'till death do us part.' However, such surmises would be grossly unrealistic.

What did indeed occur was that when 2009 arrived, heaven remembered to smile on Zimbabwe and great rivers of rain poured down, grass remembered to sprout freely and even the trees shone with verdure. Those investors who had been nervous a few months earlier began to fund SMEs and BEEs and even the beggars on the streets began to eat well, because people with money tend to share. In fact, the only Zimbabweans who suffered in 2009 were those "change-monies" who had previously profiteered off exorbitant exchange rates the way old Jewish traders had profiteered off usury.

A woman named Mavis Magwenzi opened several clothing shops in January 2009 and although she was one of the women who had spent hours gossiping about the misfortunes of Aretha Moyo and deriding her ridiculous clothing choices, Mai Magwenzi had good business sense and knew a hard worker when she saw one.

When she visited Mrs. Moyo one Saturday, her hostess had been surprised to see her. *Her poverty had detracted visitors in previous years.*

"Ahh, Mai Magwenzi! *Matitsika nhasi*? Come in, come in! Shall I make you a cup of tea? Taku! Nyari! Come and say "*makadini*?" to Mai Magwenzi! Make yourself at home, Mai Magwenzi!" *We have said before that she was unused to visitors although no one could fault her hospitality.*

"I'm not staying long Mai Moyo, don't trouble yourself. I was thinking of opening a shop in Mbuya Nehanda Way. You see Ba'Magwenzi got a promotion at his job and he's given me *start money* to get cloth in Tanzania and Dubai. We'll be making African attires…"

"Yes, I can sew very well, Mai Magwenzi. Just ask Mr. Patel, or I can show you pictures..."

"*Aiwa*, Mai Moyo. I already have enough tailors to start. I wanted to know if you could be a supervisor. You see, I'll be travelling to Tanzania on weekends and I'll still be managing the bakery on weekdays. How does this amount sound to you?" She showed Aretha a picture.

Mrs. Moyo said "hey!" like the women in African movies. The amount was more than double what Mr. Patel was paying her. She hugged Mai Magwenzi before she remembered the woman would be her new boss.

"Ahh! Thank you, thank you. Ahh, *tinotenda*! Mai Magwenzi..."

When she ran out of effusions, she sat down and remembered that there'd been a week when all she'd eaten was the tea Mr. Patel provided at 10 am and that she'd wanted to eat the spoonfuls of *manhuchu* she had served onto Takudzwa and Nyarai's plates, but being a mother, she had endured five nights of a growling stomach. Mrs. Moyo had no words.

Being a woman who'd been abandoned by her husband, she had taken all her savings from the ceiling where she hid her US dollars and promptly went to buy a housing stand. She kept a tight budget and bought bags of cement and batches of bricks with whatever extra she had. Within six months a foundation had gone down, and the house was at window level.

She kept a copy of the plans in her handbag and whenever she had five minutes to spare, she looked at the plans and then put a greater effort into making sure Magwenzi Fashions had the cleanest floors, the most hardworking tailors and the best outfits in the town.

It was to these developments that Abishai returned. He stopped by the fence of his home, which had been falling apart when he left, and asked himself if maybe Aretha had found a new man to mend her fences. No, no, he shook his head; Aretha was a good wife she would never be with someone else.

But still, a lump of cement settled itself in his stomach until he let himself in the front door and searched the living room for all signs of male habitation. There sat his beautiful Aretha, wearing a stylish java skirt and pouring through a fashion magazine. He stared at her for five minutes before clearing his throat.

"Abishai!"

Mrs. Moyo started up and then, not knowing what to do with herself, sat back down.

"Ba' Takudzwa, I wasn't expecting you."

In truth, we must credit the woman for not fainting. Truth be told, her first impulse had been to flummox the man, but then she thought of her children and considered that maybe they had missed their father, so she pasted a smile on her face and asked if he'd like some tea.

"Just get me some Mazoe, Mai Takudzwa."

She placed a tray bearing Mazoe Orange Crush, refrigerated water and a water glass on the coffee table, then she sat and stared.

"*Hezvo*, Mai Takudzwa, won't you pour the juice for me?"

Mai Takudzwa refrained from telling him that God gave him hands, but something in the atmosphere caused Abishai to pour his own drink. He swallowed it in two gulps and Mrs. Moyo took that opportunity to call the children from the respective games of *maflau* and *mahumbwe* they were engaged in.

To say Nyarai Moyo was disappointed when she looked at the emaciated man with a green duffel bag would be the father of all understatements – the girl felt cheated. When Varaidzo Matanhire's father had returned from Botswana, he'd been driving a Nissan Hardbody and he had been tall, and he had come with suitcases full of clothing from Mr. Price and PEP Stores and the back of his Hardbody had *mbare bags* full of groceries from Game and Checkers.

The thin man wearing old jeans and a golf shirt was not what she had dreamed of when she'd held her front teeth tightly under her pillow and asked the tooth fairy to bring her father back to her. She wondered if wishes had return policies.

Takudzwa, being older, had heard stories of all the fathers who came home with AIDS and wondered at his father's emaciated form. He knew already that there was no way his mother would quit her job to take care of this man, now that they had enough money to eat three square meals a day.

Takudzwa saw visions of himself having to stand in queues for ARVs and having to make porridge for his father after school like his classmate Paida did since her father had come back from the Kimberly mines with a disease her family members were calling "a long illness."

"Takudzwa, Nyarai, say *makadini* to your father."

*Nyari, Nyarai, yes that was her name*. She'd been named after his paternal aunt. *Yes*, he remembered now. His children seemed to be two pairs of eyes that stared consistently and sat with their mouths agape.

Noticing that their father did not make the effort of other adults, such as asking what grades they were in or what sports they liked, Takudzwa promptly excused himself and his sister. They rushed out of the room like the horses of Borrowdale Racecourse storming out of their cages.

"Takudzwa is in Grade 7 this year. He was first in class last term," Mrs. Moyo said, as an ice breaker.

"*Hoo nhai?*" said Takudzwa's father.

"Yes, he'll be going to St. Faith's Mission next year and Nyarai is very good at singing. Last week she..."

Mr. Moyo wasn't listening at all. He'd used the remote control to switch on the cathode ray tv that still sat in the middle of the sitting room and tuned his wife out as thoroughly as his former boss had done.

Mrs. Moyo went to the kitchen and began to cook a meal that was neither lunch nor supper but the hasty preparations of a woman who had been graced by an unannounced guest. She muttered while she worked, and if anyone had bothered to read her lips, they would have discovered that Mrs. Moyo had a great capacity for praying for the gift of grace.

She served a meal of spaghetti and mince, with a side of coleslaw salad at precisely 5:23 pm. Abishai Moyo ate with much gusto while Mrs. Moyo stared at him from the other end of the dinner table. Later, after he'd mumbled something about cigarettes and fresh air before walking out of the house, Mrs. Moyo would eat her own food. But while her husband ate, she looked at him and wondered how this… this *man* who had loved her so thoroughly when she was eighteen years old had been reduced to nothing but an audible chewer whose clothes didn't fit right.

Later, Nyari would assault her mother with a barrage of questions.

"Mhamhi, do all fathers eat two helpings of supper?"

"Mhamhi, Dhedhi must have been hungry. Does *Jubheg* make people hungry?"

"Mhamhi is Dhedhi here to stay with us or is he going to go away again?"

Mrs. Moyo hoped he would go away. So did Nyarai. So did Takudzwa. Nyarai and Takudzwa communicated these things to each other by a series of frowns and shrugs while their father devoured his third helping.

It will be remembered by the reader that whilst the other passengers of the CityLiner had engorged themselves on Steers, Chicken Licken and MacDonalds, and, on the other side of the border, Chicken Inn, Pizza Inn and Baker's Inn meat pies, Abishai had fasted out of necessity, only allowing himself to buy a loaf of bread and a bottle of Coca Cola when he suddenly felt dizzy and tasted a fuzziness on his tongue.

And so, it was that a collective sigh touched the dining table when Abishai went for a smoke. The children cleared the table and did the dishes at lightning speed, so they could go outside and play or go straight to bed whenever Mr. Moyo made an appearance. Mrs. Moyo hid her money and transferred her bed things to Nyari's bedroom – Takudzwa wasn't the only one who wondered about Abishai's status.

***

The inside of "Norman's Loaunge" wasn't as exciting as Abishai had expected. The place smelt like the inside of a brewery and reminded him of Rachel and the times they'd spent in Soweto shebeens, when he had a steady job and a healthy wallet. Ahh, how the mighty fall, he thought to himself.

The men seemed to be having fun, but being the only sober man in a sea of drunkards, he alone noticed that the radio was too loud and that the lounge smelt unhealthy and that even the *gochi gochi* that was being served was nothing but a mass of burnt boerewors and undercooked T-bone steak.

He had hoped to bum a cigarette off one of his old pals and even benefit from one of those happy drunks who had urges to buy a round for everyone, but the inside of "Norman's Loaunge" was frostier than Yeoville had been after the time he'd hit Rachel. He couldn't understand why, but he had this feeling that whenever he looked in a different direction his old friends whispered to each other before pointing toward him and whispering some more.

Panganai Muparutsa had taught at his children's school for the past decade and could recount to the other men that sometimes he'd had to pay civvies day money for Abishai's children as though they were orphans. Edson Mandaza, who lived across the road from Mrs. Moyo, added that sometimes when Mai Takudzwa couldn't afford her ZESA bill his own wife invited her to do her ironing at his own home.

"*Shuwa here*?" Bob the bar man asked, "*inga pakaipa*."

"For sure, sometimes she even came to the butchery and for years all she bought was *susu* and tripe. Sometimes I gave her extra because I felt sorry for her."

"Six years in South Africa! Look, his jean even has holes in it," said Panganai.

You know he asked me for *mudzanga*, six years in *Jubheg* and he can't even buy one cigarette. *Bva*, we're all rich men. Every one of us!"

The entire circle of men broke out into that hyenoid laughter that is long lasting and designed to break a man's spirit. This time Abishai heard the comment loud and clear, probably because it had been aimed at him like a guided missile. Abishai got up from his bar stool and decided to go home to his beautiful, forgiving wife.

His wife wasn't in bed when he staggered home at eleven o'clock. His first thought was that she was out carousing, but then he remembered she wasn't Rachel. He might have been lost as to her whereabouts, but then he heard voices coming from the spare bedroom.

"Is it a thief, Mhamhi?"

"No, it's your father."

"He's back forever, then."

She sounded disappointed.

Abishai lay on the bed and tried to sleep, but there was a heavy presence that wouldn't let him drift into oblivion. When he finally fell into an uneasy slumber, he dreamt of high-pitched laughter and heads drawn together in collusion against him. Abishai dreamt of wide-eyed girls with names he could never remember. *Is he really back Mhamhi, why is he back Mhamhi, he can't even buy a mudzanga Mhamhi.*

It was three thirty in the morning when Abishai woke up in a cold sweat. For a minute he didn't remember where he was, but then he recognised the maroon bedspread, and the word "home" was conjured in his mind. Yet the home was no longer his. Its inhabitants viewed him like he was an unwelcome apparition – if he were a spirit, they would have exorcised him. His own wife would rather share a bed with his children than suffer his presence. She hadn't poured his juice like she used to. Abishai's hands shook – he needed a smoke.

***

Two pairs of eyes watched the street as an unsubstantial man lumbered across the street with a duffel bag heaved across his back. The third pair of eyes, the mother's, rested themselves while their corresponding lungs breathed deeply – the breathing of slumber. A boy and a girl stared past the white diamond burglar bars as a man who had once been their father receded into the blackness and melted into the September night.

Unlike his children, the man's wife frowned wistfully, remembering that *once*, he had not been *so* bad. He had promised her the world and a family and perhaps there was something to be pitied there. Later, she would receive an envelope from him with HIV test results enclosed and two hundred dollars "to buy something for Takudzwa and the girl". After that she would stop praying for his return and be content with the little she had, but in that moment. Watching him walk into the darkness, her heart splintered then began to break.

Takudzwa and Nyarai rubbed their sleepy eyes and went back to bed. Each child forgot to dream of a faceless father returning with lots of money and a big booming smile. Takudzwa would forever remember this day and conjure it whenever sleep eluded him, but Nyari was young enough to tell herself it was all a bad dream. Whenever anyone asked her where her father was, she would answer, with the earnestness of a country clergyman, "*Baba? Vakaenda kuJubheg*, my dad is in Joburg."

## Brain Garusa

Brain Garusa is a literary activist, blogger, writer and reader. He is passionate about African literature. His first story Kirisimasi was published in an Aleck Kaposa compiled anthology titled, The Long Night Ending and Other Stories.

## Kufakunesu

I don't know how Tinarwo, my father, was that forgetful. He had completely forgotten all the living signs of our proximity to death. My name and his being the uncompromising link to this. *Tinarwo,* we have it, as if death was something my grandparents could put in their hands or granary or guest house. *Kufakunesu,* death is with us! Names hinting a complete surrender unto finality.

Tinarwo, my father, was impressed by my strides and successes in the bookish world. I never knew any other class position outside the top three. Just like Tambu's father Jeremiah, in those chronicles of a people whose conditions can be best described as nervous, my own father was not aware of the consequences of me being rewarded for writing the best composition in the unknown venerated Queen's language, or that mysterious mathematics. It was one of the earliest paths taking me away from myself and all things around me. Out of the four products of collisions of his sperms and Mama's eggs across a good space of five years, I was the lone survivor. And now I wonder why they didn't find me some victorious name. Takunda. Mukundi. Murarami. I don't know how I evaded the angel of death. Sometimes, I imagine myself pushing the others to the outlet valve whilst we were in daddy's loins. I think I said to them, "go, I don't want to be first". I imagine how unaware we all were, of how temporary life outside the warmth of Tinarwo's loins would be. Imagine us responding to the joyful movement of the outside of our then world. The beginning of the destructive seductions of the worlds and places we were not yet a part of. This dangerous precedence that always sought to be a part of us. Yearning for something we could not be. Something we could not touch. Something we did not know.

I wasn't aware of the happenings in the worlds of human pleasure, but I didn't want to flow with pleasure. Even those days, I impressed daddy with my successes. I was never joyful. My joy I now realise was untouchable. It wasn't something to be seen by naked eyes, touched by bare hands. I think my presence in my sorrowful mother's belly for seven months was long enough to give me a premonition to sadness. Now that I know how sad my life is, I know why I opted to stay inside her for seven months. My time in mother's womb must have been unbearable that I couldn't stay an hour beyond 2300 hrs of that 18th day of April when the country was filled by an unnecessarily cheerful mood as a response to the songs of the Wailers and the Nicodemus exchange of cloth by the golden boy Robert and the alien, Prince Charles. I regret having been born then. Having been born.

Growing up I could see the differences of the writings on my parents' facial tropes. Pretence was all over daddy's face. His over-excitement over my successes betrayed him. He was overprotective and in the sea of poverty of his home, he fought against drowning so that he could spoil me at all cost. The joy and prosperity of the new nation was not synonymous with the struggle to survive in Tinarwo's house. It failed even to offer a reprieve to a people who had been forced overtly or otherwise to dance to the songs perceived back then as liberation songs. The jewel was bitter to some who were still in the thick of struggles not recorded when histories were being told. I remember those packets of large orange sweet balls our people termed *zadzadama*. You think of those sweet little balls they for whatever reason called *maniga*. All these were for me to feast on. I'm thinking of those little bubble gums by Dandy that I chewed all day long, increasing the emptiness of my stomach. I don't think I'm wrong to think that was a source of the real ulcer eating in my stomach before the ulcer of poverty and want.

Mother's sorrow for her seed that mostly fed ants in the nearby stream was written all over her face. All my siblings departed the world a few days after the joyous African welcome offered when a new person comes into the world. They were not allowed a burial place at the homestead. They were not people enough to be rewarded with a marked grave. I grew up wondering the reasons why a baby would choose to let people anticipate her or his arrival to the world of the living, then choose death soon after arrival. I think they were bored by the clap they received after their dangerous courage which made them remain silent at birth. Legend has it that my elder siblings were very reluctant to do the normal thing for someone entering the world. The midwives, having seen how unhappy this world could be, had to force them into crying as per tradition. In descending order, they deducted the days of their existence from 6, then 4, then 2. Pain of a sorrowful entry into motherhood chewed away the beauty and joy I saw in the few photos of her girlhood and youth. She was the definition of beauty.

Regardless of my bravery to evade death, they drew me nigh unto that world I thought I had conquered through the name they gave unto me - Kufakunesu. It was an early admission of this family headed by my father Tinarwo, of the date they had with death. They had surrendered to death, so death might have been freely and confidently hovering above me. Like anyone else, I was not sure of where and when. Alas! Death followed me through the success that pleased me and successfully gained entry through the recklessness of youth that seeped through my veins as I entered the university gates in a land considered foreign. Windhoek. My father who happens to have been pretending to cling on lost me completely when he braved the last pangs of the 1999 winter, as we waited for the only bus to Harare at the nearby Guni House. This was the earliest necessary place for my last sojourning in this world. This potholed road leading to one of the few Mugabe legacies: the Harare-Chiredzi macadamised way which in turn feeds into the highway that extends Rhodes's dream into the African interior from the Cape, is obviously the umbilical cord connecting me to death. I was on a path of no return. You may want to attribute this to time and fate, but I think there is a strong bond between Kufakunesu and death. This bond pushed me into that poisoned well which everyone drinks from, as Zhakata aptly captured in that song. The nation was on its path to death, thus it entertained me on my own path to death. I was industrious enough to supplement the meagre monthly instalments from a godsent angel who pledged to pay for my university fees in a foreign land. But I was forgetful of everyone else except me. Though my weekend piece jobs gave me a surplus which I could have shared with my parents, I chose not to. Instead, I opted for the path of joy, drowning myself with toxins and love. I loved to explore the contours of humanity and worlds using energy and vivacity. I wondered why and how I betrayed a lifetime of chastity as a son to a sorrowful couple who happened to be elders in the New Church of England that had splintered from the main Anglican church based on Spiritism.

The sweetness of my new life and its expeditions and discoveries successfully gave birth to lies. Father being father believed my vacation lies, that I was studying till the day he received the call of my hospital admission. Pleasure and happiness were merciless to me. The mercilessness was so intense and carnivorous. I cannot explain how enjoyment managed to leave me a befitting citizen of Ezekiel's skeletal valley. The last time I saw myself in the mirror, the same day I realised that even the marrow was sapped in my bones, I collapsed going up the stairs to Ta's flat. A fellow from home who in her wisdom is insisting I should carry my close-to-lifeless bones to Masvingo while it is still cheaper.

Death has followed me wherever I go in this world. I could not evade it by crossing borders. Death has no need for a passport. I'm left with two choices. Waiting for the angel here or negotiating my way home, hoping I make it before the time.

As if from a dream, I am imagining daddy recollecting his memory. He is seeing the path connecting me to his lost seed on the ever-hungry soil. But by the time he wakes up, I am dying. I am fulfilling my name. The fulfilment has no correlation to space. It is closely knit to time. Death is our world-mate.

## When Mother Cries

Once upon a life, Naomi was a baby. Naomi became a girl as she marched to become a mother. Naomi is Mother, whom I grew up calling Mhamha. And the end was not like the beginning. Mhamha is no more.

I am not sure if I am dreaming or not. The dream is not far away from reality. It is so terrifyingly close to the things that cause tremors in my mind and body. I hate it when dreaming and reality are so blurred. Before these nightmares, I thought sleep was a moment to forget. Forget so that I can start afresh when a new hour approaches with a new set of fears. Fears so old, only differing at the level of propensity. But is it possible to forget Mhamha?

After a long day in the construction industry, in a land where my presence is despised and frowned upon, the nightmarish conversation seemed a continuation of what I had been thinking, lying on that old and tattered mattress I bought after realising the demands of the job needed some form of an illusion of comfort. The not so fine and cracked concrete floor was not good for my skin and tired body.

After it knocked my senses on that fateful day, I probably came to terms with the idea that comfort was destined for others surely not me. The invisible itch inducing creatures confirmed my fatalistic conclusion. I had no choice but to pour boiling water on the mattress. To kill moths disturbing a significant growth towards comfort.

Before sleep took over, I had traversed the world of contradictions as I had lived it. Having grown up seeing *maJonijoni*, as those who have flocked out of the country are popularly called in the area sometimes perceived as ours, seemingly happy; I believed then I will make it there. Having acquired a degree from the seemingly progressing yet ruined country's newest university, I thought my chances of success would be high. Optimistic of the future, I was. Reality on the other end had different ideas. Being on the ground so green but with no chance to eat the green grass, I realised the pastures were for some, but not necessarily me. It is now that I remember the first blow coming when my heroine was raped before being graphically pierced into pieces. Like me, she had no papers to be in the country. There was no room for me or anyone to raise an issue on investigating her unnatural death. Me, the complainant, is residing illegally. Being paperless has left me voiceless in matters concerning my mother's death. Is Mhamha not so important to this world we think we are living when we are leaving that her death is a non-event, even when it is not natural?

It is at this moment that I realise our cattle back home have a better destiny in the country I am currently struggling to call home. Their slaughter is accounted for. Not Mhamha's. It has left me with no choice but to leave it. My mother's situation has left me with a clear sight of how cold this world can be. My fate and that of my people was sealed without any input from our side. We are portioned to listen to the commands of fate as we watch our poor lives being swiped away like useless logs in a raging river. Rubbish just floating yet awaiting its disposal destination. The country called ours was not generous enough to have us in its plans. We're not to partake at its honey and milk sipping table. We thought being here will be our luck card. Well.

Rumour has it that, Baba being one of the earliest victims of the disease that threatened families with extinction, *shuramatongo*, Mhamha was accused of bewitching her husband to inherit the two roomed asbestos roofed house. I hear the house cannot even house clever rats. Her situation worsened when she rejected Babamukuru's advances that came veiled in the cultural practice of *kugara nhaka*. Mhamha was banished from the home she thought would be ours. I don't know my exact position to my father's relatives back then, but as I grew up, I have come to realise I'm of no consequence to them.

Mhamha died before we had gathered the mind to have a conversation about our home. My mind these days wanders and wonders if she ever saw herself outside of our home with the two roomed asbestos roofed, two beautiful huts and the fowl run. Having one's own home is every girl's dream in the land of my mother's people. What then could have been in Mhamha's mind as she toiled again from scratch in her people's land to build what we can call home. What papers was she supposed to be in possession of to remain in our original home Sometimes I think the unthinkable, of what they thought of my mother. Especially Babamukuru who wanted to inherit her. So, to them what matters of our entire family after the death of Baba was mother's thighs.

After that tragic incident, Mhamha vowed to never marry again. She also made it clear that she would look after me. She tried working in local shops but realised it would not make a difference. With the help of Baba Z, she crossed to the other side of the Limpopo. I was left in the custody of her mother, who loved me beyond measure.

A few days after Mhamha's successful landing in Johannesburg, there was a dramatic encounter between Mhamha's mother and wife to Baba Z. She accused my mother of being a whore, *hure* that specialises in killing and destroying other people's homes. Mai Z's mouth spoke unutterable words. So, let's pretend that never happened.

I'm glad Mhamha never forgot me. She must have toiled with little rest to make me become a man and change the family fortunes. I know this from experience. I've been in this land of opportunities but have struggled to provide for myself and nurse my dreams.

But life had other ideas for us. The worst it ever did was to take my mother and her mother in quick succession. This left me empty and vulnerable to the winds of instability and fear. How can one dare to dream without a mother?

Her passing away seems to have passed with a huge part of my being. There is an indescribable emptiness from where streams of hope once overflowed.

In these zinc walls that adapt to any weather condition to torture my body which facilitates the torture of my insides, mother decided to text me, and I had an opportunity to have someone to tell my troubles. I'm yet to establish the unrealistic nature of it:

*My beloved child*
*I can't ask how you are. I know you're not fine. Life was not fair to me as it is unto you. Take heart and let its blows sink. Sometimes healing comes in accepting that life has little good things for me as you wait for another sting from it.*
*I love how hope has become a distant voyeur in your life of poverty. If you allow it, your heart breaks slowly, allowing you to live a little longer.*
*Thanks, my dear child for never attempting to confuse your soul with us, the departed. As you know, we are not allowed to tell the living how we are here, so I won't bother you. If we're not in a position to tell, who are they, the living, to know of circumstances surrounding our deaths. I was devoured by the cracks of hate on which the foundations of this world let alone this country, are laid. I think you see the episodic conquests of hate in the recent outbreaks of killings of people in this land. If one day you're to devote yourself to understand what killed me, take it upon yourself to understand how this and the nation we are supposed to call home were formed. Their foundations have been watered by the blood of humanity.*
*Your loving mother.*

I was troubled in my sleep. The letter was real, and I needed to respond to it. I had no words to capture my troubles, so I scribbled incoherent statements.

*My dear mother*
*Thank you for writing to me. I'm indeed in trouble with living and existence. Why are others denied suffering with their parents watching and cheering them while they're all living, Why?*
*I don't know what to do and have no one to consult or share the burdens of my life with. The place we used to assemble during Christmas and New Year is now vast, empty, and frightening. It cannot harbour a person it once watched dreaming. I also have no courage to sit hopelessly replaying the possibilities that were never possible. The last time I slept there I felt like the place was laughing at my hopelessness as they watched the empty tomb ceremonially mad to harbour my spirit.*
*I don't know what to do, my beloved mother.*

A new letter with flashes of tear drops came as a short but powerful response.

*My beloved son*
*Those still breathing are allowed to despair, but they should try not give up on life. You know what you want to do. Don't tire of dying trying to make it happen. It's the moment you have a head-on with your fears that illusions of change happen. These illusions are necessary because they give us purpose.*
Mhamha's letter was short this time. But it's the evidence of tears that worried me. *If the dead cry, what are us the living supposed to do?*

The letter raised my temperature. I woke up sweating, not sure of where the real and unreal were separate from the scheme. Can the dead cry for us?

As I go through the dream conversations, I start thinking of the things I am already afraid of. Dreams and their ability to leave you in that pool of what we are afraid of. It's now clear to me I had so much I wanted to hear from Mhamha. But how?

I am now awake. I can't sleep again, or I may dream a response to Mhamha. I also think, what if she cries again. Wondering, I start thinking if ever I am going to know my childhood traits. I have taken up this vulnerable adulthood where my poor body is trapped. Wandering, my thoughts connect with the energetic children my eyes can see playing. There is a discouraging uncertainty in the heart on whether this joy is going to be permanent. The wish is that adulthood never interferes with this unmitigated fulfilled life.

The desire is to know if there were any traces of cowardice in my childhood. But mother is no more. And the dream is no more too. So, there is no way to ask my mother if she had noticed any traits of cowardice in my young eyes. In my young acts. I want to know.

It's her affirmation to do what is right that's pushing me. I'm no longer sure of that which is right. I was pushed out of the country by its carelessness. It failed the balance between populism and practicality. And it spitted us out of its belly. But here we find ourselves unwelcome. We are called by undesirable names that paint our unworthiness. That paint us as some sort of infringement. On some days we think of going back home. But where is home when Mhamha is lying under the earth's ever hungry belly?

Home failed to keep pace with our dreams. It has selected those it chose to move with. And we were left out. Now I only have thoughts of an unrecoverable loss that happened to me. Fate has left me off balance.

Thinking of Mhamha crying leaves me having unsettling thoughts. Unsettling. The land in which both our umbilical cords, Mhamha's and mine, were buried to rot couldn't have the boldness to sustain us standing on our feet. The very same land that allowed floating forces on its surface to chase Mhamha and me was bold enough to consume the expressionless but smiling face of Mhamha as I know it in that beautiful coffin. Mhamha. My superhero. Still. Motionless. Smiling. I imagine writing:

*After rejecting you Mhamha, when your body still had the capacity to move on its own, the land welcomed you when it's surviving inhabitants made use of picks and shovels to disturb a designated part of its own as your final place. I was there. Still in disbelief. Denial. Watching with an indifferent eye, some women, including your mother, who were in the small hut with you lying waiting to be taken to the final place - varoora, your sisters in law as dictated by the laws of your communal existence were there imitating your actions when you were still active. They burst into song, discordantly linked to the drumbeat. They danced to a song I didn't find interesting, "vana Mai ndovanoenda zvavo _ vana Tete ndovanoenda zvavo." They danced there, buttocks high up, and the rest of their bodies bent to allow the dance to be meaningful to them. Some men grouped as 'vakuwasha' were making sure that people did not go home hungry after 'planting' you, as the pastor later said in his sermon. I'm waiting for the germination of you Mhamha, but with no certainty and belief in the very act of waiting. Before he stood to give that sermon, a solemn hymn*

*was sung with a slow tempo that allowed it to stay in my heart for a lifetime. Hanging in my memory.*
*"Hatina musha panyika Hatifari kuva pano. Zvinofadza Mweya yedu kutsvaka musha unouya."*

*Thinking of this song now, I realise the impermanence of your stay on earth versus the permanence of sadness, coupled with yearning on my part. I realise how we: you Mhamha and I, your child, are just floating from one home to another, from one country to another with no guaranteed certainties of love and perpetuity. The umbilical cord failed to assert our ownership to any part of that country we call home, or anywhere in the world. If anything, the umbilical cord was a confirmation of the underground as our home. You led the way to the underground. As the pastor said, I and many others are following. Mhamha, you had no papers to guarantee your stay in a home you built with your husband. The man I called father. You had no papers to make you officially recognised in the country of your fugitive. When you were found breathless, you were only honoured by headlining the main newspapers of the countries your feet had trodden. I wish the wisdom of the hymn writer could have seen beyond us and realise it wasn't us yearning for a home far away, but the earth which desired us beneath. Underneath. Your stay in the earth's belly has a finality to it, as heralded by the umbilical cord which was left to rot after its initial bonding of our shared suffering, when my fragility was still visible. I am realising I am still fragile, but no one can see it. I think now of how you were a powerful life giver. All my life, our relationship tilted to me as a beneficiary. I tasted that which was made in the world through the umbilical cord, that string, which was buried under the earth, guaranteeing my own ephemerality. I sucked life from your breast. You toiled to make sure I went to school. I am thinking of the magical powers you possess in contrast to your stillness on that final day, trapped in that all zinc house, clueless of how to navigate the bleak future.*

## Tinashe Junias Chipenyu

Tinashe Junias Chipenyu is a Zimbabwean creative writer who is currently based in South Africa. He's an Electronic Commerce graduate from the Harare Institute of Technology. Tinashe's creative work has appeared in the Kalahari Review, Shallow Tales Review and African Writer Magazine. When he's not writing, he's watching football, tennis or wildlife documentaries. You can follow him on Twitter @_Uncle_TJ

## Restless Stalker

The elite soldier moves with hawklike awareness and murderous intent. His eyes are sharp and ultra-alert. There is something in his gait and the way he holds his weapon, that points to years of intense training. Short and of slight build, he's not immediately intimidating. But looks have been known to be immensely deceptive. History has proven it time and time again. He makes up for his lack of imposing frame with a nimbleness and adroitness that can only be a product of years of sustained honing. He suddenly stops and listens, his weapon engaged. Everything around him seems to stand still. He has been on a hunt like this one many times before. He knows what it takes. He knows full well that his opponent is no pushover. She's well trained. Very well trained. He's also aware that she isn't a soldier. Which makes her more difficult to track down. If she was a soldier, no matter how elite, he would know how to trap her. Because a soldier knows how another soldier thinks. But she is an intelligence operative and he has to think like one. The soldier must think outside the box. He changes direction, he hears a faint sound which he hopes will lead him to the position of his enemy. He must be careful, because if she sees him first, it's game over. But he hasn't survived all these years by being careless, he knows the cost of complacency all too well.

Movement to his left. He holds his breath. Is this the defining moment? Has his opponent outwitted him? He turns his head slowly, his right-hand twitching, weapon on the ready. He sees it slithering away. Must be a brown grass snake. He breathes a sigh of relief and moves on. His heart is now beating fast. It's not a good sign. Years of reconnaissance, surveillance and anti-surveillance has taught him to be wary of a galloping heart. It's an unerring signal that something is amiss. It has been too long and there's still no sign of the enemy. Chances are it's him who has become the hunted. How could he not think of this before? He is the one being tracked down now. He has to turn back in the direction from where he has come from, that's where the secret lies. He suddenly freezes. There is something eerily cold on the small of his back. And he knows what it is. A soldier of his experience knows what it is. He can feel the hot breath of his nemesis on his neck. It's all over. He has lost. "Put your weapon down." A brusque voice tells him "Slow---"

A car hooted menacingly from the road, violently plucking him out of his thoughts. It must have been the garbage collection truck. First time it had come in a month. The thought was so deep that it felt like a dream. This was not the first time it had happened. It occurred regularly. He woke up from sleep around six every morning, then spent the next ten, twenty or so minutes in a strange no man's land. Not fully awake, not fully asleep either. It troubled him, this state, but there was nothing that he could do about it. This train of thought had been happening for a while now. Him as an elite soldier stalking a lady who was an elite intelligence operative. In the thought, he was either a SAS operative or a Navy SEAL and she was a Mossad agent. It was not one of those thoughts he invited, the kinds of thoughts you willed to come. No. It would just suddenly engulf his mind and he could not control it or direct it as he did other fantasies. He could control his wealth fantasies. He could control his fantasies about women, but not this. It always ended badly no matter how much he tried to shift the scene to his favour.

Sometimes it felt like an out of body experience. He, watching himself stalking his nemesis from a vantage place somewhere. It was a most bizarre experience and, if he cared to admit, intriguing. He wondered where the thought was coming from. Part of it at least could be reasonably explained. He was a former soldier. A Zimbabwean Presidential Guard. So naturally, his subconscious was filled with images from that time. But most of it could not be explained. Who was the female intelligence operative he was always stalking and where did he know her from? Why was it he never even saw her in the thought-dream, but it seemed clear to him that he had met her before? Why was it that the thought-dream never ended well and why was it so disturbingly lucid?

Munacho stretched himself and yawned. His eyes were heavy. Painful even. Like a piece of dirt had lodged in his eyelids. He rubbed them intensely to no avail. He dragged his limbs to his small wardrobe. It was barely taller than him. His legs ached. He reached for a bottle of Visine in the bottom drawer of his wardrobe. The bottle was almost empty. He had been applying it daily. His eyes burned every time he woke up. They had assumed a permanent hooded look. He squeezed the empty bottle thoroughly, but nothing came out. He searched in his trousers which were lying on the floor, for a pocketknife, found it and cut the bottle in the middle. It reminded him of his childhood when he and his siblings did that to the bottle of Colgate or Close up toothpaste. He smiled. Crazy times. There were some little drops stuck to the internal edges of the container. He squeezed his index finger inside and dragged out just enough. He gently applied it to his eyes and proceeded to the bathroom. It was dark inside. The fluorescent light was dead, and he was too lazy to replace it. It felt like too much work, going to the shops. He did not have the time. He got in and turned on the shower. Ferociously cold water gushed out. He had noted with wry amusement, that it was always the cold water that gushed out, the warm water only ever trickled out. He was not complaining though. He preferred cold water even in winter anyway. It made him feel alive. Three minutes later, he was out. He had no time for scrubbing himself and other trivia today. He went back into his bedroom, which was also his lounge and kitchen. He applied some Vaseline on his face and slid into his work suit. He rummaged through the dark wardrobe and pulled his size eight industrial boots out. They desperately needed a helping of polish. He had no time for that. He put the shoes on. How he had misplaced the shoelaces, only the heavens knew. His stomach growled. He had last eaten the afternoon of the previous day; some badly cooked chips with too many spices and oil. They had given him a nasty running stomach for his troubles. But he was short of time. He would have to find something to eat at work, hopefully not badly cooked chips, doused in more oil than is available to the Emirati ruling elite.

Message alert: it was from the VFS. His heart skipped as he opened it. His work permit application had not been successful. Though he expected it, it was still a crushing blow. He opened his emails. Why not? Maybe there was something in there that could soften the blow, hard as it was to believe. His day had already started on a shocking note. The emails were not loading. He had no data. Damn! He took an airtime credit and bought 25MB. Enough to open a few emails. There were three messages from two African literary journals and another one from a company he had forgotten he had applied to. He heaved as he clicked the most recent one. It was a rejection. At least they had said they enjoyed reading his work. It offered some consolation, especially taking into consideration how his day had started. He clicked on the second one. This was a flat-out rejection. The editors did not make any attempt to mask the fact that they weren't impressed. And they did not ask him to consider them in the future. He had received loads of these emails. They no longer bothered him. But this morning they did. He was tired of receiving blow after blow. Every morning he woke up to a world that looked at him with mean eyes; a world that taunted and mocked him. A world that lambasted and lampooned him for things he could not change. The third one was a rejection from a ghost-writing firm. This crushed him the most. He was convinced that he would get the job. He had put his heart and soul into the test article. They stated that his test article was not good enough. His sentences were too long and convoluted and he should cut on his adverbs and adjectives. They were not hiring him and wished him luck in his future endeavours. He closed his Gmail app and walked out of the house. Life was just a pain and nothing else. Five hours ago, he had been at work and he was going back again for two full shifts. He had to. In the morning until four in the evening, he did what he liked to call his main job. Motor Mechanic. He had learned the skills in the Army. He was good at his job. The salary was not too bad from an immigrant's perspective. Immigrants did not expect to be paid as much as locals; it was normal. He had accepted it.

After that, he would proceed to his second job at the veterinary centre where he worked as an Animal Handler. He started working at seven in the evening until one in the morning. The driver — a garrulous and diminutive, middle-aged coloured guy — then took him home, where he would sleep for four to five hours before waking up again to resume the cycle. Being an Animal Handler was not an easy job. Firstly, he would clean the dog kennels, removing the excrement and then scrubbing the concrete floor until it was sparkling clean. There were more than twenty kennels and he did them alone. He subsequently helped the veterinarian and nurses who were on night shift with handling the dogs and cats while they worked on them. Thereafter, he fed the sick animals, changed their bedding, cleaned them and their cages. The work was demanding, especially after spending the whole day fiddling with spanners in a workshop with little aeration.

He usually worked with an Afrikaner guy who was short and pudgy, with calves as big as his nicotine addiction. There was no time he was not smoking. He was good with animals but very impatient with people. He would hiss under his breath every time someone crossed his path. Munacho did not know the guy's first name, but his surname was De Fries. The guy befriended Munacho and told him about his secrets. Things Munacho would rather not have heard. Drinking and sex escapades. Violent brawls. Both sides of vicious muggings. Arrests. Addiction to hard drugs. Being condemned to be homeless. And finally, being rescued by the owner of the clinic, taken to rehabilitation, and given a job. *Some people really have nine lives*, Munacho thought. *How could someone like that keep getting chances to make things right?* But that was not the worst thing Munacho heard from De Fries. It was the salary he was getting. He was earning nearly three times what Munacho was earning. Of course, De Fries was a citizen, but what made them think it was right for him to earn three times what Munacho earned? Three times. They did the same work. In fact, De Fries' work was less arduous. He cleaned the cats' cages and not the dog kennels. Cats were significantly less messy and easier to deal with. Dogs were notoriously messy and were not easy to handle. Sometimes De Fries missed work, saying he had "relapsed" and Munacho would take on his work for no additional pay.

*Relapse. What did that even mean? One word and you are allowed to stay at home as long as you want? Some of us could literally be dying and still our grievances won't be heard. We can't tell them of the "relapses"" and "slumps" we have every night alone in our rooms. They won't understand. Because they are not familiar with the trigger to our pains. Their view is narrow, and we know why.* So, he could not take his grievances to the management. First of all, he was an immigrant, an illegal immigrant. He did not have a work permit. They were literally doing him a favour employing him. They could fire him any time and he would not be able to do anything about it. A single phone call to Home Affairs and he would be sleeping in a stinking, cold cell; mosquitoes pummelling him with absolutely no mercy, or worse still, he would be at Beitbridge border post by afternoon the next day. There was no winning it. Secondly, De Fries was one of them. He was their guy and even if Munacho had a work permit, he would not still attain that status. It was what it was. He had to be content with what he was getting and hope one day his work permit would be approved.

Munacho had come to South Africa a little later than his colleagues in the Army. He was initially reluctant to leave his wife, Chenai, and child back home, but it was too risky to take them with him. It was not all lush and verdant down South. So, he had forced himself to stay in Zimbabwe. But the rapidly deteriorating economy left him staring at two options; either risking it all and making the voyage down South leaving a part of him back home, or choosing the safer option, of staying home to watch his child grow in squalor. He had made hard choices in the Army; he had to. There was no other option. But this was a harder decision than any he had ever made. By some distance. It was not because he feared taking risks. No, not at all. His line of work was about either taking risks or dying. If other people could cross the crocodile infested Limpopo, then why couldn't he? If the average man could survive encounters with *maguma-guma* then what could stop a trained serviceman from doing the same? He understood the dangers, but the odds of surviving were in his favour here. And he was an able-bodied man, with transferable skills. But leaving his two-year-old son behind still terrified him. How would he be able to cope? The little boy was the apple of his eye.

But he left them, motivated by a High school friend of his, Tapfuma, who was apparently living large down South. He had seen the pictures. Things were going on great and money was not a problem. Munacho had weighed his options and decided to go. It had been years since the friend had last come home and Munacho could see his wife and children. They did not look pitiful, but they also did not look like the family of someone "living large". But he had also seen the pictures. The guy was driving a brand-new VW Polo and a Mercedes Benz C200. He was indeed *living large.* And his family was just about getting by. *Could never be me,* Munacho vowed. His Army colleagues had become unreachable. They got swallowed by the beast never to be heard from again.

The first City Munacho stayed in when he got to South Africa was Potchefstroom. That's where Tapfuma lived. He had a beautiful four bedroomed apartment in a residential complex in the vicinity of the town. The inside of the house was a proper monument to ostentation and luxury. The walls were decorated with colourful artwork that should only be allowed at an Art gallery. There were two sets of couches in black and grey. Perched on the wall, below a "Mandela" portrait, was a Hisense TV the size of Northern Sudan. Everything in the house screamed money. Loudly. It was inconceivable how this former humble rural teacher had come to live this way. He was a Science Teacher at a school a few kilometres outside town, which did not tally with the life he was living. *What other deals was he involved in?* They spent the first day walking about viewing the town. It was about the size of Masvingo, Munacho's hometown, by his estimation. It had the same small city vibes. Everything was chilled and went about at a relatively slow pace.

Tapfuma would go to work in the morning and come back around two in the afternoon. It fascinated Munacho that he wore jeans and T-shirts to work. After his friend came back from work they would dine at the nearby restaurant, go to the mall, or sit and watch TV at home. He marvelled at how Tapfuma was fluent in SeTswana and SeSotho. Both languages flowed so effortlessly out of his mouth. Always the gregarious fellow, he effortlessly mixed and mingled with the locals. He even looked like one of them now with his newly found light complexion, permanently bald head and affinity for ear studs and bucket hats. Munacho had wondered if this would be him in a couple of years' time. Then two or so weeks later, a woman came. They were seated outside, talking, and laughing when a red Nissan Navarra entered the electric gate. Tapfuma had immediately stood up, looking a bit flustered. The car parked. A lady disembarked. Tall and slender with long, blonde hair. She wore the shortest shorts Munacho had ever seen and a thin pink top. She held a handbag and a very elegant phone in her hand. Tapfuma took the lady's handbag, slung it across his shoulder and they began to hug and kiss. The spectacle took close to a minute. There was no time to be shocked. It was not difficult to comprehend what was happening here. His friend was married to this woman, this white woman who looked almost as old as his mother. This was the reason he was living large. This was the reason he could afford to drink that expensive alcohol, wear exquisite clothes and cologne.

This white woman with nascent wrinkles on her face was the reason this rural boy was living in this comfortable apartment, hundreds of kilometres away from his struggling family. Now he understood why Tapfuma had a South African ID. He had married a citizen. A rich citizen. A rich, white citizen. *Could this be Munacho in the next three years? Never*, he vowed to himself almost audibly. He wondered why his friend had never mentioned the woman, not even in passing. And why he had never seen her pictures on the wall. Married couples loved to immortalise the evidence of their bliss and plaster it on walls for all to see. Maybe the pictures were in the big bedroom, the only room he had not entered. The two love birds finally released each other after what felt like an hour.

"MT, this is Mrs. Shava, my spouse," Tapfuma said while looking the lady straight in the eyes, a practiced smile on his face.

"Babe, that's my friend, Munacho. But we call him MT," he added, in immaculately sounding English.

"Oh, really!" the woman exclaimed. Her voice sounded like money. A lot of it. Her arms were open. Inviting Munacho to give her a full hug. He tensed a little. Hugs only ever made him uncomfortable. Especially public hugs. Never mind public hugs from exquisite middle-aged white women who smelled of expensive perfume. He took the hug though. It was strangely balmy. Now he understood why people said there was an art to giving hugs.

In the moment when the technicalities of the hug were happening, Tapfuma had gone and hauled two massive traveling bags out of the car, speaking enthusiastically in Afrikaans. Munacho was consumed with guilt in the first three days he stayed with the couple. He felt complicit in his friend's shenanigans. He could not shake away the feeling. He had inadvertently given this illicit relationship his stamp of approval and had become, if only in a small way, responsible for the quality of life his friend's family back home was currently leading. But the guilt did not last long. It faded as he got comfortable. The couple would go out in the morning and leave the entire house to him. He liked it, but he hadn't come to be a charity case. He was an able bodied family man who had come here for the sole purpose of upgrading his family's standard of living, not to sit on his backside and wait for a white woman whose wealth he could not account for to feed him. And there was no telling how pure their intentions were. For all he knew, his friend could have been disparaging him to anyone who cared to listen. He had to find something to do. Tapfuma had promised to arrange 'something' for him, but nothing was happening. He wondered if Tapfuma even cared about him finding a job, or whether it was one of those vacuous statements people said to appear to be doing something.

Munacho missed his family, but he could not call them. He could not afford the airtime. Tapfuma never offered. The only thing he brought home was expensive alcohol, which Munacho was grateful for, but he could have used some spare change. His clothes also embarrassed him, of which he only had a few: two jeans, three T-shirts and one pair of sneakers. His friend, though they were about the same size, never offered him any. Three months passed and no job was forthcoming. The City was far too small and way too white. Chances of finding a job as a foreigner there were minimal. Never mind a black, illegal immigrant. It amused Munacho that he was actually an illegal immigrant. He used to read that in the newspapers back home and never paid much attention to it, but here he was.

One day the lady came to his room. Munacho was reclining on the bed reading a rather annoying self-help book. She frowned as she entered. The room smelled. His feet were giving off a strong stench.

"MT, you have a military background, right?" she asked. She looked much older today. He could never get used to how much older than his friend she was.

"Yes, I was in the Presidential Guard," he said, trying too hard to look comfortable. The room was a mess. He hadn't made the bed in at least a week. And there were torn socks and boxer shorts on the bed. He did not get time to hide them.

"My friend has a security company and he's looking for a guard. Your military experience will come in handy."

"Oh, thank you!" *Guard.* But that was a good start.

"You can start on Monday. He's a cool guy if you ignore his random bursts of temper." *That's one hell of a thing to ignore, don't you think?* Munacho thought.

"Okay, thank you so much Sonia," was all he could say.

The work at the security company was not difficult. They mostly walked about the complex they were guarding, waiting for some daring moron to try their luck. The salary was peanuts though, for both the locals and the foreigners. It was barely enough for him to pay rent for his small one-roomed place in the locations and food. He had decided to immediately move out when he got the job. His friend's place was becoming suffocating and though they pleaded with him to stay, he suspected it was not coming from a good place.

Of the twenty-one employees at the security company, he was the only Zimbabwean. The majority of them were South African and about five, were either Mozambican or Malawian. His colleagues rarely spoke English. They predominantly spoke SeTswana or SeSotho with an occasional sprinkling of IsiZulu and Afrikaans. The Mozambicans and Malawians were fluent in all the local languages. In all areas, they identified more with the locals than him. Their feet walked sturdy on foreign soil, while he trudged along with uncertainty. There was no trace of the alien bond he had hoped to find. That unspoken connection that came from shared trauma. English was only spoken as a last resort. Most of them could not speak it well anyway, so they never really bothered. He was grateful for the little IsiNdebele he knew. Mixed with some English, it allowed him to at least get the basics across to his colleagues. He also found out that although the salary was the same, citizen or foreigner, there were some privileges that were exclusive to the former. They were unspoken rules. Like the fact that they got double wages if they worked on weekends and public holidays. Foreigners did not enjoy that privilege. The Mozambicans and Malawians had work permits, so they were entitled to leave days. He was not. He did not enjoy a single leave day in the entire two and a half years he had worked at the company. He worked on weekends, on public holidays and for no additional pay. He had asked a Mozambican colleague of his, Pedro, how he had got his work permit. The guy smiled conspiratorially and said, "When you are ready to part with two months' salary, come to me."

Munacho tried to call his wife, Chenai as often as he could. It had worked for some time. Then things started to get in the way. He would think of calling her sometimes, then somehow end up deciding against it. He felt useless. His words felt vacuous when he promised her that he would find a better job. And when he promised that he would send more money. And especially when he promised that he would come back to fetch them. There was something hollow about his promises and assurances to her. He wondered if Chenai could feel it as well. He willed his words to carry a bit more weight, but it was to no avail. Because there was nothing in them. He was not actively seeking another job. Not because he was content with being a security guard, but jobs were just hard to come by in a foreign land, especially for someone like him who did not have "papers" and was always looking over their shoulder. He also was not going to send more money.

For starters, what he was earning was barely enough to sustain his own needs. Secondly, because he had never seen anyone sending money that they did not have. So, calling his wife had become a chore. The "I love you" and "I miss you" had dried up. They needed something to stimulate them; to trigger them back to life. He could not even talk about random things without his wife bringing up something more serious. *"The child needs this, the child needs that. I need to take the child to the clinic. All my clothes are torn and worn out. I need to start a little business can you..."* Always something with his wife. It infuriated him. He however knew deep down that it was not really fury that manifested. It was shame. He felt humiliated because he could not provide for his family. He was useless. So, the communication became sporadic. And whenever they talked, they kept it short. Both were eager to get away from the awkwardness. She would complain and he would vow to make it better, but he would not.. Communication finally totally broke down. He stopped picking up her calls. He missed her and he especially missed his child but there was nothing inside. He was dead inside. The only thing that could make him tickle was punishing himself and those who loved him. So, he became a ghost. He cut contact with everyone. The deadness inside kept increasing. He wished he could cry himself to sleep, but a searing wave of shame always descended on him every time he attempted to cry his sorrows away. It was not possible.

He finally quit his job and moved to Cape Town. Not because he knew where he was going, he did not. All he wanted was to take a wild risk, maybe that would ignite a smidgen of fire in his soul. A friend had given him an address a long time back. He did not know if the guy still stayed there, but he could not care less. If he did not find him, he would stay on the streets. It did not bother him how dangerous the streets of Cape Town were. If that was how he was going to meet his demise, then *so be it.* But one thing was certain, he would go out with a bang. He would give his assailants the fight of their lives. He boarded an InterCape Bus, sat close to the window, and slept for most of the way. That was how he had come to stay in Cape Town. He had become a wanderer. By sheer coincidence he found the friend — Tomukudza. They were best friends back in the day but had drifted apart when he got married. Tomukudza was working as a motor mechanic. Three days after arriving in Cape Town, Munacho was working at the same company as Tomukudza, doing the same job. Four years later he was still there. The same level and same salary.

It had been seven years since he left Zimbabwe. He had not seen his kid in seven years and did not even have an idea how he looked like now. *Does he look like me or his mother? What grade is he in now? Three? Is he good at school? Or sports? Anything at all? Is he even going to school to begin with? Does he miss me? Does he remember anything about me? Does his mother speak ill of me to him? Do I even miss him? Has his mother remarried, or she still entertains hopes of my coming back? Is she wise enough to understand nothing will be the same again between us?*

He had lost contact with everyone. Even with Tomukudza, the man who helped him find his feet in Cape Town. It was terrible but there was nothing else he could do. *Why is life like that? Why does it find pleasure in pummelling you until you are empty inside? Until you don't care about even those things dear to you. And then, it still would not have finished with you…*

The car, a white *bakkie.* screeched to a halt outside the massive garage. Another day at the workplace. He was tired of this. He yearned for something much better. Something more comfortable. It was his fourth year applying for a work permit and it was still not forthcoming. A year ago, he had tried to buy one on the black market, but the middleman swindled him. He was never going that route again. Maybe one day it would happen, but he was starting to doubt it. These people only cared for people with "critical skills." Those with 'ordinary skills' were entirely on their own. He had finally found a possible interpretation to his thought-dream. It was very simplistic, but he could work with that until he found a more detailed one. The woman he was stalking was *comfort.* That's why he never caught her. That's why 'she' sometimes felt within his grasp, but then inexplicably slipped through his fingers. So near yet so far. That was why it always ended with him losing. And no, his mind was suggesting nonsense, he was never going to visit a *sangoma.*

## The Throes

She tightly shut her eyes to stave off the impact of the sunlight rays which were hitting at the perfect angle like arrows in a video game. She felt the yawn coming. She stilled herself and with all her might, resisted it. It left her shaking. It was one of the games she had grown to enjoy playing just before waking up. Resisting the yawn. The alarm clock chimed a second later. Her body clock has been on point lately, she was waking up at the exact same time the alarm went off. She languidly got up from the couch. It had become a recurring theme. She almost always could not muster the energy to drag herself to the bedroom. She had slept with her sneakers and tracksuit on. Probably why she was restless in her sleep. She felt tired, as if she had taken part in a cross-country marathon the previous day. Her head was splitting. She dragged herself to the cupboard, took a glass, poured some whisky and gulped it down. There was no better painkiller than whisky. It responded perfectly to her migraines and morning headaches. Ibuprofen was great but it had its limitations, so did paracetamol. Whisky did not. She stilled herself as the whisky filtered in, hitting the right nerves. Soon, she would be fine.

She removed her sneakers and left them on the exact same spot. She had worn them without socks, so they reeked of stale sweat. She took off her jacket and flung it onto the couch. She then proceeded to the bedroom and stole a glance in the mirror. She had grown a subconscious fear of the mirror lately. She did not want to investigate it. She would only furtively glance then go about her business. The pimples on her face did not make for good viewing. They were not like the ones she had experienced at twelve, which almost half her classmates had at that time anyway. These were big and not as benign. The doctor had given her a prescription with assurance that her face would be back to normal in under a week, but two weeks down the line, they were even getting worse. She had also become much slimmer than she had always been. She was naturally slender, alright, and had long legs and a long neck which accentuated her slenderness, but she had never been this skinny. She looked like a reed. Forty-one kilograms the last time she weighed herself on the scale at home.

She had immediately smashed the scale on the wall, something she still did not quite regret. It was understandable though, why she had become like that. She could not remember the last time she ate a solid meal. She did not feel like cooking. The energy was not there. She took her laptop out of her study desk drawer, an HP Pavilion that her mother had couriered from the UK. It was a beautiful gadget, she would admit. She opened it, turned it on and waited while it loaded. It did not take long. She then connected the dongle and punched in the password. She wondered why it was indicating that she had put in the wrong password. With her current memory lapses, she had decided to put the most memorable password possible: - her name. So why was it not working? Had someone tempered with it? It made her anxious. The Caps Lock was on. She swore under her breath as she clicked it off. She retyped the password and got the internet connection. Her hands were shaking. She clicked on the Chrome icon, then proceeded to YouTube. Her heart raced. *What am I getting myself into?*

She typed the key words and there it was, "The sower, the seed, and the hearts of men". The video was crisp and high definition. The sound quality, impeccable. It was forty-nine minutes long, had more than six thousand views and almost a hundred comments. She browsed through the comments first. They were mostly high adulations punctuated with a slew of "Amen!" and "Powerful!" It had been uploaded two weeks back. The preacher was in his late forties. He wore an exquisite navy-blue bespoke suit and polished brown shoes. He walked with a certitude that betrayed years of practice and spoke with that self-indulgent confidence only found in preachers, motivational speakers and politicians. His sonorous voice carried an authority with it. The congregation was of medium size, maybe 300-500 people. A significant percentage of it was female, mainly young women. Pretty young women, she painfully noted as she angrily popped an itchy pimple with her long pinkie nail. At intervals the camera would zoom in on a woman; probably in her early thirties, who was sitting alone on a comfortable couch at the front of the auditorium. She was of mixed race and could easily pass as white if not for her jet-black hair and slightly broad nose. She had that perfectly practiced smile of a supermodel. And boy, was she a stunner! That was the preacher's wife. Kudakwashe swallowed hard. The preacher was her father. She could not go any further with the sermon. She closed the laptop without shutting down. It took everything in her to not fling it on the wall. She opened the drawer and put it back. Tears were freely flowing down her cheeks.

The Geography exam was only about an hour away. She had written the African History paper two days back, which she had certainly flunked badly. She could only answer two questions and the rest could as well have been written in ancient Hebrew. She had almost decided not to go to write today.

There was really no point. She had not studied and had missed a lot of lessons the entire year. There was no way she had a shot at passing. She had tried to cram some stuff the night before, but the headache came with vengeance like that creature from her worst nightmare. She had to gulp some whisky and sleep. She staggered to the bathroom. The tub needed a makeover. It was not too ugly, but it could use some fixing. She did not care though. She sat on the closed toilet bowl, took a cigarette and lighter from the toothbrush bowl, lit it and took a pull. She enjoyed smoking in the bathroom for some reason. It was not like she was hiding from anyone. It was one of those weird habits she had nurtured. She finished smoking, stomped the stub with her heel and left it on the floor. She decided that bathing was too much work, rinsed her mouth with Listerine and walked out of the bathroom. She went back to the bedroom. She unhooked her uniform from the hanger. *Why did Victoria High School have such beautiful uniforms for such an ugly school?* She slipped into her skirt. She had to wear another one inside so that it would not fall. She then put on the blazer. She did not bother putting on the tie. It was too much work. She stole an instinctive glance in the mirror. It was a sorry sight. The phone rang. It was her mother. She let it ring out. She called again. Kudakwashe let it ring out again. Her mother's persistence infuriated her. She would not give up. She finally capitulated and answered:

"Hello, mum. What do you want?"

"Is that how you talk to your mother now?"

"Mama, what do you want, please?"

"Are you prepared for your exam?"

"Yes, what do you think?"

"Kuda, can you talk nicely?"

"Okay, I'm writing Geography today and I'm prepared. Happy now?"

"Did Mukoma Fanie give you this month's rent?"

"No, he said his wife is sick and he can't pay this month."

"And you listened to those tall tales?"

"Mama, what did you want me to do, beat him up?"

"You should have told me. I would have given him a piece of my mind."

"Goodbye, mama!"

"Kuda..."

She clicked off. Her mother's constant nagging annoyed her. She walked to the kitchen almost tripping on the floor. It needed some thorough sweeping and mopping. A lot of dust and weeks old stains had accumulated on the tiled floor. Whisky stains, tea stains, orange juice stains, whatever stains. She was not going to attend to that anytime soon. Roaches were also starting to get comfortable, emerging from the secret corners of the cupboard. She did not feel like eating anything, but she had to if she did not want to collapse in the exam room. She opened the fridge, grabbed an apple, bit it three times and hurled it into the trash can. Why did apples taste so bad these days? They used to be the absolute treat when she was young. Apples and pineapples. Whoever lied to people that those two fruits were any good deserved the guillotine. She picked up her bag and key and walked out of the house.

She waved to Mukoma Fanie's wife as she went out the gate. She then flagged down a taxi a few meters outside the house. She decided to let it go. The driver knew her. It would be awkward. She would wait for another one.

Kudakwashe was the only child of the Muzeza's. Her father was a Showers of Glory Ministry Pastor and her mother, a nurse at the General Hospital. Showers of glory had less than fifteen members, she remembered. The Church was small, and the believers were mostly from poor backgrounds. They didn't even have musical instruments or a church building. They attended the services in houses and rented a classroom for special Sundays. So, her dad hardly made any money from his job, she knew it even as a kid. His suits weren't as nice as her schoolteachers' and she would overhear him asking her mum for money sometimes. When she asked him for money, he would feel his pockets then say, "Oh, ask your mama". It happened way too often for her liking. Most of the financial burden lay on her mother. She would work extra shifts at times and her dad was the one who ended up doing all the work at home, including babysitting the child, and when she grew older, helping with homework. So, the bond between them grew. Kudakwashe's dad would pick her up at the gate at school. They did not have a car those days so he would come on foot then put her on his shoulder and ask her how her day was. She would tell him everything enthusiastically and they would laugh together, father and child. They would get home and he would heat the food he had prepared for her on the two-plate stove. *Sadza* and chicken leg sometimes, or a wing, or a piece of pork or goat meat. At times, after she had eaten to her heart's content, he would give her some coins to go and buy *freezits* at the nearby tuck shop. They did not have a fridge back then. She would then go and play with her friends. He would come to fetch her before dusk, bath her and then read her a bedtime story or tell her some folktales until she fell asleep.

Her mother was often too busy to spend time with her. When she could, she would play games and tell her stories, but the bond was nowhere near the one she had with her father. She was about ten when her mother found an opportunity to go to work in England. She had been invited by a former colleague who was already an established nurse there. She went to England and settled in Bradford. Six months later, her dad had to go too. Kudakwashe was devastated. Her best friend was gone. She pleaded with him to take her with him, but he assured her that it would be much better if she completed her primary school in Zimbabwe first. They talked about it at length until she saw the sense in it and agreed to stay behind. Grade seven was only two years away anyway. Her mother's younger sister, Auntie Tambudzai, who was in her early twenties was left in charge of the house. Kudakwashe missed her parents so much and would often cry herself to sleep for months after their departure. She missed her dad more than her mum; she was not ashamed to admit. She had even confessed that to Auntie Tambudzai who had chided her sternly for it, which confused her because it was an obvious truth. Her dad loved her more than her mother did and that was not a secret. She missed her dad's stories, his jokes, his child-like mirth whenever she told him about her day. She missed his pensive look when he was deep in thought and the creasing of his forehead when he was preaching or praying. Above all, she missed his food. No one cooked chicken legs and wings and peanut butter rice quite like him. Not even Auntie Tambudzai.

Her parents divorced when she was in grade seven. It was a bombshell when she received the letter at school. Her mum and dad wrote her letters and called her occasionally on Auntie Tambudzai's phone. She had noticed that the letters had started to become shorter, fewer, and far between. From both sides. The letter was from her mum. She was in disbelief as she read it. Her dad had left her and had married another woman. 'A mixed-race woman' according to her mother. She did not know what mixed race meant and she did not really care. She did not believe her dad could do that. He was way too nice, way too sweet. How could he leave her mum just like that, as her mother had said, without a single explanation? He apparently had come back one day after weeks of not coming home, packed his bags and walked out. It was the longest and detailed letter her mum had written her. She was telling her personal things. Things she had no business knowing. She did not want to hear about it all. It was suffocating her. She did not want to hear anything really. Auntie Tambudzai started looking at her differently after that. She became more stern, more impatient. She no longer woke up early to warm her water in the morning. And she no longer put symmetrical lines at the edges of her school uniform. She started inviting people into the house. Even at night, and Kudakwashe would hear them giggling in her parents' bedroom. Auntie Tambudzai started straightening her hair and putting make-up on her face, wearing trousers and short skirts, and going out at night. She would come back late talking loudly and filling the house with an unbearable stench of alcohol.

Her dad stopped writing her letters or calling her on Auntie Tambudzai's phone. She had loved her dad's stories about the snow that covered cars completely, neighbours who did not greet each other at all, working two shifts. She wrote him piles of angry letters putting the address her mother had given her. He did not respond. She was devastated. She threatened to disown him and consider herself officially fatherless. Silence. She threatened to commit suicide, drink rat poison, or slice her wrists like in that movie they had watched together. Silence. Kudakwashe changed her approach. The tone of her letters became supplicatory. She beseeched her dad to respond. She promised to forgive him. She asked for forgiveness herself. She promised to be a good girl. She promised to pass with flying colours and make him proud. Radio silence. She tried to appeal to his sentimental side. She reminded him of the good old days. Of their trips to the golf course, lying in the grass under the eucalyptus and pine trees, listening to the chirping of the birds and taking turns to imitate them. She reminded him of the stories he told her. "Hare and the honey badger", "Hare and tortoise", "The old hag who broke the Msasa tree with her tooth", "Leopard and hyena" She reminded him of how he taught her to ride the bike, to kick a football and to play chess. He did not respond. It crushed her soul.

Her mother tried to comfort her by sending her money. It helped a little. The money her mum made was good enough to get her into a good school. She started her form one at Victoria High School. She used to pass by that school and admire it and never thought she would one day be a student there. Her mother bought a house a year later in Rhodene, a three bedroomed house, relatively old but she would renovate it. Auntie Tambudzai got married and relocated to South Africa with her husband. Her sister, Kudakwashe's mother, had pleaded with her to stay, but she had told her off. So Kudakwashe had to stay on her own. Fourteen years old and alone in the world. Her mother deemed it safer that way. She did not trust an older male relative to stay with her. Kudakwashe thought her mum was being paranoid. Staying alone was not any better because if thieves got wind of it, they would have a field day. But she did not mind staying alone. She did not like people enough anyway. The person she had loved the most had betrayed her in the most brutal way and left a wound in her heart that would never heal.

Kudakwashe disembarked from the taxi a couple of metres from the main school gate. She walked briskly toward the gate. Her scarf covered almost three quarters of her face. She entered the gate and nodded imperceptibly at a student who was going in the opposite direction. A lot of students were moving about seemingly unbothered by the thought of anything except the impending examination. To her, everything was a blur. She felt like she was in a different place. Everything that was happening around her appeared miles away. She was feeling nauseous and desperately needed to find somewhere to sit. She decided to sit on the lawn. Three girls were sitting there, legs outstretched, each holding a sheaf of paper in their hands, their lips moving frantically and heads nodding instinctively. Making last ditch efforts to cram some key concepts. Normal people, doing normal things. *What a life!* She thought she noticed them casting surreptitious glances at her and making half-hearted attempts to suppress their giggles. They were young girls. Maybe form two or three. They looked happy. Genuinely happy. It had been more than five years since she had felt even a smidgen of it. She had known happiness as a child. It was not a concept; it was a real tangible thing. It felt surreal that it used to be her default state. It was something you could feel and experience, and live with, and define. She wanted to experience what the young girls who were laughing at her had. The person she loved the most had taken the feeling away from her forever. She had tried to recreate it. She had tried many things to fill the void. For some brief moments, she felt like she had grasped it. The year she turned seventeen was the wildest year she had ever experienced. She went totally haywire. At some point, she was convinced she was the wildest seventeen-year-old in the whole city, if not country. She had passed her O level exams, much to the elation of her mother. She did not care much about it, but she had forced herself to study hard enough so that her mum could get off her back.

For a moment, she had felt like she could fly. That was the year she learnt to drink. And smoke. A cute form six student taught her that. Suspicious was his name, right? He was in the athletics team. His thighs were a thing of beauty and his biceps, good heavens. She had winked at him while they were exiting the school's main hall. It was soon after he had received the award for "Outstanding athlete of the Year" She did not know where the courage had come from. He had smiled back and there was something between shyness and shock in his eyes. She had later invited him to her house. For the first time, she was grateful her parents were thousands of miles away. She had coughed and coughed the first time she pulled the cigarette. The young man had caressed her back. She was on cloud nine. She had pulled some more and coughed even more violently. The young man had pumped her back and they had laughed and laughed. She had woken up beside him on her bed, both of them scantily dressed. He had apologized profusely, to which she laughed heartily. She had escorted him out and that was the beginning of their escapades, which began to take wilder forms. The guy brought weed and some alcohol that she could not recognise. Sometimes she woke up in the bathroom, or lounge, alone and naked with the boy long gone. Stubs of cigarettes and empty bottles of alcohol everywhere, the radio on full blast and the TV droning away. She liked the feeling. It was liberating. For a moment, she forgot about her dad. The boy started bringing his friends, boys, and girls, some of whom she remembered from her school and others she could not recognise from a bar of soap. Some of the boys were much older than her and some of the girls, much younger. A lot of things happened. The wildness intensified. The weed became stronger. The glue became more vicious and the cocktails, more intoxicating. The three bedrooms became citadels of untethered debauchery. Things that she did not know existed happened there.

Suddenly, the boy stopped coming. Kudakwashe tried to reach out to him, but he was untouchable. It was clear he was avoiding her. She tried to entice him with money, but he did not want to hear it. The darkness returned. She sometimes went for stretches without going to school. She did not have the energy. She soon forgot about the boy, but the darkness did not go away. She reached out to her father one more time. He did not respond. He was now an associate Pastor at a megachurch, her mother had told her. And he was now being seen regularly around some popular pastors in London. The first man to break her heart. It haunted her. She struggled to sleep. She would wake up with headaches and leg cramps. That was how she learnt to overdose on whisky every night. It was the only thing that could placate the ghosts that were stalking her dreams. She wanted to forget anything that had to do with her father. She burned his pictures and clothes. She even uttered some incantations that she had read in some transcendental meditation book while doing so. But the memories would not leave. They stalked her like a psychotic lover from a crimes of passion documentary.

Out of the blue, the young man came back for reconciliation. She spurned his advances with the contempt they deserved. She did not want to go back to the wildness. It was enticing, but the phase had taken more from her than it gave. Still, the haunting memories could not let her go. She reached a point where she would suddenly feel the urge to break things. That phase cost her the family TV, radio, and microwave. She could not control her impulses. Sometimes she would suddenly scream on top of her voice. In those moments, she was grateful she stayed alone in a big house. She would scream and scream and scream until her voice grew hoarse. She would subsequently collapse in a heap and cry until she could not anymore. Then she passed the phase and she grew calmer. She would sit in the dark and think herself to a pulsating headache that threatened to pop her head open. She no longer broke things. She did not have the energy. Cooking became a luxury she could not afford. She just ate what she could. Her meals were usually fast food, chocolates, and fruits. She lost weight. No one at school asked. Well, some of her friends did, but she blamed the incessant headaches. Finally, she could not take it anymore. One of her friends advised her to visit the school counsellor – a short, white haired lady with rings below her eyes… She told her everything she could put into the words. The stuff she could say without breaking down.

"I think you are depressed, my child," the lady said.

Kudakwashe offered her a wry smile. Everyone had something to say about depression, but they did not know the first thing about what it entailed. They thought it was about suddenly getting angry and throwing things around, cutting yourself and rolling on the ground and crying and crying until you could not do so anymore. They were wrong. Depression was worse than that. It was a dark, blank expanse. It was walking in the valley of the shadow of death and not having anything to tug to for the tiniest glimmer of hope. It was feeling a void in your heart which nothing could fill. It was much more sinister than the combination of its symptoms. It was hell. It was death. Counsellors did not know what they were talking about. You could see it on their faces. They spoke about it so lightly, like it was something they could prescribe a cure for.
She had listened to the lady droning about the need for her to find a hobby like chess, or music, or playing the piano.

"You also need to find a higher power to believe in," the lady had added. Kudakwashe smiled. The lovely, little lady meant well. But she had no idea what she was talking about. This was bigger than she could fathom.

"If things don't improve, my child," she opened her desk drawer and pulled out a card. "Call this guy. He's the professional."

"Thank you, ma'am," Kudakwashe replied, smiling. The lady smiled back. She was satisfied she had done something. *Not her fault.* Every counsellor thought that.

Kudakwashe called the number about three weeks later. Her slump had continued unabated and she was still in its throes. She had not told her mother. She would not understand. She would recommend her to go and see the Pastor. Even worse, she would call a pastor to come and pray over the house. She did not remember the last time she went to church as well. *Three years ago?*

Her call was answered by the receptionist who brusquely told her to make an appointment.

She expected to see a younger man when she finally met him. One in his mid to late thirties. But the man was much older, maybe in his late forties. He courteously offered her a seat and listened as she talked. He was not looking her straight in the eyes like the lady at the school. He jotted down things as she spoke. There was something fatherly in the way he looked at her. And she noticed he was quite shy. She saw it in his eyes. Funny, given that he was almost three times her age. His response was not what she expected. He started asking random questions from her childhood. "How was your first day at school? Do you still remember it? Were you popular in school? Were you skinny as a child? Were you fat?"

She could not stop thinking about the session when she got home. That day she cooked a hot meal, for the first time in Heaven knows how long. She slept peacefully and woke up with a song in her heart. A Sunday school song she had long forgotten. *Jesus loves me this I know*. It kept ringing in her head. She sang it, she tapped her head to it, she hummed it. The sessions got better and deeper. Now she was glad he was much older. She liked him that way. He in some way reminded her of her father. Apart from that, he was also a funny guy who understood teenage lingo and issues in a way you would not expect of someone in that age range. He was also tall, clean shaven, intelligent, and dark and….and respectful.

She struggled to put him off her mind. It bothered her. He was an excellent counsellor but…

She searched his name on Facebook and was gutted when all the results it drew were of young boys wearing school uniforms or flat caps somewhere in

Gweru or Kariba or Murambinda. She hopped on to Instagram, same story. He did not have an account. She logged on to Twitter, searched his name and her heart skipped when she found his account. The profile picture was of him in his office, standing by his chair in a tailored suit. He had 415 followers and followed only 55. The ratio fascinated her even more. She clicked on his Following tab. He followed mostly politicians, sports, and film stars. She liked that. She did not see any scantily dressed, attractive lady there. He was really a man of integrity. She had first changed her Twitter handle. She replaced "RiriBabyGal" with her full name. She then followed him and waited. An hour later, she received a notification, he had followed her back. Her heart galloped. *Should I do it? Or should I wait.*

She could not wait. She clicked his DM icon and started typing. She deleted the message midway about ten times. Then she finally mustered the courage and clicked send. It was a simple message "Hi, doc".

Her heart was threatening to pop out. She could not contain herself. *What if he doesn't reply? How would I face him at the office? Would he think I'm loose? Would our relationship ever be the same? Am I crossing the boundaries?*

DM notification.

He had replied. "Hi, how are you?" maybe thirty minutes later.

It was too plain. Too formal. Too lifeless. But at least he had replied. It was a good start. Should she send another one? She had already crossed the boundary, why not?

"Hope you are doing well, my doc. Thanks for everything." She hesitated for five seconds then pressed send.

She was literally shaking all over. This was the riskiest message she had ever sent. It was not too suggestive, but it was not too innocent either. She got up from the couch, went to the cupboard and poured herself a glass of whisky. She gulped it down in one go. Her head started feeling light. She lit up a cigarette, took a long pull, then sat back down as she awaited the reply. Her nerves were still rioting, but more steadily now.

He replied. "Thank you. Goodnight."

Her heart sank. It was curt and brutal. He was really a man of principle. She cursed herself for being so rash. So loose. She had probably damaged what was growing into a solid almost father-daughter relationship solely because she could not control her emotions. She knew the man had a wife and three children, all of them older than her. There was a picture of his family on the wall of his office. She had to apologise to save herself from further embarrassment.

Maybe the man had already shown the message to his wife and they were laughing together at the little loose girl who thought every man was the same.

She sent an apology. "I'm sorry if you took my message the wrong way, I just wanted to express my gratitude that's all. I'm really sorry, doc."

She lit another cigarette. She was going insane.

DM notification. She blurted out a prayer before opening it.

"Nothing to be sorry about. Are you sleeping?"

A chill ripped through her body. She stood up. Her stomach growled, and she knew it was not because of hunger. She was breathing heavily. *How do I respond to this?*

"No, not yet doc. I will be sleeping soon though," she pressed *send*. Her hands were shaking. She regretted not adding an "and you?" at the end, so that the doctor would be obliged to respond.

"That's good. What are you wearing to sleep tonight?"

Her eyes widened as she read the message. She switched off her phone. *This must be a dream. It is not happening!* This man was surely not saying what she thought he was saying. *What was she wearing?* That question almost always led to one thing. It was a trigger to a chain of events whose ending was predictable. She switched it on again, read the message again, pouring over every single word. He wanted to flirt with her. It was an unequivocal invitation. She wondered how she should respond. Should she go all out or be a little reserved?

"Nighties, I think," she added a wink emoji.

"You think?" He added a "blush" emoji. First time he had betrayed his age in the conversation.

"Because I just might…" she was in uncharted waters now.

"Please do send a pic when you decide on the latter." Wink emoji this time. She did decide on the latter and she did send the photo.

Their next session was very awkward. Everything was forced. But as soon as she got home, the conversation thrived. She continued to send him pictures and flirt with him. Then he started making visits to her house. He would come in a taxi, not in his own car. The fact that they were doing it behind his sophisticated wife's back, added to the thrill. It made her feel special. He did not use the main gate either. He came clandestinely, in through the back gate. Even the tenant, Mukoma Fanie, did not see it. They would drink and smoke together and talk with the meeting consummating on her bed. Then he would vanish as quickly as he came. Then one day something happened. They had drunk and smoked weed together and watched "Black Hawk Down." He had an excellent taste in movies. Most of the movies he liked, she liked as well; Apocalypto, Inglourious Basterds, Sarafina. In Pursuit of Happiness. She could not remember anything after that except waking up naked on the floor, handcuffed, duct-taped, something like a leash on her neck, the man holding what looked like a whip in one hand and a digital camera on the other. It was a weird scene. She panicked. She asked what was going on but all she got for a response was a sinister grin. He took the video for about five more minutes while she struggled to free herself.

He finally removed the handcuffs and the leash and quickly bid her goodbye without a single explanation. She cried and cried that night. She knew the man she trusted had violated her. After she had slightly regained her composure and partly realised what had happened, she sent him a message, "I know what you did. You laced my drink. I will report you to the police."

"I don't know what you are talking about," he replied.

"I literally woke up and saw you taking a video of me. I could report you to the police right now or worse still, shame you on Twitter."

He replied, "If you ever dare report this to anyone, anyone at all. I will upload this tape tonight on every platform. Try me. Stupid girl." She could not believe it.

"Morris, after all we did together you call me stupid. Even after doing this to me?"

"It's Mr. Ncube for you. The only person allowed to call me Morris is my wife and at times, my children, and colleagues. Not you. Reconnect with your father and stop seeing him in everyone you meet. Take care."

She read the message repeatedly. It felt like a stab to the heart every time. Men were the same. Their aim was to dominate, deprive, destroy. She could not even cry. This was more than she could take. That night, she tried to overdose on sleeping tablets, but she failed. She could not. She was not strong enough.

Eight months later, she still had not recovered from that. She did not tell her mother anything about it. It would only make matters worse. Her mother had called her, telling her to look for her father's sermon on YouTube. She could not believe it. What use was a sermon from someone who had abandoned her and never looked back. But she felt curious. He looked different now. He looked like a stranger. He sounded like a stranger. He really was a stranger. Even her mother was slowly becoming a stranger. She had gleefully told her she had found a partner. She had been seeing him for two years apparently. A mixed-race guy of British-Jamaican heritage. She tried to be happy for her mother, but she could not. The bond between them was only transactional now. A one-sided transactional relationship. It began and ended at Western Union. Their conversations were forced lately.

Kudakwashe felt a light tap on her shoulder. It was Mukudzei, one of her few close friends. It was time for the exam. A-level Geography mid-year examination, which she knew without a shadow of doubt, she was going to fail.

## Different Shades of Brown

Laura arranged her bed again. She had always been a sucker for neatness. It was almost a sickness. She looked around the room. *Impressive.* She would later take the best photo she could and post it in a furniture Facebook group she was in. Her queen-sized bed stared back at her. It had arrived only two weeks ago. It was an image thing. People loved to portray a certain image about themselves and they used material things to do so. Some did it through cars, others through properties and still others, through clothes. She did it through beds. And dressing tables. The new bed cover and pillows she had bought looked perfectly in sync with the rest of the room. The bed cover was white with brownish edges and the pillows, which were of four different sizes, were different shades of brown with streaks of white.

The wall was decorated with beautiful artwork — four portraits that she had bought from a dreadlocked elderly Ghanaian man with a seamless British accent at the mall. "Medieval sensuality art" the man had called it. She had loved it at first glance. In some way, she felt connected to the women in the artwork. She had been deliberating on adding some sculptures to the room too. Female elephants, her totem, to put beside her bedside lamps. She walked to her dressing table. Her hair was a mess, as she would have expected. She straightened it with her Afro comb and then applied some lipstick to her dry lips. The man had just departed. He was tall and slim, with a dignified air about him. He spoke softly, his voice hardly ever rising above a whisper. He was also shy in a cute way, the sweet schoolboy kind of shy. She saw it by the way he avoided her gaze when she complimented him. But he was assured when he got about his business. She would call him 'mature' if she believed that was a word one could use to describe men. Unfortunately, it was not. Men were never that.

Her stomach growled. She needed something to eat. Should she wait until six in the evening? No, she had to eat now, or she would faint. She walked to the kitchen and took out the match box from the cupboard. She opened the box and pulled out three matchsticks. The gas stove needed fixing. It would not turn on by using the switch. She had to use the matches. It was frustrating. It was worsened by the fact that she had shaky hands. Lighting up a matchstick was never something instinctive. She had to pay full attention. She succeeded on the third attempt. Something jumped from within every time she succeeded. It always happened. Why could something so trivial make her so happy? She was too lazy to cook, so she took some leftover rice and beans from the fridge. She would have put the food in the microwave, but it has been painfully slow lately. Soon, it would stop working altogether. She needed to replace it. She put the food on the stove and scrolled through the music player on her phone. She clicked on a Killer T song. That was how she measured the time needed to heat her food. One Killer T song and it would be fine. Her phone rang. *The cocky Nigerian guy again.* She let it ring out.

Musawenkosi was in a bad mood today. The animal handler and the nurse were testing her limits. They were both uncharacteristically erratic and were asking way too many unnecessary questions.

"Doc, which animal needs feeding?"

"Doc, where do I put the used blades?"

"Doc, can you help me put in the catheter? I can't find the vein."

"Doc, please help me shave this cat. Its skin is too soft."

"Doc, which tablets…?"

It was doing her head in. She had more than five animals to perform surgery on and she had no time for such trivial things. It took everything in her to not brush them aside with brusque responses. It was already two in the afternoon. She had Church to attend later in the day and by the looks of it, there was a chance she would not make it. There were four dogs which needed her attention in the surgery room. Three of them were female and one of them pregnant. It required a caesarean which normally took her an hour to do on average. She was incredibly deft and dextrous, but even in her best form, she would not be able to complete the procedure in less than fifty minutes. She also had two male cats to castrate, for which she was grateful, because if they were female, she would need no less than an hour to work on them. Overall, she needed at least four hours to complete the surgeries. So, what the handler and the nurse were doing was making her sick. Couldn't men be professional at least once a week? She liked the two guys though, on normal occasions. They were good people. The animal handler was a Pedi guy from Tzaneen. He was a good sport. He stuttered when he spoke, which made him gesticulate with his hands and sometimes mouth, a little more than normal. Musawenkosi suspected the young man had a crush on her. And it was not only because he sent her "goodnight" messages late at night and "good morning" messages way before the crack of dawn. She saw it in his eyes. Sometimes he offered to buy her lunch, a gesture she swiftly rejected until she realised how much it hurt him, and she started to occasionally accept. She felt sorry for him because she and him would never work. Not in a hundred years.

His name was Teboho. The nurse was also a nice guy. Good-looking boy whose body showed inside the uniform that he played with heavy metal in the gym. She had seen him wearing shorts once or twice and though she was not one to be moved by physical appearance, she had to admit his legs were hewn from living stone. He had a thing for exquisite cologne and expensive sneakers. He was Xhosa, but with a SeTswana name, Oarabile. In her idle moments, she would imagine him being the one with a raging crush on her. She did not have a crush on him, far from it. He was a lot younger than her for starters. Maybe five whole years younger. Secondly, he was too beautiful. He was a pretty boy. She was not into pretty boys. She was into men. She loved her men dark, rustic and a little imperfect. Good to look at, but with a broken nose or a slight cut on the cheek. Probably why, though she did not want to admit it, she liked to watch Boxing and MMA. But she still sometimes found herself indulging fantasies about the nurse. She was glad it ended in her head at home. She never tried to make him see it.

The two women were talking too fast for Anesu's liking. They could as well have been speaking Cantonese or Aramaic. They were Zulu because that was the language they used when they introduced themselves to her. And she could hear some of what they were saying. But their pace was too frenetic. They were probably from deep KwaZulu Natal. The Zulu from that side was basically a different language from the one spoken in other regions of South Africa. She knew a little Northern Ndebele though, which helped her to at least communicate the basics and in her line of trade, it was indispensable. When they laughed, she could not help, but feel they were laughing at her. She was doing the hair of the chubby one who was the more talkative of the two. She wanted *single* braids. It would take a long time and Anesu feared it would force her to miss Church. She loved the Friday services; they were a breath of fresh air after the strenuous working week. And this one was a special Friday service. A special prayer session. The chubby lady opened a huge packet of chips and Russian sausages. Anesu's mouth watered. She could not eat until six in the evening. She and some of the ladies at her church were fasting and the pastor was going to pray for them today. Once or twice she almost capitulated and ate some hot cross buns her Zambian colleague had offered her, but she realised she would be fooling no one. Faithfulness was an absolute must in these things. The chubby lady's friend was seated in a chair close by. Too close even. She was eating the biggest and most tantalising hot dog Anesu had ever seen, the veins in her head pulsating as she chewed. She was indeed having a great time. Her lips gleamed with the oil.

"If you had done what I requested, I could have bought you a hot dog like that one," a colleague whispered in her ear as he reached for the clippers. She did not smile. She did not like him at all, the Congolese guy. There was a cockiness about him, a rudeness that Anesu could not stand. *When you are close to the line, the Devil brings a temptation,* the words of her pastor echoed. It comforted her. She would not allow the loser to ruin her day.

Laura did not answer the call. She knew what the Nigerian wanted. What every man who called her wanted. She could not do it though. She did not have the time. She needed to go to Church. It had been long since she had been in Church. She could have refused if it were anyone else, but it was her friend, Anesu, who had pleaded with her to come. Anesu, sweet Anesu. Nicest person she had ever met. She would do Laura's hair for free even when she begged her to accept the payment. Laura hardly prayed but when she did, she never forgot to mention Anesu. The girl deserved only nice things. They had met at the hair salon and instantly connected. Laura did not like the salon. The Ethiopian owner was rude, and it had rubbed on to some of the employees. She had only gone there that day because her two favourite salons were closed for renovations. That was when she met the Zimbabwean girl. Soft, funny, and respectful. A breath of fresh air. They had instantly connected and exchanged numbers. And they had been friends ever since, despite leading entirely different lives.

Laura had come to South Africa five years back, from Renco Mine where she had lived virtually her entire life. She had not come to look for work. She was on a righteous mission; to claim back her husband. Her husband had come to South Africa two years earlier and was staying in Diepsloot. He had suddenly stopped communicating and had become completely unreachable.

"He has another wife there," people told her.

"He's gone for good!" They taunted.

"You better find another husband. There's nothing to wait for."

"Have you seen South African women? Once a man sees them, rest assured he's not coming back," they warned her.

She searched for his address. One guy, her husband's former classmate, who had come home for the Christmas holidays had offered to take her where her husband stayed. He knew the place, and if his words were anything to go by, stayed close to Laura's husband's place. Seething with righteous indignation, she left her young daughter at her parents' house.

She disembarked from the Munenzva Bus at Powerhouse Bus Terminus in Johannesburg a few minutes after midday. The air outside reeked of greasy food, cheap booze and pockets violently liberated of their contents. Decrepit buses honked and hooted. Some dubious characters looked at her with lazy eyes. She stuck even closer to the man she was with.

"Don't look at them. Walk with certainty, or they will think you are easy game," the guy said, a little too sternly. They got off a Kombi at some nondescript spot in Diepsloot. There were shacks everywhere. She had seen them in movies, dramas, and newspapers, but seeing them up close was a different experience. There were a lot of questionable characters walking about. Her stomach knotted every time they passed by a group of boys. The guy she was with walked with the recklessness of someone who knew the area well and was assured of his safety. He was greeting people in different languages. Shangani, Venda, Zulu and another one she identified as SeTswana.

"Your husband stays at the end of that block of houses. The very end," the man said. Laura was shocked to realise there was already a lady tugging at the guy's elbow in a playful manner that betrayed a lot of familiarity between them. It was astounding because the man had a wife and two children back home. At least, he was decent enough to come back home during holidays.

"It's written 64 on the green door. Please don't mention my name," he said as he turned, his hands now around the lady's waist.

She passed by a lot of people. Some were washing clothes in decrepit sinks at the back of public toilets. Others were playing draughts and cards and blasting music like there was no tomorrow. The stench coming from the toilets made her want to puke and she had to jump over multiple puddles of sewage that lined the path that led to her husband's house. The people looked at her with disinterest. She liked it that way. They probably thought she was one of them. She had tried her best to not look out of place. Zimbabwean women were notorious for their affinity for wearing denim skirts together with sneakers. Nothing shouted "Zimbabwean" more than that. You could as well drape the flag around your shoulders. So, she was wearing nondescript skinny blue jeans and Adidas sneakers, as well as a new Orlando Pirates shirt. She hesitated as she got close. What if she knocked at the wrong door? She decided to do it anyway. That was what she had come to do after all. She banged on the door. A woman opened. She was tall and very light skinned. Her eyes were heavily lidded below her bushy eyebrows. She was wearing very small blue denim shorts and what looked like the South African cricket team shirt. Laura hesitated, then suddenly blurted, "*Murume wangu aripi?*" The lady did not bother responding but cast her a blistering stare instead.

Laura realised her error and then tried her best to put the message across in IsiNdebele. The woman burst out laughing. It made Laura self-conscious. She felt small in the woman's presence.

"Titus come here, what is this?" Were the first words the lady spoke. Her husband emerged from the shadows. He looked different. He had a blank expression on his face and his brownish dreadlocks grazed his shoulders. He used to be clean shaven. He was wearing a thin vest which had a riot of bright colours and football shorts. He repulsed her.

"Oh, that's my former girlfriend," he said, scratching his dreadlocks and not daring to look her in the eyes.

"You see, he doesn't know you." The woman said, making some bizarre gestures with her lidded eyes. She looked stoned. Both of them looked stoned to the gills.

Laura felt weak in the knees. There was nothing for her here. Her husband was a completely different person now. But what would she do? She did not even have the bus fare to return home. She did not know the way from here. It was midday. She turned suddenly and started walking away, carrying her small travelling bag. What had possessed her to make this most rash decision? To track down someone who could not remotely be bothered. Someone who did not even acknowledge her presence. South Africa had totally changed her husband. It was true what they said about Jo'burg being the belly of the beast. No one came back the same. She thought she heard some whistling behind her, and she instinctively turned her head. She saw a young man running toward her. It was happening. South Africa was giving her an initiation not even two hours since she had heralded her arrival in Johannesburg. She looked to her right for a possible escape route, a skinny guy in a Kaizer Chiefs shirt was closing in from that side. She had been mugged twice back home. First at Mbare Bus Terminus, then at Copa Cabana taxi rank. Both traumatic experiences. It was happening again. And this encounter already looked many times bleaker than the ones she had experienced before. She looked to her left side. There were men drinking at a makeshift tuck shop close by. She swiftly turned and started walking toward them. Maybe they could save her. They looked like nice people. They kept sipping on their bottles and laughing casually.

A crude hand grabbed her arm. She viciously shook it off but another one was already tugging at her bag. She screamed. Everything looked like it was happening in slow motion. One of them tore the necklace from her neck and the other tripped her to the ground and snatched her sneakers. It happened so quickly. She was breathing heavily. She prayed they did not strip her naked.. It had happened to a lot of women a lot of times before. These thugs were not content with taking all your belongings, their sadism would only be sated through your complete humiliation. Her life flashed before her in a ten second panorama.

*Her child, her little sweet child.*
*Her childhood in Renco Mine.*
*Her brief stay in Harare*
*Her mother.*
*Her late dad.*

One guy removed her Orlando Pirates shirt and whooped. She was powerless to resist. She heard their footsteps as they walked away. Everything was muted. It felt like a dream. She remained there for a while. No one came to help. Until a lady came with a cloth and covered her. She helped her into her car, an old Nissan Sunny. The woman was apparently the owner of the small, makeshift shop where the men were gathered drinking. She was a Tswana lady who also spoke good IsiNdebele because her mother was Ndebele from Zimbabwe. They bonded well. Laura cried in the woman's arms as she narrated her ordeal. The woman offered her accommodation and a job as a housemaid until she could raise money to go back home. Apparently, the woman had never married. She was well in her forties. She never saw the need for a man. Ever. Not once, she had told Laura while helping her to defeather a chicken, had she been tempted to get into a relationship. Occasionally a young lady visited her. She was her adopted daughter. Short and thickset girl who had the loudest laugh Laura had ever heard. She also bathed in record time.

"You are already done? Men will not come near you," her adopted mum once chided her.

"Oh? Then explain why I have three children with different fathers," she had replied. They both had broken into loud laughter.

Laura stayed at the place for three months. Part of her still missed her husband, but the woman's kindness had greatly assuaged the pain.

She wanted to go home; she really did but it was just that…things got in the way. She got hooked in some entanglements. What happened was, she met a handsome guy. It was not his outrageous beauty that drew her to him, it was the allure of money. He offered her a salary that she could not resist. She used to pass by his shop while going to the supermarket. He used to wave at her until he finally approached her. They soon became friends. Which is how she ended up in Rustenburg. He had an electronics shop in that city. The guy turned out to be destitute of all integrity and honour. Firstly, she and the other ladies whom he had recruited, had to surrender their passports to him for six months. She wanted to protest, but she desperately needed the money. So, she had surrendered her passport. It was not even an electronics shop. It was everything: a restaurant, supermarket, salon, beauty parlour. And the work was arduous. They worked for twelve hours a day. When she complained, he threatened to call Home Affairs on her.

She finally resigned after three months, with no pay. That's how she had entered the trade. She did not want to call herself a prostitute. She was just, well, doing business. Giving and taking, that's all there was to it. At first, she was disgusted by herself, but she had grown numb to it. They came regularly. Zimbabweans, Nigerians, South Africans, Somalis, Malawians. They were generally nice people. Well, they were men and their entitlement and low self-esteem jumped out at times. The need for recognition and acknowledgement. She had learned how to string them along; how to make each one of them feel unique. How to make them all feel capable of things they could not ever dream of understanding. It was part of the game. By and large though, they kept their end of the bargain, save for one or two who would try to take advantage of her status to defraud her. Two police officers tried it. They had threatened to report her to Home Affairs after she had demanded her payment. She had let it go. It was not worth it. The Nigerian would have been her fourth client of the day. It was a busy day. But she did not want to disappoint her friend. She had to keep the promise. She scrolled through her WhatsApp again. Her heart ached. It had been five years since she had seen her daughter, Tamari. She was now in grade one. She looked exactly like her father. Why was nature so cruel? She missed her. Bringing her here would be hard. Someone had told Laura's mother what manner of work she did to earn a living and her mother had vowed to never allow Tamari to come to South Africa. Now, her relationship with her mother was not back to normal, but they still talked. The phone rang. It was her friend, Anesu. She had to prepare.

Musawenkosi felt like collapsing. Doing surgeries on an empty stomach was ill-advised. Apart from it making her weak, being hungry made her extremely irritable and prone to lashing out. But hunger was not the reason she was being irritated by everything today. It was the information she had bumped into the previous night. The nurse, Oarabile, was earning more than her even though she was a qualified veterinarian. It was unheard of. No wonder he could afford the finer things in life. Why would the management approve of that? Seniority, which would have been a poor excuse anyhow, did not even apply here because she had come before him. Was it because she was a foreigner or a woman? Would they have done that to a local or a man? She concluded it was because of both. She had to add this to her prayer requests. The pastor would have his hands full. Three weeks ago, she had received a message from the VFS that her critical skills VISA application had failed because of a very small error. She cried all night and the next day. The clinic had told her that she needed to sort out the issue fast if she wanted them to retain her. Without a VISA, they would have to release her. They had already done her a huge favour by employing her without one, something which they said could land the clinic into trouble. She had heard, however, through the grapevine, that they wanted to give her job to a white intern. Straight out of college. So that was one of her initial requests. To keep her job. She also wanted a husband. She was thirty-two and single and had not been in a meaningful relationship in how long? Five years? That needed to change.

Anesu put the money in the drawer. It saddened her. The money she had brought in today only was almost equal to the salary she got at the end of the month. How did people sleep at night while they treated others like that? The salon owner had not even remotely considered increasing their salaries. There was really no downside to employing foreigners without proper documentation. They could literally break their backs working for you and you could still get away with paying them peanuts. That was the business model of most people in the industry anyway. So 'salary increase' was Anesu's preeminent prayer request. She just wanted enough money to save and send to her mother and younger sister back home. She was not asking for much. A husband was at the very bottom of her list. She was twenty-eight but did not feel the need for a boy in her life. Men were unnecessary. She was focused on making enough money to do something tangible for her mother. She had to repay her somehow. She had paid for four years of university with money from her vegetable and tomato sales. Four solid years. It pained her how it was three years since she graduated from university and she still had not even repaid a tenth of her university fees. *One day it shall be fine*, she told herself. Sometimes she did not believe it, but she would still say it out loud every morning. She picked up her phone and called her friend.

"Laura, are you prepared my friend? Let's meet at Pick 'n Pay."

"Ah, Nesu. Why not at Mugg 'n Bean?"

"Ummm you want to tempt me. Pick 'n Pay, please."

"Okay, babes!" They both laughed.

The pastor was singing Dr Tumi's 'No other God' on the pulpit when Musawenkosi arrived. Her head was reeling. She was hungry, but she had to pray. There were about eight other people in the building who were walking about praying. She went and knelt down in the corner of the building. That was the only posture her knees could take. Laura and Anesu came in about ten minutes later.

"Now it's time to bring out your prayer requests. If you had not written them yet, find a piece of paper and do it quickly, the Lord…" the pastor suddenly stopped speaking. He was looking at the door, his face quite aghast, Musawenkosi noted. What had he seen? There were two girls at the door. She knew the shorter one. *What was her name again?* Anesu or Tinaye? She was so bad at remembering names. She had never seen the taller, big-hipped one though. New to the Church.

Laura could not believe what she was seeing. This man was the much-vaunted pastor? The man who had been on her bed only two or so hours back?

"Come…come and put your prayer requests in this basket," he continued.

Laura went to sit on a chair at the back. She tore the paper on which she had written her prayer requests. She wrote another one. She read it again and smiled to herself. She carefully folded it and walked to the front.

**Ivainashe Earnest Nyamutsamba**

Ivainashe uses a classical writing style infused with directness and modern language. He is a Law student at University of Pretoria, self-published author of a debut collection of short stories called 'I was never ready and many other stories'. He is also a blogger, poet, newsreader for Tuks FM and a last born.

## An ode to my aching heart

Freedom comes with a price. Freedom comes with a choice covered in lamb's wool, and freedom comes with a price. A costly price not all can afford. A price tag so out of reach, that only a few get to embrace the ever-flowing abundance of freedom when they get it. While others get to dine and wrestle with freedom, we must make do with what we have been given, maybe. Perhaps we might spin a thread of gold from the blood, sweat and shed tears earned from waltzing with the pseudo-freedom.

> *"Mhai mamiriro aita zvinhu kudai handingazvikwanise ndiri ndega, Baba Rudo vachigara vari kumahure. Ini ndinongosara nemwana iye John asingauye kana nesweet zvaro rekupa Rudo. Imimi Mhai hamusi kunzwa zvakanaka, pari kudiwa mari. Tikada kurarama nezvekupemha mazuva ese, hapana kwatinosvika. Naizvozvo ndave kuenda Joni, pamwe ndingawane cheuviri ndiriko. Ndangoti gadzikanei ndichapota ndichikutumirai mari.*
> *Ndini wenyu,*
> *Nhamoinesu.*
> Mom, the way things are looking, I cannot allow it to carry on like this. Rudo's father is always with the ladies of the night and having the time of his life. John does not even buy his own daughter a sweet, yet he is the father of the child. You are unwell and money is required for your treatment. If we carry on like this, we will not survive. Depending on handouts all the time will only result in people shunning us. I am going to South Africa to look for opportunities, I do not know where to start and who I'll meet. I must make something out of this trip. Once I am settled, I shall send you money.
> Yours truly,
> Nhamoinesu."

As I was crawling under the rusty barbed wire, it left a souvenir wound. It drew a long line, deep as the Mariana trench. The rusty barbed wire traced down my leg like Marco Polo, from my hip down to my calf, I began bleeding, in the process of healing it left a nasty scar as a memento that whispered to eternity, *I was here*. I could not stop to attend to my wound, for freedom was calling me with the serenading voice of a Munhumutapa nymph. Freedom that subsequently translated to 'free doom' in a matter of months. The concrete jungle was preparing its ferocious teeth for yet another one of Nehanda's wholesome offspring.

"Welcome to the City of 012, the city of dreamers, where your dreams come true. If you put your back into it of course," Mama Nifah announces, with a cheerful smile that leaves one in no doubt they are in the presence of a daughter of Africa. Whose smile speaks Ubuntu, whose smile preaches freedom.

Unfortunately, the obese and diabetes-threatened den-mother is a black widow. She has recruited another school of desperate Zezuru and Ndebele daughters of the House of Stone. Who have sought the alternative route to survive in the concrete jungle of 012 by selling their bodies.

"My daughters, sex sells! It is the most lucrative and sought-after commodity in this world. They go to war just for sex, they murder each other just for sex, they poison, betray, and back stab each other just for sex... sex... sex... sex sells my lovelies," says Mama Nifah, dancing like a ballerina wearing her tutu in front of an adoring crowd, with a sultry, seductive, sensual voice laying the rose petals on the floor for special effect.

"We have what they crave for, every day, these men you see, they love to have what we have that lies in between our legs. Besides, they came out of here. They always want to come back home and play; that is why sex sells my beautiful lovelies." Mama Nifah, the Giver, walked up to her "daughters" and gave them white envelopes. In the envelopes were bank account numbers, forged identification documents and a cell phone; little did the girls know that the bank accounts were cloned bank accounts easily accessed by Mama Nifah at her bidding.

Like a flock of sheep, we all bleated *"Yes!"*

"The apple of Eve - know how to use it! You will be an overnight sensation, eat your heart out Madonna!" Laughing like a cheeky weasel, Mama Nifah knows she is recruiting another school of children who have sold their souls to the concrete jungle of 012. Little do they know, the more the jungle swallows you, the more you become numb and cold, lost and distraught, drained and wasted. What these merciless streets do is they will chew you into a pulp and spit you out as if you never existed in this world - *stay woke!*

Only time and mercy might save them, that is if they are willing to come to her aid. For the pair are selfish at times and only serve those who are willing to trade in something that is special to them for safe passage...Nothing comes for free in this world of the damned mortal men...

*"Nhai Nhamoinesu, ko zvawandisiira mutoro unorema! Chana chako ndochi chengeta sei? Iro zobo remurume wako hariuye kuzoona mwana wako... idi mwana wekubereka wazondidzimba panyama nhete. Yohwe! Zvino Tenzi wangu ndodii... ini ndodii... ndiri shirikadzi isina unoichengeta munyika ino... zvepano pasi zvandikandisa mapfumo pasi zvedi korona yemunzwa yacho yarwadza musiki wangu, rerutsaiwo mutoro wacho nhai Tenzi..."*

Nhamo, harkened unsuspectedly, gobsmacked by the stark lamentation from her mother she could only say:

*"Mhai, mosara zvakanaka. Ndiri kuno ku Jobhegi kune mari yebepa...*

Mom, keep well. I am here in Johannesburg where there is real money." The black widow with its hawking presence rounded her Sunday school children.

"Now listen, my beautiful ebony kweens... these men are filthy rich! Suck them dry, make them beg for your apple, make them work for the apple, make them your slaves for the apple. When a man is eating the apple, that is when he is weak, now exploit that weakness, make it yours and tell him what you want and he shall give you... These dunderheads are so primitive like the Neanderthals so savage, so primitive... so fragile... yet valuable. Soooo handle them with care. They are your leprechaun, hold on to his golden pot and lucky coin dearly my lovelies. When you get on top ride him like you are riding a dirt bike, ride him as if it is the last day on earth... ride him dirty and nasty, give him the satisfaction he desperately craves for... yearns for... begs for... they arrive quickly, trust me I have been in the game for the longest of time... that is why they call me Mama Nifah... The Giver."

As meek as lamb, they all sang like a Catholic choir, *"Yes Mama!"*

All Nhamo, could do was tremble like an icicle, but she needed the dead president in her pocket as soon as yesterday. As she prepared to be taken to the richest square mile in Africa, she was given everything she ever dreamt of owning from '*Mama Nifah the Giver*'. Little did she know she had signed the Faustian deal and there was no going back. The concrete cold slabs, and cold, cold asphalt… if they could speak, they would have saved her from committing to the deal. Alas, all they could do is scream in silence, *"...all that glitters is not gold."*

"Come now my darlings, stand in a single file now, the big daddies of the world have arrived." As the black widow opened her layer of doom to the escorts, the wolves of this world. Crashed racing into her spider web of deceit and exploitation, again the walls and asphalt screamed in silence, "*...all that glitters is not gold.*" Unfortunately, no one was listening; who listens to a mute wall and asphalt? Only those who have the ears to listen may hear what is being warned by the harbingers.

First outing was tremendous. An outing with a diplomat from where she came from, *The House of Stone.* He was satisfied by the services he got from Nhamo and Mama Nifah the Giver. The diplomat was keen and interested in keeping her, for himself. Risking it all to take her away from Mama Nifah the Giver - a hounding, harkening mistake the young daughter of Nehanda made to listen to the geriatric whose days on earth were numbered. Who struggles to have an erection, *thank the creator for Pfizer, their Viagra line has saved dozens of men's egos...*

As she kept on living the lavish life, the storm of Nifah was brewing like a well fermented traditional beer. The diplomat bought her shoes, Birkin bags, Louis Vuitton custom-made dresses; and she was staying in the upper penthouse that was overlooking Alexandria. Did she even care about the families who suffered in squalor, the daughters like hers, suffering? Who cares, she was living her best episode of her life in the richest square mile in Africa? The longer the rope went the more impatient *The Giver* became.

One unfortunate night, as they were having a time of their lives, serenading the diplomat. Humping and galloping on each other as if it were 1999. Little did she know, the Grim Reaper was in the room with them. Not flinched nor bothered by their nudeness gawking at his hourglass. Paying attention and taking a clear audit of each grain of sand, the Reaper was doing his job of recruiting those whose time in the realm of man had come. Unfortunately, when the diplomat's time was up, the Reaper did what he was instructed by the gods to do. Harvesting his victim like a loyal worker; and so, The Reaper did reap the soul. The old man passed over to the other side, leaving Nhamo with his cadaver as present. His passing meant the little house of cards that Nhamo had made for herself came crashing down.

The Giver, learning that he had died, the Cruella De Vil of herself gushed all over the face of the earth. Her Sunday school felt her uncouth wrath; wrath so titanic, it gave Atlas the Titan a run for his money. The Giver, as ferocious as a wounded lioness, welcomed her lost lamb back into the pen,

"Well… well… look who has decided to return back to her mother ladies… The prodigal daughter has returned… so, where is my money you dumb bitch! Bitch you better have my money… I said where is my money you dumbass whore… Where-is-my-money?" In the moment, Nifah crashed a glass vase on her head, leaving Nhamo with lacerations that covered gruesomely and extensively across her face. Frightened by what she had witnessed and experienced, she burst into tears.

Unfortunately, her bank account was linked to Nifah's account, this meant every penny that came into her account was transferred into Nifah's account without her knowledge. As she would frequently check the balance, on the mobile application, the correct figures would reflect, but in fact there was no money in her account. Shaken by what she had witnessed, Nhamo tried to send her the money. The transaction was declined…*your transaction has declined, insufficient funds available…* numbly reported the mobile application. In shock at what Nhamo had witnessed, Nhamo stammered, "I… I… I… do not understand it. My balance is reflecting that I have money, but it is not allowing me to send you the money." Nifah, still stuck in her cesspool of wrath, kicked Nhamo out of her escorting business.

Left destitute, scarred, wounded and bruised, Nhamo wandered the concrete streets of 012. All they could say was, "…we told you so… you did not listen." Dejected, betrayed and hurt, she had to pick herself up.

In the concrete streets of 012, Helen Joseph opened her hands wide like the Messiah.

"Come my daughter, what the fresh producers leave as unworthy for their clients, I will provide for you." When the sun went to her mother, Nhamo would pick up the thrown away pepper, cabbage head, onions, cucumber and other green foodstuffs that were available and looked edible. She would then wash them and boil them, add salt and eat. For a month, she was picking up the thrown unworthy perishables…*beauty is in the eyes of beholder… another man's trash, is another man's treasure…*

Nhamo knew one thing and one thing only and that was selling her body, so she decided to establish her own business. Choosing the famous Inn Capital as her base of operation was not as pretty and rosy as she thought would work out. The money was not enough; she was underpaid, the clients were rude and violent, others would not pay her. Anchoring on the sole reason that she was a woman and a sex worker she is a lesser human, the ladies who were in the same industry were not welcoming and not willing to entertain a new face. A new face meant competition and to them a loss of clients, thus the only way to save their jobs was to attack Nhamo. As always, an unsuspected turf war would brew each night at the famous Inn Capital.

*"Haaaai wena Kwerekwere-Shangani,* you think you can come onto our block and run the show*! AmaShangani* you are problem you come take our jobs and now our men *voestek! Hamba nawe Sefebe samadhodha hamba nawe!"*

Alone in the concrete jungles, Nhamo survived multiple stabbings in a single night.

One drizzly cold winter night, Nhamo's fate was placed to the test yet again. As she was standing by the corner away from the brothel, an undercover private security officer waltzed over to her.

*"Ola* my sisters, how much tonight? As you know tonight it is His birthday *ke Dezember Mos, 25 neh* it is His birthday so half price *neh?"*

Nhamo was not entertaining any chancers that night; she declined the offer. The would-be private security officer was indignant, then arrested Nhamo on the grounds of loitering, prostituting and being an illegal immigrant. In addition to the triple threat to her quest to send money home, that morning she had received a message that read:

*"Nhamo Mhai vapinda muchipatara, BP. Paida ari kwatete.*

Nhamo, Mom is in the hospital, her BP has shot up. Paida is at your aunt's place."

It had been over six months since Nhamo had sent a penny back home. As she was being driven to the police station by the private-security officer Nhamo exclaimed, "Ok...Ok...Ok! I will give you your service for free... Please do not take me to the station for booking. I will be fucked okay!" The weaselly private-security officer inclined to the offer, "Now you are talking like an adult, so why the fuss about being all boujee when you well know I am the law?"

When he parked under a tree, the cop whipped out his member that puked and oozed pus, releasing an offensive smell. The sadistic chum grunted, "Now I want you to slob on my nob... tea bag it like you mean it! Wipe it clean as a whistle, you hear me? Now go on your knees as if you are about to pray to your God! Go on now, come on now..."

Hesitantly, for her survival, she had to incline to his bidding. After Nhamo's ordeal, the chum slapped Nhamo, he spat at her and kicked her in the gut while laughing like a maniac. The man continued assaulting Nhamo, resulting in Nhamo getting a black eye. Nhamo eventually collapsed on the job. A few weeks of trying to make ends meet to no avail.

Nhamo woke up at the hospital with drips all over her and a team of frantic doctors and nurses racing to save her life. A few hours later, Nhamo was stable.

One gloomy grey cloudy morning the doctor came into her ward.

"Hello Nhamo, how are you feeling today? You were brought here by a well-wisher who had spotted your almost lifeless body on the pavement. I do not want to take much of your time... we ran some blood tests and it saddens me to tell you that you have been diagnosed with HIV and AIDS. Now there is no need to worry. You will be fine. We have placed you under treatment. Having HIV does not mean your death sentence has been signed, no, not at all..."

As Nhamo was struggling to communicate with the doctor, her lungs were running short of breath. Nhamo was struggling to get to full health, her battle with the ailment was like the twelve labours of Hercules. She collapsed again, for the illness had ravaged Nhamo severely. After a month of being in the hospital, she was fit to take her leave. The good Samaritan had paid off all the expenses for Nhamo and gave her some money to live off until she gathered herself.

Nhamo still needed a means of income that was steady and no day job was available. She needed money to go back home. Nhamo was now staying at Denning Park, where she was introduced to a new world, a world of drugs. Nhamo had moved on and was trying to get her life in order with her newfound sisters who welcomed her into the family. Though sleeping under the stars every night, she felt some sense and feeling of being appreciated, wanted and welcomed...*at last some peace in her life for now...*

As she continued her trade, Nhamo welcomed any denomination that came her way, five, ten rands, as long as it was money. Sitting along the fence of the park, Nhamo met a young man carrying vegetables.

"My brother, have mercy on my soul... may I have a cabbage head and some tomatoes. I have not eaten in a while. Are you looking for a good time? I can take any money you want to pay me..." The startled young man who was coming from Marabastad after a long day's work at the vegetable market gave Nhamo the requested veggies.

"Eh... No, my sister, I would not want to do that to you. I only have five rands on me. You are my sister and I respect you so much..." The vegetable merchant went his way.

As death appeared, he was seated along the fence looking at Nhamo and how she had become wasted, sunken and baptised in the cesspool of *nyaope* and other drugs she had been inducing through blood transfusion. A practice they called, 'Bluetooth'.

A wasted young man waltzed over to her.

"How much is *short time*?"

"Eh... fifty rands only," Nhamo responded with haste, finally a worthy client!

The newly wedded couple walked together along the aisle of death. Setting up bed under the stars in the middle of the park under a tree, Nhamo's legs spread wide open ready to receive the train of death. The young man coughed and spat blood.

"Are you ready?"

With her eyes closed, Nhamo responded "Yes, I am ready." Slowly, the sharp warm knife slit her throat. The young man started stabbing the heart, punctured the lungs, opened her stomach. Nhamo could not scream to alert passersby. She drowned in her own blood as she silently recited the lyrics of Ephat Majuru. *"Hama dzangu tinoda mugariro wakadiniko pasi pano..."*

With no one responding to her internal chant, even death who was overlooking the stabbing would not chime together with Nhamo. As an independent woman, she responded to her own chant, *"Tinoda mugariro... mugariro wakanaka."*

The young man continued to stab Nhamo's body everywhere his hands could land; he was delivering the job that he was hired to perform by death.

*"Mudiwa mwoyo wangu, tasvika pasarungano rwerwendo rwedu. Chishuwo chemwoyo wangu changa chiri chekuti tisununguke tochengeta Paida, ndini wako Nhamo...*

Dear heart, in this melancholic demise all I wanted was us to be free as a bird and to take care of Paida, yours truly Nhamo..."

## Yours truly I am gone

In the heart of hearts, my soul and mind all play different roles as I hear from a distance not so far, but close by, the banging of the front door. My sole refuge is an empty, dirty with grime and algae-stained bathtub. The banging of the door grows louder and louder. The horrific tormenting voice of a humongous Oompa Loompa Afrikaner man rumbles behind the door, speaking in a tongue that sounds as if someone is chewing stones. Eventually, I hear the thudding sound of his thunderous-boisterous footsteps leaving the door. For now, I am safe.

I hear and feel the violent vibration of my cell phone - it is him, the terror of a human being. The wretch blows up my phone. I am harkened to answer the harbinger of death's call. I know *if I answer I am a goner*. All I can do is look on and act natural. My heart of hearts is racing and pacing. I am in no man's land. I left my uncle's place in haste and I did not bid him goodbye. The man was on my case each day, *"Shamwari handingagare ndichikuchengeta mazuva ese, iwe uri dambudziko kuna amai vako... M*y friend I cannot be taking care of you all the time, you are a burden to your mother," that's how my hope for a place of refuge went flying out of the window like Noah's Raven.

I tried living with them for a month, but I could not carry on the way I was treated. I was given a place to stay, rent free with warm food every day. A roof over your head is a blessing, but it was a blessing that felt like I had been forced to hug a porcupine with its quills. The quills were dipped in the poisonous skin of the Amazon poison dart frog. I had to let it go, so I did the unthinkable and fled my uncle's home, because I could not take it anymore.

As I prepared for my semester test one evening, I slept around "1am", but thirty minutes into my sleep, *Sekuru* burst into my room and switched on the light. Wearing a face of a man ready to go to war he bellowed, *"Muzukuru nekukura kwako kudai unoziva vezera rako vane mhuri, vavakushanda iwe uchiri muchikoro. Uri kuremedza amai vako iwe. Uri dambudziko kuna amai vako iwe. Rema remwana ndiwe. Unoda kuti ndikupe mari? Yekuti uzvichengete? Ini ndine vana vangu..."*

He was challenging why I was still in school and not working like my age mates. I wanted to respond, but as the needy visitor I was tongue tied and could not rise up to challenge him, so I apologised instead.

One morning, the merciless South African winter was blustering me as I waited outside of the house for *Sekuru* to give me a lift to campus. When he finally emerged from the house, he looked me right in the face and then looked away chewing his teeth, without uttering a word to me. En route to campus, *Sekuru* lapsed into yet another lecture *"Muzukuru unoziva uri wega muno muJoni handiti? Saka ndakaudza amai vako kuti ndiri kungokupa mwedzi mumwe. Mwana wenyu anofanirwa kubuda mumba mangu* and he leaves my family in peace not in pieces *handiti. Saka chitoona kuti watowana imba yekugara nekukasika, wova nezuva rakanaka,"* I boarded off his car, and as he sped off, I wondered what that was for.

While I was walking to the entrance of the main campus to my right, I stood at the back of the mob of praying students. As they were praying I could only hear one line, *"Ishe kwamuri ikoko ivaiwo neni namai vangu.* Lord, wherever you are, please be with me and my mother."

During a meal one evening, Sekuru looked at me for a minute or two and asked, *"Muzukuru ndine mubvunzo, zvaunogara wakango nyarara unenge uchifungei, dakungo ziva hangu?"* He wanted to know why I was always quiet.

I giggled cordially to defuse the tension first, then explained, *"Haa sekuru kungo nyarara hangu, dzimweni dzenguva ndiri kufunga nzira dzandikwanise kushandisa kushambadzira bhuku rangu kana richinge razobuda, Mwari mubatsiri wangu. Zvimwe nyadenga ungandi tambidzawo tsiye nyoro ndikwanise kutengesa chipo changu chekunyora ichi kuti ndiwane raramo iri nani muno muJoni".* After explaining that I was brainstorming ways to sell my upcoming book to try and make a living, Sekuru looked at me with the corner of his eye while trying to fish out a strand of meat that was stuck between his teeth, and exclaimed "tis-tis!"

You know kids are kids, but they can be used as tools to administer hurt and pain like a doctor. One of his kids waltzed into the room, started rummaging through my stuff and fidgeting with my laptop. The brat broke my laptop, and in the laptop, there was a manuscript I was working on. *Well, there goes my dreams and hopes of maybe making it big in Mzansi, again flying out through the window like Noah's Raven. Hopes and dreams of coming back. I sincerely do not think so, in as much as I tried to keep my cool, the pain, I could not hold it any longer.* As you know in Shona culture, *"Unova ne hunhu kana uri mumba mevanhu,* you have to have respect when you are a visitor".

The drama with Sekuru's house continued until I called my mother to inform her I was leaving her brother's house, *"Mhai! Zvekwa Sekuru zvarema, ini hangu ndava kubuda mumba mavo..."* Mom responded *"zvakanaka mwanangu"*, and as I was leaving campus making my way to Sekuru's home, I recited the lyrics from the Dendera King, Simon Choppa Chimbetu *"Tomuvhunza muvhunzo uyo kumatenga, isu touvhunza chete touvhunza, kuti sei Mwari muchitipa nguva yakaoma..."*

I packed my bags and I left *Sekuru* and his family. The maid tried to talk me out of it. As I held back my tears and battled the lump on my throat, I explained *"Ah, mainini zvepano zvandikandisa mapfumo pasi, hupenyu hwangu hungatopinda mumasango ndakatarisa, ndati zviri nani ndiende hangu. Ishe vanondichengeta kwandiri kuenda."* She was shocked with my stance, *"Asi munenge mangoita hasha henyu Muzukuru, Ambuya vanotofara nemi mufunge, kana zvirizvo aiwa patsvene itai zvinosungura mwoyo wenyu muzukuru."* I just did not know what to do. I was going crazy. All I needed was a moment with my thoughts where I could hear myself think; I might have come up with a plan to save myself. I could feel it; I was morphed into a sub-human being.

Did I tell you that I am a law student at the "Harvard of Africa?" A cool way to brag when you are with your peers who do not see the madness that is happening within that glass building.

Did I tell you today marks the tenth suicide case in one month and today marks the sixteenth female student who was gruesomely raped. So, it is between you and I, being a young Nancy Drew myself. After digging deep and conducting my own investigations, I reached out to the Youngman. It is a gruesome story, so please bear with me on this one. I must be as clean as a whistle, as blunt as a judge and as precise as Excalibur. The lad I reached out to, weeping and distraught, ghostly and pale, I could feel the cold... cold... air of dismay and disdain crawling out of him. As he was mustering the courage to share with me his awful sad story, I nearly jumped out of my skin, when he said to me:

> "...this is only going to take a few minutes. I know your story and where you come from. I know that your government does not send money. Even your embassy has no money to sustain you guys. I have a better proposition for you. I was desperately inclined to his proposition; I knew I was signing a Faustian deal with Lucifer himself. What would you do when there is no option for you to take? I felt inclined to respond positively. I would take the opportunity and see the results at the end, I mean I want to survive in this dump. So, he came and picked

me up in front of the University's main gate. I hopped into the beautiful chariot of gloom and doom... everywhere, its soulless treads left a trail of deceit, despair, and disdain. So, he warmed up my seat for me. He looked at me with a devilish eye and grinning joker smile. 'I am warming up the seat for you so when we arrive at the place you will be well warm and ready.' I nervously agreed, what was racing through my mind was that God help me, God help me. We drove into this secluded estate, far away from civilisation and there was no cell phone reception. We boarded off the car, my only refuge for safety. As I was walking away from the car, I looked back at my refuge, my sanctuary I could hear it speak and it said to me, '*...peace be upon you, may the cup of mercy runneth upon ye sacrificed lamb the lamb's wool of protection you have left it with me I shall keep it safe for you as I wait upon your return....* We got into this mansion that had occult symbols, Baphomet, the up-side down cross *"the Cross of Saint Peter"*, the Black Sun, and the symbol 666, among other occult symbols, some of which I had never seen before. I was welcomed by a group of hooded women who removed my clothes and started oiling my body. One of the mysteriously hooded people exclaimed with authority, '*...prepare the lamb for the ritual is about to commence...* 'in a commanding voice that could snatch the soul out of any mortal.

Harkened by the gripping story I could not bear it anymore. The young boy's marble eyes sought for mercy in my eyes. I could not deliver what he was yearning for. *I too am a mortal man like you and a Zimbabwean trying to survive in these lands that are not ours where even if we cry to the white men god and his son. Our cries only reach the ceiling and come back, where even trying to call unto our ancestors they can deafly hear our pleas of mercy.* The Youngman carried on.

"I was stripped naked and I walked into the centre of the room where there was a table made from white marble. I had to lie down on my back on the cold... cold... table and there came the Priestess speaking in a language I could not recognise. A language I had never heard before, though she was in a trance state. She poured oil all over me and the only words I could hear were 'sacrificial lamb'. The ritual began, then this humongous, towering human being was the first to walk to me and bend me over. I could feel my buttocks opening. As he inserted his huge veiny penis inside of me without any lubrication, I felt my sphincters breaking. Blood trickled down between my inner thighs as they took turns to rape me. The only words I could say were, 'hear me lord... as I pray... hear me lord... save me lord... I am feeling low.' I felt the warm hands of a woman holding firmly my shoulder and she reached up to my left and she whispered my name. I knew that creasing rough voice despite having my blindfold on. It was one of my supervisors, who said, 'Thank you, my lamb, for you have done our lord's work,' as she inserted her strap-on inside of me. I could feel my sphincter muscles collapsing as she grunted and forced her oversized strap-on inside my worn-out rectum. She carried on performing what the... the... others had been doing for the past three hours. What I remember is that I passed out... I woke up in the morning, naked and in the middle of nowhere, my anus swollen, and an envelope that was written *THANK YOU*. As I opened the envelope, there was a bloody one-hundred-rand bill. The blood hardened on Mandela's face... so much for freedom he fought for. They are out here abusing that freedom..."

A harrowing story it was, I... I... I... I could not believe my ears and eyes what they had heard, and I only took a deep sigh and I ejected from where we were seated. As I turned my head he said, "do not tell anyone about this..." with beaming marble eyes begging screaming HELP ME!" I only nodded and went my way. I was in shock. Later that day I heard commotion from outside people looking up and some were waving their hands hysterically while others were holding their cell phones. It seemed as if they were taking photos and videos. I curiously slid from my chair and I made my way to where the commotion was.

As I was arriving, I heard a loud thud and students screaming, others crying, many taking photos and a video of the splattered brains; and the slowly dying young Zimbabwean man who had a spark in his eyes. Who had a light in his life unfortunately the light switched off without ever realising its full potential. Walking with haste to go investigate who the victim was. Wrestling my way through the hoard of students, gobsmacked by horror, and choked by terror. I made it to the front of the hoard of students to my shock and disbelief, "You of all the people, YOU!" Before he took his last breath, our eyes crossed and he heard me saying, *"ko wazviitirei nhai? Wazviitirei, inga wani tiri vekumusha kumwe chete? Zvingangei kurema, mutoro wacho uno rema asi ndino mira newe kani. Zvino mai vako ndovatsanangurira sei...*why did you do it, why did you do it? The weight might have been heavy, we come from the same place. I would try my level best to stand by your side..."

I saw him breathing his last, *"Mwana wamai wofamba zvakanaka asi ndanga ndine chishuwo chekukubatsira, zvino ndozvawafunga. Zvawafunga ndinogamuchira nemawoko mairi, zvandapihwa nashe ndogaamuchira handi rambe...I*s this what you have decided? What you have decided I receive with both hands open. What has God given me, I receive I will not refuse…"

As I was leaving the horrified congregation and the campus security was trying to hold back the swarms of students flocking to the scene, the paramedics were arriving at the scene, *"manonoka munhu watoenda,* you are late he is gone".

As I was walking away slowly making my way to the library, I heard my phone vibrate. Investigating the message slew of messages that had arrived like a goods train that is bound to Mozambique passing through Marondera.

The chain messages read:

*"Zvepasi zvandikunda, zvepanyika zvandiremera, mutoro wacho wandidzimba pamwoyo, chandichararamira pano panyika ndechei. Ini hupenyu hwacho hworevei. Zviro zvacho zvobatsirei ini wacho ndorevei, ndoremedza mai vangu, ndoremedza shamwari dzangu, iro Degree racho rorevei muno muSouth macho havatidi, kumusha kwacho hurumende yacho inotidzvinyirira. Kuti mwana weku Zimbabwe achawanawo zororo rinhi? Zvatiri nhapwa kumusha nekumasango toendepi… kuna musiki ndokwega kwangosara. Ivo vokanga steak isu tokanga waya. Vanodya chingwa isu torwira mafufu zvorevei ini ndabvunza ndini wenyu, ndaenda...*

…the labours of being here on earth are heavy, the labours ache my heart. Why must I live in this wretched earth? My life, what is my meaning, I burden my mother, I burden my friends. What does this degree mean here in South Africa and back at home? Here in South Africa, they do not want us. In Zimbabwe, the government oppresses us. When will the Zimbabwean child ever realise peace? As if we are slaves here and back home. They eat bread and leave us to fight for the breadcrumbs. They eat the juicy steaks while we eat foul intestines. I ask what does it all mean? Yours truly I am gone..."

The hulky, bulky, clumsy Afrikaner landlord returns late in the afternoon and instructs me to leave his premises in an hour or he will kick me out using force, looking at me with a threatening eye…. I have delayed my rental payment by three months because the invisible horsemen derailed everything, even the flow of money from Zimbabwe to here. In this COVID-19 season I do not know where to go. Who to turn to in this concrete jungle, like my fallen brother I have become like him, the sacrificial lamb. Meek and ready for the slaughterhouse of this concrete jungle that chews you and spits you, and bays for the next prey like a Harpy Eagle.

## A passage through the tumultuous, boisterous sea

Freedom is a choice that comes with an expensive price tag. Purchasing freedom involves leaving your homeland, like Icarus flying too close to the sun and constantly hoping that his wings' wax does not melt. The pursuit of freedom is like stealing fire from the gods of Olympus as was done by Prometheus. The narrative for freedom is like a penitentiary experience; a journey of a slave who is running away from a cotton plantation. Only to crash land into another cotton plantation that has a new master who is xenophobic, racist and who is not concerned about your welfare. It is imperative to understand that there are two worlds when one embarks on a journey into a new territory. Understand intimately that there are those ones who come from an affluent family that are immune to the meltdown of the economy of Zimbabwe. Then there are people like me who rely on the antagonistic aggressive system to survive in the new lands. Thus, prepare yourself for an exhilarating journey of a middle-class black Zimbabwean. The people who have seen it all, done it all, and survived it all in these lands where the only source of solace and mentorship is the asphalt and concrete that teach you the value one carries.

A first generation middle-class black Zimbabwean who has left his homeland for a couple of reasons. The first reason is to escape the harsh economic demise, a catastrophe that the country is spiralling into. Thus, pursuing that dream of hopefully making it out to the other side, God willing, you secure a better paying career, drives one to leave their homeland. Knowing the way Zimbabwe is going, there is no future for those who subscribe to the sacred pages of freedom. If one would focus on those who are in the creative spaces of Zimbabwe, the porous legal fraternity of Zimbabwe that does not protect the rights of women and children. What about the rights of creatives, where piracy has been the demise of many talented creatives that Zimbabwe births annually? Culminating further in this psychological journey, leaving Zimbabwe is a conscious decision that one takes. A conscious decision that is backed by the family, the immediate nucleus. Anchoring on the faith that their beloved son might make it over to the other side. When he makes it to the other side, he will hopefully open the doors of reprieve and optimism to the family. The madness of Zimbabwe destroys families from their nucleus because the conditions are unbearable. Albeit bearable to the gatekeepers and their offspring because they are the ones who are controlling the system. A system that they have fashioned to best suit them, not the people, thereby perpetuating a severe class system. It might rival the system of The French society that was led by Louis the XVI and his wife Marie Antoinette.

Being a first-generation immigrant is a baptism of fire, where you must learn the ropes fast. If you do not learn the ropes fast, you are cooking a recipe of uncertainty and demise. This is based on the sole reasoning that as a first gen, you cannot go back home and claim to start afresh or anew. "You have made it over the river, now make things work." With the contemporary struggles of Zimbabwe, you must be versatile or fibrous to survive in the lands that are not yours. Yes, you may have relatives, but the reality that must be understood intimately is that they too are trying to make ends meet. Thus, if you bubble and submit your concerns or struggles before them, you are in a way burdening them. In this submission, they too have their own children who need to survive. They too have their own circles of immediate family that need their help. Therefore, as relatives we become antagonistic in the submission that, "young man the time is now upon you to make ends meet on your own in order to survive in the area you are in."

I realised that I needed to be versatile and that I could not rely on the degree only to survive in South Africa. I could not manage problems that I was going through from rent payments, grocery and clothes purchasing.

At the same time, I needed to make it through the academic course. Admittedly, the quest to establish a means of income while in school took a toll on my attention span. Studying law is not for the faint-hearted; it needs one's full attention and commitment. In a nutshell, a student is forced and expected to adapt to the abrupt changes in their new life, and if they do not change it is unfortunate for them, because the new environment will spit them out before they know it. A law student wakes up, goes to school, comes back, sleeps, eats, and repeats that cycle. Menial jobs, such as working at fast food outlets are a lucrative avenue. However, the problem that surfaces is there is competition against the local student. A student who has the same experience as you. The competition places one into the crosshairs of a xenophobic attack and scorn from the local people, especially for an aspiring graduate of law.

As is spoken by Jesus Christ in the Bible, *"one cannot serve two masters at the same time."* As spoken by the begotten son of man, it would be difficult to serve two masters. Thus, one cannot put their academic journey on the line. If everything was conducive in Zimbabwe, a child would not be driven to pursue the alternative channels to make the stay in university worth every moment. Thus, at times thoughts of being a drug mule would orbit around me because the money is fast, and it does meet your needs. Yet again, the moral question would be, "should I be an accessory used to plague my own kindred?" On top of that, you would be putting yourself in the crosshairs of the law. The hands of justice have a unique way of catching up. The negative energy of such deeds would haunt any conscious mind for the rest of their life. It is a cataclysmic barrage of thoughts that holds one hostage.

In Shona culture, it is bad to be a burden to other people, *"Kandiro kanoenda kunobva kamwe,* a plate comes back to where it came from." Similarly, the concept of karma haunts an individual when they know in their heart of hearts that this is not the way I was raised by my mother. As a conscious Shona person who is studying law, I carry a particular identity. Whilst I acknowledge that no society is perfect, I have a responsibility to ensure that when people see another Shona person, they must remember that Shona people are honest, kind and hard working. Then one is driven to pursue cleaner avenues to establish that sustainable financial flow so that they may focus on their studies.

Exams do come and as a student you are ill prepared because you do not have the prescribed textbooks. In the campus bookstore, one is gutted and gobsmacked to learn that the price of the textbook is the same as their rent. Then you are driven to use library textbooks, but there are eight-hundred students for a particular module and the library only stocks three copies of the latest edition. The old edition is no longer valid because the content in the book is outdated. It is at that moment one realises they are alone.

On the other hand, the landlord is blowing up your phone asking for his rent and you are two and a half weeks late.

"My brother, when am I expecting the rent to be deposited or else, I am deactivating your access into the premises..."

"Well I am going to camp on campus then, let me go and sleep in the library."

It is an outrageous experience, not for the faint-hearted. That Zimbabwean instinct of 'just keep pushing, it is going to be alright one day'.

*The prayers of my mother are the only asset that keeps me alive in these lands that are not of my clan's name, even if I try to call unto my gods, they will not be able to hear me. Well, the white men's god and his son do not seem to answer my cries... look, the Zimbabwean people have been suffering since 1982 to this day...*

In the life of an international student from Zimbabwe including countless others from other countries, misery and bleak uncertain financial futures torment us.

A survival instinct brought people together, before the pandemic "Coronavirus" waved its ugly head. The university departments hosted various symposiums right through the week, from engineering to theology to marketing. Due to allowance money coming at uncertain times, students kept themselves abreast of the events taking place on campus. We attended all the functions, day and night, collecting the uneaten food that would last us for days, or we would go without food. Some of the food was thrown away, so we attended the conferences with empty lunch boxes and harvested as much food as possible, from sushi to tiny rolls, to anything consumable.

When the landlord denies me access to my room, I must use the library as my bedroom for the night. During the night I study and catch a snooze for just an hour or two, because the security guards wake you up reminding you that you should be studying. They have no time to listen to explanations of your situation. Some security guards do not understand English and my struggle.

As the journey continues, to survive in my part of the world, you create relationships with the security officers of your respective faculty. Some of the security guards understand the plight of the black student. When the library is closed, he opens the doors for students to camp inside and make sure by four in the morning they are up, and they have vacated the library. Such noble helpers are appreciated, because they too understand the plight of the black international student who is battling to earn an A4 piece of paper on graduation day. That is if they survive the tumultuous journey.

It is a convoluted reality that one is forced to accept, but must not get comfortable with, because you draw yourself into the pool of mediocrity. Friends one would have, but they too have their struggles, so the only way they can support you as an individual is give you moral support. In that moment you hear the... the... voice of Steven Bantu Biko, "Black men you are on your own..." In that moment again the harkening voice of Malcom X reminds you that you are more than your problems, "Today it is time to stop singing and start swinging. You cannot sing up on freedom, but you can swing up on some freedom..." They cannot solve your problems in the scary haunting passages of life; you ought to rely then on your instincts.

Indeed, the institution offers campus jobs such as tutoring spots. Unfortunately, in the faculty of law, we just read, memorise and know how to argue or submit a plausible debate about a case. The skill of analysis can only be unearthed if one reads a lot and appreciates how others present their cases. The legal fraternity is totally ajar from the other fields such as engineering or accounting that have a fixed formula for calculating gravity. This is again a precarious situation if one pays attention to it intimately. If one is not strong willed, they are bound to panic and even call it quits. Again, that energy of surviving all odds that has been ingrained into our DNA brings us to be who we are. Jokingly laughing at our pain, us Zimbabweans say, "If I survived 2008 man, I could survive anything". Though to survive the pain, you need to find coping mechanisms. Just sitting and doing nothing is impossible. You need something to get yourself out of the barrage of madness that you are always consumed in. The semester results come out, and when you see you have a fifty, you are content with it, because what matters is to pass and a fifty is a pass. It is a beautiful madness where you hide the vast emptiness behind a smile. You reach a point of not making a video call with mom because if you see her, your heart aches. You are constantly blaming yourself if *I had not left home, maybe things would be better.* Then reality slaps your face to remind you that you are at least over the river now and must rely on what you have.

I am an articulate young man who delivers a unique way of writing. In my quest to realise a sustainable income, I am nudged to write an anthology and in its first production it sells well, by the way in the middle of Covid19. Then the doors begin to open because I decided to follow my instincts by relying on my skills and talents. Now I work for Tuks FM as a newsreader, I am a self-published author and a law student at the University of Pretoria. Having a literary work as a student, no, a black international student who comes from one of the worst places in the world now, *Zimbabwe,* you realise it is not a mistake nor a fluke. The universe is watching the journey of a *first gen* immigrant...it is tough and not for the faint hearted...you must be brave.

I have seen and done things I regret at times, but I had to do them to have a sustainable flow of income, so that I may pay my tuition fees until I obtain my masters'. The more my projects gain traction, the better my life in South Africa. Hello, my name is Ivainashe Earnest Nyamutsamba, I am a first-generation immigrant based in South Africa, and this was a snippet of my story. *Keep moving forward...*

## A K Mwanyekondo

AK Mwanyekondo is an emerging writer. His first appearance on the literary scene was through the short story, 'Migoti neMigwaku' in Gangaidzanwa, a compilation of short stories published by Essential Publishing Co. AK Mwanyekondo is an avid reader, he loves the works of Yvonne Vera, Ngugi wa Thiongo, Virginia Woolf, among others. This is his second appearance on the literary scene.

## The Interview

- Jon Paulo! What are you doing here at this time?

Musa was surprised to meet with his gateman inside the house. His surprise emerged from the realisation that his shift ended at six in the morning but the clock was fast approaching eight. A lot of ideas and accusations began to fly in his mind.

- Nothing sir. Actually I have just finished my shift and I took it upon myself to check if everything is where it is supposed to be. Madam has taken a tendency of leaving the taps running and the stove on. I wanted to…

This calmed and relaxed him, even though the thoughts of Jon Paulo stealing the little things they were likely not going to miss did not entirely leave him.

- Madam! The funny thing is that she will deny having opened the taps or using the stove.

Musa chuckled at this remark, not sure of how to respond to this. The gateman, Jon Paulo, joined in on the laugh, his being nervous and forced.

- Thank you for taking on these extra tasks. It is not easy for anyone, including you, to be working outside of your stipulated hours.

Jon Paulo wanted to ask what 'including you' meant. Was he entitled to certain privileges he was not currently getting, or it meant the honour and dignity of being a gateman that required knees to remain fixed on the ground? He would have wanted to know, but he found his tongue stuck and lips glued, afraid to ask. What terrified him even more was the answer. Either of the two caused his bones to ache. After a long pause, he changed the subject.

- By the way, when did you return from your trip? I mean the business trip. We were not expecting you till Thursday, right?

Musa was stunned that Jon Paulo had remembered. One, that he was away on a trip, a business trip. Two, he was supposed to be there till the end of the week. Three, the accusations became more pronounced and clearer in his mind, he was here to loot! Musa never managed to shake off the myth that Jon Paulo and all his low level employees were intrigued and keen on pilfering at each opportunity. Subtle forms of resistance. This myth was unfounded though, Musa's family had been with Jon Paulo and his family for more than a decade, his loyalty and commitment was never questioned. Not even once.

- I am surprised that you remembered Jon Paulo.
- You mentioned it once and I cared enough to remember. Not to forget, I mean.

The fog of the accusations momentarily cleared, leaving questions. More questions. Madam, his wife, had forgotten when he was supposed to be coming back. In fact, she had even forgotten that he was away. She would call asking, summoning his presence if the marriage was to survive only to be calmed when he told her about his trip, the business trip. Was his wife getting old or the marriage was being sustained by insecurities? These were the questions Musa pondered on, not sure which answer he preferred.

- She is forgetting things lately, Musa ejaculated. This wasn't directed to Jon Paulo, these were the thoughts he didn't want to nurse and attract, but they kept appearing in his mind. Jon Paulo picked on this and decided not to inquire.
- Did you manage to bring some clothes for my little one? I mean my children? I asked you to but…
- You know, my mind kept telling me that there was something I had failed to remember. To think that I even went to the children's clothing section, but I quickly discarded the thoughts as unknown desires for another child. Musa interjected, his voice getting elevated as he tried to mask being disappointed at himself.
- I understand. It was a business trip after all.

He saw the look of disappointment on Jon Paulo's face, the dissatisfaction he didn't want to admit. Jon Paulo too was trying to hide that this was yet another expectation not realised.

- There is something we can do about it. Yes, there is. I will add the money on your salary, then you and the wife can do the shopping together. That will be much better isn't it Jon Paulo?
- Thank you, sir. I am afraid Madam will not agree to that. She already believes what I am getting is too much, making me the most rewarded 'door opener' in all of East Africa. Glorified door opener.

The gateman giggled, it was unhappiness that took over him yet he continued smiling.

- Madam can be difficult, but her heart is in the right place. How about I give you the money now, maybe you can forgive me for forgetting. It will be our little secret huh?
- Thank you sir, but it will make everything else difficult.

Jon Paulo would have wanted... loved to elaborate what his remark meant, but Musa neglected this remark. To Musa, it was one of the many things Jon Paulo said that he couldn't comprehend, despite his esteemed academic pedestal. He thought of his qualifications for a moment, education that spits gold had taken him to the depths of lavish delicacies he never dreamt of during his youth, during the days of the naivety of his youth.

- Do you miss your home sir? I mean home. Jon Paulo's voices snapped Musa from the wandering his mind had descended to.
- Everyday Jon Paulo. Every fucking day! There is no day that goes by that I am not tormented by memories of home. Some of my beloved relatives, I am sure, no longer remember my face. Just a name, a name with a virtual face.
- But sir. You look so happy here. You have created a name for yourself. I pride myself, to my friends, that I open Musa Chihota's door and clean his wife's car.

Jon Paulo remembers how his friends laugh at him for degrading himself by washing another man's car, although the roots for their resentment emerge from the sense of joy that is in Jon Paulo's heart. His friends always express a certain revulsion for the foreigners which Jon Paulo doesn't share, and for that reason he becomes an object of ridicule for forging an alliance with the devil that has chained them! Jon Paulo claims to be unbothered by their ridicule, but the truth of it all, it creates a turbulence in his mind. One he is not sure how to console and provide comfort. For this reason, Jon Paulo finds himself falling, sinking, drowning in a deep and frightening abyss.

- That is thoughtful of you Jon Paulo.

Musa Chihota didn't know what he was complimenting Jon Paulo for, but to him it felt like the right thing to do.

- I know Zimbabwe has ripped and torn many people apart, forcing them to escape or at least think about escaping, but it wasn't for me. I had sworn never to call another country my home. I wanted to remain close to the bones of my ancestors and my umbilical cord.
- So what happened? Was it crime? Did you call the president names?

Musa chuckled at this statement because he knew Jon Paulo intended it as a joke, but it was true that there were people who had lost their limbs and life because of their political standpoint. He had witnessed an entire village burn to the ground, the pain of memory of bodies screaming and wailing still kept him awake at night, the smell of raw flesh being fried made him a seasonal vegetarian especially during the days the voices in his head got louder.

That is why he goes to bed drunk, that is how his wife thinks of herself as unlucky and cursed. She shouldered the trauma he didn't want to admit existed, making her marriage exist not on lies and infidelity, but silence. A loud and deafening silence.

- Nothing of that sort, Jon Paulo. I had a successful business I invested all my youth in. This made leaving, the choice to leave quite difficult. The burning of the nation was like a hurricane that could be witnessed from a distance and I had envisaged it long before it happened. In the end this pushed me to look for ways to ensure that my family didn't suffer. Fortunately, this coincided with my job interview here in Kigali. Not so many people are this lucky!
- That was brave of you. At least you had an option, a choice and a decision. Most people are reactive rather than proactive. So what do you miss the most about home?

Musa wanted to ask why he was being probed about his past life. For the past thirteen years Jon Paulo had never asked about his past. They did talk, but nothing of substance. Musa picked that there were wounds, a confusion that Jon Paulo intended to heal with words, his words. Another thought was that he was on the lookout for an opportunity, a gateway from being a 'glorified gateman opener'. Why now? At the same time, the questions about home interested him. They ignited a certain fire inside his heart, a fire that quickly got cold when his wife and children were around. The unholy alliance consisting of his wife, children and other relatives they talked with virtually, were not interested in tales of a Zimbabwe. Their rationale was that he left for a particular reason so there was no need for him to bore them with stories of a home he willingly left. The fact that returning was another option he could embrace if only he could summon the courage and confidence, made the alliance's argument solid and provocative. Return, to the alliance, was a simple decision which could be substantiated by a plane ticket and a message that the prodigal son had seen the light. To Musa, returning was not easy, returning was even more difficult than leaving, yet staying here in a foreign country continued to stifle and chain him. On the other end of the conversation, Jon Paulo hoped these questions would make it less difficult. He was wrong.

- There is the laughter of my Sekuru, which makes me smile on rainy and sunny days. I miss my relatives. I miss church, singing in Shona. There is the food. I know this sounds crazy, but I miss being angry at the government. Walking barefoot in my childhood home. A lot of things, Jon Paulo.

A wave of nostalgia made him smile, remembering, the intention to remember had been the fine thread holding him intact as well as a sharp knife piercing in his heart, making him want to scream.

- Do you like it here? Sir. Do you enjoy being here?

Jon inquired. Jon Paulo was caught in web, a labyrinth further chaining him as he tried to find his way. Yet everything remained difficult.

- Honestly, I don't. I can hardly call this place my home because I do not have a connection of any kind with Kigali. There is the local cuisine that still makes me sick even after decades…

Jon Paulo's mind drifted off, he ceased to listen to his boss' explanation despite having posed the question. This was what his friends had been telling him about the foreigners, milking their resources and opportunities for their own selfish reasons.

- *They are not even grateful for being here, for being provided with chances missing in their country.* He remembered the statement from yesterday's conversations.

This brought to memory their proposed solution. To force the foreigners back to their homes. Dead or alive! Jon Paulo remained indifferent, not sure where he stood regarding this radicalism. Everything remained dark, improbable and difficult.

- Anyway, what about you Jon Paulo. What is your story?
- I have no story except being a 'glorified opener of doors'.
- Come on Jon Paulo. Did you go to school? Have a degree, perhaps?

This question opened up a past, a history he had locked and buried deep in his soul. Jon Paulo lived each day as it came, liberated from the pain of memory and the disappointment of owning dreams. Though unspoken of, as if the memories had been disremembered and succumbed to the joy of amnesia, they remained vividly imprinted on Jon Paulo's mind. Musa's question had summoned these memories, it had called out to them, providing them with the attention they desperately desired. Yet the words, the will to transform these memories to words failed him. He couldn't speak, he looked at Musa's face with a blank gaze, without emotion. Jon Paulo remembered his childhood days, going to school, spending more time at home rather than at school because there was no money to cater for his tuition. He remembered cursing his father for failing to be a man. Mzee had failed to move with the changing times that required looking for work, any type of work. Instead he embraced what he thought to be his destiny, being a high priest at the cost of providing for his family. Though he never showed his anger directly to him, there were times he would have dreams of murdering him in cold blood and enjoying the entire experience. The burden to send him to school befell his brother who couldn't do much himself. Jon Paulo's thoughts took him to a time when his feet had caressed university corridors, but the same semester he began his Pharmacy degree, Acel, his elder brother, got ill. His health continued to be critical and unstable which meant once again, the ability to progress was put on hold. Mzee could have helped him but the gods, his gods didn't intercourse with another deity which Acel believed in. This enraged Jon Paulo. The anger he had bottled for years erupted, in a moment of grief and disappointment he struck his father with a flaming log during the funeral. It was this act that decimated his relationship with his father. After the funeral, news reached Jon Paulo's ears that during a period of 'enjoying his youth' he had impregnated a woman he hardly knew except the contours of her body. His wife. Thereafter, his path was clearly carved and laid out. Fucked without redemption. Words could not be released, he continued staring at him with a blank gaze. Musa knew what his silence meant, he didn't have the energy to ask Jon Paulo to come out of his cocoon. To him, people like Jon Paulo were lazy, not eager to work hard in order to change the complexion of their lives.

- I am familiar with stories of people like you Jon. But let me tell you something, your family has to be your duty now. You are in your home country, so some things are relatively easy to navigate. Your children will not be required to go for VISA screening or be ineligible for certain bursaries. Give them, try to give them the opportunities that were shut out to you. Break the poverty cycle Jon Paulo!
- By being a door opener sir? I think not.
- Is it easy? Never! But the struggle is worth it.

The words 'but the struggle is worth it' kept ringing in Jon Paulo's head. Which struggle? He would have wanted to ask, to know, hoping that the answer would help him locate where to anchor hope in a harsh and unforgiving world. That is the way of the world - to be a dreamer, a visionary for a struggle he hardly knows its existence. Victory, possible victory was not even possible. He decided to leave, to go home before these thoughts left him, he needed to hold these thoughts in his hand, to flip the pages of their soul hoping that such an endeavour will present to himself who he was. Somehow these thoughts were the anchor of his sanity, yet they were difficult to hold.

- Let me make you a cup of tea before I leave.
- I can make my own breakfast, Jon Paulo. You don't have to worry about that.

- Allow me. You need to rest before the meetings come raining on you. I will make your favourite eggs.

Scrambled with a subtle lemon flavour. Musa remembered that on top of the list of things his wife was forgetting, was his fondness for scrambled eggs with a dash of lemon. She sometimes asked the maid to make breakfast bacon, forgetting that he was allergic to pork. It made his face swell and blister.

- Have a nice day Jon Paulo. Greet your family for me.

Musa took a huge bite of the sandwich, it was divine. Better than most hotels and fancy restaurants he had ever been to.

*Tomorrow's newspaper will have an article with the headline:*
**African Icon Found Dead!**

Today, Musa Chihota enjoys his delectable sandwich.

## These Were the Voices

i.

Your name is Grace. You wanted to curse the Lord and His Mercy so that you could die, because what your life had come to was no longer worth living for, yet death failed to fully embrace you. The tongue needed to release words overflowing with insubordination against the Holy Ghost who had neglected his promise, to be your *Mweya Munyaradzi*. All the same, you remained outside your gate, outside the borders, inside the belly of your wretchedness. You waited until you could no longer wait or afford to wait. Hands kept waving at the *matatus* speeding past you like a ghost, an unliving soul that could be felt but out of reach, out of touch. You began to pace back and forth at the front gate of your borders, hoping to calm yourself but failing at each attempt. You saw your colleagues getting onto a *matatu* even though you had arrived first. The waiting continued, waiting for your turn. Waiting was your fate and destiny. Waiting for death to ferry you to eternal damnation. Waiting for the *matatu* to take you to work. At work you would be required to wait for your payment and gratitude that sometimes came on the $40^{th}$ sometimes on day 51 of the month. You are tired of waiting, of remaining expectant, you were a phantom pregnancy.

The decision to walk to where you were supposed to have been an hour ago was not yours to decide, it rained down on you like a hailstorm. Perhaps if you had made the decision an hour ago you could have been there by now. By now you would have begun the usual routine, voices pronouncing your worthlessness. These were the voices that got louder tearing you apart with each whisper. Whispering was their life purpose. Tormented by these voices, you found your hands shaking, head split into two by a terrible headache. That is how you had let a hot cup of coffee escape your hands to bounce on the lap of the shareholder. His thighs are still tattooed by fresh burns. Your boss, Potiphar's wife, is yet to bring out your transgressions. You continued to wait for an altercation. A scolding that was yet to come.

You opened the gate with vigour and violence, perhaps you wanted to announce yourself, the windows vibrated and shivered at your arrival. Potiphar's wife was already waiting for you at the reception. It wasn't instinct or intuition, but the realisation that you are always late, always. Potiphar's wife was smiling, displaying her teeth she considers to be her best feature along with the brain and everything else starting with a 'b'. Breasts, bone structure and big eyes. You wanted to return the smile but the energy failed you, the only thing you managed to do was wipe the sweat dripping from your brow making your face sticky, unnecessarily sticky. That is how you began to blink unusually fast, a sign and symbol of panic with a flavouring of terror and sprinkles of disgust. Disgust. These were the voices being whispered inside of your head for it was a time, a season and an age of whispering voices.

Your eyes embraced each other. Potiphar's wife staring at you, her eyes filled with admiration but another closer look at you quickly eroded the feeling of veneration because your dress code, your choice of clothes on this particular day and many others consumed by time, forced an invitation to embarrassment and ridicule. A leather jacket you had worn every winter for the past three years. The leather succumbing to a premature old age emerging from use, overuse. Black suede shoes that hadn't seen suede since the manufacturer's hand yet they seemingly remained new. Hair. Supposed to be natural meant it kept aiming, pointing and poking at the insects flying and buzzing in the air. The jeans. Potiphar's wife remembered the black jeans because she had bought them, hoping to replace your favourite faded marron slack. Favourite meant the only one you possessed, still wearable. Now, the black jeans had ceased to be black, existing somewhere between grey and off white. It was the blue thread, green thread and red thread used to patch different holes that disgusted her. As Potiphar's wife feasted on your dress code, a dress code speaking a tale of being a wretch and a wretched, you were stunned by her radiant smile, the gap between her front teeth completely annihilated you, both body and desire. There was nothing you could do about that except. Desire Potiphar's wife. Potiphar's wife did not have a husband called Potiphar, neither was she a wife to anyone. In fact, her name was Helen. Just Helen. But you had nicknamed her Potiphar's wife because in your mind, you think Potiphar's wife must have looked exactly like Helen. The voices in your head would say, 'I will never flee like Joseph'.

Potiphar's wife was flaunting her new car keys. You remember the day the 'beast' embraced Kigali, she had called an informal emergency meeting that had a celebratory mood synonymous with the end of year party. At this meeting slash party, Potiphar's wife went on and on about being amongst the three people in Kigali with the latest Range Rover, she with the limited red edition, the only one in Africa. The voices in your head broke down, they wept miserably as you remembered it was day forty-seven of the month.

ii.

Anesu Mufakose. *He is with you; he continues to be with you as death destroys you.* Your name is Anesu Mufakose. Your whole body sings and rattles when you descend from your slumber, your sleep. The sleep that you do not own but owns you. Both king and master, it determines what you see and feel. You are a slave, a subordinate, a mere thing with a beating heart. Heart. A heart without beat and rhythm. You do not wake up. Rather, you are startled, terrified and shaking. Shivering. You gasp for air, like someone being baptised in deep frightening waters that give out prophecies of forgotten dreams. The time is 05:47, thirteen minutes before the hour six in the morning, five forty-seven. The orange shimmering light is greeting you through the glass window, the window of glass or simply put the window, it is calling out to you. Reluctantly you embrace the sun with your eyes.

The insides of this coffin you call home are liberated from outside influence. This coffin you live in resembles both death and dying. It is difficult to stretch your hands out without compromising the structural integrity of the walls. You allow and are allowed to die three times before the cock sniffs the morning breeze. That is how you die for the first time, confined to a space that was not meant for confinement, for life and for living, but you are alive. Your beating heart and heaving chest confirms this. Guarantees this. Two. The toilet seat is broken, the lid perhaps stolen, probably being used for another purpose. You are the lid of a broken toilet seat, uprooted from your home, neglected by the ties that anchor you to this soil. This coffin is a forgotten backyard toilet, with a roof that drips water, a place that has become an embodiment of living and suffocating. The divide between the two blurred, fine and unperceivable.

Three. In this coffin, the remnants of diarrhoea are scattered everywhere, time and space have taken away the foul smell, leaving you plagued and cursed by a stench of misery, wretchedness and looming death. This place. Home. Rats, sometimes black, rarely white grace your humble abode. Tossing the reminders of a terrible diarrhoea and cholera to the rags you use for protection from the cold. Today you woke up, the reminders and remainders plastered on your left jaw. Shit, eternally glued and grafted into your identity. *Shit*, the reincarnation of your umbilical cord. You stare at the orange shimmering light, fast transforming to gold as the sun continues to rise, a celebration that you survived night and darkness. Night and darkness, transporters of mourning and weeping. You did weep and mourn, you are certain that today is not the day you will experience joy. That comes in the morning. For you, reality continues to hammer your invisibility. You are a ghost robbed of life and living, your dreams simply allowed to continue sleeping.

i.

You stood at the front gate of where you used to work. A few minutes ago, you opened the gate with such vigour and energy, right now you carefully close the gate, hoping it won't make any noise. Counting on being unseen, to become invisible. Holding the box with the few things you had owned, one lunch box that no longer had a lid, a cup covered in dust and oil. You remembered bringing the cup for the time you would have coffee. But there never was a situation that required coffee or tea or any related break. So the cup remained on the shelf, gathering dust, hoping against hope that one day, someday it would be put to use until. All hope, crushed, soiled and never to be realised. You are the cup, with disappointed dreams.

The conversation with Potiphar's wife, your boss, former boss, continued to reverberate in your head.

- *You can't work here any more*

- *I cannot allow you to continue working here*

- *You no longer work here*

- *It is best for you to look for someplace else…*

Four reasons. Same outcome. A fourfold impact. You were without employment, you could have a cup of coffee or tea at any point you liked, if only you could afford water, sugar and teabags. The words continued to torment you, it felt surreal that just like that you had become dispensable. Words uttered by Potiphar's kept echoing in your ears.

One.

- *You can't work here anymore*

This had been said. Said in response to your tendency to arrive at the workplace at your given yet unchosen time, this dismissal was conceived by your unprofessional disposition. Potiphar's wife had carefully singled out this reason, to justify, to convince herself that there wasn't anything at fault with her

decision, or the underlying reasons for dismissing one of her hardest workers at the House. The Publishing House. The only justification you could summon and release from your tongue was:

- Sometimes. I have to walk because of money.

Potiphar's wife realised this was a valid and big enough justification. It was not her intention to delay her payments, but somehow, every month, she forgets to file your papers with others so every month your payment is delayed. In response, the boss weaved out another reason, another blow, another death.

Two.

*- I cannot allow you to continue working here*

Potiphar's wife was both architect and victim of forces and policies that killed you. She whipped out a newspaper with the headline, Rwandan Government to Hunt Illegal Migrants. This began a conversation, a dialogue that sounded like an interior monologue.

- You see. The immigration officers will bleed both you and me dry when they come. That is why we (pointing at herself) have decided to let you go. I am afraid that when they do come and find someone from, where are you from again?' You want to say 'Zimbabwe' but the 'Zi' chokes you and you start to cough violently. The reminder of home, the remembrance of dying grips on your neck. You can't breathe.

- Okay 'Zi'. I am afraid it will present worms in a can, they will want to look at our funding partners, the integrity of the books we have published. By integrity, this will be a way to check if they are politically correct, but you know. We try to present human narratives as they are experienced and lived amongst our own. I can't be in jail; I will not come out with a manuscript. So no, I cannot allow you to continue working here.

You remember the article; it was the one that had propelled you to put your papers in order. The newspaper article was an old article, dated two years ago. Potiphar's wife remained at the door, telling you to go. *Where?* You would have wanted to ask, to know, to believe there was some place for you to go to. A place where you are both needed and wanted. *Where?* Where did not mean, your now former place of work.

Three.

*-You no longer work here*

This was meant to relinquish any obligation to meet your needs. All payments due were no longer Potiphar's wife or the House's responsibility. That is how you were released with an old lunch box that didn't have a lid, an old cup that had lost its colour due of lack of use, and a notebook with the notes on every manuscript you had read and a couple of poems you had authored over the years. You no longer worked at the House, but the characters you met in your journey remained with you.

ii.

Eight at the back
Two in front
Double nothings in between

Harvest.

2008. The year is 2008. The country ablaze, the economy on fire and fresh bodies scattered and littered in the streets, your grip on reality continues to evade, so is your grasp on dreams and their probable realisation. Looking, staring attentively would tell you that the realisation of both dreams and hopes was beyond you. Beyond your reach. Two years after graduation, the grey suit had become grey. Yet. You continued, hoping.

Before your eyes, Harare had become a melting pot, boiling and spilling the contents in the fire. There was no hope for hope, for dreams except survival. Survival through eating yet another dog, another life. Another soul. You decided to leave, for there was no living happening. Remains of corpses could be found on the mouth of a dog, a mother seriously contemplating frying her children without oil in order to survive the day. Fathers, completely broken down and stripped of dignity as they visualise and envisage their entire fleet of wealth spending nights on end in the bars. Walking the streets, holding so tight their sexuality. Survival and death. There was sickness in health.

Your mother could hear nothing of it. Home kept stifling and choking her too but for her, now was the time to hope, to believe and to have faith. For you, the hope and faith she exuded had. Emptied. Dry.

A drought, with no rains on the horizon. Zimbabwe.

- You can't leave me here!

Amai Mufakose kept screaming, calling out to the prophets of old, Nehanda and the ghost of her departed husband. All these cries did not move you. You remained steadfast, home was no longer home. It had been transmuted to prison, to a slave ship taking you nowhere with the possibility of not even arriving.

- Take your umbilical cord. She cried during her early morning ablutions.

You knew the prayers were not directed to a god who seemed to have failed to meet all her needs and expectations. They were directed at you. The *you* she was claiming to be abandoning her, the *you* that had drunk from the poisoned chalice of servitude constantly being forced down your throat by them, by them you mean *them*. The *you* that was her reason for living, especially when everything and everyone else had left her. The *you* that was not keen on listening or hearing. The *you* that believed grace could be found in sacrifice. Sacrifice hinged on putting your life and trust at the mercy of strangers. Foreigners.

Mufakose

Mufakose, any situation can kill you. Killed you. Wretchedness, true to its identity, sucked hope, life and living from your soul. Leaving an emptiness and realisation that your expectations and reality are running parallel to each other.

Hope. Met you when you arrived at Kigali International Airport. You met someone who believed in the gravity of your qualifications. You got yourself a job, a dream job that allowed you to dream one more time. As is usually the case, there was darkness looming in the shadows, death and dying watching from a distance. Waiting to kill and to steal. That is how you become Mufakose. Home choked you to death, foreign lands stifled and suffocated you. It happened before you blinked, before the gold shimmering light of morning caressed and tainted the sky, beautiful. News had managed to reach you. How? You no longer remember. You identified her by the red floral dress, the one she bought when she took you to university. The whole journey, she kept chanting blessings and the faithfulness of the Lord. She rarely bought new clothes, but this was no ordinary journey, this was her and her son treading on top of a pregnancy that spits gold. Education. Now. Her body was mutilated, several knife cuts were tattooed on her body, her palms lying next to her feet. Head without a neck. Beheaded, lying scattered away from the scene. The article read:

> *The state is committed to bringing justice to the opposition supporters who are terrorising people in order to push their own agenda of regime change. Reliable sources suggest that the opposition supporters are getting financial support from the diaspora. Their allies…*

i.

Flattering Butterfly

You are holding an old red box. Inside the box is an old lunch box that no longer has a lid, a white cup dipped in dust, a journal that you had used and other small and tiny things such as fancy pens with dried glitters, a tattered copy of *How to become a Book Editor*. Your legs are moving, but you are failing to focus. Without realising, you had been standing in the middle of the road. Not concerned with oncoming traffic that could have hit you if it wasn't for the sounding of the horn that brought you back to the world as it is. As you continue to walk, you begin to hear voices. You haven't heard these voices before but you knew exactly who they were, they were characters from manuscripts never accepted for publishing, most of them continued to gather dust in the storeroom.

***Character One:*** (in a calm and still voice) If yesterday you had so much power and dominion over me, today you cannot afford to look at yourself in the mirror. For you have become nothing, a forgotten wretch.
***You:*** (raising your voice) I was just doing my job. Doing what was expected of me which meant, reviewing manuscripts that made way to my desk and providing a short review to the Senior Editor.
***Character One:*** (the voice starting to elevate from anger) It is not the Senior Editor I have a problem with, it is you, Assistant Editor. It is you who wrote in your journals and I quote, "The main character is under-developed, without emotion or any relation to human aspects as we know them. He remained untethered and unconnected to the world…" You think I was underdeveloped. I had no soul or a beating heart? Huh?
***You:*** I remember you. You are the protagonist from (pause). That story of a man who returned (pause). From the war soon after independence was announced. He stood at crossroad of war and peace, his disposition to violence during a time of alleged peace twisted his mind. The place-less-ness he felt as he failed to land any form of employment took him to the depth of solitude, the realisation that they had continued with their lives as he put his on hold weakened his knees. His peers and colleagues suckled from the bosom of independence with greed. The same people he had saved from the colonial diseases laughed and ridiculed him for having slaved away his youth in the *bhundu*. In the end he

went on a killing spree, murdering in cold blood top government officials under the mantra of 'Exorcising Independence'.
***Character One:*** (you could feel him getting closer, speaking right in your ear.) Oh so you do remember. Did you make an attempt to understand the root for my desire? For my alienation? It was the period of the Uhuru, ululations and whispers were everywhere, yet I remained stuck and closed out to the celebrations. The trauma I probably felt? (he exists, leaving you with questions making your head spin.)
***You:*** I did highlight that the story, your story represents the lives and experiences of many Africans, most who are being gagged by independence. Look at myself, living. No. I am not living. I am alive but not living. Yes. Alive. 3000 kilometres from home, for what? Fired on a whim or because of an unfounded fear. Like you, I lock myself in darkness because only that. Darkness is my mirror, you are my mirror, untethered and unconnected to my surroundings. The quest for independence that probably killed your children and wife is the same liberation (you begin to sob). The same liberation… (enter character two).
***Character Two:*** You lost your job today, didn't you? What went wrong?
***You:*** Sadly, yes. Life is what went wrong, as with every one's. I could have gone home, but the borders I live in are opened at nightfall, that is how they keep everyone in check. They do not allow unemployed people, so they make sure all the doors are shut during the day.
***Character Two:*** You will remember today as one of your darkest days. Tomorrow might be even worse, but it does get better.
***You:*** (in a subdued tone) I wish I could believe that. I really do, but. I have experienced very little pleasure in life, I am beginning to think I am a statistic, just a statistic. You know. They say 49 out of 50 people who leave Zimbabwe end up in working and living conditions better than the ones they were exposed to at home. I am the one, the one outlier, the statistic. Who are you by the way?
***Character Two:*** My maker never gave me a name (pause). I never got to feel the world or anything.
***You:*** I seem to have forgotten my name. Several times, I hear someone calling out my name, but I am not so quick to respond. Are you the woman who dies in the opening scene?
***Character Two:*** You remembered. I didn't think you would. You know the book got published elsewhere, but I wasn't a part of it. They said my death had

no bearing to the story, because it wasn't investigated, and no one mourned me. I simply died and was forgotten. So there was no point in such a story, my story.
***You:*** Oh yes. That is the story of us all. Constantly dying each day…
***Character Two:*** What did you think of me?
***You:*** The sad thing is I agree with the publisher. However, I wouldn't have ripped you out of the pages of the novel. I would have made your death the closing scene, as a reminder of us who continue to die, our deaths never avenged by justice or simple mourning. You and I are one.
***Character Two:*** Thank you for your kind words. I hope we get to meet again soon (she exits and character three enters).
***Character Three:*** (weeping) It's a shame. Tragic even! Whilst others are broken down by ruthless assessment of the editor, I. My own life and entire existence never got to be reviewed, to be seen. Potiphar's asked you to read my story, but the moment you realised it was about incest was the end of it all. You occupy a high moral ground that you couldn't allow your Christian principles to be tainted by a father who shakes in pleasure, leaving seed in his child's womb. Becoming a grandfather to his own child, son in law to his wife and husband to his child. All this was too impure for you? I need answers!
***You:*** How was I to go through the pages of trauma so beautifully captured? I wasn't in a position to read it without breaking down, without bringing to memory my own similar experiences.

iii.

For a while Holy, you were father to Grace, your beloved daughter who was keen to be like you in every way. All this is in the past now, it happened before you were born again. Your name wasn't Holy but you were known as Holy because your fascination with the kingdom of heaven stood out, more than your name. You would speak the language of angels with zeal and passion, like a Zealot. You didn't seem to care that your wife was a drunkard, a chain smoker and a woman, because the community and yourself continued to hold on to the faith that she would change, she would become like her husband. She didn't. Ridiculing their misplaced faith, the wife, the profane wife would wake up early Sunday morning and roll a huge blunt of weed to carry her till lunch. You would look at her through the mirror whilst buttoning your shirt as she licked the ends of her homemade cigarette and making sure that the contents were airtight.

- Pray for us Sinners, now and at the time of our death, your wife would call out to both father and daughter as they embarked on a journey to Jerusalem whilst she continued to descend in vulgarity.

You developed a special relationship with your daughter, bound and united by your growing and unwavering faith. Your inner person's faith grew exponentially yet the physical Holy developed unworthy yet enticing and inviting desires. You began to notice your daughter's transformation into a woman, her blooming sexuality derailed your faith, feeding you with desires that could only be quenched by, release. That was your birth rebirth. You were not drunk on this occasion, what was certain however was your flaming passion and burning sensation for release. A disease had taken over your soul as you slid inside Grace, sweat dripping from your forehead onto his daughter's lips, panting and shaking from pleasure and revulsion. Your wife shouting and cheering as you arrived, as you experienced your own crisis.
- She is a piece of flesh. She is just a piece of flesh.

That night, you spent the night in the shower, trying to wash away your sins but the disease you had buried in the depth of your heart was strong. Five years later you were hanged for being a paedophile.

i.

Those who came to see you, who had been summoned to such a spectacle got more than what they had expected, a memory they would keep sharing till word reached and caressed each ear of their circle, their circles. Your actions elicited a thousand emotions, your kind felt pity for you but there was no way to help you except by hesitating, hesitating to stretch their hand. Some laughed because you were neither a friend nor an acquaintance, this liberated them from desire to be compassionate. *Chawana hama hachisekwi* so they had every reason to vividly display their ridicule, not intent on hiding their pleasure. At one point you kept running back and forth as if warming up before a big match. Tired from exhaustion you would sit down, your head supported by your palms. Before your breathing stabilised, a vortex of energy would hit you, forcing you to jump up and down, as if chasing away invisible bees or embracing a gospel shut up in your bones. You became Jeremiah. Your actions became erratic, sometimes you appeared to be reasoning with someone who was not keen on listening, sometimes you would be the one not so eager to listen to a voice

whispering in your ear. Now, many were surrounding you. Taking pictures and videos. Different and many captions were making waves on Twitter, Instagram and Facebook.
- Woman loses her mind on the street.
- Crazy woman talks to herself. Madness in Kigali.
- Migrant attacked by demons in broad daylight. The end of time is here; rapture might be tonight.

Exhausted, you pass out on the road. They continue looking.

ii.

Home.

You work in a restaurant in Kigali. There are many food outlets in Kigali, making this one and you unremarkable. This one is a bit different however, the waiters are careless and carefree, they are young and desperately aim at being wild. Some miss the entire target, many of them hit the bullseye. You try to ignore the noise, the constant screaming and shouting, laughing and synchronised singing. This is what your days have become. Frequent intercourse with a silent noise, a noise that carries no sound, only sound infiltrating the air like bugs. Mosquitoes. You don't bite, neither do you make a sound, but all the same they think you are irritating. There is a message buried deep in the silence of your workmates, in the subtle yet loud rolling of eyes when you pass or cough. That, 'he is not supposed to be here' look haunts you each day, but there isn't much that either you or them can do, except to co-exist, to simultaneously live with each other's revulsions. The screaming and laughter continues, as with every other day you remain unsurprised and unbothered. You are the oldest, which becomes one of the reasons they probably are not fond of you. They, your workmates. You hardly say anything to each other, except make sure that by 12:30 lunch is ready, enough to cover for an unexpectedly busy day. Your days are always busy.

They, the children slash waiters, have their way of doing business. Just finished writing their Senior 4 and Senior 6 exams, looking for someplace to spend their days before progressing to the next stage of their lives which for some is university. The most unfortunate ones repeat from Senior 3, because they had been ploughed by the exams. This, their working in a restaurant, means a place of escape, a place to grow up. The girls and women come to work wearing strips and strings that don't leave much to the imagination. Some leave home wearing decent tops which they tie into a knot when they arrive, allowing their navels to blow imaginary kisses to the customers. Them, the customers like it. Unaccustomed to flat and smooth tummies, they completely lose themselves. They, the waiters are drawn and attracted to the attention. They allow the men to brush their fingers on their navels and other parts of their bodies they dare to. The men remain fixed on the navels, afraid of being too daring.

She will jiggle her breasts when delivering their drinks. By the time she goes home, her pockets are full and overflowing. Both of them pleased, her body sexualized, his pockets sucked dry. The men and boys are not completely forgotten in such escapades. Both men and women, exhausted but not tired from their unions. They seek someplace to be free, to forget and be without worry. For women, the place is this restaurant where men, old enough to be their lastborns are the waiters. Waiting on them. They come wearing tight shorts that seem to trace their masculine anatomy, a symbol of dominance and pleasure. The women seem to agree. They order their food, in the most sexual and erotic ways, their friends whom they have asked to join them like it this way, the waiters like it too.

- I would like to have a big and hot sausage. Please make it hot, I want to blow on it before it fills my insides with pleasure, this is how the women order their food.

At this, the waiter cups his own sausage in his hands and the women, both old and young, scream. The women are also generous, the male waiters leave with their pockets full of money and a list of women who placed private orders. It is funny to think about. Tomorrow, they will wake up in university hostels, memories of having worked here, forgotten or abandoned or both. It is usually both. So you. You, with nothing that appeals to the eye, are not allowed in the front stage. Your job is to cut the onions.

All your options had run out, seriously questioning life, survival and existence. That is when you met Helen. The owner of the restaurant. She asked where you were from, and the answer you gave was what she loved more than the person.

- Zimbabweans are known to be hard workers. Do your job, don't ask questions and I will make sure the immigration people will not lay a finger on you. You did your job, kept your mouth shut and the immigration people haven't laid their finger on you. As promised.

You hear the synchronised screaming and shouting outside, it isn't the usual. You realise it has an echo, a reverberation out of the ordinary. It has voices, new voices you haven't heard before. There is no one on the front stage, they are congregating outside, taking pictures and videos. You normally don't like these kinds of gatherings, but today it is calling out to you. Like a magnet.

There is a woman, passed out on the pavement. Different voices pronouncing and proclaiming what might have happened to her.

- She is talking to demons. Demons cannot be reasoned with; they beat her to death.
- Lies! She is insane, can't you see she is a foreigner? It must be her people who want her home. So sad what our ancestors can do.
- Maybe this is a stunt, want to direct attention from our pockets. When we get home, we will have nothing.

There is an energy that consumes her, you sneak through the crowd much to their surprise. You ask if she is alright.

- *Handisi kuziva.* Everything is changing. The congregation has stopped taking pictures, looking and observing what you are doing, in awe and surprise. In amazement.

You put her backpack on your back and ask her to hold the box.

- We are going home, you say.

## Untitled

…stood at the window, curtains wide open, a bucket on top of her coffee table to stop the rains from dampening her carpet. There were complete and unfinished paintings used to decorate the room, it was almost difficult to see and touch the wall without stumbling on a painting, sometimes wet. Martha clenched the iron burglar bars as she marvelled at the rains that were gracing the soil, and the tiny droplets of water dancing on the window, making her head turn and spin with ecstasy. Martha caressed the window, intending to touch and hold the tiny dancing droplets, but they were on the other side, close yet distant. The roaring thunder and flashing lightning pushed her to the far end of her one-roomed apartment. She admired the beauty of rain as it fell down, in contrast to balls of snow. The dancing droplets wiping away the dirt on her window, made her forget her fear of torrential rains. A fear that was unfounded, but it remained true to her.

Her mother was named Martha. Her father had named her Martha and she was known as Martha, but the two were quite different. Whilst Martha, the mother, had long hair the colour of gold flowing down to her shoulders, Martha the daughter had short black kinky hair that failed at every attempt of reaching out to her shoulders. The complexion of Martha was pink, almost pink. Words rolled out of her tongue with ease, carefully expressing the 'ts' and 'rs' with affection, a sign of flirtations with the English language conceived at her birth. As it turns out, Martha had no physical qualities borrowed from her mother, especially the ones she adored and positioned at a pedestal; the flowing hair and white skin. Tainted by her father's genes, Martha's complexion was that of overripe berries, much to her mother's chagrin.

- I don't understand why and how she turned out to be darkness when half of her is supposed to be this.

By 'this', Martha meant her blonde hair, a key aspect of her beauty. 'This' referred to her skin the colour of milk, which according to Martha was a symbol of perfection and royalty. Such abhorrence of her daughter's uniqueness began her experimentation of turning her into royalty. Days on end she would dip and drown her in lukewarm oil, her justification being that the oil would suck all the blackness from her, leaving a smooth and perfect white skin. At first Adam was furious with his wife, but her tenacity and determination quickly overshadowed his anger for these experiments. In the end, he only ensured that in these purification and distillation processes, the child was not harmed; though most times he had to nurse burns, broken bones and severe rashes. The height of her hatred of her daughter's appearance was the reason she decided never to have other children. Martha did get pregnant again and again and again, but the children simply disappeared, and Adam never asked what became of the children. Afraid to know the answer, he kept his mouth. Shut!

-Ah! Adam, I am not interested in raising a black ant-farm here in Boston. This was the only justification Martha gave to appease her husband's silence.

For these and many other reasons, Adam named her Martha, to remind her wife that despite significant differences in their appearances, Martha was her child. She had begotten her and was bound to her till death. Martha had accepted this, the name being the only tie and connection between her and Martha. Nothing else. Martha, bound to her daughter by a name, only a name, thereby denying and rejecting any other form of link between her and her daughter. Adam became the only link between the two, without his presence Martha, the daughter, never acknowledged the presence of Martha, her mother. This was a comfortable situation to the mother, for she had sworn never to waste words and energy talking to her daughter.

The previous year that had recently gone to sleep was the most difficult Martha had to endure. Mary, her husband's sister, had made sure that she died, against Martha's consent. Martha had spent many days on end praying for Mary's soul and health, but her maker had other plans; amongst those plans were failure to heed her benedictions and ablutions. Mary had taken Lazarus with her. They departed together, their graves next to each other as if to spite Martha who felt alone, ignored and absent. A Fading Light. The year had consumed Martha's beloved aunty, Mary and her son, Lazarus. The loss left an indelible mark on her heart. At first there was rage, a violent rage. Martha made herself bleed, shouting even in her sleep:

-If you had been here they would not have died. They would not have died! Martha cried, tossing herself on the ground. The state of her grief and grip on reality continued to fall. On the fourth day after the burial of Mary and Lazarus, she woke up so early in the morning with a veil on top of her head, clenching her right hand, which was holding a mustard, Martha sojourned to the graves. The morbid mood of the graves and graveyard which made her skin

crawl, today represented a place of hope and belief. A possibility that miracles are not only possible, but they walk in the lives of the distraught, crushed and childless.

-Lazarus! Arise. Arise Mary! Arise, arise. Martha called out to her son and beloved aunt, summoning them. Martha had harnessed the authority and confidence that was used during creation. Let there be light and there was light. Let there be Mary and there was Mary. Her voice was full of authority and an energy that almost terrified her. The chanting and prophesying of a possible yet doubtful resurrection continued even when her faith significantly declined. Hoping to summon the dead back to the land of the living, Martha had her eyes closed, senses attentive and expectant to the rumble and quacking of the earth, waiting for the graves to split into two, spitting and vomiting their contents. She spent the rest of the day reciting these words. In her heart she had summoned the faith to move mountains. To her grieving heart, playing fetch with mountains was a much more difficult task than breathing life to a body that was alive a few moments ago. She did hear the rumble, the soil blazing, sending a sharp pain from her ankles to the groin. It was the screaming of Mary and Lazarus's throaty laughter that brought her to her knees as she embraced them, their bodies trembling after resisting being sucked, pulled, consumed by death. Only that this was not real, as Martha's mind feasted on a grand reunion, her mind churning and spinning stories of Mary and Lazarus who braved death. Her physical body, void of its soul, was being immersed in the cold, the tears had ceased but the voice was still intact, pronouncing high pitched shrills. Alone and lonely, forgotten and abandoned. Even the birds fled from this scene afraid of their own demise. Death.

The rage and panic did not stay with Martha for long. When they left, only a fraction of Martha was left, bones visible and prominent on her body, the dreadlocks she had taken ages to groom were like dangling strips of torn and tattered clothes hanging on a madmen's body. Her feet could still walk, hands could still touch and hold, but there was no life left in their movements. Martha had become an unliving soul. When the rage left, it paved the way for a subtle form of grieving. Grief taught her that instead of praying for the second coming of Mary and Lazarus, she was supposed to cherish the happiness and the shine they had lit up her life with. With this came an emptiness, a reality that happiness was probably six feet down. For her, this was the worst. It came with the revelation that she would be required to down antidepressant and other nerve calming medication till her last day.

The flashes of lightning followed by a pitch black darkness reminded her of solitude and abandonment. She found herself curled up in a vacant corner with her knees supporting her chin and her hands firmly embracing the legs, waiting for the pills to kick in. A white sheet appeared in flashes before her, it calmed her. Its appearance became fixed, the white sheet ceased to be fleeting, it had become stagnant like a pool of water. Tiny droplets of water appeared on the white sheet with tiny wings of unusual colours - blue, pink, black and red. Martha stood from the corner she had curled up in, searched for her brushes and began painting.

This year, the one that followed her self-proclaimed Year of the Fading Light was carrying on with bringing misery to her life. Old age, looming menopause and death were catching up with Martha at a rate that further crushed the possibility and potential to make it as an artist. The fact that no one was really interested in purchasing her paintings weakened her knees. Mary and Lazarus had departed, leaving her with an emptiness that had taken hold of everything she knew and understood, an emptiness which became a mirror image of her life and interpretation of the world. With her paintings strapped on her back, head supported by her palms, her dreadlocks caressing the insides of her ears, oversized shoes tied so tight to make sure they do not escape, jeans tight as shoes, but with distinct holes intended as fashion, but later overtaken by age and being worn far too many times; elicited a scruffy look close to madness, closer to a destitute. She was wearing a pink top with the words 'Paida' printed on the bosom. She was not sure if it was intended to show her navel or it was yet another reminder that she had outgrown her clothes, most of her clothes. Martha painted her face black, black lipstick and eyeshadows, her nose ring made her look like a thing to be feared, but before she could make others scream, she was terrified by herself and what she had become. A Martha.

As soon as she got out of the Zimbabwe Art Gallery, she went to admire the sculptors at the entrance. Admiring the artwork, the finely chiselled stone modelled to make a man with a bulging stomach and protruding nose was a marvel to her. She strolled in front of the art gallery, brushing her fingers on regular stone made special, and a mark of beauty by people like her, people she wanted to become. Martha turned her head from the left and slowly turned back to the right, trying to identify that which was before her, but nothing came to her mind. Everything, every form of the stone remained vague and abstract. It came to her that art; any form of art was not meant to be understood. Art needed to be felt, savoured on the tongue like tasting fine wine. She stopped to take a look at the subdued eagle. Martha allowed her fingers to touch the eyes, feel the texture of the stone smoothed out of its roughness only to present an eagle, facing down as if in mourning. Looking up by looking down, this was her, subdued and void of all hope. Seeing such works of art being advertised quickly brought the realisation that she was failing and fading as an artist. It wasn't jealousy that made her stand a distance from these sculptors, it was more of disappointment and unmet pleasures that brought her down, further and further down.

*-The morning after the storm carries a blazing sun that vanishes the narratives of hail.*

She recalled the quote from a book she vaguely remembers. The quote had sung songs of hope and optimism, expectation and release. Unfortunately, these feelings of positivity didn't last. The encounter with the curator in the Gallery had made her sink further to depths that were not easy to come out from, depths she knew so well. The man had lifted her painting with his index, a clear sign of disappointment and repugnance, he scanned the frame which were pieces of wood glued together by far too many nails probably hammered by an amateur. She.

-You didn't allow the paint to dry before moving this thing.

He called it 'this thing' because it failed at every test of being regarded as a painting. 'This thing' she had spent the entire night working on, carefully singling out each colour to properly synchronise and capture the beauty of a woman staring at a sunset with its fading light. The curator picked another painting with tiny yet colourful droplets of what appeared to be water scattered on a white sheet, for a moment he thought of it as beautiful and fresh but quickly, he noticed the lack of coordination and consistency in the colour of the droplets making him frown and throw it carelessly on top of the others.

-The colours you used do not usually blend with each other, as you would have wanted to. I can see the eyes, what I think are the eyes anyway. If you want to be serious with painting, perhaps go back to kind…"

Martha could not allow him to finish. She simply grabbed her painting from him, her long nails scratching the sun and further diminishing the light it was supposed to give out. Before she opened the door, she turned back to him and

asked a question. A question she had dreaded to ask anyone who had belittled her work, energy and life.
-Sir. Are you an artist? The man chuckled before responding.
-Better. I study art.

What worried her the most was the dwindling nature of her savings. She had put all her eggs in one basket, only that there were not many eggs. In fact, it was just one egg. Home. She saw cars speeding into second street, witnessing a police officer being bribed by drivers who had intentionally or unintentionally ignored the stop sign. From where she was seated, Martha could see a thousand windows facing her, some with clothes left to dry, others shut with curtains closed; no life allowed in, no life allowed out. A thousand possibilities laid before her, people with dreams being met or crushed brushing shoulders with her. Hers, lying idle and lifeless on the ground, same as the maker, she, who could not control her nerves without downing blue and white pills, green and yellow pills and plain white pills with names that cripple her tongue at each attempt to pronounce. Fluvoxamine. Sertraline. Escitalopram.

It wasn't Martha's intention to visit a foreign land which was supposed to be home. The breakdown of her marriage and the finality of her divorce had left her with nothing, no identity, an absent home and a fading soul. All this had happened in the Year of the Fading Light. Edward, the husband to Martha, lawyer, Mary's brother, and the father of Lazarus had popped the bubble she had been living in. To finalise her disintegration, he had delivered the news of a looming divorce during the period of her mourning and grieving.
-I can't do this anymore. I can't Martha, said Edward.

Edward carefully rolled out the words, stressing each syllable, hoping that she hears it the first time. Counting on saying it only once for these were the words that shouldn't be repeated. Martha was not sure what 'this' meant. Perhaps it meant the mourning which seemed to have consumed her body and soul. Perhaps he was referring to the constant screaming and breaking of mirrors even after telling her to learn to control her rage and anger. Perhaps it was failing to show up for counselling sessions despite confirming that this time she would attend. Perhaps, perhaps.

-I feel suffocated when I am with you. I am gasping for air every time I am close to you. Every time I remain in this marriage. Edward continued with his plea after realizing that no response was going to come from her.

Clarity! This meant the marriage, this meant her proximity to him. Edward's response had ignited a raging and consuming fire inside of her, it was her turn to respond.
-I can leave! I can leave Edward. All this hurting is quiet noise to you huh? I can leave this minute, maybe you can breathe. Just maybe…

Without notice and notification Martha grabbed an empty cup close to her, the impulse gene took over her one more time. Martha did not pause to realise the damage she might cause, she just let the cup fly to his left temple making him bleed, the cup lost its handle during the struggle. What followed were books, plates, and newspapers, but none of them reached him, none of them had the same impact as the cup. The now broken cup.
-Remember Martha, I also lost a son, an heir and a sister. I need consoling, I need comfort." He tried to get close to her but hesitated, he was held so tight by an invisible grip. Edward was suffocating.
-My two favourite persons are lying fresh in the ground Edward. Martha screamed at him, eyes clenched, seeing only darkness, feeling an intense pain.
-Two favourite people huh? Where am I? Where am I?

That was the finality of the divorce. The fact that Edward was possibly her third favourite person made it relatively easy. It quickly confirmed his suffocation and the judge granted the divorce. Was it true though, that he Edward, was her third favourite person if he is lucky or were these words uttered during the height of grief and a disappearing sanity?

In a year, Martha had become a divorcee, alone, without a child. Untalented painter, unemployed, old, she felt death's presence lurking in the shadows. The divorce came with other realisations. Boston was no longer home, her home. It carried in its belly memories, tales of a fleeting love, tried desires and unmet pleasures. The only place she could turn to be a vague and abstract home, the country her father had met Martha. Zimbabwe.

By the time she got back home, it was already pitch black. Martha hadn't expected to be away till nine in the evening, but the transport situation had sucked the life out of her. The long distance she walked made her soaking wet, sweat falling down her forehead, her armpits starting to stink as if she hadn't bathed in ages. The paintings, her paintings were still strapped on her back like an infant. The paintings still needed to be tied to her back because they were not in a position to walk. She was doubting they would ever walk, let alone sprint, let alone on their own. Her landlord had slid a small note under her door. Martha knew he probably waited for her till he gave up. She was so close to giving up. Giving up.

*Mobhadhara rent sisi kana kuti mofamba famba!*

This is a different language, a language she never heard her parents speak. A language she desperately wanted to learn. Martha did not read and could not read what was on the note, but somehow she knew what was being asked and required of her. To pay the rent which now was due. Not wanting to sleep with the burden of a debt staring back at her, she searched for her wallet. Martha was confident there was nothing inside it, but she needed the confirmation to determine the finality of her state. Homelessness was close by. Calling out her name, looking for company and comfort.

Before boarding the plane from Boston, where she had lived all her life, Martha took the opportunity to research the country she was going to call home. All she knew was that her parents met in Harare, Zimbabwe, nothing else. The relatives, his relatives remained buried in the bosom of their secrets they never shared with her. During the rare times Martha and Adam were cosy to each other in her presence, they talked about a past. Martha would say,

-I love you my African-American. Mr Martha Jackson. Martha said this whilst rubbing her soft hands on Adam's beard he insisted on breeding. Like Hussein. Like Border Gezi.

-You know. I am the only person of Zimbabwean descent, spent half of my childhood in Tete, the rest in Kigali. I went to school in London. I have walked this earth more than Johnnie and his whisky. I married my love, my life, the centre of my existence. Martha from Boston. Adam found pleasure in narrating his diverse background.

-My global citizen. I love you, Afropolitan. Martha would respond by sitting on her Afropolitan's lap, hands wrapped around his neck. Martha would watch, hoping that this feeling and moment of affection would include her. But she kept watching and waiting, till their death. Although it was never confirmed by any certificate, it felt like they were swallowed whole on their way to the supermarket. Nothing was heard of them, they simply vanished, disappeared from her life without leaving clues only emptiness and longing.

A mother, an overbearing mother who went at great lengths to burn, toast and fry her skin and an unusually silent father, was her childhood and the greater fraction of her life. That is how she had met Mary. Mary whom she pronounced as 'Meri', a confusion of both Mary and being merry. In Meri she could see a friend, a sister and possibly a mother. They connected on an emotional level that made Edward almost jealous. She laughed louder with Meri more than she did with Edward. Without realising, this became the foot tracks to her divorce.

News of making, buying and selling money were everywhere and under the illusion of alleged protection, she wiped clean her bank account, which didn't have much. Edward and his lawyers presented such a case that left her with nothing. She had nothing, so Martha quickly accepted her fate and demise. In her mind, the making and selling of money would give her a certain advantage because that way she could live and earn a living by selling her forex. Unfortunately, the situation had been grossly exaggerated or she simply misinterpreted it. Martha learnt the hard way, that the American dollar she had was only vital before use in Zimbabwe. It fast became useless once sold. It failed to earn her a living, and her ability to sustain herself had dwindled faster than she intended. This state of misery stimulated the rage she had tried so hard to keep at bay, to keep in check, not giving it comfort. However, the situation required anger and rage. She needed to be angry, but there wasn't any scapegoat to carry her sins. She was alone, a fading light.

The American identity Adam took pride in left Martha in the air, legs dangling and failing to embrace the ground. Adam had met his opportunity to spread his wings when he met and married a white woman. This tie and union made him an American citizen and little Martha was born on American soil, further reinforcing her identity as both American and un-American. Seduced by the sweet experiences of a diaspora narrative, Adam renounced every form of identity that tied him back home, accepting his renewed and refreshed surname, Martha's. That is how both father and daughter became a Jackson. Whilst this was a noble cause and a thing to die for, for many parents, little Martha remained an outsider both at school and at home. She never suffered from unnecessary bureaucracies of visa inspection or torture from the immigration people, yet she remained untethered from any form of spiritual and cultural connection of her identity. Probing her mother was useless and talking about the past with her father was just as useless because home, Zimbabwe was not home to either of them. It was a place that choked them to death. That is how they were liberated from the pain of memory. Right now she was back to her supposed home, yet her feet were still swinging from left to right and the left again. A pendulum. Swinging that generated motion but remained fixed and unmoving. There was the pain of language, the desire to let her tongue rollout one Shona or Ndebele word became an obsession; she was fixated on the idea of conversing in any of the local languages. Instead, she kept walking, running and hunting blind folded. Every effort she made to acquire a Zimbabwean identity had been crushed without any sign of resurrection. One, she didn't have her parents' documents, and two, she vaguely remembered what her hometown was.

-*Zita rasabhuku ndiani?* Who is the chief of your hometown? The workers at the Registrar's would inquire. Her response remained the same with each attempt which meant a pronounced silence. The insults conceived by the silence remained the same too, though they stung deep and more painful at every utterance.

"Please go and bother the people who bewitched you and allow us to do our work in peace. *Pengerai kwamakaroiwa!*"

Three, there was no money to speed up the process. Four, her paintings remained strapped on her back, disabled and blind and hard of hearing.

Out of respect for the man who had given her a place to stay, even though for a while, she began packing her stuff, afraid of a possible altercation if the rent due was not sorted by sunrise. An altercation would direct unwarranted attention and she didn't like that. All her life she had been without any form of spiritual connection. The circle was now complete; as of tomorrow morning, she would not have a shelter on top of her logs. Homeless.

It didn't take her a while to finish packing, something had whispered to her not to unpack everything when she arrived. Martha could feel her canvass calling out to her. This time she didn't resist. With her eyes closed, she reached out for her black brush, dipped it in black paint and started painting. All her pain faded away, her uncertainty and fear of death evaporated, leaving with her a passion, a burning desire to keep on painting till the end of the world. Dawn...

## James Wanangwa Kajumi Kuwali

James Wananga Kajumi Kuwali is a denizen of Malawi, Zimbabwe and the People's Idiosyncratic Republic of Brooklyn. Raised by a journalist father who surrounded him with books, magazines, and other reading materials, he took to reading and writing early. James is a part-time accountant, chef and writer.

## The Republican

I hated this place. I had never quite figured out why I was here. Then. And now.

I hated the cufflinks. I hated the stuffed shirts. I hated the stuffy rooms. I hated the de rigueur dark scotch that had been aged beyond a teenager's lifespan and yet still tasted like not-ready-for-prime-time ramen broth, spiked with bathtub liquor. I hated the pretentious snifters, and the affected way one had to hold them as they downed that noxious swill. I hated the way I had learned to refer to myself as 'one' in casual conversation.

I hated the imposing antique furniture; it was uncomfortable to sit on. I hated the thick stone walls; they were claustrophobia, embodied. I hated the visually overpowering damask draperies which, even when open all the way to let light in, seemed to envelope the rooms with an unremitting and fundamental darkness. I hated the overstuffed floral furnishings, and how they reflected the English's strange need to bring their gardens, already over-designed and tended to the very last geranium bloom, indoors.

I hated the gilded…everything. No kidding, the only thing not fringed with gold trim were the human beings in the place…and then a substantial number of them found it fit to gild themselves anyway. Tiaras, ostentatious brooches, and copious medals and ribbons for gents whose experience of war seemed to have been forged at a comfortable distance from the front lines was the uniform here.

I hated, hated, hated, I tell you, the mildly pervasive house 'smell' - a faint perfume wafting throughout the place, redolent of generational conquest, privilege, grand theft, petty intrigue, bergamot, tasty pastries, and…centuries. It hung over the whole place like a fog. The armies upon armies of cleaning staff could not wash it out.

This was all before 'one' had to deal with the stultifying minds and personalities of the Buckingham Palace mandarins. The prospect of another social gathering in this setting was always daunting and exhausting, in advance. But today, the additional obligation of being 'on the program' as a speaker was what had me sweat like a prize pig at a barbeque, over and above the standard agita these events imposed.

So, I took a moment, to collect myself. And to stop, quite literally, sweating the small things. Things like 'being on the program to speak'. I tugged down the cuffs on the suitably blah shirt I had worn for this occasion and checked that the geometric Ndebele art cufflinks Seydou had gifted me were just so. With the appropriate weight of misgivings and apprehensions weighing down my shoulders, I prepared myself to enter, once more, unto the breach, and kill it. I need not have bothered with the affirmations.

***

My personal assistant, Naz, spotted me or, more accurately, they sensed my entrance into the room and bounded towards me with the purposeful velocity of a premium racehorse, in all their non-binary gender glory.

"Heya, Boss!" they said, with typical enthusiasm.

"Hey Naz…"

"Are you ready?"

"When am I ever ready…for anything?"

"NVM," he said, in true zoomer fashion and led me into the maw.

To call Naz merely my personal assistant was to pay them short shrift. They made sure I had my shit together, that I was free of worry, and that I was sufficiently caffeinated. They were also a constant ray of sunshine that permeated the hushed tones, performative modesty, constant bowing and scraping, and other environmental motifs of the dungeon-like warrens that officed the senior Household staff. It felt good to have a brown-skinned fellow traveller in that world.

In the office, Naz was like a wild, young stallion let loose amongst a stable of geldings long put out to pasture. They sported the exact same attitude and energy at work as I had seen when I was enjoined into playing in the junior staff's football league or attending the lively and raucous gatherings 'downstairs' in the bowels of the Palace. I had even unwisely gone out on the town to the amusingly named pubs that were their redoubt, where they could cut loose, and cut a rug, away from their supervisors, and the possibility of one of The Family cruising the dank and unsuitable places, like the Ball and Cock.

The Palace still had not learnt how to process a masculine gay African man…so Naz was a further bridge that broke their brains. I appreciated, and loved, Naz. They non-verbally dared haters to talk smack and be ready to get slapped. No one talked back. They made me feel young.

***

I often wondered how I had ended up here. Sey wondered why I stayed. Or to quote him exactly, "Honey, why, why and why? Why do you insist on staying if you hate the institution as your bleating on about it would suggest?"

As to the former, Bjorn, settling into his then-new Senior Partner role at the boutique investment firm I had run emerging markets trading for, had asked…nay…told me to do it. It was an unstated condition of my promotion to the senior partnership tier that I 'do my three years' at the Palace. Something about how the partnership's access to the 'right people' required that one of us attend on the Windsors. Funny enough, it had never, ever been Bjorn's turn to eat shit in the name of 'client development'. Anyway, I took it on the chin. I was nothing, if not a compliant colonial subject, as Sey liked to say. Sey had that way about him. A way to just express things succinctly, pointedly … and frightfully accurately. I had no rejoinder…he had a point. Eight years later, I was still at the Palace.

As to the latter, all I had for Sey were facile, half-baked explanations that framed the whole situation a matter of cold, unsentimental career advancement.

Was it really for the pay? No. There wasn't much in the way of dinero from serving as…and I always have to check the title to get it right…the Keeper of the Privy Purse. The money was ok, but there was more to be earned elsewhere. I had taken a major pay cut to be here and, suffice it to say, the pecuniary benefit from this 'gig' was a piffling fraction of what I could be bagging in The City. Amongst the standing offers I had was a gig to stand up a London office for an offshore bank domiciled in Angora, helping people like the people in this room to fleece their fellow citizens. Then there was the 'Executive Vice Chairman for Government Relations' engagement for a deep-pocketed German investment bank, something that involved going to conferences in Davos to talk up petro-dictatorships and lobby HM's Government towards dodgy ends. The partnership also offered up significant pecuniary benefits, were it not that my presence there did not threaten Bjorn so much. There were ungodly sums to be made in any of those settings. Yet here I was, working myself to the bone for pittances and in service of an anachronistic institution.

So, was it the random and weird privileges? No. There is something to be said for being able to get in for free and ahead of the line at the Balmoral tour. And seeing Her Majesty descend from up on high to walk her high-maintenance corgis and dispassionately look upon her subjects.

Sey and I argued about the gig from the first day I reported for duty. Then after that, frequently and spiritedly. It was the only thing of substance we ever argued about.

He would say something like, "Babe, please do not insult my intelligence by telling me that it's about money. Just … don't …stop it."

I would deflect, gaslight, and project. Anything to not concede that he was right. But he was right.

***

I had already attended the more formal and somber farewell ceremony a fortnight prior. On sufferance. It was held in an ornate State Room, with an actual throne and the Sovereign sitting on it.

For that occasion, I had had to pull out and rock all the finery that came from nearly a decade of service or, as Sey would describe it, subservience, to the Crown. So out came the pins and the titles that had been bestowed upon me, the only one of which I could reliably remember was Lieutenant of the Royal Victorian Order, simply because I found the inherent irony delicious. I, a son of the African soil, descendant of the people Victoria herself had considered lower than mere chess pieces, was now here, with her descendants either playing nice with, or trying to strike up an acquaintance with, me.

There, I had endured an evening of small talk with a motley assemblage of senior Family members, the grandest of grandees, and perfumed popinjays. I 'circulated', hobnobbing and schmoozing with people who were addressed as Counts, CEO's, a physicist, a man of the cloth, and sundry notables.

Still seething at being passed over for Lord Chamberlain, I had to entertain inane conversation like, "Oh, is Malawi next to Mali?"

"No, Lady Chichester, Malawi is as far away from Mali as London is from Warsaw," I said, in my most placid voice, stifling my less politic, and caustic, wtf voice.

The word 'stifling' would capture my time at the Palace. It was a stifling environment that called for one to stifle oneself (again, referring to myself as 'one', sigh). Everyone down from the Sovereign to the scullery maids had to stifle themselves to exist and work in these spaces.

I thought about this place. My history in this place. My experiences. My connections. My unprecedented successes. My heart-rending disappointments. My place in this place…that was also a palace. I thought about the village in Mzimba. About the distinctly different bustle, industry and…life back home. I had yet to reconcile how I came from there to here. That kind of reflection was best left for retirement. Today, we 'get on with the job', as my masters, benefactors and social validators liked to say, as if 'the job' was chipping away at the coal face and not…being royal and entitled. I did not understand this thing. Why was this person, this family, this bloodline…chosen? Why did their tentacles reach so far as to reach our village?

I also pitied them in the same breath. I was not the first to describe them as goldfish in the most expensive fishbowl in the world. I feared that more time spent here would make me more like them: vestigial organs, in human form.

If I had neglected to mention before, I hated this place. I kept hearing Sey's pained voice.

"Bae…why? Why? Why do you still give those toffs the better part of you?"

I had no answer to that question. Sey had an unimpeachable point.

Seydou was a conceptual artist, which meant that he made beautiful, life sized, but odd, objects d'art.

I understood little of Sey's work when we first met and felt like I understood it even less now. He would putz around in our backyard for several weeks, emerging, like a lion spent from the burdensome task of hunting antelope, with something funky, and dare I even say it since I lack all aesthetic sensibilities...arty.

On the outside, Sey was built like a tank. On the inside, he was all gooey and soft, a fact Sey knew and protected from view except only to his closest friends. At home, Sey was a quiet presence. In social settings, he bloomed, becoming, for the night, a rapier wit, bon vivant and raconteur, especially when recounting the stories of his youth in Abidjan. He would regale and connect. It all redounded to my benefit.

On those nights, I had little to do other than be the arm candy as Sey regaled and charmed his way through the proceedings. Tonight, I would have to perform that social labour myself. Sigh, and groan.

***

I was not much of a public speaker. I was not much of a public anything. I loathed being the center of attention. If there was a stage upon which one --- there I go referring to myself thus again --- had to stand...I would rather set it to arson. Yet tonight I meant to do it, and to do it well. Once thrust upon the stage, I had to make a good show of it. And I had to pull out my best poker face so no one could tell how pissed off I was at being passed over.

Naz, ever attuned to my insecurities, broke into my reverie.

"Boss…you're on."

"Urgh…OK…let's go and slay this," I said warily, understanding that Naz would not let me go into the belly of the beast without sufficient warning or preparation.

Sir Michael had asked me to make remarks upon the occasion of his retirement. I owed a lot to the man, and so, despite my misgivings about public speaking and my saltiness at being passed over for the job he was leaving, I obliged.

Major General Sir Michael Phillips was, like me, a 'commoner'. He had risen fast and high in the Royal Marines and was on his way to achieving high command when, like me, his superiors had offered him up to the Palace. We had bonded as outsiders who were both not privy to the 'real' networks and the opaque rules of engagement that governed this doll-house world, and our indifference to the Kremlinology about this family. We both came to the job as a means of obtaining a promotion at our 'real' work, and both stayed at it.

A Geordie through and through, Sir Michael never shed his background, even as he mingled with the high and mighty. He was an unusual presence in that world. He was an abstemious man, stentorian in voice, burly in body. He did not suffer fools, gladly or otherwise.

So, I had prepared, to make sure my comments appropriately captured the man, and his long and tireless professional efforts. I had even reached out to his wife, Jenny, to obtain specific cute anecdotes about his life to deliver to the crowd.

I walked up to the improvised dais, an ornate wooden artifact that some community in India, or Fiji, or Argentina, or the Susquehannock Nation, or the various nations of 'British' Africa, was pining to get back, because it meant materially more to them than what it was being used for now.

***

I nailed it. I spoke about how he had mentored, supported and gloried in the professional achievements of his charges. I spoke of how he was a man of honour, a sage, a consummate professional...

"Sir Michael is a mentor, a guide, a judge, an advocate, a hard taskmaster. A kind, competent and visionary leader. He is, and I believe this is the first time this word has been said at such an occasion, a mensch. A good man all around. Father, husband, grandfather, HM's liege Lord of life and limb, boss, and…I hesitate to say this…friend…?"

I waxed rhapsodic, throwing out a litany of praise and platitude. I tossed out a bon mot here, some mawkish recollections of our work together there, sprinklings of war stories from our time slaving away 'under the stairs' at the Palace. I was vamping on the stage.

"I hope it is telling that I consider my professional experiences with Sir Michael to only be the second-best experience of my working career. The best experience has been to know the man. To get a measure of him and realise that the measure is full to overflowing. To know that, even in the honoured place he occupies in this rarefied constellation, he remains humble and down to earth. A Geordie through and through…"

I could see the old man tearing up. That was my cue that my work here was done. I wrapped up my comments.

"It is a singular honour to have Sir Michael as a boss, an honour to know him as a peer…and a privilege to be able to call him a friend…and not get decked for it."

At this the room erupted in laughter. I had practiced that closing line for days and was gratified that it 'landed'. This was the kind of crowd where 'dad jokes' landed, to rapturous laughter. It was not a 'tough crowd'.

I stepped down, relieved that I had pulled it off. Sir Michael hugged me, in a show of human emotion that he typically was uninclined to show. The other staff clapped vigorously as I walked to the back of the room, discomfited by all the attention, trying to shrink into my clothes. I was walking towards where Naz stood, when I was buttonholed by Vanessa Jones, one of the press wags who covered the Palace for a living and had had lucrative TV gigs under the job title of 'royal watcher'. She was here to fish for the latest juicy gossip to throw out to her readers in the Murdoch-trash-media-industrial-complex, like chum to a shiver of sharks.

"Vanessa, I'm not biting."

"Aw c'mon, any comment on all these mishigas with the Family?"

"No comment."

"Ok, but…"

"Vanessa…no fucking comment."

There were material benefits to talking to the tabloid press. Great steak dinners and decent wine to be had from feeding the insatiable royal news tabloid gaggle. They were a permanent presence on the edges of Palace life, trawling for some fresh dish on the royals, frenzying over the latest Baby Watch - apparently, now a proper noun – and spilling an inordinate amount of ink on the latest installment in a series of breathy takes on unborn ducal spawn. I found their obsession disquieting and creepy. I also just couldn't be arsed. The whole ecosystem was tedious, tawdry, and toxic.

"I'll get you yet. Nice speech by the way," she begrudgingly granted.

"Good to see you, Vanessa. I've got nothing for you."

"So…nothing for me? Really?"

"You are asking if I have some vile and vapid vituperation delivered in velvet prose and dulcet commentary on clearly biased public news forums? Would I be willing to engage in that? You know my answer, Vanessa."

"I'll get you yet, mate…"

Naz noticed the situation and scurried over from across the room to rescue me.

"Nice speech, Boss. Vanessa, kindly sod off, would ya?"

Always polite, that Naz.

***

The speaker who followed me was quite something. And by 'quite something', I mean not a lot.

Lord Llewellyn was a doddering old fool who had all the right breeding and connections, but not the smarts to punch his way out of a wet paper bag. The junior staff rather unkindly referred to him as Lady Lew behind his back, an allusion to both his obvious homosexuality, and his hilariously strenuous attempts to suppress any signs of it in the office.

As a card-carrying sodomite in good standing, I was, of course, privy to the more spicy and salacious details of his 'weekend life' from the well-sourced and efficiently distributed bulletins Sey occasionally stumbled upon in the gay whisper circuit of London. It did not help that his assigned nickname in the landed gentry's amusing habit of 'endearing' diminutives, was Lynnie. I had once heard someone describe him as a human harrumph, as apt a description of someone as I had ever heard.

His family line, unfortunately in his telling, ran on all the wrong sides of the bed of the dalliances and romances of kings and queens. He was the product of a storied line of younger sons, cadet branches, furtive affairs, and morganatic marriages. The upshot of that provenance was an embarrassment of riches showered on the family by guilt-ridden fathers who would not formally acknowledge their issue, but rather throw passels of pounds at 'the problem', where a fatherly hug would have sufficed.

Lady Lew had a gloriously luscious mane for a man of his advanced age, with only the naughtiest flecks of grey daring to show themselves, on occasion.

As far as I could tell, the qualifications that he, or to refer to him by his 'appropriate' name and title, Lord Sir Llewellyn Pierre Bourke-Archer...the twelfth Lord and Master of The Harrowgate Commons, Knight of the Most Noble Order of the Garter and on and on, had 'earned' to possess his exalted positions was merely emerging, alive, whole, and male, out of the right womb. That was Lord Llewellyn's CV. He had begged to be in Royal service, treasuring the ostentatious livery and servile attention he got from people for providing servile attention to The Firm.

And now this man, only fit for service as Master of the Household, organizing parties and tending to the laundry and linens, was being handed the top job ahead of me, and many other more qualified people. I was instead offered the role of principal private secretary to one of the young Princes, an offer I peremptorily rejected.

Apposite to that, Sir Michael had been dragooned into the Household's service by his superiors in the Royal Marines, an experience he often analogised to being swallowed by a black hole. Duty was his calling card. Entitlement was Lord Llewellyn's.

Sir Michael had once memorably said of Lord Llewellyn in a private moment, "Even in his prime, Lew was never *at* his prime."

The contrast could not be starker. Sir Michael had to be forced to accept a fancy grace and favour house that the insiders thought more befitting a former head of the Household than the humble cottage he had saved for with Jenny, who was even more down-to-earth than her husband.

Lord Llewellyn, on the other hand, swanned through the Palace, attended to by a coterie of fawning assistants whose job functions, other than making Lord Llewellyn feel regal, were obscure to the rest of the Household. And in his leisure time, he repeated the routine at home, lording it over his own considerable household. I had once taken Lord Llewellyn up on his offer to visit his house for the weekend. It was not anything that any ordinary human being would recognise as a 'house'. It was a vast and lush country pile, itself a dwarf of the main family seat occupied by Lord Llewellyn's older brother, the Duke of something or the other.

Once there, I spent a depressingly foggy and soggy weekend, drinking dank ales and indecently expensive wines, and pulling on nasty cigars in the proverbial smoke-filled room. My hunch was that the experience was designed to exorcise the unacknowledged psychic toll of days spent shooting innocent, unsuspecting animals in the face, for sport. Bollocks on top of bollocks, served with a side dish of bollocks, is how I would describe that experience.

I was upset at being passed over for Lord Llewellyn, keeper of clothes and costumes. I did not understand why, other than me being Black, and African, I did not qualify for the 'top job'. The establishment could appreciate my labours on their behalf, but heaven forbid that I rise to the top. But I was not one to wear my feelings on my sleeve. Far be it for me to satisfy people's stereotypes by being the 'angry black man'.

***

Lord Llewellyn cleared his throat so dramatically that he expectorated. And then he mumbled stuff, in an accent too rarefied to even be called Received English. He went on, interminably. His speech was a damp squib, and all were happy to get to the end of it, most of all the person delivering it.

The speech, such as it was, was a synecdoche of the poor wisdom of appointing such a spent force to such a demanding role…and of the unspoken social factors leading to the passing over of the man standing front and centre to where the old man floundered at basic communication. A lifetime of trite and banal pleasantries in country garden party banter did not translate well to rousing speeches in front of audiences that lived out in the world.

Despite, and in spite, of all this, I played my part. Gregarious, indifferent to slights, pretending to not be bothered when one of the Family referred to me as "the black one". Being passed over inexplicably for a walking scarecrow. It was not about my race, they all sought to assure me. They could not proffer any other sufficient explanation. I pretended to believe them.

Sir Michael reluctantly took to the stage to deliver his remarks. He passed out the requisite thanks and platitudes. He was surprisingly loose, for such a laconic fellow. He extemporised and kept the audience rapt as he reflected on the meaning of duty and service, before turning to address me directly.

"Young man, of all the people I have worked with, I have the utmost respect for my military peers…and you."

It was my turn to stifle a tear. I knew where he was going to go next. He had told the story to me before. He recounted the job interview he had subjected me to. He noted how recalcitrant I was. How so obviously not into it I was. And then he got to the punchline. I remembered the verve with which I had blurted those words out.

"I am a republican!"

"Well," Sir Michael said, swirling his snifter at just the appropriate time, in just the appropriate way, "he didn't so much say it to me as he barked it at me."

More soft laughter ensued.

"I asked him to sit, offered him some tea, and suggested that we start with his CV instead and maybe he could approach our future work with less 'Mau Mau' energy. And I was sold, I told him to report to the Palace for work ASAP. Sotto voce, I admitted to him that I, too, was a republican."

More requisite laughter issued forth.

"This young man is the future."

Then he lowered his voice, "He is our future," he pronounced gravely, lifting his finger up for effect. "Of all (and here Sir Michael paused for effect), and I sincerely mean, all the people in the Household I have worked with, he is the cream of the crop."

Here, the laughter in the room dimmed noticeably. The audience whispered at this rather naked and brazen put-down of Lord Llewellyn, who was standing right next to me. He steamed. I cringed. We sat there, stoic, stewing in our mutual discomfort. After he had got that uncharacteristic jab at Lord Llewellyn, Sir Michael concluded the rest of his speech with the standard pablum of farewell speeches.

"The monarchy. The monarch. The family. The establishment. All of us. We represent the absolute best of this realm" etc. etc. etc., all of which the audience politely clapped to, as I resisted the overwhelming physical need to roll my eyes back all the way into my cranium.

The speech ended with the requisite exhortation to "just get on with it". Someone at the back of the room launched into a badly sung -even by the standards of that drunken celebratory standard - *For He's a Jolly Good Fellow*, followed by some insipid hurrahs, as can only be delivered by people who had drank too much of that witch's brew they had in the snifters.

Why was I even here?

I had brushed up against, boned up on, and tried to game the invisible rules of power, relationships, and politics in the Palace and yet I knew that I was fated never to get the whole labyrinthine maze. I had thought I could navigate the bullshit and come out of it with a great career, some fuzzy 'cache' and my sanity. I had only obtained some nebulous 'cache', losing both career and sanity in the process. I preferred the more visible rules of power, relationships, and politics out in the normal workplace. In the Palace, there was a formal Order of

Precedence for both the family and the household…and then all these other informal rules.

That was Sey's fundamental question: Why was I working in spaces where people referred to me as 'the Black guy'? I had no good answer before the event, and even less so afterward. I said the requisite farewells and excused myself from the gathering.

***

Minutes later, a sleek grey Jaguar pulled up to the receiving area and a door was opened for me by a uniformed page. These were the few perquisites of the job. Pages and Jaguars. I collapsed into the back seat, unresolved questions about my life purpose swirling in my head. It was the better part of an hour before the car alighted on the driveway of our cute little countryside fixer-upper cottage.

I knew that, per custom, Sey had cooked anyway. Sey laughed risibly at the idea of palace retirement party food serving as 'dinner' for an African man. Before I had left for the office in the morning, he said, in his inimitable way, "Man shall not live by canapés alone, but by whole fried fish with cassava and bitter greens. Man shall not find those things deep in the bowels of Buckingham Palace. Those things are to be found back home."

I found Sey lounging in our favourite chair, in deshabille, as was his wont at the end of long days spent being creative. He did not look up from his reading, continuing to inhale the massive tome he was reading.

"Hey babe…" I hesitantly said.

I gave him my best puppy dog look in inadequate recompense for my not following his advice - writing a resignation letter, packing up our few belongings, and returning to the motherland.

Sey looked up and smiled. He knew that come Monday, I would not be wearing a power suit to deliver my resignation in huff and indignation. He looked at me for a long time, dropped his eyes, sighed, and made for the bedroom.

"You realise what day today is?

"…www…well…is that a trick question? Today is Wednesday. Did I forget something?"

"Here's a clue…ten years…"

I was stumped. It was not a birthday or anniversary that I was aware of, and I was primed to remember such anniversaries.

Sey, the fatigue in his voice palpable, snapped back, "The calendar? The calendar where we marked this date ten years ago?"

It immediately dawned on me. He had the calendar on his office desk. On that calendar, we had both marked this date, in this year, as the date by which we would have wrapped up our lives and careers in the UK. The other thing marked on it was our two countries of origin, with a question mark symbolising the unresolved part of the plan: where we would live. Sey then pointed to the same date three years hence, where he had simply written 'Abidjan'.

"That's where I will be this time. I hope you can be there with me. When these toffs release you from your gilded prison, I would like to have you back. I'll get your pajamas."

I smiled. Once again, I had a reprieve that was only as good as how good my next streaming selection would be, so I scurried to the remote.

"You better pick something good to watch on Netflix. No Palace dramas, thank you. I think we have had enough of that," Sey said as he made his way upstairs to attend to my basic needs.

I took a moment. To reconsider the day. To reconsider my career decisions. To reconsider this improbable life. To reconsider my priorities. For Queen? And country? What a fat bag of bollocks. Seeing the disappointment in his face tonight, I had started penning that resignation letter in my mind for the first time. It would take some time to extricate myself, but not three years. I owed Sey, and myself, that much.

Then I busied myself about the urgent business of trawling our Netflix queue for something 'good'.

## Leaving Las Vegas

The long-abused cell phone, tattered boarding pass, and other sundry detritus came streaming onto the filthy TSA inspection table in involuntary compliance with the brusque airport security guy's demands that Zi empty all his pockets. So, he emptied them, right down to the last speck of months-old bubble gum. The authority-hound, a bulldog whose mien and bearing seemed a tad excessive for the situation at hand, dug into every little thing, turning everything inside out in a way meant to denigrate Zi's basic humanity.

"Sir, I'm gonna need you to turn off that phone, right now," snapped the gussied-up mall cop.

Before being harshly commanded to turn the phone off, Zi noted the pings of several texts, missed calls and emails. He turned the phone off and handed it to the government agent. He would get back to those messages once he had cleared security.

***

Awaiting the eventual end of the agent's unduly thorough search of his effects, Zi recalled the odyssey that had brought him to this point. MMQ-ORT-ATL-JFK. Malaika-Johannesburg-Atlanta-New York City. The week that had elapsed from then to now felt like a dog's lifetime.

"Really wish I had listened to John," he rued to himself, referencing his more sensible Prime Minister's Office colleague's entreaties that they stay in the hotel booked for them at Atlanta's Hartsfield-Jackson Airport for their 6 am connecting flight to New York.

"Let's check out the sculptures in the other terminal, maybe a couple of drinks, call it a night and catch some zzzs," John had suggested in his typical maturity. John was a boring man, as his name hinted at, and mighty proud of that – it had served him well in life.

Zi agreed to wander amongst that airport's epic collection of Shona sculptures, an experience that always sanded off the edges of the colonoscopy-like experiences of intercontinental travel and airports. And he agreed to indulging John's passion for vanilla milkshakes, a passion John came to in his early fifties. John was like a baby when he had two milkshakes, they sent him into a near-sugar coma, and so he excused himself early.

"My brother, the night is a new-born, let's live a little!" Zi said in his best cheerleader voice, knowing that the much older man would most likely politely decline.

***

There was a whole night to burn before the NYC flight and Zi could hear the bars, strip joints and clubs of the Southern Mecca calling his name. Also, the moment he hit 'post' on his Instagram picture standing next to a sculpture of a buxom lady, his Atlanta friends started blowing up his phone and mentions. So, he wandered out, solo, into the balmy Atlanta night, ready to delight in its famous pleasure dens, immortalised in a thousand and one hip-hop music videos.

At that moment, Zi had available to him an entire universe of possibilities that would not have ended with the Premier turning up, in the flesh, with the Deputy Mayor of Atlanta to spring Zi from a holding cell. In hindsight, those voices calling him out into the night were decidedly not emanating from the nebulous 'City'. They were in, and from his head. So, the things that happened that raucous night in Atlanta had happened. It was the kind of thing that personal brand or image management cognoscenti would technically term 'not a good look'.

Zi's crowd had not started the fight that spilled out onto the disgusting, piss drenched back street behind the bar. In fact, Zi didn't even hear the original racist epithet that initiated the melee. By the time he came back from the pisser, things had devolved into impugnment of genital endowments, 'yo momma' taunts, and headbutts. Once battle was joined, though, they took to their self-defence with gusto. Blows and bruises were handed out and received, in equal bloody measure.

Once sprung from lockup, Zi was sternly instructed to leave town, leaving his battered friends behind in the gulag-like conditions the 'land of the free and home of the brave' loved to consign people to for minor infractions, priming them for the shakedown that was 'cash bail'. Unfortunately, the benefits of high political patronage did not extend to them. The Premier banished Zi from the UN General Assembly delegation and ordered him to take his vacation early. Essentially, go to the corner and think hard about what you did.

Letting down The Premier was always a wrenching experience because the man was incapable of anger, only of deep disappointment. And if Zi's stunt du jour was especially bad, he would drizzle a soupçon of "what would your dear late father think?" on top of that guilt salad, knowing well that any invocation of both Zi's late father's prized memory and his high hopes for his promising, but wayward son was sufficient to chasten Zi for a few months. He felt duly chastened.

But, whatever, no use crying over spilt absinthe, right? Hence, he had found himself headed for Las Vegas four whole days earlier than planned. Zi promised himself he would not hear voices of the night calling him out there.

"Yeah, right," said the voice in Zi's head, not sounding at all chastened.

***

The Premier had a lot on his hands. His Excellency, the State President, and owner of all things in Malinze, was away for three months, putatively, on one of his increasingly frequent overseas sojourns. He had taken a new wife and meant to show her the world.

The new First Lady was a recent upgrade and had all the looks and features typical of the women His Excellency liked to cadge away from their spouses to service his need to feel young. Bouffant hair, ostentatiously garish 'African' prints crowned with sky-high shoulder pads, and altogether too much eau de parfum and powder. She skated about on impossibly high Louboutin pumps, drawn from her reputedly vast designer shoe collection, which would make Imelda Marcos envious, legend had it. It all looked architecturally impossible that she could walk in those shoes and not stumble.

Every once in ten years, His Excellency liked to upgrade to a newer model, and when last that happened, she drew the dubiously lucky straw. The prior, superannuated First Lady had recently had a divorce settlement foisted upon her before being consigned to the sidelines whilst the latest model had her turn in the lights. And she was an actual fashion model, albeit indecently young compared to the old goat who was always pawing at her on national TV. She combined naked ambition with the common sense of a child. It made for a heady brew of tone-deaf moves. Shopping junkets to the fashion capitals – London, Paris, Milan – and all similar global points between, betwixt, and beyond.

State House apocrypha and accounts, passed along on WhatsApp like samizdat, claimed that residence staff had overheard Her Imperiousness utter the words 'let them eat cake' when there was a brief shortage of the staple maize meal. The story was quickly picked up by the online scuttlebutt outfits and an inevitable meme to feed WhatsApp group chats worldwide was born. Incidentally, a well-known Italian fashion designer and maven of the global jet-setting elite had started to 'summer' at a Lake Malinze resort, not because of the pleasant weather, but because they wanted to be close to their cash cow. She would turn up at some blighted locale or the other, in incongruous fineries, motorcade in tow and her skin lightened by illicit 'pharmaceutical' products to within an inch of still being considered negroid.

It was just as well that she had His Excellency's attention. Entire adults had been born since 'His Excellency' had mentally checked out from governing. The resultant national tailspin looked set to be finally arrested by the strenuous exertions of The Premier, the only Malinzean who had both the independent political status and nous for His Excellency to consider a peer and listen to. His Excellency always paid due respect to The Premier's work remediating the effects of His Excellency's rule by repeating to all and sundry what the Premier's basic philosophy was: "There's work to be done."

Into this mix, came Zi, causing problems.

***

Thus, one week after the clusterfuck in Atlanta, Zi finally found himself launching into the snaking trajectory back home to Malaika. He looked at the sheaf of papers showing his full path. The first leg, LAS-JFK, was about to take off in a little over two hours. Zi arrived at the airport happyish but was now starting to get annoyed at the airport security people. He travelled two hours back into his memory, to when he was getting into an uber to head to McCarran International Airport, after enjoying one final lunch and the attendant idle chit chat with Jack, with whom he had spent a decent chunk of his week in purgatory. Jack's presence that week had been a salve to Zi's mood and a welcome break from all the governmental drudgery Zi had been consigned to as penance for his sins.

Zi's mood had been low, generally. Although he had been the point man for the Premier in the preparatory committees, his antics in Atlanta had left him frozen out from all the key discussions related to the UN talkfest. Zi could only busy himself with the prosaic tasks of administration. Like clearing up his e-mail or responding to the anodyne requests of minor government functionaries or finally getting to addressing the copious marginalia that The Premier annotated any document presented to him, even damn expense receipts, with.

Jacques Johnson Bourgeois III was Jack's government name, the combination referencing the legendary African-American boxer, and Jack's Louisiana Creole-royalty predecessors, who liked to pass their high-falutin names on to subsequent generations ad infinitum. Jack hated the name, for its comically on-the-nose invocation of economic values he loathed and for the assumptions people made about him when they heard it.

"I'm gonna get this stupid name legally changed!" He would protest, loudly, each time the appellation made an appearance, even for such mundanities as presenting his credit card for payments.

Whereas Zi arrived in Vegas worn, harried, and spent, Jack arrived looking fresh and rested, like summer fruit at the peak of its ripeness. His already flawless caramel complexion was...glowing, even Zi had to admit it. This was mainly because Jack was fresh off a month-long stay at a 'wellness' facility in some beautiful part of Utah that was simultaneously blessed with pristine white 'Christmas' snow-capped mountains and intense sunlight all year round. It was a 'rich man's rehab', places where A-list celebrities and the well-heeled would check themselves into, and check out, in the wake of committing some embarrassing inebriated or drugged-out social faux-pas, leaving their public relations flacks to incredulously blame 'exhaustion' as a catch-all culprit for the excesses of their paymasters. Generational wealth meant that Jack got to dry out regularly at such Xanadus. This year, the recovery idyll selected by Jack's emotionally spent parents, was an Edenic place called, of course, Harmony Hill.

Jack copiously posted pictures of his time there. He was always attuned to his sacred duty as an 'influencer' to feed the insatiable beast of the social media engagement-industrial complex. His currency in that world was ever flashier 'content', dished out from increasingly 'exotic' locales with the discipline and dispassionate efficiency of a Model-T assembly line. His ravenous rabble of anonymous 'followers' demanded, nay, needed, constant reminders of vicarious 'lifestyle experiences' they would never themselves experience.

A well-composed image of him sitting cross-legged in yoga pose on a small hill, in pensive expression, staring out into the near distance as though entranced by an embarrassment of Oprah-esque epiphanies, trended worldwide that day. It garnered more 'likes' than whatever boilerplate the White House social media pages had posted that day about fundamental issues of life and death. Even Zi, a professionally jaded soul, had to relent and hit 'like' on the exquisitely curated images, followed by a trailing stream of heart emojis for effect.

That was Jack. He sold the dream, and he sold it convincingly.

Jack filled Zi in on the details of his most recent sojourn. Jack was eternally obtuse about the fact that his life experiences were not the norm for the average addict: Individual cabanas, hipster baristas serving gourmet coffee and tea, and an actual guru flown in from India were part of the course. The latest and greatest new wave rah-rah-rah about 'the hard work of healing' was served up, months ahead of when the plebian spirituality seekers would even hear of its existence in the canon. Jack had even found time for furtive assignations there, as always coupling his discarding of one addiction with the servicing of another. It was an entirely different world of empathy than that afforded the black and brown men Zi had made acquaintance of during his overnight stay as a 'guest' in DeKalb County jail.

And it worked, sort of. For about two months after such time-outs, Jack was a paragon of sobriety and productivity. Beyond that, things would always follow that familiar grinding path down to the next expensive treatment.

"I'm coming over there, or you meet me in Vegas and that's that!" Jack had bellowed into the phone when word reached him of my Atlanta misadventures and my semi-banishment by The Premier. Soft-spoken giant as he was, when Jack insisted on something, it meant it was going to happen.

"I'm already heading there, so join me," Jack offered. Zi groaned at the thought of the ostentatious neon signage, waterfalls in the desert, or ersatz miniatures of renowned world landmarks. Or any of the other signature markers of 'Vegas'. So, with misgivings about heading to the global capital of vice and coming fresh off suffering professional setbacks on the back of shady places, Zi took the gratis ticket, boarded the plane, and headed towards the devil's playground.

***

They ignored the lights, the loud noises, and the appealing 'sights', carnal and otherwise, of the city this time. They eschewed their regular vampiric existence and welcomed the beautiful dawns that were the natural spawn of early nights. Early nights wherein the wildest thing to happen was dinner followed by a couple of hands of poker. Vegas had world-class food by the plateful. Even some of the casino buffets were haute cuisine lite. The mornings were especially awesome when one bothered to leave the cacophonous Vegas Strip and enjoy the natural beauty and piercing sunlight of Nevada, trading in the dopamine hits of slot-machines for bird and insect song. In that bounty of early and energetic days of clarity, they traded in their inveterate cynicism for the pollyannish innocence of gawking tourists and fully embraced the Potemkin village that is Las Vegas.

That last day, they had lunch before Zi headed to the airport, just the two of them. They both behaved at lunch, involuntarily downing fruit juices in lieu of the regular stiff drinks. It was no easy feat. Jack was an area 'our guy', the informal, at-large, non-resident mayor. Jack always roamed with an entourage when in Vegas, many of whom Zi knew. To a man and a woman, they were all walking pharmacies, always loaded with, and on, various powerful prescription painkillers, drugs, and other poisons by the bagful. Opiates were the religion of the masses who clung to and flitted about Jack and his considerable money like barnacles to a ship's hull. Yet, to both the surprise and chagrin of those masses, Jack and Zi kept to their mutually assured sobriety. They elected not to indulge, which was an upgrade from their default setting: overindulge.

To make light of it all, they made sobriety jokes throughout lunch. They both agreed that the perfect accompaniment to the frisée-lardon salad appetizer was a tall glass of iced lemon water. They also agreed that the head-on shrimp in their main course looked too depressed to not be accompanied by a nice dry sauvignon blanc.

"Shrimp. They are such lushes…" quipped Jack.

Zi laughed his head off. Jack laughed his own head off. Thus, went lunch, a light affair, reflective of the rare sense of peace they were both feeling. It ended on a slightly sombre note with Jack expressing his concern about Zi returning to Malaika while the protests were ongoing.

"You can't work remotely for a while?"

"Not right now, but we think we're finally getting a handle on the problem."

"Are you sure you will be safe…?"

"I would tell you if I felt unsafe."

The two best friends hugged for a while, before giving each other 'dap'. The Uber to the airport pulled up alongside them, Zi jumped in, and Jack faded into the distance on the street curb. It had been a wonderful week, all things precedent considered. Something gave Zi disquiet about the week to follow.

***

Zi came back to from his fugue state to the jarring sound of the security agent still barking at him, for some reason not immediately visible to the naked eye.

"Sir, Sir, Sir!" The agent instructed in a hectoring tone that defeated the entire salutary purpose of the word 'sir'.

"Please gather your belongings quickly and move away from the security area!" He ordered, the 'please' performing so much labour in the sentence.

"Sir, please... blah blah blah," more gratuitous orders followed.

"I can't. I am arthritic. Birth condition, you see." Zi finally responded to the repeated provocation. He just could not resist needling the man's fragile ego. Bad idea.

He'd always been singled out for 'random inspections' by TSA agents, so this was old hat to him. The upshot of years of 'random' searches was that he had perfected his own 'civil disobedience' routine, down to a 'T' for days such as this one, when he was on time and could thus afford to put up a show. He performed a slow, deliberate, and ritualistic de-robing and then re-robing of his shoes and belts that would have put a Tokyo geisha to shame. He had time today.

Zi's non-compliance with the now irate agent's tactics drew more state police agents to him, like vultures descending on a rancid corpse. One would think they had found a reanimated bin Laden in Zi's laptop bag, the way they were huddled and chattering excitedly. Occasionally, one would emerge from the huddle to ask Zi a silly question, then return to whatever national security strategizing they thought they were doing. This was starting to be more than the usual harassment Zi was accustomed to in these situations.

"Sir! Please step into that room!" the guy thundered. A network of pulsing red veins resembling the Zambezi River delta was starting to crawl across his pale forehead. His minions moved in on Zi to emphasize the seriousness of the situation.

A humiliating body search ensued. Agent Temper Tantrum took it upon himself to personally carry out the ritualistic invasion of Zi's body. No contraband was there to be found. No explosive devices. No… that was never the point. The humiliation and cruelty were the entire point. The pretence that it was all a result of blind 'luck' was insulting in its disingenuousness. Zi made the mistake of mouthing off. That earned him an 'upgrade' to a highly invasive full body x-ray scan followed by a maladroit wanding with jabs directed at his short and curlies, as though he could fit a tactical nuke down there. The work of white supremacy could not be done unless the chap jabbed at Zi's holy of holies.

But he had to be wiser. He could not afford another international incident. The Premier would sack him this time. He knew when he was outnumbered and decided to withdraw from the drama and play the compliant subject. Sort of.

So out came the English grammar school accent and social graces. He acted out an award-worthy performance of apologetic regret about causing them so much inconvenience. He flashed the old ivories at the attractive middle-aged agent who seemed as flummoxed as Zi was at the extent of escalation. That seemed to do something. There was one more huddle, and he was a 'Sir' in good standing once again and allowed to go on his way. Having gathered his clothes and effects, he passed by the instigating agent.

"Thank you so much for your service, sir. You could at least have bought me dinner and taken me to a movie first, if you planned on getting this intimate with me," Zi quipped, a minxish look on his face.

A gaggle of old retired white ladies, clutching desperately at their slot machine winnings, giggled with a mixture of pure mirth and red-faced embarrassment at this exchange. Zi was extremely self-satisfied that he had got his own petty dig in where it stung his interlocutor. The look on the TSA guy's face as he registered the meaning of the nonchalant look on Zi's face as he said that was its own special, priceless reward. He looked about ready to rendition Zi to some 'black site' in an unknown corner of Poland. He spoke one more time at a safe physical remove from the uniformed goons, but within their earshot.

"Cosplaying at war coz they don't have the gonads for actual war…"

The old white ladies were now rolling on the floor, laughing. Zi had slaked his need to meet pettiness with pettiness. He winked at the agent and casually sauntered off, bathing in the rage he had induced on the Dollar-Store stormtrooper.

***

He had got his digs in but emerged from the tense exchange with the TSA supervisor highly irritated, anxious, and angry. He loaded a song on his playlist… just to obtain some measure of zen. DMX, poet nonpareil, barked a Nietzschean aphorism into his ear, "To live, is to suffer. To survive, well, that's to find meaning in the suffering!" The haunting tale of long dissolution followed by an awakened consciousness and a return to the normal world spoke to him, for obvious reasons.

His next route was JFK-ACC, New York to Accra, where he would now only be able to connect with the Premier's delegation at the closing plenary of the African Union conference, when all the interesting stuff was over. Then on to ACC-ADD, Accra to Addis Ababa, for his next assignment. From Addis, they would be ferried to Abyei in South Sudan on a UN transport, and then back to Addis after barely three days. He had no idea what to expect from that part of the trip. It seemed self-evident to him that helicoptering into a tense situation for three days was not the best way to address entrenched generational conflict. With Malinze taking over the annual chairmanship of the continental organisation, there would be trips like these to the infamous hot spots of the continent, marketing as a selling point the maintenance of relative peace in Malinze. He was always awed at the enormity of the work on their hands. They were not running a corporation; they were running an entire country. Serious stuff. Serious stuff wherein nothing was predictable, and everything was possible. Who the hell knew what was in store? The prospect of it was both intriguing and anxiety-inducing. He hoped he would acquit himself well, with wisdom, and make the Premier proud.

He had let The Premier down. That weighed on him. There would be a reckoning when he finally re-joined the team, and Zi was looking forward to it like an ulcer. Right now, he would happily have taken the ulcer. His anxiety at having to face the sangfroid wrath of the Premier was rising. That much was unavoidable. Jack had provided some useful heuristics for thinking through the situation, as a person well versed in disappointing father figures. Jack repeated what the nice counsellor at Harmony Hill had said to him about projection into the future being the source of psychological anxieties in the present.

"So, let's not, shall we?"

"Yes, we shall," Zi had responded, quietly.

After all, Malinze was a boring and peaceful non-entry in the Almanac of World Unrest. It was one of those African countries that 'behaved'. Not too much hunger, that didn't play well on TV. Just the right amount of conflict, enough that could fit in a five second news spot, and no more. Lions, friendly folk, mountains, and the lake was the country's brand. So, he knew that at least things would be well once he got back home. The Premier had reached a back-room settlement with the leaders of the protests, the credit for which the Premier dutifully delivered to the absentee President. The protest leaders had assured him of no more than three additional days of peaceful protest, to save face and to mollify their restive followers. That was the prevailing status quo, as Zi understood it.

***

Zi joined the tired masses ambling desultorily towards the boarding gates. He knew what they were feeling. Whatever one's background was, leaving the circus that is Vegas to go back to real life, whether that be child-rearing, meetings in skyscraper conference rooms or working the till at a big box megastore, was disorienting.

He thought about the news developments back home during the week he had been drying out in Vegas. Why was the coal mine on Malinze Island such a big deal? Why had religion vaulted over so many other bread and butter issues to become such an animating issue in only six months? From Zi's perch in the Prime Minister's Office, it was difficult to tease out the signal from the noise. Suddenly, people had acquired an unusual fervour for the belief systems of the Middle East. Ironically, the various peoples of the Middle East knew and cared nothing for the belief systems of aMalinze.

There was a proliferation of loud and brash American evangelicals, who seemed to see the country as a place to sell stale dogmas that had reached their sell-by date back in the USA. They found a ready market in the ruling classes. Certain strains of puritan Wahhabi Islam were gaining adherents, particularly amongst young men who found the staid religious observances of their parents insufficient to explain their persistently low status in the social firmament. All this added to the permanent push and pull of centrifugal and centripetal forces that buffeted Malinze – the global business interests, "aid workers", sex tourists, and such. The country was teeming with foreigners, and it was open season for strange and parochial agendas. The country seemed noisier. The air crackled with a foreign feeling. aMalinze had been defined by a congenital calm. But now ennui, anxiety, anger, rancour, and violence had seeped into the body politic, like a shot of poison into the national bloodstream.

Zi wanted to talk to the Premier about it, after the ritual raking over the coals was done with. He was looking across the chess board and seeing something thematically disturbing. A country being captured by non-state foreign actors. What he couldn't quite put his finger on was the why. Why Malinze? Why now? He would be home soon and be knee-deep in it. He passed a bookstore that had its TV turned on to CNN. They were saying something about Malinze. Before Zi could catch what they were reporting on, they turned to some 'news' about one or more Kardashians. And Zi tuned out. Messages and calls were accumulating on his phone. He planned to address them once he was safely ensconced in his window seat.

***

But it was one of those news days when the entire world seemed to be on crystal meth. The chyrons blurted out one shocking thing after the other. The news anchors were like flies blessed with a mound of waste in the heat of summer. They alighted on one story only so long before they just had to hop over to the next juicier one. The protests in Malaika had made the international news, but then only barely and briefly, wedged between several hot stories. After all, 'massive but completely peaceful protests in Africa' is not a news lede the media can do much with. A coup attempt in a central Asian country had raged hot only to just fizzle out. A fading all-American football player who hadn't taken well to being dumped by his social media celebrity girlfriend for a caddish British actor had attempted suicide. A prominent US 'family values' congressman had been involuntarily outed as gay...and more. And there was a breaking report of another mass shooting of an as-yet indeterminate level of carnage at some shopping mall. Such and such. It was gory. Zi averted his gaze. Then he noticed something else in the bottom corner of the split-screen being beamed live on the TV.

He noticed home.

***

"Please turn that on," he breathlessly instructed the bartender at the nearest sports bar in the terminal, pointing to one of the overhead TVs in the bank of screens showing sports coverage. CNN was featuring the Malaika protests and 'monitoring reports' from various sources. They even dispensed with the split screen and were fully focused on the story. The CNN correspondent was breathlessly trying to keep up with events.

Part of the throng had suddenly, and without warning, advanced towards the Parliament building. Then they breached the cordon line. The wide, large ornate entrance of the building could probably handle eight people entering abreast, but it was not built to handle a scrum of angry citizens. The door gave way. Scared parliamentarians and staffers rushed out in attempts to evade the marauding hordes. The CNN correspondent went quiet. There was nothing to narrate. No words could encapsulate what was happening. The chaotic spectacle narrated itself. The split-screen coverage alternated between the fortuitously close vantage point of a street-level witness cell phone camera and a longer panoramic shot that Zi surmised was being recorded from a window in the tony Michaels Hotel on the opposite end of Kwacha Park. The tension hung over the park. It begged to be broken. The authorities broke it.

The mass of protestors was set upon by helmet wearing and baton-wielding riot police, who began to administer a world of hurt on the protesters in blithely excessive ways. It was like a scene from some dystopian caricature of third world political chaos. Except it was live, and unscripted, and real. In his own country.

A commercial break came on, but Zi barely noticed what was being sold to him. He took the opportunity to check his now constantly beeping phone. There were messages and missed calls galore from family, friends, and workmates alike. The understandably rattled TV anchors cut into the commercial break midway to say, "Viewers around the world, we have to return you momentarily to Malaika in Malinze where an astonishing scene is playing out there in the protests by members of the Muslim community in that impoverished country…"

The crowd near the Parliament entrance had been pushed away, way back, back beyond Haile Selassie Avenue and the riot police were patting each other on their backs on a job well done when one lone figure lugging a nondescript object that Zi readily identified as a plastic grocery bag returned into the wide frame and slowly crossed the cleared threshold.

The shot zoomed in on the protester, dressed in basic shirt and trousers, not the 'Islamic garb' that most of the other protesters had worn. He launched into a brave solitary harangue directed at the riot police and the parliamentarians behind them, a cigarette wedged insouciantly at his lips. The riot police walked towards him with disquieting relish, truncheons at the ready. The young man was unfazed. He casually took something out of the plastic bag he had brought with him. Via the magic of HD TV, Zi immediately recognised the yellowish liquid in the full vessel as petrol.

Before the CNN crews could figure out what was happening on their live feed and just as the police bore down upon him, the young man made two quick movements. He picked up the bottle with his right hand, and in one fluid motion, sprayed some of the contents on the police now ringing around him. This stopped his flustered attackers for just a second, which was all the time he needed to splash the residual liquid over his own head with his right arm, flick the lighted cigarette at one of the terrified riot police with his left hand, and ignite the cigarette lighter that had also been in his right hand. The young man was engulfed in flames, as were the riot police ringing him.

Zi stood there transfixed and watched the screen with hand on mouth. The terminal public address system blared.

"This is the final boarding call for passenger Ziwani Kaunda booked on flight 342 departing Las Vegas to New York LaGuardia. Please proceed to gate three immediately!"

Zi did not, or could not, hear it.

"Final checks are being completed and the doors of the aircraft will close shortly. I repeat. This is the final boarding call for Ziwani. Thank you."

The notifications droned on and on, until about the sixth time, when Zi finally shook his head as if to physically clear the shock and confusion. Then he made to gather his things from a nearby barstool and head to the plane. He was not going to Accra from New York anymore. He knew that the Premier would not be staying in Accra either. Everyone would be finding the fastest way possible back home to Malaika. He would be needed. There was work to do. All hands-on deck.

He walked almost all the way to the exit…then turned back and went straight to the bar.

"Scotch neat, please. Matter of fact, make that a double."

Nothing like a live broadcast self-immolation to justify a jump off the wagon.

"Fricking shrimp. Such lushes…" he muttered to himself, in gallows humour.

The bartender handed it to him, and he knocked it back in one gulp. Then he ran out towards the boarding gate, which was just about to close. As the irritated flight attendants hustled him onto the plane, he heard the last announcement, "...end of boarding for Delta flight 342 now leaving Las Vegas for…"

***

## Nobuhle N Nyoni

Nobuhle is popularly known as uBu. She is a personal blogger; you may find her work on www.becomingubu.com. She is a self-published author and her first book is titled The Kings That Didn't Need This Queen and it's about the many relationships she went through in search of validation. In the final chapter she tells you why this was.

Nobuhle writes for change and shares lessons that she has learnt through making her own mistakes and therefore she jumped at the opportunity of being a contributor in Amanda Marufu's book titled 24 and Reclaiming.

When she isn't writing she is helping people brand their businesses and grow their social media platforms too. She does this via website design, social media management and graphic design. Connect with her via @becomingubu on Instagram, Twitter, Pinterest and LinkedIn.

## Just Ask For Help!

When I moved to South Africa I was 25. I had been tossed from one home to another all my life and I thought it was finally time to settle down and build what I would call my home. I imagined I would create my world, the very one I was denied back at home in Zimbabwe and prove myself to those who doubted my ability to survive this cold world. My determination was strong, but I had no idea what was waiting for me on the other side of the door.

In the first couple of weeks of being in South Africa, everything felt easier. I still had a little cash on me to do small things and it was great. Then the cash ran out and I was back to leaning on someone, my sister. My sister has a heart of gold, she understands how life works; today you may be on top of the world and tomorrow you may be right back at the bottom. If there is one thing she is amazing at, it is making you feel at home. Regardless of that, I was uncomfortable asking for even little things like airtime.

Here is why.

We lost our parents when I was 7 years old, making her 13 years old at the time. After their passing we were separated; she went and stayed with our aunt. I was at my grandmother's for a while before my uncle took me in. My uncle attempted to reunite us and it was great, but she could not get along with my uncle and so she left. The separation caused a major rift between us, because for a while I did not know where she was, then when she finally got in touch she was now based here in South Africa. Our relationship was never the same, so I was never sure if it was okay to ask for things, even when she said it was.

Dependency in general is a beast for me, because of past personal experience. Remember I mentioned being taken in by my uncle? He had two beautiful daughters and those are my loves. However, I had to watch them get their requests granted and mine being shelved. It was very painful and I found myself housing a lump of anger for most of my childhood. Then one day, I accepted that this was my reality. I could not bring my parents back and I had to suck it up. In the same breath, I vowed to never be dependent on anyone no matter what.

So here I was; in my sister's home, jobless and cracking my head on how best to get myself employed so I could make some coins. I would have sleepless nights trying to figure out how to make money. At first I tried to braid hair, but the problem was that I needed to go out and approach people. Those who know me will attest that I am not good at starting conversations with strangers. I freeze up, my tongue feels heavier, my words do not come out. So that was a fail before it even started. I was back in a jam.

My sister could tell that I was struggling, so from time to time she would make an effort to make me happy. From buying me ice cream to topping up my airtime and insisting that I let her know if I needed anything.

I moved out of her place a few months later, to cohabit with my then boyfriend. Boy was that an epic fail ladies and gentlemen! I may have hallucinated myself into a happy ending that was never coming my way. We stayed in Benoni and the residential complex we stayed in was home to many foreigners.

We started as very closed-off people. I remember one Christmas we went out and bought a few treats, cooked for ourselves and chilled watching television. The complex manager came and knocked on our door, and I will never forget what he said to us. 'Why would you hide yourselves indoors during a time when we should be coming together and celebrating making it thus far into the year. Come join us!' I wanted to decline, but I could not resist the genuine look in his eyes. It was a great day! We shared food, stories and we danced until we couldn't feel our knees.

On this very day, we created relationships with people who had our backs when we needed help and vice versa. It did not feel so lonely after that, I even started babysitting our neighbour's son. I don't know about you, but being trusted with a child is kind of a big deal to me. He just loved me, so it made it so much easier. I made a bit of money from this little gig too.

Keeping your business private is very different to keeping yourself completely closed-up and living in a foreign country teaches you this in one too many ways.

After man X and I went our separate ways, I had secured a very good gig as a blog manager and content creator for a UK based company. I was making better money and I could do life on my own, finally. I was very excited about my new journey. Man X had helped me with his old furniture as he was moving to a friend's place.

In the third month of living my best life, I got the shock of my life. It was payday and as usual, I sent out the invoices for me and the other writers I had recruited for the blog. Initially, my boss said he was tied up and would process payments as soon as he could. Then it became days of little to no communication.

You can imagine the anxiety that I was living in, not to mention that the other writers were asking after their money. Then I started digging up on this boss man, only to find scandal. First of all, he had lied about his name! He had also ghosted another person online without paying them. I also found out that he had paid another guy who worked for him, yet we were still waiting for our dues. This was a man whose brand was all about women empowerment; I should have known it was a scam! I then realised that I was in trouble and that my money was not coming. The money he owed me was meant to cover my monthly expenses including rent. I had never been more anxious in my life. Not only was I the only female in this communal home, I was also the only foreigner. Xenophobic attacks had just started in South Africa at the same time and I imagined how terribly things would go for me if I were to be thrown out. People were getting burnt alive and tortured.

I had to explain to the other writers what was happening, and I am thankful that they understood the predicament we were in. I went ahead and messaged the boss man, telling him that I knew he was a fraud. Just after I sent my message, he deleted all the work I had done; I am talking about all the social media accounts and the company website that housed all the articles that had been published! I however needed to make a plan for my rent, because my landlord was knocking on my door daily and I was tired of giving them excuses. The people I had built relationships with helped where they could. I had not spent all my money from the month before, so I was just a little short.

Just when I thought things couldn't get any worse, the only other client I had shut down their travel business because of the xenophobic attacks that were happening against Nigerians. The South Africans were angry because a Nigerian had allegedly shot a taxi driver. Nigerian businesses were looted, buildings were burnt down, and lives were taken. The Nigerians also retaliated and started looting South African stores in their country. The rivalry was really bad. I was depending on this client to at least get me through the month, but that went up in smoke. What miracle was I to work in 30 days? I could not do much, so I had to do the one thing I hated doing, asking for help. I wanted to pull my hair out. I remember lying in bed and contemplating suicide. It all felt very heavy and I felt like I was destined to be a failure. However, the love I felt around me stopped me from going ahead with it.

I called my sister and asked for her help. I was anxious but she said to me, 'It is not a problem, come and stay with me until you find your footing again. This is how life works and we have to have each other's backs.' I slowly started getting comfortable with the idea of asking for help when I needed it, the feeling of having someone ready to assist you in whatever way they can to see you happy is one that I had forgotten. I had gone through life asking and being made to feel like a burden and this was new to me. So I had to move again!

My sister was not the only person who was going to teach me this valuable lesson, the universe brought a stranger into the equation. Thank God for technology, right! I met Tory when I was deep within pain. I was lost and trying to find myself and I am grateful that he saw the real me. I met him when I was still with man X and I was a ball of anger, insecurity and fire. I would get stuck because I struggled with asking for help. I would tell my story and then wait for him to offer to help. I would get frustrated if he didn't and find myself lashing out instead of just communicating my needs. One day he said to me, 'You know if you ask for help I will help you when I can of course.'

I wanted to act stubborn, but I knew he was right. There was no way I was going to get out of the space I was in all on my own. He is the reason why I design websites today, because instead of throwing money at me every time I was stuck, he saw the value in teaching me a skill. A skill that till today puts money in my pocket. He also opened my eyes to other skills I didn't realise I had, some that I also offer as services today. Imagine if I had shut the door when he did not do what I felt was help, where would I be?

We have all met people who suffer from this problem that I am still unlearning. I would like you to know that asking for help does not make you weak, it does not mean you have failed. It simply means you have reached a point where you need an extra hand to get to the top of the hill and it is okay. May I also point out that you didn't wake up and become this person, some events led you into this cage. There are many reasons why people end up here, but most link back to childhood experiences where the adults in their lives constantly tell them they are a burden or refuse to acknowledge their needs.

'You were a mistake anyway, now you are costing me extra money!'

'You are always asking for things, do you think money grows on trees?'

'I cannot wait for you to leave my house, I am tired of you."

These words stick with people and harden them to a point where they never want to need anybody else ever again. I have met people who would rather suffer, go hungry or be homeless before they ask for help. They vow to themselves that they have what it takes to save themselves no matter the situation. Determination is one thing, being stubborn is another. Nobody is designed to carry all that weight all on their own, but the scars run deep. I eventually had to learn that all those times someone made me feel like I was a burden, it did not reflect on who I was, it reflected on who they were.

I was a child who needed help and guidance and my carers chose to be cruel. I realised there was no need for me to hold onto it any longer. The strength I thought I was showing was just weakness and it was weighing me down. The complex in Benoni I previously stayed in had Zimbabweans, Malawians and Nigerians and I saw Ubuntu in practice. A group of five young men stayed in one apartment, they called each other brothers. I thought they were related by blood, but they were not. If one could not afford the rent or electricity that month, the others would cover for him.

I was shocked the day I found out that they all met in South Africa and because they were all Malawians, they stuck together. I saw this pattern with Zimbabweans and Nigerians too. Today I want you to know that it doesn't matter where you go, you will always need help from people. It is impossible to survive all on your own. You will at some point need a hand and there is nothing wrong with that. Again, I say it does not make you a failure, it doesn't make you weak, it makes you human. In Africa, our biggest magic trick is Ubuntu, which means, 'I am because you are.' We are each other's strength.

## What It Means To Be a 'Foreigner' In South Africa

The South Africa I heard of from my little sisters sounded like heaven; every time they visited they came to tell me about how different it was in this country. Of course, they only sold me what they got to experience, the nice food, the nice restaurants, the green grass and the affordable fashion. If we are being honest, they had me at food and fashion because a girl got to look good whilst well fed. I suffered from FOMO - Fear Of Missing Out - and at the time I did not have a passport, so it was just a dream.

When I eventually got my passport, you know who would not stop thinking about travelling to South Africa? This girl! Before sleep stole me every night, I would find myself fantasising about my time in South Africa, I also started saving up for the trip. I would spend time on the Mr. Price and Legit websites planning to buy things that I didn't have money for. I saw myself in the best restaurants, the type that I saw Instagram influencers in. Listen, my imagination went as far as me meeting a fine boy and it ending as a sad love story because I had to return to Zim.

Yes, I laugh too when I think about it!

When it was finally time for me to visit, l could barely sleep and this was due to two things, anxiety and excitement. I was going to be travelling alone and I had no idea how it would turn out. On the bus trip into SA, I did my best to not lock eyes with anyone in case they picked up on my fear. I imagined they would trick me into handing over my money and phone, so how about we just avoided it altogether. The trip was refreshing, I remember crossing the border and the first thing I saw was green grass. I wanted to message my little sisters and say, 'You were right, it is so green!' That tells you enough about what we have back at home. Yikes!

My anxiety shot up to a thousand when I got off the bus and walked into Park Station in Johannesburg, there were so many people. Most of them looked very dodgy too! If there is one thing that has always been a topic when it comes to South Africa, it is the crime rate. All I could think about was getting out of that place, then my phone ran out of battery ladies and gentlemen. Fear gripped me hard. I could not cry because that would attract attention, so I continued to put on a brave face. I had to, but where was this woman I called a sister? An hour or so later she arrived, and I just wanted to go home!

This encounter made me realise how brave my sister was to live in a city so packed with people, a city with so many dark corners and in each one you could see a group of people at the far end in rolled-up woollen hats. The city centre had more vendors than I had seen back at home; where were the nice places I had heard of? It felt like I was walking into a movie scene where I was guaranteed to be robbed. I held my breath and kept to my sister's side until we got to the taxis, then off we went.

My first experience was different from what I had been told by my other sisters. I tried out a Kota and I say this delicacy needs to be protected. A Kota is basically a quarter of the loaf of bread, it is hollowed out and then filled with French fries, Russian sausage, cheese and sauces of your choice. When I say carbs are heaven this is what I mean, such a filling and tasty meal and my little sisters knew nothing about that. I learnt that you are better off leaving your phone at home if you would like to have it longer. I went shopping and for the first time, I got dizzy because the choices were too many! I walked in a mall until I was sure I would wake up with blisters on my feet. It was my experience and I went back home with a story, but I was so young and so much reality went over my head. I didn't see through the cracks until later.

I would hear people speak of xenophobia, but for some reason, it did not sink in. I could see how this was problematic, I could see the cruelty of burning another person alive. But when I heard of it, all I prayed for was that my sister would be safe, and I didn't care to dig deeper. I didn't realise that this was a very big thing that would continue to affect Africa. It did not occur to me that the actions of those that came before us had dug a hole for my people. My excuse is that I was a child!

My semi-permanent move, because I do not think this is my final destination, exposed me to who I am in this country. To South Africans, I am the reason they don't have money in their pockets, I am the reason their applications are always denied when they apply for jobs, I am the reason that they are poor, I am the reason they cannot provide for their children. I am also the reason there is a high crime rate in their country. My nationality brings them so much sorrow and anger. I am not a fellow African in their eyes, I am an alien they would like to zap out of existence. As a Zimbabwean, I do not deserve freedom, a job or peace in South Africa, I do not belong here.

I once went to get my nails done at a salon and everything was fine until I was asked the one question we all dread, 'You are not South African, are you?' The chit chat we had before died, it was as though there was a wall that was placed between the stylist and I. I could tell she was uninterested in finishing the job, as though the hands she had complimented before were now a disgusting sight. I was very uncomfortable. I wanted to ask questions but realised I was the only 'foreigner' in the salon at the time, so I let it go. That encounter made me realise that the hate South Africans have towards us runs deep.

When you watch the news and you hear the vile things they say about us, they are not joking, they are not sorry, they mean them. Their anger sits with us. In 2020, just as we were pushing the hashtag #ZimbabweanLivesMatter on Twitter, South Africans started their own which read #ZimbabweansMustGo and with each tweet, I felt my heart die a little. I read things such as, 'Zimbabweans life must matter in Zimbabwe, not in other countries,' and 'Foreigners must go home and fight for their countries and stop being cowards. Their being here has magnified all our social ills, even the blind can see.'

Tweets from people I did not know had me feeling unsafe in my walls. I do not encourage you to search for this hashtag, it guarantees you so much heartache. At this point I want to give props to our colonisers, they did an excellent job of turning us against each other. The amount of black on black hate that exists is not by mistake. It was carefully planned and laid out for us to bite, and here we are today killing each other. Imagine setting someone alight and singing and dancing as you watch them scream and cry for help. How can you watch them burn to death and then head home to sleep with a smile on your face? A fellow black man? A child, a woman with a child on her back, all because you are convinced they are the reason for your troubles.

Let me walk you into the reality of this country.

When you walk into a restaurant on a Wednesday afternoon, the waiters and waitresses are black, the people behind the counter are black and in the kitchen? Also black. But when you look around to see who they are serving, 80% of the tables have white people. You will order and leave and they will still be seated, ordering without flinching. They can afford to turn the restaurant into their office for a full week if they want. The people waiting on them are being paid R2 500 as a basic salary -if they are lucky - plus tips. Some do not have a basic salary, the tips are their pay.

If you have a basic salary that large, you consider yourself highly blessed! To make ends meet you have to make sure to wait as many tables as possible, you may also need to work overtime. When it comes to overtime you get paid double the hourly rate, whatever it may be. Let's just say by the end of the month you have made between R2 500-R4 000, you have to pay your rent, buy food, put aside transport money, buy toiletries and take care of your personal needs. 30 days of slaving for coins!

When you walk into office buildings, the cleaners are black, the front desk manager or receptionist is usually a white person, in the offices, there is a mix of races. Sounds fair right? It is not! You will find that people sitting next to each other in that office space are doing the same job but are getting paid different amounts of money. I know a black person who shared the same position with a white person who barely worked, they offloaded their work on them. The white guy would get all the credit, and earn more money! Organisations pretend to be diverse for external support, but when you take a closer look you realise that it is all just a hoax.

I have a relative who has been working for a company for years as a tea lady. A position opened up in the company for a front desk manager as one of the managers had submitted her resignation. She applied for the role because she had the required qualifications. Her application landed her in a disciplinary hearing, where they told her she was overstepping boundaries. You can guess the race of the person they wanted for the role can't you? The disciplinary hearing was a reminder of where my relative belonged and that they should never repeat that. Imagine that!

I have only pointed out a few scenarios, but I know of more. The point I am making is that we are fighting one another for coins. Africa is rich, but we are here caged and working for our colonisers. We hate each other and call each other 'foreigners,' yet we never had these borders to begin with. Once upon a time, we were brothers and sisters, but all that melted away when we were colonised. Our anger is misdirected and yet it feels like nobody is trying to correct it. The hatred we hold for each other seems to be fuel for our leaders to do absolutely nothing.

Dear South Africans, Zimbabweans are not leaving home because they want to crowd any other country. It is because life is hard for them in Zimbabwe. They are just looking for a way out to provide for their families. Believe me when I say that I would have never left home if all was well, it had become tough for me. The Zimbabweans you fight are feeding a whole family back at home and paying school fees for children; they barely spend any money on themselves. Families have been separated because of the disaster that is the Zimbabwean government, so when you kill them you have stolen a breadwinner for a whole family. Think about that.

Why don't we fight for our rights? We have tried and you too have witnessed what happens to us when we try. How many times have you watched a video of people being shot in broad daylight, women being beaten down, children being chased when Zimbabweans voice out their opinions and their rights? How many times have you seen journalists and activists being arrested for speaking up against corruption? I know you have read the stories on abductions, and how both men and women are tortured for speaking against the regime. So you tell me, what should we do next?

Here is something else you may not know.

Every time there is a protest in Zimbabwe, the people who suffer the most are the poor. Those that stay in the high-density suburbs, the townships, are the most helpless and therefore they become targets. For days on end, the police will flock to their neighbourhoods, they will rape women and beat men up. They will punish them regardless of them being in their homes. Imagine watching your daughter and wife being raped right in front of you before they beat you to a pulp. The same police officers will come back around election time to remind you who to vote for. You would think they are paid good money for this, but they too live in houses that are one storm away from falling apart. They are just under command, so they do as they are told.

Do you remember when we said #ZimbabweanLivesMatter and we exposed the many injustices we have faced as Zimbabweans? Do you remember that the president came out and said that everything was fine in Zimbabwe, then they imposed a hard lockdown so that people could not protest? People went ahead and protested and they were arrested. Then we begged for the president of South Africa to help us and what did he do? Nothing! He instead sent our president's friend on a diplomatic trip to have some drinks and chat. Do you honestly think that your president has no idea of the state of our country?

Our leaders are here pinning us against each other, throwing in hints to make you believe we are the enemy yet we just want to be home. We want to return home, but what hope is there for Zimbabwe right now? Imagine if we forgot the borders and chose to come together and fight against all these dictators disguising their rule as a democracy. Imagine if we took them down and demanded that they leave so we could all live fair lives, so that we could all work and earn the money that we deserve. Education would be free again, hospitals would be functioning again, we could run big establishments and watch our dreams come true. I speak for all Africans when I say this.

I know this is just make-believe, but for those of you who may wonder what it means to be a 'foreigner' in South Africa, this is what it is. It means that when you are asked for your name, if it is not English or South African your heart is going to beat so hard it might fall out of your chest. It means that when you are asked to translate something into a South African language if you get this wrong, you might die. It means if you stay in the townships, you are better off paying your rent on time and minding your own business because you may be set alight for delaying the payment.

It also means you may die without seeing your family for years. Your dress code will have to change so you somewhat 'match,' with the culture; it turns out they can pick us out from our dressing too. Anxiety is your best friend because every single time you leave the house, you do not know what you will come across in the streets. Every stare you receive feels like death is looming. There is no peace in your heart, everything you do feels like a battle for freedom that will never come. Did I mention the anxiety that comes with publicly listening to Zimbabwean music? That makes you an easy target too.

I do not know if it will ever get better, if we will ever see each other as equals or as allies in this fight for our rights as Africans. It is my biggest wish that we take down the borders and come together as one to stand up for ourselves, to claim back what is ours and finally have the freedom we deserve. I hope one day South Africans will stop calling other Africans foreigners whilst advocating for those that were not born on this land. I hope for peace, love and unity.

## It's Not Always The Final Destination

I moved from home because I wanted better, I was searching for an opportunity and I believed it was waiting here for me. As human beings we are dreamers, we are planners, we also love having control over our lives. And I think it is the love of control that has us missing out on the lessons we need to learn, not to mention the opportunities that come our way. I had a plan, and that was to get to South Africa, get a job, work for at least a year, save up to buy event management equipment and go back home and take over the industry!

Solid plan huh, yet three years later I am still here. I was employed as a part-time worker for a total of weeks in those three years and as for that equipment, let's forget I ever mentioned it. My plan was an absolute flop, but the universe's plan seems to have worked out just fine and I can tell you this, I never saw it coming! My move to South Africa was for my personal growth, it was for me to find who I am and own it.

Let me walk you through the things that have changed since I have been here.

I was a wobbly Christian when I left home. I was raised in a Christian home and Sunday was church day no matter what. I remember this one time my brothers and I went out drinking, we came back home at 6am and we showered and got ready for church. Did we catch the word that day? Nope! But we were present, those were the rules. Even then, I wasn't sure if I was truly myself, I altered many parts of me to try to live up to the Christian standards. It didn't help that at some point I was given a leadership role in church, talk about pressure!

I am a singer. I wanted to be a superstar, but the pastors said, 'Every gift is for God's work so use it to glorify him.' I managed to force one gospel song out of myself and I cannot even remember how it goes. Every song I wrote was far from my Christian faith. I believe that music is a language, that it is meant to heal people, bring people joy and laughter. I saw no problem with secular music, but the church said all those that listened to it were going to hell because somehow they were being drawn into evil every time they listened to it.

I felt suffocated by the idea that everything I did in my life had to include God and give him glory. I often felt guilty for doing things that I enjoyed, or merely thinking about them. I couldn't dress the way I liked without being called in for a 'talk' by a church elder. I was an unhappy child, trapped in Christianity and in a cycle of trying to please society. I look back now and oh how I wish I had chosen myself over anybody else a long time ago! Over the last three years, I have had the time to reflect on all these things.

I have managed to walk away from Christianity and allow myself to just be. The hardest part about this journey was silencing the guilt and undoing the fear of 'burning in hell.' I listened to what I wanted, I spoke much more about the music I recorded, I wore the things that I liked and this was the beginning of my bloom. I never believed in 'praying for homosexuals so they could be saved,' and I finally stood up and said, 'Let them be, they are humans and have rights just like the rest of us.' I do not know if I would have gone through this change if I had never left home.

I learnt to trust myself, to believe that I can do whatever it is I put my mind to. I had gone through a series of failures that were always thrown in my face by my relatives back home. People do not realise the power of their words, but they hammered my failure into me so much that I started to believe that I was nothing but a failure for not living up to their standards. I was never meant to live up to their standards, I was meant to live up to mine. I was meant to fulfil my destiny, my purpose, my dreams. The time I spent alone searching for direction opened my eyes to my capabilities.

I wasn't meant for a 9-5 in a cubicle or a hospital as they wanted, it is not who I am. They chose to turn their backs on my skills and talents, when I pursued them myself they called me mediocre. They said I was headed towards a disaster and poverty. At some point I started to see it, I started to speak it into my life too. And believe me when I say, it is okay to close doors on your relatives too, toxicity is toxicity. I curate the energy I keep around me and I am no longer afraid to walk away from bad energy, if anyone tries to dim my light so they can shine I am out!

With every hurdle I face, I am reminded that I can jump over it and land on my feet. With every challenge, I see the strength that is in me, I see that I can go as far as I want to go. I am my limitation, not the world, and not another human being. My focus has shifted from trying to please people to making the change I want to see in the world. That is why I write, that is why I will sing, that is why I will speak when I am asked to. I am here on this borrowed time to make a difference, and my goal is to make sure it is done.

I started blogging five years ago. I had no idea what I was doing, I went with the flow, copied other bloggers and hoped it would bring me traction. It did not work. I did not have a voice, everything about me was just random and noisy. I moved from a random blogger to an angry blogger; every blog post was sad, dark, and painful. I was stuck in my past and I couldn't find a way out until 2020. This is when my healing process began, this is when I started reflecting on the things that hurt me and those that shaped me. I started questioning my beliefs and tracking where they were coming from. I faced my trauma, my pain, my ugly side and with each step, I wiggled my way out of a cocoon.

My writing has evolved since then. I shifted from the anger and worked my way to peace. I talk about my highs and lows, I tell people the things I have learnt and I help those that are stuck in the past to break free. I imagine if I was still home, surrounded by the same noise and pressure to be someone else, I wouldn't have found myself. As a matter of fact, I may have self-destructed from depression and anxiety. The journey of becoming, as I like to call it, is a never-ending one, and I know I shall continue to open up new doors for myself as I go, but I am grateful that I was awarded the chance to experience it.

I never got to graduate from a university like I wanted to, and that led me to believe that I was not as intelligent as those that did. I looked down on myself and I never dared to speak up in the presence of those that were capped. I felt like I belonged at the bottom and was worth way less than they were. I was very small-minded and I limited myself, on most days I thought I needed a miracle to make it through life. I was the miracle I needed and now I know it.

If you are reading this and you are just like me, let me remind you who you are!

You are your light, shine so brightly nobody can stand it. You deserve to speak up and voice out your opinions just as much, they are valid too! You can do whatever you want to do, yes you will fail but learn from the mistakes, get up and run your race. You are your own competition, your story will never be like the next person's so stop comparing the two. You get to cap yourself, but it will always be up to what you decide to do with your life. I say choose yourself, choose to do what needs to be done, choose to be brave, choose to be you.

My social life died when I arrived in this place, but I guess I needed it. I needed to figure out the things that were important to me. If you asked me what was important to me three years ago, being rich and successful would have been my first response, but not today. Today, I know that having the people I love and that love me for who I am is important to me. Sharing big and small moments with them is what matters to me. I know now that I do not need a designer shoe or bag to be counted. I just need to be myself and those that share the same energy with me will come around, those are the people that matter.

I finally understand that a simple life comes with more peace, and when you chase the things that bring you joy you are happier. I lost friends because of the changes that I made in my life and that is okay because in the process I gained those that align with who I am. I too have learnt to be a better friend, to respect boundaries and to love unconditionally. Healing from past trauma has also allowed me to see how I made it difficult for people to love me, I had to unlearn those habits and traits. This is not to say I am a perfect human being today, but I am a better one.

I know that my time in this country is almost up. The lessons I needed to learn I have learnt, and that is okay. I wrote this for those who are starting to feel like their time in a certain space is up and are doubting their feelings. Stop. Your conscience is never wrong; most times when we doubt it we find ourselves in trouble. Chances are the experiences and the lessons that were awaiting you in that space have passed. Do not be afraid to close the chapter and start afresh, because in doing so you are opening up a new phase.

I will not act like it is not a scary thing to do because it is, you are jumping into the ocean and hoping for the best. You are walking away from your comfort, and you have to shape a new one. Think about it this way, what if by not moving you are blocking yourself from your big break? Exactly! I for one am excited about the new chapter and I cannot wait to spread my wings and fly. I know it won't be easy for me, but I am not willing to pass up the chance of being happy and I know my big break is awaiting me at the next stop. I hope you find courage too. CIAO!

## Flavian Farainashe Makovere

Farainashe is a Zimbabwean born writer who fell in love with words at a tender age. A writer by day and a reader by night, he is passionately committed to daydreaming. According to rumour, when not writing he will be in the kitchen playing a wanna-be chef's role and creating his own recipes (or so he claims). His writing opens up a glimpse into his life, addressing African stereotypes through his experiences and issues as he strives to create a life that inspires others.

They found him alone. They found him ready to give up and let the water take hold of him after holding on for the whole night, but they found him. The excitement of being found almost made him want to let go of the thorny branch he had been holding on to the whole night, water reaching up to his shoulders. If only he had known, if only he had known that things would end like this. If only, then he would have learnt to hold his tongue. But did he have a choice?

***

It was a liturgical requirement on the program of service to at some point pray for all nations. The service on this particular Sunday was held at the Africa Unity Square. ‘Open service’ it was titled, a stone’s throw from the Parliament building. He read from the Holy bible, Psalms chapter 33: 12 to 22 and 1st Timothy 2: 1 to 6.

He closed his bible after reading and began “Like all other things of Divine Institution, prayer is commended by benefits as varied as the aspects in which it can be considered. It is our duty and only symbiotic element or mode of communication between our almighty Father and us.”

“Our Lord Jesus Christ has mentioned that it is a privilege for us to speak to our Lord, for God to supply our daily needs. It is necessary for the full heart to find some mode of utterance, a happiness for in prayer we enjoy that Holy matrimony from our Heavenly Father through Jesus Christ.” He paused and took a sip from the glass of water the usher had placed on the pulpit.

“On that note, we want to pray for those in authority, those nations that are suffering right now as I speak.” Pastor Lovemore Mavhura of the End Times International Ministries was on the rostrum.

“Father in the Mighty name of our Lord and Saviour Jesus Christ we come to you this morning, humbling ourselves as a nation and church. Your word says blessed is a Nation whose God is the Lord. Most of us in this nation are looking up to other things for fulfilment and completeness - forgive us Father. Prepare the hearts of those who don’t know you lord so that when your word is being planted in their hearts, they may turn from their wicked ways. We pray for the East and West, for the North and the South, including our own country Lord, that you may give us good governance.” He stopped as if something had taken over him, his body, his mind.

"Lord you choose and appoint Leaders for your people. Good and honest leaders and not greedy, corrupt ones who don't want to leave office and continue to suppress their own people. Those who cause suffering and pain day in and day out. Removeeeee! Remove them ooh Lord, those who are wicked and who kill for the sake of clinging to power even if the ballot box has spoken, the people have suffered enough!"

He shifted, took out a handkerchief to wipe the sweat off of his forehead and switched to tongues only he could understand.

"*Re ka taa aa aa, re bo sata mandere*, thank you Lord, thank you Jesus. You have heard our prayers in the name of Jesus who is the Alpha and Omega we pray thee .... Amen!" He rambled in a theatrical voice.

Was Pastor Lovemore Mavhura really filled with the Holy spirit? He had spoken in tongues, bellowing through the microphone in the middle of the city centre for everyone to hear. Who did he think he was to speak such words against the ruling party and government in broad daylight and this was not the first time he had handed out sermons and prayers that spoke ill of the government.

Several times, the government of his country had been defeated at the general elections by the opposition party – Movement for Democratic Change popularly known as the MDC, and each of those times they had refused to leave office by rigging the results and threatening the masses. Each time Morgan Tsvangirai, the leader of the MDC party appeared, supporters would flock from cities all over, filling the streets in support of the new young leader. Never in the political history of the country had such a humble young candidate been so liked or inspired the spirits of the people.

The party was growing and had already set itself apart by its clear-eyed commitment to reform and campaign against corruption, gender-based violence, inequality and good governance. It spoke of a new corruption-free Zimbabwe, of a new policy centred on conciliation, trade and ideal shared sovereignty. A sound vision for a country which used to be a breadbasket for Africa but had now deteriorated. The country was now in shambles like books of a firm maimed by an unqualified accountant, all in tatters. Morgan wanted change, he instigated for change at its totality, for stability and fairness. He knew well that he was dealing with hard-liners opposed to any movement towards transparency and efficiency. People who had brought down the country and its industry, people who feared peace more than war. But for how long was he going to keep the momentum, as rumours were already emerging that he was being sponsored by the western government to bring confusion and chaos to a peaceful country. Rumours were coming out that the new party was paying people of influence like pastors and community leaders to bring about this fake democratic change and influence the masses to go against their government.

That night in a small, neat office on the top floor of the Karigamombe building, James Mabhunu, an ex-government associate, squeezed the phone with both hands and slowly repeated the words coming from the other end, from his high command. His was the biggest of the small offices on this floor, with his title nailed onto the door – Head of Investigations. A lone certificate was hung on his empty office walls, recognising him for twenty-five years of dedicated service as a Criminal Investigation Department head for the Harare Police Force. Though now officially retired and running his own private investigation firm, James was still as much a worker of the government and the ruling party.

He gathered his crew quickly. "Our orders are to kidnap this talkative Pastor Love-Love and find out by any means necessary who is behind him, who is telling him what to say to the public and brainwash them!" he snapped. It was an easy job, as they had been doing many grab-and-go kidnapping jobs lately. At first they were tempted to grab him before he got home, but it was mid-September and a lot of people would be roaming outside of their houses to cool down from the summer heat. The less witnesses the better, so they opted to sneak into his house and wait. It was an easy job, a two-man job, so they waited.

As soon as Lovemore got home that night, unlocking his front door, he knew something was amiss, something was not right. He went for the switch of the dining room light, but it was too late. He was greeted by a shiny silver pistol to his face which made him freeze for a moment, and before he could think of what to do next, someone grabbed him from the back with thick hands and yanked him violently to the floor.

"It's nice to meet you Pastor," the man said in a guttural voice.

"We have been waiting for you."

The pastor tried to kick and fight back, but he was no match for the two men. One of them took out a syringe filled with a clear liquid from his small bag and drained it into Lovemore's veins. Within a minute, he was knocked flat by the content of the syringe. They quickly packed him in a body bag that they had brought with them and carried him outside, making sure no one was close by to witness their work of art. Opposite his house, they had parked a Black V12

Mercedes Benz with tinted windows and no number plates, but just a sticker on the front screen written – Dindingwe Car Rental. They folded him and shoved him into the trunk and drove off to the cabin in the farmlands where the rest of the crew was waiting patiently.

When reality finally sunk back in, he did not remember how he had been stripped to nothing but his underwear. He had been placed on a thick metal table with holes drilled into it and ropes used to tightly hold his ankles, waist and wrists. It felt like déjà vu, like he was dreaming. It reminded him of his days as a soldier back in the guerrilla war against the colonial regime. Lovemore, like any other young adult during the colonial times, had felt it prudent to join the war. As a young teacher in 1974, he had helped forty other young boys with the aim of getting to Mozambique for military training. He and other young men had done the Maoist guerrilla tactics training in Tete Province. The training was not easy and most who joined were greatly disillusioned once they had reached the training camps in Mozambique, discovering that the ZANLA, the military wing of the Zimbabwe Africa National Union were far from being the romantic freedom-fighters party they had hoped for. Longer training periods were no longer possible, so they ended up doing six-months training, where the concept was to break an individual's mind before recreating and wielding them back as fighting forces with the rest of the comrades. Their names were taken away and they adopted new Chimurenga names, as this would safeguard their identity when they went back to the front. Lovemore's name had been Maxwell Hotshot Joborinjo and after the training he had been deployed to sector 2 under commander Josiah Tongogara where he had met some of the comrades who were now in the presidency and cabinet of a new Zimbabwe.

When the war ended, many were deployed into the regular army, air force and police. Young boys and girls who had not completed their education were encouraged to go back to school and those who wanted to pursue other avenues did so. Pastor Lovemore Mavhura was one of those. He had seen and witnessed enough blood and suffering and wanted nothing more to do with it, so he opted for bible school and was ordained a pastor. He wanted to pray for all. Yet here he was again, tied down to a table and labelled an enemy by those he had fought side by side with before.

It was James Mabhunu, popularly known as Jimmy who brought him back to reality with a shot from another syringe – a different one this time. It was a poke of Sodium thiopental, the truth serum which they hoped would make it faster for him to confess. Who was he working for? Was he part of the opposition party which was trying to tarnish the president's image or was it the Western governments that were paying him to cause confusion and incite violence among the people?

The room was dark except for a little light that was above him. He tried to lift his head, without success, a dozen needles danced their way across Lovemore's forehead. He felt the pressure in his brain as the floor swayed beneath him, dizziness followed and his vision became blurry. His heart began to thump loudly at an increasingly rapid pace, he was sure everyone around him could hear it – the drug was beginning to set in. He tried to say something, but it came out as nothing but a guttural bark.

"Can you hear me Lovemore?" Jimmy asked.

"You have been sleeping for two days," he continued. It had only been six hours, but with the sodium in his veins, it was hard for Lovemore to tell how long he had been knocked out.

"We just want to know the truth, that's all. Who sent you, who are you working for, comrade?"

"Sent me where?" Lovemore croaked his first words after some time, so hoarse he was not even certain he had spoken.

The reply came in the form of a punch to his gut, ''Don't waste our time here, who is paying you to spread this propaganda?" – a scream came out but no one outside of the sound-proofed room could hear it.

"See, the choice is yours. You can either tell me now and we let you go or you can tell me in ten hours or in two days when you are half dead, but you will tell me."

They hooked car battery jumpers to his body, with one of the clips secured to his right nipple and another to a finger on the same side. Suddenly, Lovemore leapt in his bonds and screamed his lungs out, Jimmy had just sent the first electric charge through his body. They wanted to know who was paying him to tarnish the image of their government. They were not going to kill him, he assured himself, but the shock that followed changed his mind, an instant and frightful electric shock gripped his body, with bolts of electric currents ripping his flesh. His cries came from deep within his chest, rabid animal sounds that twisted into hoarse moans by the time they left his cracked lips. He yanked, before passing out.

It was shortly after midnight when Lovemore regained consciousness. The back of his head was throbbing with pain, he bit out a curse and moved his hand to inspect the injury – except that it did not move. He was now tied to a chair and something was restraining his arms and legs. His clothes were back on and there was no one in the room. His eyes were bloodshot and there was a sharp pain in his head. He wanted to scream off the pain, but did not have the energy. He struggled with the rope that tied his hands behind the chair until it broke, and his hands were free. Lovemore scanned the small room again to make sure no one was watching him. He moved closer to the door and pushed it open slowly, as quietly as possible – it was showering outside. The opportunity to escape had availed itself. A wave of dizziness and disorientation overtook him, but he did not have the time to nurse his wounds. He stopped and surveyed the area for guards. He smelt the whiff of cigarette smoke and became alert. There was a big man dressed in camouflage sitting on a makeshift seat made from stones with his back to Lovemore, an FN rifle placed in front of him.

Was he alone – not holding a walkie-talkie, no visible communicators, no earphones. If he was part of a team, he should have been carrying his assets. However, the soldier was relaxed and had a small side arm, by the looks of it a 9mm Beretta. Was he alone? Lovemore inched closer, using his hands and feet in a roping sequence. If he moved any closer, he would give himself away. He clenched his jaw, squeezing his eyes shut for a second and trying to remember everything he had learned during the war. He waited for air to fill his lungs; his lips quivering with anticipation before throwing himself at the gunman hoping to tackle him. It was a bad idea, because the noise alerted the gunman and he turned around. Lovemore hit the man at knee level rather than the waist, which proved too low. Instead of being knocked off his stone stool, the gunman dodged forward and grabbed Lovemore with a steel grip. Lovemore managed to grab the pistol, but with a powerful blow the man knocked the gun from his hand and five meters away it fell. It was then that Lovemore realised he had made a blunder; he had underestimated the man. The man was 1.8 metres tall, heavily muscled and landed blows like a trained boxer, each punch carefully aimed and powerful. The most he could do was to protect his head. With his body left exposed to the crushing blows, he knew the gun man would eventually make him unconscious. He stepped out of position, slammed himself against a tree trunk close by and dropped his hands. The big man was more pleased than puzzled – *free meat,* he thought as he moved in for the kill.

Lovemore gulped air, his body shivering. A glance at the gun man told him the man was going for a single roundhouse punch to the jaw with all the immense upper body strength he possessed and just finish him off. Lovemore retreated just out of distance, dropping to the ground with exquisite timing. The gunman missed, fist connecting to the tree trunk and Lovemore heard the reflexive expulsion of breath as the man plunged down in pain. With fast movement, he tied the big man's hands with the sling from the FN rifle, he moaned in agony.

"On your knees, on your knees!" Lovemore commanded.

The big man did so, moving reluctantly, "I think my hand is broken!" He cried in a low voice.

"Not my funeral!"

He patted the man's pockets and extracted a military style pocketknife and some cash.

"Man," Lovemore mentioned as he opened the knife, "We are going to play a little game here, I need to know the truth and nothing but the truth." His war days memories were starting to come back. Memories he had tried so hard to bury and not think of.

"Are you alone?"

"No, we are many," he lied.

Lovemore knew he was lying. He had learnt the art of lie detection during the war. A tremble in the voice in one case study. A tone of voice that was too assertively smooth in another, a twitch around the eyes or licking of lips – there was always something.

"So, you are alone huh!"

He extracted a towel from the gun man's bag, tied his mouth to the back of his head.

"I don't have time to waste."

Lovemore now had the rations from the man – some cash and a pistol with 12 rounds of ammunition. *Where to next?* was the question. He was no longer safe in his own country, a country he had left everything and fought for. His own countrymen, people who used to be his comrades, were now hunting for him. He had to escape, he had to get out of the country otherwise Jimmy and his band of troopers would find him and kill him. He had no time to waste.

Lovemore took the bag and headed for the road, trying to move as fast as his feet could allow. A long-distance haulage truck would be his safest way to travel. Two borders were of interest, Plumtree to Botswana or Beitbridge to

South Africa. Southwards from where he was, the mountains of Selukwe ran a road so mathematically straight, it ranked among the world's best measured miles, and long distance trucks used it as a shortcut to the Beitbridge border post. He had no choice but to hop over the fence and into neighbouring South Africa without getting noticed; to brave the treacherous crocodile-infested Limpopo river that divided the two countries. Did he really have a choice? After all, he would not be the first one. Thousands of Zimbabweans had flocked into the diaspora, running away from the once breadbasket that had turned to a basket case. People who were running away in search of a better life for themselves and their families, for without the involvement of the Zimbabwean diaspora the nation would be in an even more forlorn situation. A lot of people had died trying to cross over the unforgiving Limpopo river and its many flooded streams. For those 'Jumpers' fortunate enough to survive the crossing, the *Guma-guma* criminals would patiently wait for them on the other side of the river and show them the worst of what South Africa had to offer. The *Guma- guma* boys would prey on the newly arrived – scouring the length of the border fence to rob them of their meagre belongings and rape the women. The South African police had also intensified patrol on their side of the border trying to stem the flood of *Zim* illegals in light of an upsurge in the irregular migration and smuggling.

He heard the changing of gears of a long-distance *gonyeti*, haulage truck, and moved closer to the road, waving it to stop. The truck stopped and he jumped in. The *gonyeti* were the safest mode of transport he opted for. It was at 02:00am according to the radio on the truck.

"Beitbridge border post," Lovemore announced.

He asked the driver to drop him off two kilometres from the border post, thanked him and handed him a $20 note. It had been a sleepless night and he needed to rest before he continued with his journey. He could not afford to feel safe as long as he was in his own country. He knew they would look for him, they would find him and shut him up. Shortly before sunrise, he found himself in a thick forest where he sidled into a massive anthill and quickly fell asleep.

Lovemore was woken up by dogs barking at him. The owner of the dogs – a retired teacher, thought his dogs had encircled a bushbuck, maybe a kudu or rabbit until he saw Lovemore. The dog owner was herding his cattle along the Shashe river.

"*Dumelang Mmna.*" Greeted the man.

Lovemore knew nothing of *Setswana,* a language commonly spoken around the borders around Zimbabwe, Botswana and parts of South Africa. The teacher had encountered a number of such incidents – many undocumented Zimbabweans had used this route to enter South Africa illegally.

"You look exhausted my friend, going south?" the man asked, in a matter of fact way.

"You know at this hour of the day it's not safe to cross. The white farmers on the other side will be patrolling and the S.A.D.F are just as heartless when they are checking for illegal immigrants."

"Around 4PM will do," he advised.

The retired teacher informed Lovemore that in the event that he had managed to escape the immigration police, the only stumbling block would be the hippos and crocodiles. Since the river is up to the brim with crocodiles hibernating in the small streams and hippos only came this far around 6PM when they would go grazing, it would be better to cross before they came.

"Let's wait until that time and I will show you the safest crossing spot." Things have gone wrong, things are now sour my friend, even us retired folks can feel the pinch."

"Uuum even I thought I could resist the pressure, but failed." Lovemore humoured him.

The country had surely gone to the dogs, with many choosing to brave the rapids, the crocodiles and watchful border guards. Many were preferring the diaspora where degree on no degree, everyone would end up with menial domestic jobs.

Many had decided to rather face the xenophobia attacks in South Africa, where the locals accused them of stealing their jobs, than to be treated like dogs in their own country where the future looked bleak.

The conversation went on and on until 4:00 PM.

"My friend, I will go and show you the crossing spot," said the retired teacher, after he had shared his lunch with Lovemore. Was it really a crossing point or just a spot with less stones?

"Good luck and journey mercies." he bid Lovemore.

"You need to move faster, the white man up the stream usually opens up his dams around this time." He warned Lovemore before disappearing into the bushes.

Lovemore now faced the confluence of the Shashe and Limpopo rivers - a stretch of over a kilometre of water. He jumped in and moved as fast as his legs would allow him. The water was knee deep.

Lovemore was halfway when he turned back to check for his new friend, but he was gone.

When he faced the front, the water was now waist deep. In the blink of an eye the water was up to his shoulders and fighting to carry him with its current. He pushed his feet from the bottom and with all his strength, he tried to bounce back up. The first time his head had gone beneath the water he was not alarmed, because he had been a diver before and was not scared of a little water. His eyes searched the area with undue haste looking for his friend, for anyone to help him, but no one was there to help.

The current was too powerful to fight and his stupid lungs did not give him any choice but to inhale. would it be air or murky water.

Lovemore was not ready to die, to come all this way only to die drowning. To survive the liberation war only to die trying to escape the same country he had fought for.

He found himself clutching on a thorny branch that hung into the river close to the edge - he could not continue, so he held on. It was an unpleasantly cold night, the type of coldness that reaches into your bones. The wind matched into the picture torturing trees and furiously blowing like a sneezing monster. The whole night he was there, holding on as his life depended on it. He tried to fall asleep but the occasional barking of wild dogs close by broke the silence of the night. All his clothes were gone, and how so he could not tell. Naked, depleted and terrified he cried for help, but there was none to come. If only he had not escaped and died at the hands of Jimmy and his goons, at least he could have died a more honourable death, a death fit for a soldier.

A jeep drove past in the early hours of the morning. It was the white farmer and his workers doing their routine morning patrol.

Lovemore shouted, with a faint voice ready to give up and let go. He was pale and exhausted and eyes swollen nearly shut. The jeep went up the stream, but before long it came back and stopped close by. Had they heard him? Was it his instinct or just a coincidence? The boss and his laborers approached the bushy tree where he was holding onto. The white man was huge and had fur all over his body. He instructed one of his laborers to get into the water and grab Lovemore by his arm. The water had subsided a bit but was still very much dangerous. He swam in and shouldered Lovemore to the riverbank where they pulled him out of the water.

"*Wat Kom Jy?* Where are you from?" Asked the white man in Afrikaans.

He only got the *Kom* part and translated it to 'come'. He pointed to the opposite side of the river.

"*Kan jy Afrikaans praat?* Can you speak Afrikaans or not?"

There was no reply for a moment then the words came out as if they were painful to say.

"I can speak English only," he pronounced.

"Oh my friend if you can't speak Afrikaans, life is going to be very difficult for you. All bosses around here need people who speak Afrikaans!" The white man responded.

He drove away, leaving his newfound refugee with one of his labourers who could also only speak Sesotho. Thirty minutes later, he came back with his old clothes and shoes which they gave to Lovemore to wear, with a question.

"Need a job?"

"Yes Sir," he replied.

"Farm work, 20 rand per day and you pick tomatoes for now, okay?"

"No problem sir," he agreed, as if he had a choice.

"You are very lucky, we had to make sure. 300 bodies were retrieved down the river just three days ago. The river is very dangerous and people don't need to take chances. My view mirror told me there was something hanging on to the branches – thought it could be a fish or crocodile."

And just like that Lovemore Mavhura, an ex-combatant and ex-pastor was now a farm boy in the diaspora.

## Painted Feelings

"You call it madness, but I call it love..."

My mother once told me that. She said she had read it somewhere in one of those poetry books she had cared enough to burden herself with when she escaped Zimbabwe in the middle of the night, after her family had been butchered by Colonel Perrence Shiri and his fifth brigade soldiers. She said if you take something to heart, someone to heart, they will stay there forever. I do wonder about the veracity of her statements, but then again, my mother lived a life away from the rules that society had tried to nurture into her, the lessons culture had schooled her to always follow, so I will never know. I miss her and wish she was here to gift me a line from all those books she loved to read so much, to advise me what to do now that I am at a crossroads. Is all love like madness or is my madness really love?

The therapist's office sat at the far end corner on the 8th floor of the London Study Centre, with a large window that overlooked the British Museum. Three of the large walls were covered in books as if it were a lawyer's office and the fourth wall was neatly lined with pictures and certificates of what he had achieved in his career. A small signage set on his table announcing him as Dr. Samuel Bishop Adeyemi – Psychologist.

He nodded at us to sit on the couch, on the other side of the shiny mahogany table between us as he sat in his comfy armchair. His face had been flawed by time and collapsed with age, into a pile of tissue that held onto his eyes and nose. This was our second and hopefully last session with the old therapist. It was Zuri's idea to see a therapist that might help us in deciding the way forward. I did not want to do this, to be here to discuss our personal issues with a stranger. But did I have a choice?

"Your situation is a unique one, but it's not my job to judge if the two of you should be in a relationship or not," he began with a mellow, almost professional baritone that commanded attention. His voice was deep, cultured and you could pick up the traces of his Nigerian origins from his accent. He removed his glasses and wiped imaginary sweat off of his big forehead before he continued.

"What is very clear is that your love for each other is very real."

I looked at Zuri who was sitting next to me with her long legs crossed, hands in her lap and nodded my head in agreement with the doctor's words.

"But is love enough Dr. Adeyemi, will it be able to sustain us?" Zuri questioned.

"I do not think we can find a way to fix this. We are related, Thando. And nothing we do can change that," she continued; her voice soft, almost fragile as if her heart was about to break. She sniffled as her throat started to close and tears welled up in her eyes.

I had met Zuri two years earlier at the London Metropolitan University while doing the final year of my Bachelor of Arts degree. It was those gorgeous eyes that drew me to her the first time I saw her in the corridor and she asked me for directions to her next class. She looked nervous and seemed to be having a hard day, but in spite of all that sadness written all over her face I could see the beauty engraved in her - was she new, why had I never seen nor noticed her before? One could tell from her coffee-stain-like beautiful skin that she made an effort to look good, to look this amazing. I must have gazed at her for too long, her eerie eyebrows inclined slightly and I yelped at being caught staring. Her Kikuyu mother had truly done justice by naming her Zuri, for she truly was beautiful.

When she came closer, I had noticed her sherbet sweet lips and the light in her eyes caught my attention, so luminous and penetrating that when she looked at me, I felt as if she could see right into my heart, into my soul and read the secrets buried deep within. All my illusions and preconceptions faded away and I knew I had found the one I had been looking for; or was it her that had found me? The thing with love is that it arrives when it's supposed to and I knew love had finally shown up in my life. Three days later, we went on our first date where she seemed to find more words than I did, where it seemed I had forgotten how to speak properly and that is when our relationship started. But here we were now, seated in a therapist's office just eight weeks before our wedding and trying to save whatever was left of our relationship. I wanted to blame it on her Uncle, her late Father's brother who had given us a pre-wedding gift as a fun way for us to discover our African roots together, a gift that had turned out to be a curse.

I never had the privilege of meeting my father, not that my mother even knew who he was. My mother was one of the few lucky people who managed to escape from her beloved country after her whole family had been killed by the fifth brigade soldiers at the command of Prime Minister Mugabe. During the Rhodesia war, the Zimbabwe African People's Union had split into two groups in 1963 and even though at the beginning of the war these two groups had started with a common goal, things quickly changed. As a result of the split, nationalist parties emerged to challenge the white government with ZANU which was led by Robert Mugabe recruiting in the Shona speaking regions and ZAPU which was led by Joshua Nkomo recruiting from mostly the Ndebele speaking regions in the west. The two groups, even though fighting for a similar cause, quickly became enemies on their own.

Following the rise to power of Prime Minister Mugabe after the war, his government in 1983 felt threatened by what they called the dissidents – disgruntled former guerrillas and supporters of ZAPU. In order to get rid of his enemies, he ordered a purge whereby not only the dissidents were killed, but all Ndebele men of fighting age were considered potential dissidents and thus automatically guilty of subversive activities. The government ordered a crackdown using a special kind of army that had been trained in North Korea, used different methods, wore a different uniform and only reported to the Prime Minister directly. It was this army the government used to purge these innocent souls and over the next four years they killed anyone related to ZAPU soldiers and marched those left behind to re-education camps. Entire families were herded into grass thatched huts, which were then set alight stealing the innocent souls' ability to breathe.

"The people of Matabeleland need to be re-educated," the Prime minister had declared. The Soldiers would routinely round up dozens of innocent civilians and march them at gunpoint to a central place, like a school or borehole. There they would be forced to sing Shona songs praising ZANU.

It was Professor Hayward, her father's work mate who felt pity and helped her to slip away into the night, careful not to be seen or heard as they made their way towards the South African border. Decades after escaping, she would narrate and recall those fateful nights, still haunted by the suffocating darkness, the last images of her family and the sounds of gunfire echoing in the dead of the night. She knew nothing but death awaited her if she stayed, so she agreed to pack a few belongings and face the danger and death lurking at every step. Escape they did, in the middle of a cold night where a horrific army of blackened spooky clouds did not hesitate to launch an attack of heavy murky rain. When they saw the silhouettes of the patrolling soldiers from afar, they would lie down and drag themselves over the muddy terrain, making their few belongings wet, but they made it out of Tsholotsho and into South Africa. Once in South Africa, mother and a few other girls were put on a ship transporting Ivory to the United Kingdom.

When she escaped to the United Kingdom, mother turned to prostitution for a living. She would later write in her diary that she left me, that it wasn't easy at first, but she had no other option. She would stand every night on the corner of Oxford Street in Soho, London's red-light district, just six blocks from the university she never had the privilege to attend. For months on end, she would wake up next to a stranger and use all the hot water in hopes of washing away the rancid smell off her body, her temple. After months of selling her body, she became a professional of sorts, forgot how it felt like to be happy, to smile or love, too used to the breath of stinky hairy men with fantasies of quenching their thirstiness on her sixteen-year-old body. She got too used to all the emptiness the men she met poured into her and with being too used to the job came the recklessness. That's how she ended up with me, an unplanned pregnancy, an unwanted child whom she didn't know what to do with at first. The concept of love was too foreign to her yet with time, she learnt to love me in her own way. She named me *uThando*, meaning love, after her dead brother whom she said I reminded her of. She refused to raise me to become someone else's war and burden, someone else's weight, so she loved me enough not to become like the men she did her kind of business with. Just enough to make sure I did not become a side effect of the messes and mistakes she had made. My mother was not a strong woman, but she kept us safe, she knew what it meant to build, and build she did. She built in me a strong character, a gentleman, a different man to my father - whoever he was, wherever he was.

This is what had brought us here, sitting on a therapist's couch with the lady I had hoped I would spend the rest of my life with, the lady I still hoped to spend the rest of my days with. It was her Uncle's fault, her Uncle's idea of a pre-wedding present for us to take one of those My Heritage DNA tests that tell you how much of your blood is European or East African, together, and discover our African roots before spending the rest of our lives. The results came back with more truths than we had expected, than we had hoped for – Zuri and I were related, brother and sister, sharing the same Father.

"Have you told anyone about this since the last time we met?" Dr. Adeyemi questioned removing his reading glasses.

"No, we don't know how to say it, and truth be told I am not sure I want to." I fretted.

"Two weeks ago I was planning our honeymoon but now," I stopped, trying to hold myself from breaking down.

"Now I might lose the love of my life."

I knew telling people I had just discovered the woman I was about to marry was my half-sister would complicate things. It would make our love madness. If I could, I would have overdosed myself with sleeping pills hoping that when I woke up, if I woke up in hospital I would be someone new, someone who didn't care as much as I did for her.

"You won't lose me," she said, choking up on each word and trying to hold back the tears from suffocating her. "If anything, I am terrified of waking up one day and your love for me has expired in the middle of the night because you remembered we are related."

"That will never happen Zuri, I love you and I don't know how not to. I give you my word."

"Words are not enough; words will never be enough. I want to be the air in your lungs, I want to remind you to breathe easier."

I moved closer and took her hand into mine.

"Then let me be there for you. Not only to land you a hand or an ear, but to be your spine, let me be in your life forever."

She turned to face me, our eyes locked and smiled, for she knew we were painting the same picture in our minds, in our hearts. That day we walked out of the therapist's office hand in hand, our hearts imprinted with each other's fingerprints and with a secret we would take with us to our graves. Some will call it madness but we call it love.

## My Father's Shoes

He leaned his face towards mine and I could smell the mildew aura of a dead cat mixed with cheap homemade beer coming from his mouth.

"*Wam potooo potom potom*!" He shouted brusquely in a language only he could understand, opening a small brown dirty bag made from goat skin and holding its contents with his thumb and forefinger. He held it close to his weather-beaten face and deposited the contents into his nose, inhaling it as if his life depended on it – he waited and then a sneeze followed.

He shook his head and a lank of his lustreless Rasta fell around like strings of rotting straws and another sneeze followed, "*Yebooo, siyavuma Makhosi!*"

He took a sip of the home-made beer that smelled like cow urine and handed over the cup to me with instructions to quaff it up. The strong pungent taste of the beer made my tongue numb and for a minute my vision became blurry.

A smile cracked open his thin bloodless lips that were as black as the night, and he licked the remaining contents of whatever it is he had taken from the dirty bag - satisfaction filled his face.

Babu had been our village traditional healer who would treat all ailments for as long as I could remember. He lived deep in the forest and only came down to the village occasionally when there had been a death, a ceremony to welcome the spirit of an ancestor home or when his presence had been requested by the elders - *abadala*.

He closed his eyes as if going into a trance and after what seemed like eternity, he came back to the land of the living, mumbling to himself with a ghastly smile.

"I see, I see a bad spirit upon your head," he mumbled.

"The ancestors are not happy; they are not happy."

"What can we do Babu, what do we have to do to rid us of this bad spirit?" Asked my father's older sister *Babakazi*, trying to hold back her tears.

"A goat, we need to slaughter a goat," he said slowly as if struggling to let the words out.

Over the years, as the village chief, my grandfather's yard had become the place where most ceremonies and meetings involving the council of the elders in the village would be held. Him and the other elders would gather under the trees for shade, drink cheap beer while settling the villagers' quarrels over farmland or other small issues.

On rare occasions, they would invite the village traditional healer to perform rituals that needed someone who communicated with the ancestors, rituals that were beyond their understanding. This day was one of those golden occasions where they had been graced by Babu's presence; gathering to rid me of bad luck and the death spirits that were calling me from beyond.

There are days when I do not feel like collecting new memories, days when my heart feels like a fifty year old gas stove waiting to explode, days when my anxiety holds me hostage in my own bed. On those days I hide my pain like treasure in a chest. I carry my thoughts to keep me company and I show no weakness. I try to remember the words of my father, "Melusi, *mfana wami*, crying is for weak men, and in this house we don't show any weakness."

It was then that I learnt not to process my feelings, of the toxic pressure my culture puts on us to suppress our feelings. On those days, I try to remember that so many people want what I have. That I am where the grass is greener, that I am privileged - but am I really?

On those days, I wear my trauma on my skin like a tattoo, I speak of my trauma as if it were a fairy-tale, as if the gods intended for it to be so, so they can see us through. I am just tired, I want to go on, to strive, but I am just tired and there are not enough hours in a day to do the things I want to do. To pursue the goals the world has set for me, to run after my dreams and if I am to be truthful, this makes me angry, but anger is not an emotion I can afford as a young black man. To be angry, just like self-care is a luxury I cannot afford as this will only make them see me in the same box they have always wanted to place me in - an angry black man, an immigrant, a thief who is here to steal their jobs. This is what it means to be us, to be me – having the world going up in flames yet still be a sanctuary for others, a provider, a superhero on the outside yet afraid of my own feelings when I close my eyes at the end of the day. This is what it means to be an African man, to be physically strong, to choose dominating your surroundings over the ability to love and care for others.

I do get to rest my eyes occasionally, and on those few occasions I dream of long mornings by the beach, of eating lobster for dinner at a roadside joint. I dream of a cabin at the southern tip of Grenada, as away from all distraction as possible, but before I finish dreaming, the familiar dulcet voice of Sarah Parnell brings me back to reality through the speakers of the London underground train, "The next station is Walthamstow Central, where this train terminates. All change please." I quickly grab my bag as reality sinks back in, and stand up moving closer to the door as I know one of the escalators is out of service and being late for my second shift of the day is not something I can afford to do. This is my daily life; truth be told, I just want to make my dead father proud wherever he is. For if my father is ever to be proud of me, then it would mean that for a second, for a minute, for just a day I would have lived a better life than he did.

How much we have come to know of ourselves is of utmost importance, but how we treat ourselves is even more important. Now I am not sure about you, but for me knowing of this is much easier than feeling or acting towards it. By this I mean an emptiness, loss, a worthlessness. All I know is that there is something so wrong with this picture I carry with me. After all, men were born to live, right? But the more I carry on, the more I live, the emptier I have come to feel.

The Doctor diagnosed me with clinical depression and recommended I see a therapist. "How could that be?" I had questioned the first time he told me.

"Is depression not a white man's disease?"

After all, seeing a therapist was out of the question. Why would I waste time and money which I didn't have, talking to someone about my emotions and being asked silly questions like, "*Do you love yourself?*"

How can I love someone I have only met in passing. If I struggle to deal with my own emotions head on, why would I want to open those borders of myself to someone else I hardly know, for them to trend in that space of mine. Maybe healing is something I will never be able to flower because hate is entangled in my roots.

This is what has brought me back home. *Ekasi - Abadala* summoned me.

"We need to rid you of this bad luck, my grandfather *Ubabamkhulu* said in his matter of fact croaky voice.

"We have to appease the ancestors by slaughtering a goat and brewing beer."

My decision to leave my home country was irrevocably sealed the day I made a conscious decision that I would live a different life to that of my father and his father before him. I was raised by my grandmother, *Ugogo*. I never got the glee of meeting my own mother whom I killed the day I was born, my first breath in exchange of her last - a cocktail of severe bleeding and eclampsia they called it. Her people never forgave me for taking away their only daughter, their museum of laughter. It is a hatred I have had to carry with me every day of my life. It is a hatred that comes with a unique kind of sadness; being hated for no reason, for something you did not have control over. I never really got to have a relationship with my father either. I grew up hearing of my father's survival until it became my own.

I was only twelve when death stole him from us. It was on a Saturday morning and the sun had just risen, not that it mattered as it was in the middle of winter. The clouds were slowly gathering, ready to cough out just enough rain to freeze my veins and make my small body quiver.

On days like these *Ugogo* would always make a fire in her time chiseled kitchen - *ekhishini* and prepare *ujeqe* for us. Warmth had just begun to flood the room as the fire came alive when death came uninvited. They found his lifeless body hanging by the neck on the aged Marula tree near the cow shed. Its branches looking like arms ready to hug you, to invite you to one of its branches and give away your desire to live. The village elders called it *Ulaka lwababphansi* – the wrath of the ancestors, said that the ancestors were not happy, they brewed beer to cleanse the home and appease the ancestors.

It was then that I first learnt of the romantic relationship the men in my family have with death. Of how attractive she is and seems like the perfect escape, of her raven black hair and how it caresses her dimpled cheeks and brushes her kiss inspiring lips slowly when she whispers. I do hear her calling me from the other side when I lay in my bed at night, "Comeee , come dance with me," she mumbles in her alluring voice. I can never forget how death loves my people. There is just something so amazing about her eyes, always seeming so big and bright, so passionate. I often fantasise about my own funeral when she cuddles me, not that I want to die, but I do not want to live either – I just want to stop existing, to stop processing being a hostage to my thoughts.

This is what has brought me back home.

Father Mukonori, the priest from *Ugogo*'s church once told me that it was an evil spirit that possessed me that steals my joy and makes me feel this way. "Anything is possible through prayer, my son," he would always say. I would be lying if I say I paid attention to these conversations I used to have with him every time I visited home. To be honest, I would say I only attended these meetings to make *Ugogo* happy. After all, growing up I had been introduced to god by one of those Catholic priests at Cheshanga boarding school and made to believe that god looked like an old gentle white man, more like Mr. Ginsburg, our headmaster who would once every year in December disguise himself like Father Christmas. But the white men whose butts I wash for a living in London are not gentle at all. If anything, they are mean and uncompassionate, so why should I believe in their gods? Is there a point in believing in their god when he is so small, they wear him on chains around their necks? Why should I believe a word that comes out of Father Mukonori's mouth?

I am not sure if I do need my spirit to be cleansed, or whether it is something that only a physician can understand. If only my father was here, maybe he could have used this therapy more than me. Maybe he could have learnt that the remedy for pain is not always more pain, that you can never have a breakthrough if you are afraid to break. I cannot blame him for all the pain and trauma I carry with me, for these shoes he left me to wear on my own; it was the only way out he knew. It was the way society raised him and culture nurtured these thoughts in him, that you can never show weakness, that you have to suffer gracefully, that to be a real man means to have indestructible strength and not prioritise your emotions.

What I do know are stories of my father. Of how he learnt from a young age how to provide for his family through the work of his hands. My father was a farm foreman in the large fields of Mr. Nicolson. It was in these large fields that he grew anxiety and depression which stained his fingers and carried it home on his back and in his wallet, cuddling together with his next to nothing salary. I would like to believe it was then that depression was given new names – laziness they called it. Said it was more a spiritual thing rather than a biological one. But then what do I know, I am just a little boy who wears his Father's shoes proudly and has nothing to lose except his mind. I do not know where to start, but I know exactly where I do not want this to end.

## Lazarus Panashe Ivan Nyagwambo

Nyagwambo is an emerging writer whose works have appeared in The Kalahari Review, AFREADA, The Shallow Tales Review and Munyori Literary Journal. He is currently working on a short story collection.

## Vessel for Misery

Luke feels the weight of his flesh on his bones as he swings open the door and lumbers into the apartment he shares with five other African students; currently six with the recent and unwelcome arrival of one of Ngoni's friends who has been squatting on their couch. The apartment is eerily quiet at one twenty-seven in the morning; the silence endowed with an ethereal essence of the red glow of the neon light from the Kolan Hospital sign that spills through the open window to the apartment's living room. The light matches the stagnant heat that chokes the air, clinging limply to his body and clogging his pores. A vague figure, the shirtless form of Ngoni's friend whose name he cannot not remember, emits soft snoring sounds from the shadowed couch that sits just underneath the window. He walks quietly to the kitchen and opens his designated cupboard. As if sensing the presence of food, his stomach utters a low growl. *Fuck!* The packet of Indomie noodles that he had left on the lower shelf of his cupboard is not where it is supposed to be. A sudden wave of emotion, the undercurrent undoubtedly anger, but the surface of it something much sadder and fraught, sweeps over him and before he can control himself he slams the cupboard door shut. The bang echoes in his head, reverberating off a space that was now hollowed out in his current state of exhaustion. He carries himself to the living room and as he is about to open the door to his bedroom, his eyes spot something that he had not noticed before. A bowl. His bowl. The pasty remains of a meal are smeared around its interior. He sighs, unwilling to contemplate the possible implications and afraid of what he might do to the sleeping man on the couch in his volatile state.

In his room he collapses onto his bed. The springs of the thin mattress that he got from the previous occupant of the room dig into his back, but he ignores it. His body does not have the energy to contort in protest. He reaches for his right pocket before remembering that his phone is not there. He unzips his trousers and slips his hand into his underwear. The cell-phone is wedged between his testicles and his right thigh. After having walked for so long with it there, he had tuned out the discomfort and forgotten he had put it there.

Mehmet. For everything that had happened, he blamed Mehmet.

He blamed him for how much he hated his job. He blamed him for everything that had happened today, the boy having instigated the incident that initiated a sequence of events that led to his current predicament. He blamed him even, in some abstract way, for the misery, the misfortune that had been lying in wait for him the moment he left home, set for what he thought would be academic conquest, professional triumph, a better future. To him, the boy had become the embodiment of what he felt was no doubt a cruel conspiracy against him, a sadistic plot to make his life this vessel for misery that it had become.

The thought of the boy releases a surge of venomous resentment that turns his blood to grit. *That little shit!* The boy could be no more than sixteen, yet it was unequivocally clear, in the crooked way that his lip curled up on one side when he spoke to Luke. And in the arrogant way he pushed out his chest, that he considered himself Luke's superior; a sentiment which stung more because it was not entirely untrue.

Mehmet was related to the owner of the small workshop where Luke worked, whose primary business was manufacturing a variety of steel parts that were used to make large scale kitchen apparatus for hotels - furnaces, stoves, counter tops among other things. That, in addition to being the only non-black of the four workers at the workshop and the fact that even though he did only a fraction of the work, his salary was nearly double that of Luke and his colleagues reinforced the boy's sense of superiority. The factory manager, although he did not encourage it, did nothing to quell it. Luke doubted whether the boy had even gone to school and if he had, he had likely not progressed very far. His infrequent exchanges with Mehmet in broken English that only at a fundamental level could be considered conversation, often revolved around what were clearly fabricated tales of *fiki fiki* – sex, with many girls, a number of which, he liked to add, were African. It was unlikely that Mehmet, with his narrow head, his protruding forehead and eyes that were set too far apart underneath a single brow; Mehmet who looked a lot like something in the earlier stages of the evolution of Man had ever seen a naked woman in person, let alone touched one. He could easily have forgiven the boy's ignorance, even tolerated his incompetence, but his arrogance which often ended up interfering with their work, he found insufferable.

The work was taxing and the remuneration too modest to compensate for the ten back-breaking hours he spent daily carrying and cutting heavy pieces of metal. He was already starting to feel a constant pain in the small of his back that he could not afford, in the literal sense of the word, to be fretful about. Regardless of how he felt about it, it was the only job he had been able to get after spending six months searching for employment. Without a work permit, finding any kind of administrative job was virtually impossible and already most of the blue-collar jobs were filled with African students employed illegally, with no work permits. It was a classmate of his, a loud Nigerian boy whose eyes shifted only slower than he spoke, who had eventually found him the job when one of the people he was working with finally conceded that it was not worth it and quit. Luke would have been apprehensive about taking on the job under such circumstances, but his situation was already far beyond dire.

Mehmet may have been the subject of his imputation after he arrived in Cyprus, but it was Gloria, the exuberant lady who worked at the agency that had helped him apply for the scholarship, whom he held responsible for his having ended up there to start with. Charming, perpetually laughing and pleasant faced, it was impossible to think of her promises of abundant job opportunities at high paying firms as anything other than guaranteed, even going so far as to reinforce her assurances by inviting several students to testify via a conference call during the luncheon that the agency organised prior to their departure. He wondered now whether she was malicious enough to pay those students to give false testimonials. It certainly couldn't be beyond her, if she was able to do what she had done to him and hundreds of other bright eyed, hopeful students. But he did not dwell too much on the thought because his present circumstances only allowed him to think of the present and on a few occasions, the future. So, every day he woke up at five-thirty. Every day he boarded the six o'clock *dolmuş* from Gönyeli to the bus terminal in the CBD in Lefkoşa where he would board another one for the ninety-minute ride to Famagusta. His boss would come with Mehmet and pick them up at the bus stop together with his co-workers, the Nigerian classmate and a withdrawn Zimbabwean whose name, Emmanuel, was the only thing he knew about him, and they would drive to the factory.

Today, he and the other workers had needed to offload a delivery of metal sheets. Normally such tasks would be executed by the three of them, opting to avoid working with Mehmet's frequent grumbling and immutable condescension. But the sheets were too heavy, so they had asked Mehmet to help them. The boy only complied after Luke had threatened to go and tell the manager that he was refusing to offer his assistance. Halfway to where they were stacking the sheets, a good thirty meters or so from the delivery truck, Mehmet, whether deliberately or accidentally, abruptly let go of the corner that he was holding, leaving the full weight of that end of the sheet to Emmanuel. If he hadn't been caught by surprise, Emmanuel might have been able to hold it on his own long enough to safely set it down, but instead he dropped it and the sharp edge of the sheet cut his leg.

About thirty minutes of commotion ensued: frantic calls for an ambulance and the manager repeatedly screaming directions into his phone to the rather remote workshop; Emmanuel howling in agony until he eventually passed out; Mehmet staring, ashen, at the steady spread of blood soaking through the clothes that they used to try and wrap the gash in Emmanuel's leg through which they had seen a brief flash of white before the blood started oozing. The ambulance finally arrived and Emmanuel was taken to the hospital. Their manager followed in his own car, leaving the three of them to finish the rest of the work and handing the keys over to Mehmet in case he was unable to come back, then the boy could take them to his house.

Luke was not surprised when Mehmet, hands in his pockets as if nothing had happened, casually announced, "Boss go. Now, me boss. You work." The two of them knew that attempting to reason with him was futile and would only waste more time, so they resolved to finish the task of unloading the truck on their own, which ended up taking twice as much time because they needed to take frequent breaks. While they did the offloading, Mehmet sat in a chair by the door of the workshop, playing games on his phone.

It was nine o'clock by the time they finally finished work, two hours later than his usual dismissal time and an hour after the last *dolmuş* that could take him home had departed. He was waiting for an hour at the bus stop before a grey Mercedes with tinted windows and two men finally stopped to pick him up.

"My friend, where you are going? It is very…ehhh…how you say *karanlık*?" The driver, a dark-haired man with a full beard and an army cut, was wearing a windbreaker in spite of the heat. He thought for a moment and then exclaimed suddenly, "Dark! It is very dark." He smiled elatedly, pleased with himself, revealing a set of teeth that were the colour of dry grass from too much smoking.

"Gönyeli, *abi.* Are you going there?"

"Ahh Gönyeli. *Tamam.*" He turned to his companion sitting in the passenger seat and said something to him in Turkish. Luke managed to pick out the word *guzel* – beautiful and *arkadaş* – friend. The other man looked at Luke briefly before he smiled and nodded. Then the driver said, "Ok my friend. We will take you."

"*Çok teşekkürler abi.* Thank you so much."

After Luke had got into the car, he heard the thudding of the car doors as they locked. Instantly wary, he tried to roll the windows down to no avail. He had nothing of value on him except his phone. Even that was not worth much, a cheap Chinese brand that he had brought with him from Zimbabwe, but he could not afford to lose it. It was the only way he was able to communicate with his parents. He knew his mother would worry if she was unable to contact him ritualistically every other night. So he discretely took it out of his pocket and slid it into his underwear, placing his satchel which contained his work suit on his lap to conceal his movements. While he was doing so, the driver said something to him.

"*Ne*? What you say?"

"You speak *Türkçe* my friend?"

"*Kuçuk.* Only little Turkish."

"Why you no learn my friend? *Türkçe* very easy."

Luke smiled politely, "No time *abi.* Too much school." The lie, unrehearsed, unpremeditated, flowed from his mouth so effortlessly. It was a small fantasy that he liked to indulge himself whenever he could, but the truth was he had not attended lectures for the entirety of the last year which was supposed to have been his second. The costs of paying for his school fees, despite his fifty percent scholarship, had finally become too much for his parents in addition to paying the fees for his younger siblings back home, with his sister who followed him also sitting for her O' level Cambridge exams that year.

His father, knowing no more than the fantasies that had been fed to them by Gloria, had asked Luke to find a job and at least pay the fees for that school year while they concentrated on finding the funds for his sister's exam fees. Luke had agreed, initially believing that it would be easy enough on the basis of Gloria's claims, but after he had been dismissed by an impatient and rather bemused secretary the first time he tried to submit a CV to an engineering company, it dawned on him that maybe he had been too rash in accepting his father's offer. And then as the number of bemused faces that scoffed him out of upmarket executive offices increased and the quality of jobs he applied for decreased, he had come to realise the worst: that the dream that had been sold to him by Gloria was a lie. At that point, his parents' hopes had soared too high for him to bear bringing them crushing to the ground, so he lied that he had finally found a job. The plan then had been to defer the semesters for that year to the next and when he did eventually find a job, use that income for his subsistence and rent. The first signs that that might have been ill-advised planning on his part came when, every time he called his parents, their complaints about how much harder things were getting became more and more reiterative. Eventually, his father told him right out that going forward he would need to support himself because things back home had become too hard. By then it was too late to rectify his mistake and he could not bring himself to tell his parents the truth. It would devastate them. And in any case it would change nothing. They would still not be able to pay his tuition and he would now also be in trouble.

"Sorry?"

"I say what is your name?" The driver glanced at him through the rear-view mirror.

"*Benim adım* Luke. What is yours?"

"*Benim adım* Emre. And my friend here is Mehmet."

He wanted to tell them that he knew someone else named Mehmet, but he did not know how to say the words in Turkish and he was sure they would not understand him if he spoke in English. Instead he just said, "Nice to meet you."

They had been driving beyond the city limits of Famagusta for some time. The road was now flanked on either side by panoramas of fields that were dotted with rolls of hay. The man sitting in the passenger seat suddenly said something in Turkish. The driver peered at him again in the rear-view mirror and nodded. The car slowly came to a stop and parked underneath a highway lamp, its orange light illuminating the interior of the car.

Luke watched, alarmed as the man in the passenger seat began to unbuckle his trousers. Not knowing what else to do, he attempted to open the doors. Emre clicked his tongue and shook his head, a delinquent smile etched across his face. "My friend think you are very good looking."

By then Luke's heart was clattering against his chest, its deafening beat filling his head until he could almost feel its vibrations in his temples.

"Don't worry my friend. We just want you…ehh…help. You are good friend so you will help us no?" As he spoke, the passenger pulled his jeans down and reclined his seat. 'My friend no girlfriend. So you will ehh…" Emre did not know how to say the rest of the sentence in English. He curled his hand into a loose fist and made a quick up and down motion. "You understand?"

It was clear what he wanted, but Luke looked at him and shook his head.

Emre clicked his tongue again. "You no help my friend, no go to Gönyeli okay? You stay here. Here nowhere."

He tried to read the driver's face, searching for some sign that maybe this was all a bad joke but it was stern, serious. They meant what they were asking him to do. The car dashboard showed that it was now past eleven. If they left him here he had no idea how long it would take him to find another car or if he could at all. It was unlikely that any other person would be willing to pick up a strange black man at this time in the middle of nowhere. He could tell the two men were aware of his situation.

"Please *abi*. Don't do this."

In response to his pleas, Emre opened the glove compartment and took out a small white tube. Luke recognized the K-Y logo on the side. He sighed, defeated and took it.

Even though they had given him some wet wipes to clean his hands afterwards, they still felt sticky. Luke once again heard the disgusting moan of the man in the passenger seat as his sickeningly warm substance slowly dribbled onto his hands. The stale smell that subsequently filled the car still clung to the insides of his nostrils and the back of his throat.

As soon as they reached Lefkoşa, he told the men to drop him off. He would walk the rest of the way. "But this not Gonyeli my friend." He stared at the driver. "Okay. Goodbye my friend. *Görüşürüz*." But he had no intention of ever seeing them again.

He turns over in his bed and closes his eyes to sleep. He cannot afford to dwell on the past. Tomorrow he needs to get up early for work.

## This Game for Two

Your thumbs quake as they feverishly rise and fall onto the smooth glass surface of the screen of your phone. They contain in their tips the climax of your anger, seething, intractable. Your lips move soundlessly – *plus two six seven* – as you enter your husband's phone number into the dialler. They suppress a cascade of words, protests, insults and lamentations, the words of one who has been wronged. The dialling tone seeps into your ears, falling amongst the clutter inside your head.

"Hello." He sounds unenthusiastic. You blow hot air out of your nose. Something else to add to the clutter, to fan the flames. Your anger is inflated, pushing aside reason. It needs to be released. It doesn't matter towards whom.

"*Sha!* I have had it with your sisters. *Ndavatadza.*" Not how you had planned to start the conversation. You had no plan, only words and tumultuous emotions. If you took time to plan, maybe the blood that had risen from your feet to your head would start going down and you did not want that to happen. Not until you had had your say.

You can hear him exhale on the other end of the line. It sounds like an echo in the static hollowness of the long-distance call. *How dare he? How fucking dare!*

"Tell me what happened."

*No no no.* You deserve more than this jaded inquiry, this half-hearted acquiescence of a response.

"I'm sorry. Should I not have called you? Am I interrupting your precious resting time again?" The words do not come from your mouth. They are forged somewhere at the pit of your stomach, heated, laced with bile and then discharged into the microphone. You hope that they have not cooled by the time they come out of the earpiece on his end of the line.

From the way he responds, it seems like they have. He repeats once again. "What happened?"

You pull the phone from your ear like it has bitten you and you can barely resist the temptation to shatter it and watch the pieces fall like rain. You press the red button that ends the call. Red. The colour of everything around you. The colour of your emotions. You sit down then stand up. One foot taps the floor impatiently. Your left hand drums absently on the coffee coloured sapele nightstand beside your bed. Even the seconds ignore your urgency, choosing instead to go by at the pace of a snail. *Hakudyiwe rinopisa nhasi.* Your eyes are lava. They could melt everything they touch. You close them.

He waits for two minutes. Two minutes too long. The call screen shows you; a before version of you, arms outstretched, smiling, lighter, unstressed, before his sisters and his mother conspired to ruin your life. You would not let them. He is standing next to you. He is smiling with his mouth closed underneath the shadow that his farmer's hat casts over his face. His khaki shirt is stretched over his paunch like an overstuffed *changani* bag. Behind you, the Mosi-oa-tunya gleams in the sun, shying underneath the veil of a rainbow. That was a good day. And a great night. You wait for the call tone to ring itself out, exhausted, unanswered. He would have to work for your cooperation now. *Men!*

You finally pick up on his third attempt.

"Where had you gone?"

You can play this game of pretend as well. You can play it much better than him and he knows this. "I'd gone to the kitchen to drink some water." He says nothing. "How was your day?"

"Busy. Long." You can see right through him. He will not guilt you into submission. "How was yours?"

"Fine. Your sisters were here…again." You wait for him to digest the statement, to turn it over in his fickle little head and examine its slimy surfaces and consider all the possibilities it held.

"What did they want?" He sounds slightly more alerted, more anxious. *Good.*

*What did they want? My blood!* Since your husband left for Senegal it felt as if his sisters had been out for your blood. For starters, they blamed you for him leaving, claiming, as you deduced from their thinly concealed slights and bits of conversations eavesdropped when they thought you weren't listening, that you had urged him, or when they felt particularly spiteful, that you had even suggested that he take the job outside the country. Why? So you would inevitably be left in charge of his finances to spend and waste as you pleased and you would have more time to freely be with your fleet of lovers.

*Seriously? Lovers?* You who had been a virgin until the night of your wedding. The accusations were too ludicrous to warrant any kind of concern or response, a simple case of affinal jealousy that should have dissipated with time. After all, in a family with so many women, three of them without husbands, all looking to the same man as their provider, there was bound to be friction. But what were at first whispers behind closed doors subdued by the restraints of faux politeness slowly turned into blatant, even abusive, persecutions and you had had enough.

Of all the people who had something to lose as a result of your husband leaving, was it not you who stood to lose the most? Who was it that spent countless nights in a bed that felt cold and empty, mourning the corpse of the shadow next to them that was a constant reminder of something they no longer had? What would that whore, your husband's younger sister, know of it? And the older one, her womanhood has certainly since dried up like a pasture in the thick of the dry season. Let them leave you please. What could they possibly understand of a husband's sacrifice to leave his family so that he could give them a better life, what with them not having any? *Asi ka!*

It was they who wanted his money, you often pointed out to your husband even though you had the feeling that he did not take your observations seriously. They thought you held the keys to the kingdom, so to speak, and refused to share his wealth with them against his wishes. To them, you were the villainous *muroora* who had fed their brother medicine to make him discard them as they felt he had. If it were not for you, they saw themselves living lavish lives, their children going to A-class schools, never wanting for anything, all courtesy of the hard work and constant toiling of your husband. *Jesu! Ishe wangu! Some people ought to be ashamed weduwee.* They did not even care about his welfare or whether he came back or not, they only wanted to reap the fruit of his labour. You were just in their way. But you would not let them. You would not let them touch even a single *kobiri*. Over your dead body. Let them talk.

"What else could they want?" You spit fire and venom into the phone.

"I don't know Constance. That is why I am asking." You squeeze the device in your hand. You need something to suffocate, to extinguish. He only uses your middle name when he is trying to antagonise you. It is his not so subtle way of letting you know that he thinks this is not a conversation worth having or not the time to have it. But he would have it nonetheless, now, whether he wanted to or not.

He does not have a monopoly on passive aggression. "*Iwe* Prosper. Are they not your relatives? You should be asking them what they want and not me. I am an outsider in this house, why should I be involved in your affairs? I do not want to use my words please. If you don't want to talk to me properly just hang up the phone." He does not hang up. A victory. Small, ultimately insignificant, but a victory.

The silence stretches across national boundaries, from the Savanna dry lands to the saline, humid air of the West African coast. It is his voice that finally breaks it, taut, controlled, to stop it bursting. Like you. "Can you please tell me…babe?" The last word sounds misplaced, like something he had forgotten was in his mouth and only found when he was not expecting it.

"They said they came to see your mother."

His mother had come from the ninth circle of hell to torment you. Old age your ass!

She came to live with you shortly before he left. Even then, with him present, she'd been a bit of a nuisance. Nothing serious then, no more than an itch in a sensitive area that could not be scratched while people were looking. High blood pressure. Arthritis. Cataracts. This pain here, another one there. The woman was a petri dish of diseases. Dangerously close to her expiration date. And she took full advantage of her illnesses and then some more. The most maddening of it was her cravings which always conveniently seemed to never be whatever you had cooked that particular day. If you cooked green veggies, she wanted *muboora.* If it was sweet potatoes, she wanted butternut. She supplemented these tedious demands with a newfound pickiness that she had acquired after your husband's departure – the very next day in fact. That morning she suddenly could no longer drink tea that had no milk yet when you all had breakfast the previous morning she had no problem finishing her cup of black tea with lemon. She could no longer stomach having sadza with beans. Her palate was suddenly revolted by porridge that did not have peanut butter and pieces of bread in it.

And his response to all of this? "She is old." *Old? Old you say?* Is she the first person to have got old? Is she the first person to have lived this long. Was Baba not almost a hundred when he passed? Did he mean to tell you that this woman who was barely past eighty, who still had the strength to walk to the kitchen to tell you that she wanted *muboora* for dinner was old? *Please.* You are not a remote control whose buttons ought to be pushed.

Because of their mother's sickness, your sisters-in-law often found justifiable cause to come to your house to attack you, to abuse you, to make snide comments and wave their loathsomeness in your face. Where they found the audacity to actually board two busses and come into your home just so they could run their filthy mouths, you would never know.

"*Hanzi* I am not taking good care of her." It was close enough to what they had actually said. At the very least it was implied. They said the old skank looked a shade darker than usual. Wasn't quite as jovial. She was not eating. How was that your fault? Did you make her grow old? And on top of that, no doubt to spite you, they took a list of things she wanted so that *they* could go and buy them for her. You did not sew her mouth shut so that she did not tell you what she wanted. If she found you too hostile to talk to, it was her problem.

"Was it not just a joke?"

You grind your teeth. *This man.* "Of course they disguised it as a joke but there's no doubt what they meant. They meant every scornful word. After all I have done for this woman, can you believe they would have the audacity to say such a thing." If it weren't for you, would she keep getting so goddamn fat?

"Are they still there?"

"No, of course not. They left. They took your mother with them." You pause. You hesitate. You are tired. "Prosper…I think you should come back."

He sighs. "We have talked about this before."

Talking about it meant you suggesting it and him refusing. It was almost a game now. You toss the idea. He ducks and runs away. But you have had enough. Inasmuch as you enjoy the improved quality of life that comes with him working abroad, at what cost does it come?
What did it matter if you could afford to buy all the most beautiful designer clothes when your insides had turned to mud? What use was it being able to afford a fancier car if you could not even go where your heart was? You could not keep living this life where your happiness was always tomorrow, never today.

"I mean it Prosper. I can no longer take it, being abandoned here. I can no longer bear to always wonder whose mouth utters the words that bring a smile to your face when I am not around; whose hand cooks the food that you eat; whom you think of that makes your blood run hotter. I am tired of missing you. I don't care if we don't make as much money. It is not a bigger house that I need, it is to be closer to you, to have you touch me, to feel you against me. I…I am all alone here. I cannot carry on like this. We cannot carry on like this."

The words come out of you like a waterfall. You had felt their presence somewhere in a part of your heart that your resilience had kept safely vaulted. But now that vault has been broken. For a long time it was being chiselled away by each ghost of a happy memory, each murmur of gossip from your sisters-in-law, each complaint from your husband's mother.

You were suddenly no longer angry with him. All you wanted was to have your husband back.

He does not say anything for a long time, but you can hear him breathing on the other end, hear him replaying your words in his mind, magnifying them, studying them, considering them.

"Okay. I will think about it."

*Note: The names of the people and places in this story have been changed.*

## A home shaped hole

There's a home shaped hole inside each one of us. And mine is the shape of a teapot.

Why else would I be writing this from Zimbabwe, a country that for so much of my life I've only ever viewed as an inadvertent geographical prison I needed to escape, the misfortunate teapot shaped little chunk of earth that I was unlucky enough to be born and bred in?

We all try to fill our holes with different things. Sometimes, it's with food from back home or the closest equivalent. I don't know how many times I have seen people cooking 'sadza' with semolina. Other people like to surround themselves with compatriots, forming communities, clubs, student bodies that are essentially miniature versions of life back home meant to reconstruct the familiarity of being in one's own country. Instead of fully immersing ourselves in our new lives when we go abroad, a piece of us always stays behind, one foot in the new life and the other in the old.

I suppose to give greater significance to my decision to return, you have to understand why I left in the first place. I mean, beyond my need to finally board a plane for the first time and test how 'strong' I was by determining, once and for all, whether or not the experience would make me vomit, as so many of us are told we certainly will by people who, strangely enough, have never been on a plane themselves. I didn't by the way, thank you very much. Or the fact that the longest distance I'd ever travelled prior to that was the two hundred and eighty something kilometres it takes to travel to my village in Mutasa. It was more than my desire to experience the fabled diaspora for myself: the place where people went and the sun, an entirely different celestial object altogether, turned their skin from peppered ebony to the colour of paw paw; I wanted to smell this air that once it entered your lungs it changed the way you talked so that when you returned, it was to Zim-bah-bway instead of Zimbabwe and Har-rah-ray instead of Harare; I wanted to see with my own eyes these clothes that when worn, turned good girls into whores and good boys into gangsters, clothes that were worn not only on the body but on a person's very character that hid even their manners underneath their foreign fabric. It was not just that I wanted a better education and better opportunities. More than wanting to go, I wanted – needed – to leave.

In order not to turn this into a sob story about the pitiful circumstances of my life – which is more challenging than you might think because self-pity is a bitch – let it suffice to say that my living conditions, emotionally speaking, were far from ideal and I had good cause to want to run away from all of it: a frigid family comprising one emotionally distant individual, an impassioned rivalry with another, and a stepmother I can only describe as the work of the devil. Add to that the natural struggles of adolescence and bickering amongst extended family members that you will find in any Zimbabwean family. Ah, I tried *amana.* I'd like to add, for the sake of these individuals, and if anyone else is wondering, that the first two of these things have since been fixed, but god that woman still grinds my gears. You know those people who, when they're not making you wonder how they exist, you constantly feel the need to apologise for their existence the way you would if say someone you're associated with were to say something homophobic at a Pride Parade or do the Nazi salute in Germany?

Sorry to digress. Naturally, the last place I wanted to end up was back here. Even if things didn't go quite well in Cyprus I would have rather gone to a different country. Home, as far as I was concerned, was now behind me and I was never turning back.

**The Fabled Diaspora**

So I'd finally made it out. My early days were admittedly daunting. I'd never been outside the country before and not only that, but all of a sudden everybody was white and nobody spoke English. Now, my factory settings were set to introverted, and it was hard enough interacting with people while I was still in Zimbabwe, but this...this was like being at my high school dance all over again except of course the hall was an entire country and there were girls everywhere.

Funny story, so originally, I was meant to do Architecture and not Civil Engineering. I get to Cyprus; I go through the registration process easily enough and it's now time for me to attend my first class. I'm a little nervous; it's uni, it's new, it's change. I don't like change. I walk into the class and…lo and behold, not a single chocolate coloured person. Not one. It's all vanilla in there. I didn't even sit down. I pretend I am lost and go straight back to the Student's Office and change my program there and then. Four years later, I had a degree in Civil Engineering that I don't know what to do with, because writing is now *bae*. Of course I didn't just pick the first program that came to my mind. Engineering is the closest thing to architecture except it's just less drawing and more calculating. And there were black students. It wasn't too big a price to pay in my opinion.

In retrospect it's silly that I would change my career, something that I'd been planning to do for the previous two years, all because there weren't any black people in that class. I can't justify my decision now, but then, it felt like it made all the sense in the world.

I've recently found an appreciation for African literature. I don't know if it is because most *good* writers - *boo hoo romance* - almost collectively, masochistically choose to depict the less agreeable traits of the human condition, or maybe it's just the kinds of stories I enjoy. Anyway, if you read African literature and if you pay attention to the stories about Africans going overseas then you'll notice that they are seldom ever happy tales. Shout out to Americanah by Chimamanda Ngozi Adichie and a certain alligator who recommended it. Maybe it's a Pan-African thing: *Africa is the best and everyone else is an asshole.* Maybe it's just reality, but I find it hard to believe that every African immigrant has suffered the way the people in some of these stories do. I don't know about the other stories that are going to be in this book, but I'm willing to bet a fair share of them are going to be grisly. Or maybe it's just the immigrant's way of filling their home shaped hole. By romanticising their idea of what they left behind and almost demonising the idea of migrating.

In any case, my own personal experience was nothing like that. The Turkish, who are the inhabitants of the Northern part of the island of Cyprus on account of some ongoing political hoo-ha with Greece and the UN, *more of that on Wikipedia*, are actually generally quite friendly. Amongst what little smattering of English that the majority of the population speaks, almost everyone knows and frequently uses the phrase "My friend" when referring to foreigners. And we quickly learned to call them "*abi*" – brother. Or the antonymous *abla* for the women, but my interactions and those of many others were with the men. The women mostly kept their distance. Aside from the ones I talked to in shops and banks, my trophy white friend's roommate, *I'll get to that*, and one particularly audacious hijab clad lady who asked to touch my dreadlocks and take a picture with me, I don't recall talking to many other Turkish women. Oh, and the MILF that was our landlord's wife. I'd like to think it was more of a cultural thing that they kept away from men, not just African ones. My point is, they were nice enough people. The ones that exhibited some signs of prejudice against us were the exception rather than the rule.

There was one incident that I think maybe raised some red flags as far as racism goes.

**The Phone Incident**

One great thing about not being in Zimbabwe is that things are so much cheaper. And another thing, despite this particular aberration, is great customer service. Seriously, most of the people I've met in retail outlets in Zimbabwe look like they don't get paid enough to give a tenth of a shit. I bought a phone, an LG G4 which was a *latest* back in 2015. The guys at the shop, hereinafter referred to as The Shop Guys, were nice enough the day I bought it. They had to be with the amount of money I was giving them. Hell, I had to live on noodles and *ekmek* for the next few months. A little less than a year later, my phone died. Just switched off and wouldn't switch back on. After a little digging, I found out that this was actually a common problem with that particular product line. Fortunately, or so I thought, I had a one year warranty on the phone so I took it back to the shop. Boy oh boy.

It was hard enough trying to explain what the problem was in the first place because The Shop Guys barely spoke English and I don't think I knew more than ten Turkish words. So, imagine trying to say that this was a common problem and they should replace my device and send the broken one back to LG because they were aware of the problem and were actually willing to send a replacement. Try typing that into Google translate. They eventually understood the 'Phone die' part and agreed to 'You fix problem' which I yelled repeatedly while I waved the warranty slip madly in their faces. They took the phone and told me to return two weeks later.

I returned three weeks later. 'No fix my friend. Phone no problem.' I was bemused. Was he saying that the phone had no problem, which it did, or it was not *his* problem, which it was? I was too upset to remember the exact details of what went down, but there was a lot of Google translate saying some pretty nasty words, some more waving of that poor warranty, thoughts about doing something drastic like shitting on the store floor or breaking the front glass. In the end, we eventually came to what I thought was an understanding but turned out to be just a way to get me out of the store and I guess stop drawing the attention of the other customers. He told me he would send the phone to some sort of parent company in Turkey. Okay.

When I came back several weeks later, said parent company hadn't yet come to collect devices that needed repairs because they hadn't accumulated a significant enough number. And then some more weeks later they'd only just collected them and it would supposedly take a week to ship them back. That day I did happen to see a phone on the shelf that looked a lot like mine, but I did my best to believe it was someone else's. And I was using what little resolve my anxiety allowed me to shout at these people, so I didn't have any left to ask if I could look at that device. Long story short, it took a month for my phone to be shipped back and wouldn't you know it, they didn't manage to fix or replace it because there was no discernible problem with it. And my warranty had conveniently run out so I would have to pay if I needed to get it fixed. Slick motherfuckers.

I finally gave up and just got a new phone. My G4 was never fixed or replaced, yet on more than one occasion when I visited The Shop Guys, I saw a lot of other Turkish people having their phones given back to them, all fixed up. And yes, some of them did get replacements. Is it possible that this was because of the particular problem with my phone which was virtually unfixable and that there was nothing more sinister at play here? Heh. Does the sun set in the East? Did the catholic priest really not touch the choir boys?

There were other small things, like a person at a counter in a supermarket ignoring you, a barber complaining about your hair being too hard to comb or a group of people looking at you and saying something to each other which was clearly about you. Of course it's entirely possible that I read too much into some of these things, but that's just part of it isn't it? Part of being an immigrant. I constantly felt this insecurity, this otherness that caused me to always be on the lookout for any signs of racism and/or xenophobia and to see them in places where they might not have been.

**Other Diasporans**

There's this joke. If you go anywhere in the world and shout something in Shona, you're bound to get a response in Shona.

There were so many Zimbabwean students, not just at my university, but all over the island. But in spite of the program switcheroo incident, I actually didn't befriend a lot of them except for a few classmates and housemates after I moved off campus following one unpleasant incident involving jollof rice, some hair, me and a Nigerian. More of that in a bit. It wasn't just that I'm naturally withdrawn, but I also didn't see the point of leaving Zimbabwe only so that I would surround myself with more Zimbabweans abroad. Yes, I know! So why did I leave the all-white class? Call it shock, I don't know. It's like those babies who cry the first time they see a white person. Whatever, I wanted to befriend people from other countries and in this I managed some degree of success. I got my trophy white friend who is now just a friend who happens to be white, befriended a coloured Kenyan guy to whom I am eternally grateful for his role in my academic success, and I was somewhat familiar with a few Pakistanis and Nigerians. Ironically though, at the end of my diasporic tenure, the opposite had become true. I just wanted to be around my compatriots.

Ah. Nigerians. I don't think you can talk about the African Diaspora without talking about Nigerians. During my first three semesters I stayed on campus. It was all well and good during the first year because I had Zimbabwean roommates, but after my first summer - during which I greatly came to appreciate Zimbabwean weather - I was moved to a different room and my roommates were all Nigerians. The first of them was your typical God-will-make-me-prosper prayer warrior. The only gripes I had with him were his unwavering need to convert me to Christianity despite my best blasphemous attempts to discourage him, and his morning prayers which had to be done at four a.m. and were loud enough to have awoken Jesus before his three days were up. The second was a quiet guy who had the nicest, shiniest Afro and always smelled really really good. He loved two things: anime and checkered shirts. And then there was Femi.

Picture an arbitrary Nigerian. Big, loud, club ranger, perpetually wearing sunglasses, tacky ones with golden rims, looked like the kind of guy who'd be behind the keyboard when you got that email from a Nigerian prince wanting to do some business with you. The only thing he was missing were tribal cuts on his face. Femi loved to cook. Nigerian dishes mostly. And he was quite good from what I surmised the one time he gave me some of his food before we had lived together long enough to decide that we would not like each other after all. He wasn't a bad person to be honest. I just didn't like that he frequently had his friends over and they were always making noise when I was trying to read, watch a movie or sleep. And almost conscientiously, they never failed to leave a mess.

One day, Femi cooks a pot of jollof. This was around the time I'd decided that I wanted to get dreadlocks so I was keeping my hair long. And the thing about our kinky curlies is that they're very brittle and I didn't care enough to invest in looking for remedies that prevented breakage. It was too much of a threat to my masculinity. So, whenever I combed my hair, bits of it always ended up all over the room, including on Femi's desk. And he'd complained about it previously but what was I supposed to do; leave the room every time I wanted to comb my hair? Actually that wouldn't have been a bad idea. But I disliked Femi and I was more than a little glad that it annoyed him. So this day Femi is having his jollof. I didn't comb my hair while he was eating, obviously. But I had in the morning so I guess a strand of it fell onto the floor and then decided to go on an adventure that would ultimately end on Femi's plate. It might not even have been my hair, come to think of it. Oh he was mad. And me being me, did my best to aggravate him even further by pretending I couldn't hear him shouting.

The slap was swift. A flash in which palm collided with cheek in an explosion of sound and pain. I couldn't react, except for one tear drop that took it upon itself to display my humiliation which was very promptly and discreetly wiped away. At five feet four, even if I'd wanted to hit back, I was no match for Femi who stood a good foot plus above me. I just pretended nothing had happened and continued watching the movie I was watching, my ears ringing, the entire left side of my face burning and plotting various convoluted revenge schemes all of which involved feeding Femi his own penis.

So to all my friends who always wondered why I hated Nigerians, now you know.

**The trophy white friend I mentioned earlier**

What's the point of going abroad if you're not going to send pictures back home of yourself and your white friend? Bonus points if they're the opposite sex and then your parents will already start wondering if their white *muroora*-to-be will be able to cook sadza, or if she will agree to wear *zambias* and *doeks*.

I know I've kept calling her a trophy white friend, but she means a lot more to me than that, I promise. But, when I first started talking to Zerya, I would be lying if I said it had nothing to do with the colour of her skin. I was now in my second year, so a little wiser, a little braver. She was a classmate of mine from Syria who'd transferred from a Turkish university and was one of the only four girls in my civil engineering class. I think the other two were from

Jordan and one was a Vhitori, straight *outta* Great Zimbabwe. Most of the people in the class were Arab guys. Our friendship was birthed under the guise of being study partners, but soon we were socialising outside of school and going out together. I remember specifically the day we went to the harbour and I couldn't imagine why she'd asked *me* to go, because at that point we knew very little about each other. But I'm glad we did. Maybe she wanted a trophy black friend. We black men are notorious for our…err…prowess in certain areas down south. Or maybe it made no difference to her at all that I was black and I was the only asshole.

Whatever, Zerya may have even been one of my ever changing list of best friends at a point. I certainly hung out with her more than anyone else. The boat cruise, the Nicosia paintings, Gloria Jean's Café, Bibliotheque, Dereboyu. Most of my good memories are the ones I made with her.

In case you're wondering – and I know you are – our relationship was only ever platonic. And no I never wanted it to be more. Why? I just didn't, simple as that… Okay fine, she had a boyfriend, but that really made no difference. I just never saw things going that route. All the same, it was probably better that way. There was a rumour at one point that she and I were dating, which I guess was started by some of her fellow countrymen who couldn't fathom why she hung out with me instead of them, and I may have not been as upset by that as I should have. But I don't think she was either. That's as far as it ever got and you know what? I have no regrets.

I'm glad we became friends and we are still close to this day, even though I haven't seen her in over three years. I'm probably closer to her than anyone else I was friends with over there.

**Why not stay?**

I mentioned the home-shaped hole before and trying to fill it. Well, guess what? The only thing that can actually fill it is home.

A graduate at only twenty-one, my entire life ahead of me on a red carpet that stretched into the stars, I had everything I'd set out to get. I had my degree which I'd not only got with the Turkish system equivalent of a first class grade, but had also managed to do so at the top of my class. In addition to that, I had an offer for a full scholarship to continue at the university for my master's and another from a Turkish firm that was looking for bright young African students like myself to do a kind of apprenticeship after which I would be guaranteed a job in their organisation, travel and living expenses all paid. It wasn't that they were generous or even that they were particularly impressed with me really, they would have taken any African student. It just so happened that their recruiter was friends with an engineer in the company where I did my internship. But I wanted to go home.

I didn't have an especially negative experience being an immigrant. In fact, I enjoyed myself for the most part. I can't say that I was lonely. I had a few friends and plenty of acquaintances. I had a relationship. Financially, I had no complaints. No longer a student, I now had plenty of time to be a tourist. It was easy enough to extend my stay illegally after my student permit had expired. All I needed to do was stay out of any kind of trouble that warranted police involvement. I was, for all intents and purposes, happy, or at the very least, fulfilled. Yet…

**Because of Chompkins, Chimombe, Buttercup, Lobels, Cerevita and other things**

Adding to the list of what I would say were overall amazing experiences I had in Cyprus, I also went camping one time. It was with a group of Zimbabweans who were friends of a friend and this guy just invited me. Why not? Pictures, the outdoors, a road trip, drinking and chilling. Sign me up. The experience was as fun as it sounds.

But then on the day we were scheduled to leave the campsite, something happened. Nostalgia. Bittersweet, eye stinging, heart melting nostalgia. I remember we were all sitting around the table having breakfast. I don't know exactly how it started or who started it, but we found ourselves talking about the food from back home that we missed; Chompkins chips, Charhons biscuits, Lobels bread, Buttercup margarine, Chimombe milk, Cerevita, you name it. I've never felt more sentimental about this country than I did that day.

I'm not going to tell you that this prompted my decision to come back, because it didn't. I already had my return ticket by then. But it made me realise just how much I missed these mundane things that I took for granted before I left, that after I'd only been here a few weeks I stopped caring about.

What I felt wasn't some sense of patriotism, it was much more profound, imminently much more forlorn. It was a desire to fulfil some longing that up until then, I'd never quite acknowledged I had, even though it had always been there. It encompassed, without being completely comprised of the things about Zimbabwe that I missed; the weather, the familiarity, the food, *kombis*, not feeling like an intruder all the time. I missed the banality of being where I belonged.

### Home Again

I'm not a patriot. I hate the state Zimbabwe is in as much as the next person and I complain as vehemently about how hard things are. I concede that life abroad is so much better. I too, bemoan the rampant corruption, the directionless government, the unemployment, the poor economy, the condition of our infrastructure. And honestly, given the opportunity I would leave again. But always with a view to come back. Because in the end, there is no place like home.

## Samantha Rumbidzai Vazhure

Samantha is a UK-born Zimbabwean who grew up in Masvingo. She works as a regulatory consultant in financial services, but is currently on sabbatical, pursuing her interests in writing and publishing. She resides in Wales with her husband and two children.

Samantha has written and published poetry collections in chiKaranga (Zvadzugwa Musango) and English (Uprooted) as well as a novel (Painting a Mirage). She also compiled an anthology of short stories by Zimbabwean women – Turquoise Dreams. Samantha enjoys writing realistic fiction and advocates causes she is passionate about in her works – discover more on her author website www.samantharumbidzai.co.uk. You may connect with her on Twitter, Facebook, LinkedIn, Instagram and YouTube.

## Barcode

You have been living in the UK illegally for eight years. For that reason, you still live with your older brother Lovemore, and his wife Benhilda who despises you. You think she is frustrated because you, a younger brother to her husband, have children, but she does not.

Lovemore returned from an untimely visit to Zimbabwe last night. He had gone to bury your mother who died mysteriously. You stayed up late discussing the details of how everything went and *zvirango*, the rituals that remain outstanding. You had become detached from your mother due to distance and the never-ending allegations of her witchery. Most of them by your own wife, Saru. You are still processing her death and feel numb. Flashbacks of the day your mother bid you farewell at Harare International Airport relentlessly plague you. "Kumbi *mawanangu, usatikanganwa zvinoita vana vevamwe*," she had counselled you to never forget your roots like other emigrants did. You feel guilty for letting her down.

It's 4am on a Thursday and your alarm has sounded twice. Your chronic nightmare, the details of which you cannot recall has been interrupted, again. You are certain the bad dream has a deeper meaning. A message. But you cannot decipher it and this frustrates you. As you peel off the duvet and climb out of bed, the first thought on your mind is, how on earth you are going to progress your life. You need your wife and two children back home to join you in the UK, but how in the world will you achieve this? Everyone you know who is doing well seems to do so because of couple teamwork. Your wife Saru seems distant when you phone her these days, and you've heard your childhood best friend Ngoni has been spending a lot of time with her. You are worried she has given up waiting for you.

The 16-seater van that shuttles you to the strawberry farm arrives at 4.40am, so you hastily make your way to the bathroom. The shower gently sprinkles your skin like confetti, and you allow a moment of gratitude for the privilege of running warm water; something most people take for granted. They have never had to bathe from a bucket, sometimes with cold water because the electricity back home is intermittent; and sometimes the firewood has to be saved for cooking. Your mind shifts to reminisce about your good times with Saru, how you met her at the University of Zimbabwe when she was an undergraduate and you were completing your master's. How you quickly fell in love with her while she took her time to warm up to you, until the love eventually blossomed. Then you sent cows to her father as your token of appreciation, and to seal the relationship in marriage. She gave you two beautiful children. In that moment of gratefulness, you yearn for Saru's touch and her laughter.

The thoughts tear your heart apart, but your mind cursorily shifts to the local girls you see regularly. They glow more and are self-assured, *but the risk is not worth it*, you tell yourself. But the truth is, you can't afford them. Your mind returns to the present when the ten-minute timer sounds on your mobile phone and you depart from the warm shower room to get dressed. The temperature drops as you enter your lunchbox bedroom where the central heating bar does not work. It broke some two years ago and despite complaining about it, Benhilda insists it is on her to-do list and she will get it fixed soon. You fleetingly wonder why Lovemore does not pull his weight and fight your corner. Their three-bedroom semi-detached house in a quiet cul-de-sac has a larger spare bedroom, but Benhilda uses it as her dressing room and it is where her friends sleep when they rarely visit. The radiator in the guest bedroom works and you are often tempted to break the rule and camp there overnight, but the risk is not worth it. You swiftly plaster Vaseline onto your goose-bumped body and pile on layers of thermal clothing in readiness for work.

In the kitchen, there is leftover food from the previous evening in saucepans placed on Benhilda's Parry six-burner gas cooker. Her pride and joy that she gloats over to anyone who will listen. You pause for a moment wondering whether she would prefer it if you ate the leftovers or her bread. Either way, she will pass a subliminal comment implying you eat too much; despite the fact that you spend all day at work, and you contribute more than half your pay towards the rent and bills. You decide to serve rice with chicken sauce and coleslaw, and you leave the chicken alone. You ladle as much food as you think you'll manage to scoff down in five minutes onto a deep plate, including the coleslaw which you know should not be microwaved, but you like it warm.

While the leftovers are heating up in Benhilda's Menumaster programmable microwave which must be kept spotless, you need to make a sandwich to have for lunch later. Benhilda recommends one slice each of the ham and cheese. The sliced bread she likes to buy is neither white nor thick, because she's on yet another diet. You have given up wondering why she never buys the food you like despite contributing money towards the communal grocery shopping she insists on. *Would it be better to make two sandwiches with one slice of each, or one sandwich with two slices of the ham and cheese?* You decide on the former and brace yourself for the inevitable attack after your 16-hour shift. Having recently submitted your monthly contributions to Benhilda, you hope the money might ameliorate her wrath towards your little indulgence. *She loves money.* With that thought, you decide to fish out a small piece of cold chicken from one of the saucepans and throw it straight into your mouth. *Ha! Too much Royco,* you internally detest the over-spiced offering.

The microwave tings and you devour the leftovers for breakfast, ignoring the heat of the nutriment that sears your pallet. You wash down the food with a pint of 'value' orange juice from the corner shop that Benhilda says you should have. The Tropicana is reserved for her and her visitors. You used to have it anyway, but she began buying the type with juicy bits which you loathe. The shuttle will arrive any minute now, so you quickly wipe off drops of sauce and crumbs scattered over the cooker and kitchen counter. As your swift arm hoovers beside the sugar basin, instant coffee and teabag canisters, you suddenly remember that the farm no longer supplies teabags. Discretely, you extract two from Benhilda's tea cylinder and stuff them in your trouser pocket. You unplug your discman from a socket where it was charging overnight and stuff it in the nearest pocket of your coat that you have unhooked from the porch. Grabbing your foil-packed ham and cheese sandwiches, you shut the door behind you and head out to face the day.

It is May already, but the mornings are still bitterly freezing, so you put on the long weatherproof parka coat that Lovemore handed down to you when you arrived in the UK. You have a moment of appreciation for Lovemore because he has given you so much, including the opportunity to escape hunger and poverty. It is his benevolence that makes it possible for you to feed your family back home. You slip on your worn synthetic knitted gloves, breathe in the crisp fresh air and wish for a proper UK summer this year. As you patiently wait for the work shuttle at the corner of your road, you decide to send Saru a text message. There is no mobile reception at the strawberry farm, so you reach for your old brick Nokia phone from an inner coat pocket, remove your right-hand glove and text her, hoping to see her response now rather than later, after work.

*Mukoma Lovemore arrived safely last night.*
*Thanks for all you did for amai's funeral.*
*He tells me you're doing a great job with the kids.*

*I miss you baby girl.*
*You are everything to me.*
*We'll soon be together.*
*Promise me you're hanging in there.*
*For me. For us.*
*I love you.*

No response. This has become a normal occurrence. Occasionally, you call Saru and your children pick up her cell phone and tell you their mother is "not there". You take those opportunities to make intentional conversation to get to know them better, but when they are not requesting new clothes or money, they don't have much else to say to you. You resolve to phone home tomorrow night after work.

The white van arrives on time and Lechoslaw slides the door open, jumps out and folds his seat so that you may get into the back. His brother Stefan is driving and exclaims his usual greeting in a strong Polish accent.

"Good morning Zimbabwe!"

You chuckle and respond, "Hello hello Poland!"

The van is packed with foreigners, like sardines, with nearly all continents represented by workers with no papers. They will all be paid cash in hand at the end of the week. The rate is £3.50 per hour and way below the minimum wage.

"*Sei sei blaz* Kumbi?" Tindo, another Zimbabwean cheerfully greets you from behind your seat. You tell him you're okay, but his facial expression reveals he does not believe you. He inquires how your mother's funeral went and whether Lovemore had a safe trip back. You strain to relay a few funeral details, then quickly change the subject - the current exchange rate and the most reliable Zimbabwean to use to send money home these days. Before you know it, the white van arrives at a farm, somewhere in mid-Kent and the shift starts promptly at 5am.

Your least favourite supervisor, Karen, is on duty. She is a hefty and bossy middle-aged blonde who reminds you of the cold and confident whites back home. The ones who are less humble and not as reserved as the ones you meet in UK malls; the over-courteous UK ones who say "sorry" even when it is you who has bumped into them. Karen's face is plastered with several layers of make-up to conceal her mulish wrinkles, and you hate to imagine what time she woke up to take on the poorly executed task. You wish her rainbow-coloured face would exude some positive energy, but it does the exact opposite. Karen flicks her bob numerous times unnecessarily to assert her presence. You have heard some of your colleagues claiming she does it to attract male attention. Your attention. She cracks a dry joke as she separates you from Tindo, to ensure you focus and maximise your output. *There is nothing attractive about that*!

You fish out the earphones connected to the discman in your left side pocket and press the play button. Your favourite *sungura* CD begins to play and inevitably aggravates your concoction of grief and nostalgia. You miss your late mother more when Simon Chimbetu's *Samatenga* plays, and you fight off your tears. Stubborn tears that you wipe off with your forearm and thoughts of gratitude. You vigilantly pick the strawberries and immediately zone out, as you normally do.

At 10am, you make your way to the canteen for a 15-minute break where you can rest your legs if you're lucky enough to find a vacant seat. You arrive at the canteen and all seats are taken. There is a free socket, so you are able to charge your phone instead. Tindo is already there, making a cup of tea. He has a whole box of teabags and freshly baked *magwinya* that his live-in South African girlfriend, Ntokozo, made.

"Have some *mudhara*, I can't finish these on my own." You pretend to hesitate then accept the offer and thank Tindo profusely for his kindness.

"By the way, you said it's your birthday this weekend, *tiri kuita sei baba*? How are we celebrating?"

"*Hapana ufunge, ndakachona*." You explain that you are broke, having co-funded your mother's funeral. That is not the real reason why you won't go out. The truth is, Benhilda has a university student friend who comes to braid her hair every now and again. You overheard Benhilda saying Michelle will be braiding her hair all day on Saturday, and you want to be around to look at Michelle. To bask in her presence and hope she connects with you, somehow. You know you are not Michelle's type, but you hope she notices you anyway. Even if she does not notice you, you want to gaze at Michelle, allow her elegance to hypnotise you, and permit those mental images of her gracious beauty to intensify your Beef Strokenoff.

You agree to meet up with Tindo on Sunday instead, to watch the final English Premier League match of the season. Manchester United is playing Everton and you would not miss it for the world. United already won the league last weekend, but there will not be much more football on television thereafter.

You will walk over to his place, a 30-minute stroll from Lovemore's house. It will be more relaxed there, plus Ntokozo will have gone all out with the cooking and cleaning. She will have bought a lot of beers and will join the match cheer. Ntokozo is a nurse who tries too hard and hopes for marriage. She probably pays the rent and most of the bills for their modern three-bedroom house in an upmarket neighbourhood.

On Friday morning, as you wait for the white van, glimpses of your recurring night terrors download into your consciousness. You are being chased by white men, but Saru and Ngoni are there laughing at you. You feel upset and wonder what the meaning of the nightmare could be. The white van promptly arrives at 4.40am as usual, and the usual *hello Zimbabwe, hello Poland* ritual takes place.

You sit on your usual seat and expect to hear Tindo, but after a minute of silence, you turn back and realise he is not in the van. You immediately send Tindo a text message to find out what's going on. He replies that he had to call in sick but will explain the full story on Sunday. *Iri bho mudhara, see you on Sunday!* you respond as you settle into your seat and the van enters the motorway.

You immediately notice flashing blue lights behind you, then Stefan and Lechoslaw break into a desperately rapid and nervous Polish dialogue.

*"Co się dzieje? Co się dzieje?"*

*"Nie wiem! Mamy przejebane!* We're fucked!"

A few seconds later, the loud wail of an impatient siren brings your shuttle to a sudden halt. The Polish brothers talk quicker as if they are arguing, and the flashing blue lights keep dithering behind you. After ten or so minutes, four fully armed policemen disembark from their unmarked van and walk up to yours. One of them, tall and heavy, asks the driver where he is going so early in the morning. Stefan responds pensively that "we are going to work."

"Do you have your driving licence on you?" Stefan pretends to look for one, but eventually says he forgot it at home.

"Step outside sir. What is your full name?"

As Stefan steps out of the van and spells out his last name, the mist waltzing out of his mouth spells trouble. The police officer repeats Stefan's name into his walkie talkie.

"Can you confirm your date of birth sir?"

"Twenty…twenty thirrrd…" Stefan stammers and his eyes begin to water.

"Twenty third of what?" The officer calmly probes him with the patience of a parent who has finally caught their child in the act of a long-suspected transgression.

"Ummm. Twenty…I'm not sure."

*Oh shit!*

One of the other three officers inserts his torso into the van through the driver's door and asks, "Do any of you have identification documents?" As he slowly scans our faces for an answer, we remain shtum and blank. He reaches for his walkie talkie and calls for backup.

"You have the right to remain silent. I am arresting you on suspicion of being immigration offenders. Anything you say may be used against you at a later stage." Within minutes, another unmarked van with flashing blue lights arrives. Four more huge police officers walk up to the van, this time with a pack of keen and curious Alsatians. And just like that, you have been seized.

As you watch the drama unfolding, your nightmare suddenly becomes alive. The white van is confiscated and removed by a police tow truck. Fifteen of you are cuffed and sent to Brook House detention centre to await deportation. As you travel to the removal centre you had never heard of, neatly tucked away behind Gatwick Airport, you accept your fate as one might give in to death, and realise that your dreams have been shattered.

When you arrive at Brook House and they uncuff you, you quickly send a text to Lovemore:

*Mukoma tabatwa, they are sending us back home.*

*I'm at Brook House near Gatwick.*

*I'm not sure how long I'll be here for.*

*I will need money, toiletries and food.*

*If you could pack some clothes too.*

Within hours of arrival, you realise that the detention centre is full of foreign criminals and asylum seekers who have lost their cases, awaiting deportation to their countries of origin. The place is chaotic, and you wonder how you will survive here. You have already discerned that it can take months and sometimes years for deportation to take place. You are placed in a cell with a Russian armed robber and a Nigerian asylum seeker.

The Russian criminal constantly swears in his native language, hitting and kicking walls - you find his presence intimidating and energy sapping. He sleeps on the top bunk of the bed you share with him. The Nigerian asylum seeker is in unswerving dramatic prayer on the bottom bunk of the other bed. The top bunk of his bed is empty; its recent occupant was rushed to hospital after attempting to end his life only a few days ago.

"*Fada Gaad*, in *de* mighty name of *Jizos!* Send down thunder, lightning and a spiritual whirlwind to abruptly end this my problem!"

"*Piz-dets!*" the Russian swears in response and punches the wall.

"No weapon *dat* is formed *agains'* me shall prosper, in *Jizos* name!" Inspired by the energy of that moment, you inadvertently answer "amen", then the Russian screams, "*Idi na hui!*" and punches the wall more vigorously than before. His knuckles begin to bleed.

"Equip me father with a heavenly machine gun to free us from this nonsensical situation. *Bhratatatatata!* I am coming for you with my spiritual Mafia! *Bhratatatatatatatata! Rabalashabala libirikishabahiska!*"

You quietly observe the two in consistent hullabaloo and struggle to focus on how you will navigate the future.

As the Nigerian chants in tongues and sprays his surroundings with spiritual bullets from his heavenly machine gun, male officers storm in to first aid the Russian.

"Oh not you again! What have you done to yourself Feliks?" The aid murmurs in frustration as he forcefully restrains the Russian criminal. The Nigerian man intensifies his indecipherable speech.

"Oh for fucks' sake Adebiyi! Just shut up will ya!" The aid pushes the Nigerian out of the way and he lands on the floor with a loud thud.

"God forbid!" is all the Nigerian manages to say, then whimpers quietly with his head between his knees.

The detention centre staff are physically and verbally abusive, and completely oblivious to the dangers of mixing criminals with non-criminals in the cells. Those who express their concerns or "complain too much" are kicked, pushed or spat on in the face by the staff. It is best to stay put in silence and watch the clock ticking.

The food is inedible. Those who have been in the detention centre for months contemplate suicide daily.

Lovemore arrives that evening and promises to get you a good lawyer, which he does. He brings you essentials to live on, but most of them are stolen on your second day at Brook House, during a short stroll outside for fresh air. The lawyer is paid thousands of pounds to ensure your deportation hearing is expedited. The days in the detention centre are long, but the nights are even longer. Feliks induces tangible fear for your life with his thunderous intimidating rants, and Adebiyi's sonorous theatrical prayers intermittently startle you out of your sleep. He even sets his alarm at 3am to demand his freedom and to rebuke this bondage in the name of *Jizos*.

You spend your birthday in the detention centre and Lovemore returns to celebrate with you, this time with Benhilda. Like you, they are devastated by the state of affairs. They have brought a small birthday cake from ASDA, a midsized suitcase full of your clothes and a few things to take home. The gesture brings tears to your eyes. Before they leave, they promise you everything will be okay and will do everything in their power to get you out of there.

After a week in the hellish detention centre, your lawyer confirms your departure the following day. That night, a concoction of excitement and the usual racket keeps you half-awake till the early morning hours. Adebiyi, who has now warmed up to you, his African brother, is distraught that you are leaving so soon. He prays for your "journey mercies" all night and asks God to favour him too. Feliks screams and punches the wall and ceiling above you in response, and the predictable cycle of drama unfolds. The detention centre officers turn up to offer first aid and to quiet things down. You finally fall asleep.

When your alarm sounds at 6am, your eyelids are heavy and reluctant to separate. A barnyard rotting-manure-type odour slaps your nostrils as you return to consciousness. *That burst sewage pipe needs fixing pronto*, you cogitate. Through crusty eyes, you seem to see a dangling figure resembling a rattan egg-shaped hammock swing. Unsure whether you are still asleep, you rub the remnants of slumber off your aching eyes and the fog of exhaustion slowly begins to dissipate. It becomes as clear as day that a body is suspended from the metal railing of the upper bunk of the bed across the cell. Anchored by a thick leather belt tightly wrapped around its neck, the lifeless mass of flesh has long succumbed to asphyxiation. It rocks ever so gently and peacefully, like a hammock swing resisting the gentle nudge of a patio breeze. Its buttock nearly touches the concrete floor and its legs outstretch in your direction. Beneath it, a small puddle of urine mixed with a final deposit of faecal matter explains the offensive reek. When you tilt your glance upward to corroborate your fear, the rigor mortis on Adebiyi's face confirms to your horror, that he has left the building.

The gruesome sight thumps your being, forcing you to emit the loudest screech of your lifetime. You offer a substantial helping of pungent vomit, some of it splattering onto Adebiyi's legs. You abruptly get up and knock your head viciously against the upper bunk. The tears stream down your cheeks, and you roar even louder. Feliks wakes up to the shocking sight and immediately slurs loudly, "*Gav-no! Gav-no!*" He slaps his own face frantically and an army of staff storms in to control the commotion. You are both immediately removed from the cell and prepared for questioning by police. A few hours later, after it is determined that Adebiyi's death is not suspicious, a prison welfare officer asks if you are well enough for the long haul flight back to Zimbabwe that evening.

"Of course!" You affirm with an air of annoyance. *What kind of question is that?*

The flight takes off at 6pm, and immediately after the seatbelt signs are off, you make your way to the hospitality gallery and demand a full bottle of whisky from the tired looking flight attendant. She senses your desperation and hands you four miniatures, two of which you pour down your throat in quick succession. She hands you two more and you return to your seat where you pass out shortly thereafter.

You arrive at Harare International Airport with just a bag of clothes and a few cheap gifts bought by Lovemore for your family. You find Saru, Ngoni and your two children waiting for you at the airport at 6am. Your daughter, Tambu, is now thirteen and your son, Farai, is eight. You burst into tears when you see and hug Farai for the first time. He seems shocked and overwhelmed by the quickly unfolding events. He is limp and expressionless but occasionally smiles nervously. Saru was carrying Farai's pregnancy the year you left for the UK. You are shocked that Tambu who was only five when you left is blossoming into a fine young woman. She does not speak much, but seems happy to see you. Saru seems jumpy and more talkative than usual.

Making your way to the airport parking lot, you notice an overfamiliarity between Farai and Ngoni; it stings your heart with jealousy. "Daddy Ngo, it's my turn to take the front seat because when we were coming here it was Mhamha, and when we went to the movies last week she was in front again...'

"Ok, you can sit in front!" Saru abruptly stops Farai from spilling more beans.

Wearing a shiny alabaster-blue oversized suit, a pink shirt and snow-white trainers, Ngoni stretches out his right arm and dramatically unlocks his Pajero SUV. "This is the latest model *mudhara! Dziriko kuUK here idzi? Hapana ati aanayo muZimbabwe iyi*! I'm the only one driving this in Zim my friend!" He goes out of his way to point out the high-specification frills on his "latest toy", the 18 inch platinum rims, camel leather upholstery handmade for him in Gauteng, power mirrors…you zone out as Ngoni rambles on. You couldn't care less what his car can and cannot do. Saru cheers him on and chortles in excitement, "This is definitely the only one in Zim!" She adds.

"*Hauna nzara here mudhara?* We can pass through a food court if you want. It's obvious *hauna* cash *ka iwe. Ha, kudzingwa munyika yaQueen ma1 chaiwo.*" Ngoni arrogantly offers to buy you food, then chuckles at the fact that you have been booted out of the queen's kingdom without a penny to your name. You decline the offer. It's too early, you are still sick from the shock you woke up to at Brook House and everything is happening too fast.

"Change that CD Farai, *raakubhowa*. Play Joe Thomas. It should be in the glove compartment." Saru calmly instructs your son from the back seat.

"No, play the dancehall mixtape. *Isa* Turn me on *ya*Kevin Little," Tambu interjects. This is the only time she has spoken since you hugged in the airport arrivals, and the realisation of how much parenting you have missed out on hits you, hard. You internally promise to bridge the gap between you and your children. Anything to salvage the inevitable transactional relationship that has been dictated by the long-distance.

Ngoni drives you home via Warren Hills to see your mother's grave. The sight of a fresh heap of soil, wilting flowers and a small placard with her name ruptures your heart. Sitting beside the grave with your legs and arms crossed like a child in a naughty corner, you expel loud shrieks and gasp for air for what seems like an eternity. As you mourn for your mother, the trauma of Adebiyi's untimely death sets in. Saru and Ngoni try unsuccessfully to console you – they are clueless of the grievous emotional turmoil that has culminated in that moment. About two hours later, when your energy runs out, you eventually agree to leave.

When you arrive at your house, Ngoni hangs around a little longer than you would expect. You have not been with your wife for so long and desperately want to rekindle your intimacy. It is all you have now. Nothing else. When Ngoni finally leaves, you sense hesitation each time you try to touch Saru. She seems to wince upon contact, but you are not sure whether it's been too long, so you decide to take it easy and give her time.

You spend the rest of the day wandering around the bungalow that took you eight years to build. Four bedrooms, a lounge, dining room, kitchen with a pantry in Cranbourne. *Not bad for a boy from Mbare.* The house looks a lot smaller than it appeared in the pictures and it seems older than you imagined. Some of the building work was done with such palpable negligence, parts of the house have begun to fall apart. Could you be unfairly comparing it to buildings competently erected in the UK? The ones that are built at the speed of lightning, yet come with building guarantees and warranties on structural and latent defects for at least ten years after the work. You know you will not find the cowboys who duped you, so you push the thought to the back of your mind and focus on remaining positive.

Later that night, you embrace Saru in bed and tell her how much you've missed her. The goosebumps that used to infest her body when you whispered sweet nothings into her ear are utterly absent. You notice with mild indignation that her skin remains silky smooth… and glowing. Her expensive human hair extensions drape over your chest and she looks delectable. After a lot of talking, she promises you that everything will be okay. She is no longer used to sleeping with a man and your sudden return, albeit exciting, feels strange. You decide that as you have not had sex with her in eight years, an extra night or two of waiting won't hurt.

You stare into the roof with no ceiling and notice a lizard creeping across *marata* directly above you. *Could Saru be the "cowboy" and not the building contractors?* After attempting unsuccessfully to process how badly your life is unfolding, you notice that Saru has long fallen asleep. With hope for a better future together, you also succumb to much-needed sleep. In your dreams, Adebiyi visits. Hanging off the top bunk, he lifts up his head and offers an invocation, which you complete with a litany of hope.

The next day, you go shopping for groceries with the bit of money Lovemore gave you. Saru tags along and nonchalantly throws little luxuries into the basket. Chocolate, crisps, biscuits and the more expensive brands of everything. When you ask her what proper food she normally buys, she proudly announces that Ngoni usually sorts that out, because the money you have been sending home was never enough.

"This is what we're used to now," she titters without realising the offence she is causing. "Oh, and I love Savanna dry!" She announces as she loads two six-packs of the dry cider onto the full trolley. So, your wife who did not drink when you left now drinks but forgot to mention it. You decide to not dwell on the new developments. *Coping mechanisms*, you internally call out and dismiss her unpleasant surprises.

That evening when the kids have retired to bed, Saru seems to loosen up as she chucks down ice-cold Savanna dry. You finish off the whisky miniatures from the flight back home. You both reminisce about the past and how much you've missed each other. You gaze at her deeply, hoping she looks back at you, into your eyes, but Saru avoids eye contact. When she is halfway through her second six-pack, she changes the channel to a late-night music show on DSTV. She gets up to dance to Afro-jazz, writhing in a manner you're unfamiliar with, pulling up her skirt to unveil silky thick bronzed thighs. *Wow, a bit raunchy.* You find her behaviour distasteful, only because she is your wife, but it somewhat turns you on. You get up to waltz with her momentarily, then drag her to bed before she passes out.

Towering over Saru who now spreads herself naked on the bed, you stand firm and keen, like a tall oak tree hugged tightly by heartless ivy. She whispers, "I want you" and you will oblige her. Saru's glowing skin diffuses an inviting essence that trebles your thirst for her. Engorged with desire and grateful for the overdue invitation, you neck her passionately and whisper the sweetest things in her ear, "*Ndokuda* baby. *Uri wangu iwewe.*"

With flagrant urgency, you thrust in and out of her with rampant unapologetic vigour. You find that she is as vast and dry as the Savannah she has been drinking. In her state of disorientation, Saru whispers "Ngoni" and what you had hoped to be an oasis of pleasure quickly turns into a sea of heartbreak, betrayal, confusion, doubt. You immediately deflate, like the untimely detonation of a balloon that was gliding gracefully in the air before landing on a vicious opuntia spine. Unconscious of her carelessness, she passes out and leaves you wide awake to soak in your severely bruised ego. An ego bruised beyond repair, by a million glochids flung by the same ruthless cactus.

In the weeks that follow, Saru's detachment from you becomes more conspicuous than the presence of a skunk, and so does Ngoni's. He declines your invitations to spend time alone with him. Time you hope might reveal what you already know, the trouble you smell. Ngoni says his thriving businesses are doing so well and require his perpetual presence. Yet he seemed to have the time for Saru when you were away in the UK. Saru only agrees to sex with you when she is drunk, but you can barely afford to keep her drunk without a steady income. She disappears for hours on end most days and sometimes returns home drunk.

"Saru, are you seeing someone else?" You confront her eventually.

"*Siyana neni iwe, zirombe!*" Without denying an affair, she attacks you for being a useless douche bag.

A dark cloud of sorrow envelopes your being as you live day by day without a solid plan for the future, in a marriage that is shattered irreparably. An aching heart makes death feel so close. Too close. Your sporadic thoughts often wander to Adebiyi. Perhaps you should have beat him to his idea. What use is it, to be back home to such chaos? Then your thoughts saunter to your own mother's death, a wound that might never heal. You realise then, that your children are far too young to handle the loss of a parent. A hefty and unnecessary complication you decide to avoid.

Tambu and Farai are your only sources of hope. The only reason you have not taken your own life. When they are not in school, you familiarise yourself with them, by learning their favourite food, colours, music, tv programs, sports. But some days are harder than others. When they ask you why you cannot get a job or start a business like "Daddy Ngo", your ego is battered beyond measure.

You consistently wonder how life could possibly turn out this bad for you, despite how hard you worked for everything. Your bachelor's and master's degrees, all reduced to meaningless framed pieces of paper hanging on the walls of an unhappy home. You visit your mother's grave often; you seem to find solace there.

About two months after returning to Zimbabwe, you are shopping for seeds and garden tools at a local farmer's co-op. You have decided to keep busy by growing your own fruit and vegetables in your half-acre garden. You bump into the mother of your ex-girlfriend. Rudo was your high school sweetheart who you quickly forgot about when you met Saru at university. Rudo went to Africa University in Mutare after high school and the distance fizzled out the relationship during your undergraduate years.

"*Amai makadii henyu,* how are you Mai Moyo?" You greet her warily. You are aware that Rudo was heavily invested in you when you broke her heart all those years back. You want to ask Mai Moyo what became of Rudo, where she is now and whether she is happy. You wonder if Rudo ever stopped loving you, whether perhaps there might be a glimmer of hope for a friendship at least. Something to hold onto. You wonder how to ask the question. *How is Rudo? Where is Rudo? Is Rudo still there? Is Rudo married now?* Anything could have happened to her. After exchanging pleasantries about the weather and the rapidly declining economy, you blurt out, "*Mufarise* Rudo. Pass my regards to Rudo."

"Oh, did you not hear? Rudo died three years ago *mwanangu.*"

"What? What happened?"

"*Zvinorema mukuwasha*. It's tough, my son in law. She took her own life after she caught her husband cheating."

"Aaagghhh. Sorry *shuwa*. I didn't know. How are you coping?"

"Our lives will never be the same without her, but we believe everything happens for a reason. With God's grace we will be okay."

"Are you still in Sunningdale? Maybe I'll come and visit you one of these days."

"That would be wonderful *mwanangu*. Joyce is there. She would be happy to see you." Mai Moyo says with a promising smile.

In the days that follow, you silently grieve for Rudo, your mother and Adebiyi, and get on with gardening. Thoughts of Joyce begin to infest your mind. She is Rudo's younger sister. The one who used to take your love letters to her. The one you would send to ask Rudo to meet you at the local shops. She was beautiful then and you wonder what she looks like now.

***

Benhilda has been sending you more messages than usual. One evening, she and Lovemore call you to make an announcement that leaves you elated, to the point of forgetting the predicament you're in.

"We're pregnant!" You cannot help noticing the tension in Lovemore's voice as he feigns excitement for the imminent baby. Benhilda subsequently becomes unnaturally friendly, but you play along, hoping that something positive might come out of the interactions. At the very least, this child could be the *cease and desist* that might heal your toxic relationship with her.

One morning, about five months after your deportation, a ray of hope in a text message ignites your life force.

Benhilda: *I think I have found a solution...*

*If you change your name and get new IDs, you can come back.*

*Michelle has a British passport and says she can help us.*

*She will write a letter of invitation as your "fiancée"*

*And she will provide whatever is required to get you back here.*

Your prayers have been answered! Benhilda sends you money to begin the exciting new journey. You are very aware that she needs you to return so that you can supplement their living costs, more so now with a baby on the way. You will be the childminder on night and weekend shifts, and your days off work will be spent looking after that child. You do not care, because that existence seems a million times better than being with a wife who no longer loves you. A wife having an affair with your married childhood friend. An affair you cannot prove, yet it is beyond reasonable doubt. Life in Benhilda's comfortable home is a welcome relief from the intermittent electricity and clean water supply that have become an unfortunate daily reality in Zimbabwe. You slowly begin to detach yourself from Saru and anything to do with her.

After a few visits to Mai Moyo's, a friendship between you and Joyce blossoms. You open up to her about your grief and the trauma caused by Adebiyi's death, a conversation you have not been able to have with absent-minded Saru. With her own relatable loss as a reference point, Joyce offers a sturdy shoulder to cry on. Like a flower ready for pollination, she is receptive and bright. She exudes irresistible warmth that guarantees her a throne on your mind. That inner space left vacant by Saru in your right striatum is now possessed by Joyce. She lingers there with majestic charm as a rent-free inhabitant.

Joyce works at the Zimbabwean Department of the Registrar General. With the promise of a relationship in the UK, away from your wife and the bitter Zimbabwean economy, Joyce accelerates your applications for papers. She bribes officials for a new birth certificate, then a passport, all in your brand-new name. She knows friends who forge bank statements and other supporting documents for the UK visa application.

When the papers are ready, Lovemore sends money for a ticket. You cannot help wondering why Michelle is being so generous. You know she would not charge anyone for such a favour because her parents are wealthy. You wonder if she might have the slightest feelings for you, and if not, whether the fake relationship could be turned into a reality. You shamelessly begin to create a space for Michelle in your heart. If things do not work out with her, your plan B is to import Joyce. You wait with bated breath for the journey ahead.

Eventually, you announce to Saru your imminent return to the UK. She feigns disappointment and instantaneously announces she is pregnant. You wonder if it's yours and swallow the immense disappointment that comes with the prospect of yet another mouth to feed. One you might not be responsible for. Deciding to not dwell on the matter, you focus on the brighter future ahead.

***

Your flight lands at Gatwick Airport on a frigid December morning. As you walk towards passport control, memories of Brook House, just next door, fleetingly return to plague your mind and you hope you never set foot there again. The bone chilling arctic blast rouses your scepticism, but knowing that Lovemore, Benhilda and Michelle are waiting for you beyond the customs declaration hall calms you down. The prospect of a warm shower, fancy food cooked by Benhilda and a new niece or nephew excites you. The mystery behind Michelle's benevolence electrifies you. Your fantasy runs wild as you imagine visiting Tindo with Michelle on your arm. You imagine Michelle and Ntokozo cooking and laughing in the kitchen, the aroma of food wafting through the open plan kitchen to mesmerise you and Tindo watching a football match in the lounge. The thought brings a smile to your face. 2004 promises to be a better year.

You're awoken from your daydream when the UK Border Force officer calls you forward. A bead of sweat forms on your brow and you pray your nervousness is not apparent.

"Passport please."

You hand over your passport, with the visa page open.

"Confirm your name."

"Takudzwa Hove."

"Why are you here?"

"To visit my fiancée, Michelle Nkomo."

"Where will you be staying?"

You parrot Michelle's off-campus address.

"How long have you and Michelle known each other?"

"Twelve years."

"Is she here, waiting for you?"

"Yes."

"What is her mobile number?"

You are exasperated by the officer's *silly* questions and unnecessary bureaucracy. You are certain the immigration officer already knows Michelle's number. *It is clearly stated on the invitation letter!* Making great effort to hide your frustration, you provide the mobile number which you memorised in anticipation of the interrogation.

The immigration officer reads something silently on his computer and calmly asks you to take a seat on the side. You are so confident that everything is in order, so you roost on a bench and impatiently wait to be released. A large digital wall clock confirms it is 6.30am. After an hour of sitting in silence, a different UK Border Force officer finally turns up and takes you to an interview room. You convince yourself that this is normal procedure, and that all is well. In the interview room, you find another immigration officer waiting for you with your suitcase. That seems strange; your heart begins to pound like it must escape your chest.

"Confirm your name please sir."

"Takudzwa Hove."

"Is this a genuine passport sir?"

"Yes it is."

"And are these bank statements real?"

"Yes they are."

"And is this your suitcase sir?"

"Yes it is." You respond with an air of annoyance. You wish the officer would stop calling you "sir". *It is patronising!*

"Has anybody other than you ever used it?"

"No."

The officer reaches for his portable scanner and scans a barcode. It is the barcode they stuck on your suitcase when they deported you eight months ago. The scanner reveals your real name, Kumbirai Gaza, and the immigration officer points it to your face.

"Who is Kumbirai Gaza, sir?"

You feel sick and without thinking blurt out, "my cousin". Within seconds, the other immigration officer walks over to you and shows you photocopies of your genuine passport and old visitor's visa to the UK.

"Is this you?"

"Yes."

"Sir, you signed visa application forms, and on those forms there is a declaration that tells you the consequences of making false representations. Before I make a decision, I need to refer the case to the entry clearance manager." Both officers disappear for half an hour. During that time, you engage God and all your ancestors, begging them to hear your entreaties. You sense the spirit of Adebiyi hovering over you like Casper the friendly ghost. He prays with you, demanding all sorts of ammunition from *Gaad in Jizos name.*

The tension you feel could explode your veins. You fleetingly wonder if you should attempt to escape, but the sight of butch police officers rambling around the airport with German shepherds quickly thwarts that idea. You see your officer returning, but you cannot read the decision on his face. You feel bloated as he begins to speak.

"Thank you for being patient sir. I have reached a decision." You shut your eyes momentarily and meditate one more prayer for clemency.

"I am denying you entry into the UK because of the forged documents you used for your application. You will be transferred to Brook House now, where you will await deportation to Harare. We have informed your family outside that they can meet you there this afternoon. Is that ok with you Mr. Gaza?"

***

One year later, you arrive at Harare International Airport.

## Tariro

It's 4pm on a Friday, two weeks before the last semester of my final year. The end of my journey at the Kent Law School beckons. My existence is plagued by a slight impatience, and I am fatigued emotionally, mentally and physically. I should be elated that the end is near, but a vestige of anxiety afflicts my soul. My incessant financial woes continue to irk me, plus I have a few more exams to write. I check-in to the campus library for a bout of last-minute revision. The noise in the student village on a Friday afternoon is unbearable regardless of the exams in progress. When I log into my student portal, I am faced with yet another email from the bursar, and I know exactly what they want.

> *Your tuition fee is in arrears of £3500 and if you do not pay in full by the end of this semester, you will not graduate with the class of 2000.*

Just then, I receive a text message.

| | |
|---|---|
| Landlord: | *Hello Tariro.*<br>*Will you be able to pay the rent for this month and clear your arrears from last month? Need it by Monday or I have no choice but to ask you to leave.* |
| Me: | *Yes. I'll deposit the full amount in your account by next Monday.*<br>*Can I just double check the total is £900?* |
| Landlord: | *Yes.* |
| Me: | *No problem.* |

Actually, this is a problem, because I am not sure where the money will come from. Most of my income comes from braiding the hair of black students and other professionals off campus, but the last few weeks have been quieter than usual.

Mhamha is a healthcare assistant at a nursing home, a job I detest because it dehumanises her. She is overworked and emotionally abused for doing her best. When it is not one of her colleagues trying to sabotage her hard work, it is her boss trying to downplay her efforts, so that she can never be awarded a pay rise and never have the confidence to leave for a better job. A few weeks ago, she was embarrassed in front of everyone at work for opening a new packet of incontinence pads when she could not find the one her boss had recently opened.

"A sick elderly patient exploded Tari, soiled all their immediate surroundings and desperately needed changing. I had to open a new packet of pads!" Mhamha had cried into the phone. Then they called her all sorts of names: cow, monkey, ape! *For a packet of pads?* That had been the last straw. When Mhamha called me, I had been watching TV and an advert for "no win no fee" litigation claims had just appeared. When I got off the phone with her, I immediately called the lawyers and explained Mhamha's situation. They took down her contact details and said they would get in touch with her.

Mhamha and I left Zimbabwe six years ago when my father died of AIDS. She ran successful businesses, but due to the failing economy, she could not sustain them on her own. Mhamha uses her meagre income to fund my tuition fees and she contributes towards my living expenses. She tells me not to worry, because together we can do it and she is "praying for a miracle". Afflicted by wobbly optimism, I wonder if I believe in miracles.

Later that evening, as I walk back to my room, I make a phone call to Moses to find out if he managed to sell the clothes I buy in bulk to resell. Moses is a philandering Zimbabwean socialite I met on a cleaning shift. Sometimes I clean offices on weekends to make ends meet. Moses is single and in his late 30s. He exudes the impression that he is doing much better than he actually is, a tedious lifestyle choice. During weekends, Moses hires expensive supercars to go clubbing, in order to attract the most beautiful women who would not ordinarily look at him twice. After Moses tried unsuccessfully to bed me, he offered to help me sell imitation designer clothing I bought a few months ago from a wholesaler in Turkey. He flogs them to the women he sleeps with.

"All the clothes were taken on credit and I'm doing my best to chase the arrears." He assures me, but I do not believe him. It always feels harder than it needs to be, chasing for debts. Sometimes I suspect that he was paid for the clothes, but he won't hand over the money so that he keeps our attachment intact. *A trauma bond I don't need right now!*

"I really need the money, Moses, or I'll be evicted next week."

"Don't worry I've got your back babes! Worst case scenario, you can move in with me. I promise I won't touch you." *Moses disgusts me!*

My maternal cousin Byron lives in Gweru. I sent him an assortment of ten Nokia and Motorola mobile phones that are scarce in Zimbabwe. He assured me that the phones would fly within a week because they are in high demand, so I am relying on him to make that imminent flight possible. Five of them are on contract and I am still paying for them. The other five I bought using money from hair braiding. My own phone is in serious disrepair, but I cannot afford the luxury of a brand-new mobile phone. After six weeks of silence, I decide to text Byron for an update.

Me: *Have the phones been bought sha?*

Byron: *I managed to sell 3. There is an issue with 4 of them.*
*Some guy came to buy them with a cheque.*
*But the bank is saying the cheque is fake*
*and we cannot trace the buyer.*
*Sorry sha. I still have the other 3.*
*Pastor Manu from my church says he wants 1.*
*And our neighbours want the other 2.*

My heart shatters and I fail to respond. Mhamha will counsel me to forgive and forget. She says it is the best way to maintain peace between her and her sister, Mainini, who always seems to overstep our boundaries. Mainini was told by *mapostori* in Zimbabwe that all her luck went to Mhamha who "uses dark powers to obtain that luck". Mainini and her children feel entitled to our property as a result. We succumb to any offences they toss our way, when they wrong us and don't take responsibility for their actions. *It is exhausting!*

On Saturday afternoon, my regular client, Lizi, texts and says she needs an urgent hairdo. I thank the heavens and confirm I will see her tomorrow. I text Moses and blackmail him into ferrying me to Lizi's house.

"If only I had the money you owe me, I would call a taxi." He confirms he will pick me up at 8am.

I have two exams next week and a final paper the week after. I push my worries to the back of my head and begin to revise. *Just in case I fail to make the time later in the week!* Two other clients have already booked me for Monday and Tuesday.

**Sunday**

At 8am sharp, an obsidian black Mercedes S-class parks in the car park beneath my window. The cooing and whistling by the young students outside makes me peep through the window. I catch a glimpse of Moses getting out of his transitory vehicle, and like a peacock he radiates magnificent offence to other men. The girls, like peahens, are drawn in to take a closer look. He is wearing an oversized brilliant-white cotton tracksuit with the letters FUBU strategically embossed in red velvet throughout the attire. Matching FILA trainers and a red velvet cap accessorise his outfit. A pair of multicoloured flat top shield designer sunglasses sit awkwardly on his tiny face, and I think he looks obnoxious. By the time I arrive at his car, he has already given out his phone number to a few 'chicks'.

"*Ndeipi*. Nice ride."

"*Ndeipi sha*, I was out with my crew last night. You know how I roll!" Moses chuckles then licks his lips as he eyes me up and down. "You look edible, as usual," he adds.

"Oh save it Moses!" He enters Lizi's address that I text him the previous day into a gadget I've not seen before. It begins to instruct him on how we will get to the address.

"Sha you can't tell me that you're not turned on even a tiny bit by this car. Ha, what do you think?"

"Are you telling me there are women who would sleep with you because of the cars you drive?" He laughs uncontrollably then is perplexed when I tell him, "Cars don't fascinate me much. My father had plenty of nice ones and I grew up riding them. I am more interested in what's inside that chest and that mind, thank you very much! I'm intrigued by that machine though. What's it called?"

"Oh, that's a satnav! Stands for satellite navigation. You've not seen one of these before?" Moses responds excitedly, because finally there is something about him I find interesting. I roll my eyes, a presage to tame his excitement. He quickly resigns his quest then discusses his favourite African music instead. I confirm I love *Loi* by Koffi Oloide and *Etat Major* by Extra Musica. He inserts a *Kwaito* CD from South Africa, which I listen to with interest. "That's Mandoza...that's Mzekezeke...this is still underground stuff Tariro, but it's gonna blow up!" he interjects as each song begins to play. Sometimes Moses works as a DJ at his favourite nightclub. I am fascinated by some of the music and he says I should come out with him sometime.

"Ha, I can just imagine *matako ako* clapping to *Ndombolo* in Club 19! Mmmm that backside of yours! When are we going out?" Moses grins and jolts twice in his seat as if the thought of my 'backside' sends electric shock waves down his spine. Clenching the steering wheel and stretching out his arms in the most exaggerated fashion, he presses his back firmly into his seat, squeezing his thighs together as if he has an ant in his pants, then peeks at me for a reaction.

"Never!" I respond coolly to bring the conversation to an abrupt end before he gets silly ideas. "I'll text you when I'm done so you can take me back to campus." I add as Moses pulls into Lizi's driveway.

"No worries babes. See you later!"

Liziuzayani is a Malawian religious extremist in her early fifties. She always narrates the most bizarre stories about herself or someone she knows in a concoction of English and Nyanja. I probably miss a lot of essential detail, but there's always enough English to ensure my comprehension. Lizi was trafficked to the UK three decades ago and only managed to liberate herself when she married Dereck, now a retired English man who goes on two-week-long fishing trips every month. From what I gather, Lizi is a glorified housekeeper who now has the luxury to work shifts at local farms only when she wants to.

The last time I braided Lizi's hair she was devastated because the pastor of a Pentecostal church she was attending in London had fled to Nigeria. She had taken out a £20,000 loan after some coercion by the church leader to help build a new place of worship, "in exchange for a high position next to God in heaven". With this pastor out of the picture, her ambitions were doomed. She also had a lot of explaining to do to Dereck.

When Moses pulls into the driveway, Lizi runs out to greet me with the excitement of a mother who has not seen her child in a long very long time.

"*Moni* Tariro my *dhiya*! *Muli bwanji?* She greets me in Nyanja.

"*Ndili bwino. Kaya inu?*" I respond that I am well if she is, as she taught me.

She leads me into her very retro home, full of old things scattered everywhere, most of which belong to Dereck. After exchanging pleasantries, we head over to the guest bedroom and settle into our hairdo, and Lizi launches into the predictable lamentations of her life.

"Guess what, I found a new church that is solving all my problems."

*Oh, here we go!* "Really? Tell me about it, Lizi."

"Of course, I will tell you. That is why my father named me Liziuzayani!" She pauses as if to gather her thoughts then continues. "So, I don't know if I told you, that each time Dereck is away on his fishing trips, something strange happens to me. It all started when my underwear mysteriously vanished from the hanging line outside where they were drying. Only a few months ago my *dhiya*! It happened when I heard that my brother back home, Kapeni, had been visiting witchdoctors to bewitch me. *Ha*, those people back home are so jealous! After all I've done for him. I pay school fees for his five children and I send him money for food."

"Oh that's terrible! Are you sure your own brother would do that to you?"

"Oh yes! Are you not African?"

"What does he stand to gain by doing that? If he is indeed bewitching you, you could get too sick to provide for him and his children, so it doesn't make sense…"

"Nothing makes sense where I come from. Anyway, since the disappearance of my panties, I've been experiencing a strange thing, for months now. A baboon jumps out of my wardrobe and gives me sex!" She says, seemingly horrified by the words coming out of her own mouth.

"What? A real baboon! Here in England?"

"Yes! It happens every night as long as my *mzungu* is not here." Dereck is her *mzungu*, which means 'white person'. I pause for a while, trying to comprehend her story, holding back an outburst of laughter because her peculiar tale sounds almost comical, but Lizi looks too serious to discount, and I am gradually overwhelmed with compassion as she carries on. I refrain from rebuking her claims and probe her further instead.

"So you are being raped by a baboon?"

"*Iyayi,* it is not rape. Pastor Fashana says it's a spiritual thing… which he is treating."

"A spiritual thing? How does he treat it?"

"He comes here to sleep over when *mzungu* is away. He puts me in a trance and I sleep peacefully until the next morning."

"Oh! So what does he do while you're sleeping?"

"I'm not sure. All I know is I am covered in thick liquid between my legs that I must wash off in the morning. I think it is the liquid that keeps the baboon away."

"Does Dereck know about this?"

"Oh, why would I tell him something like that? He already thinks us Africans are mad animals! Why should I give him ammunition to look down on me worse worse? Ah, nooo!"

*Fascinating!* Too perplexed to offer any meaningful help, I allow Lizi to ramble on to her heart's content, and my mind wanders off for what feels like hours. I create minute partings of her hair and attach to it small strands of dark brown curly synthetic fibres. The electric movement of my wrists drives the interlocking process my fingers have become so accustomed to. It is to me like a driver who climbs into their car and unconsciously arrives at their destination with no memory of how they got there. The agility and precision with which I complete the task always mesmerises my clients. Hair braiding is my passion and my clients feel my energy, through my hands and into their hearts.

We take a break at lunchtime because Lizi insists I must eat something for energy. She prepared *kondowde* with stewed sea bream before I arrived. We heat up our food in the kitchen then make our way to the lounge where Lizi prefers to eat. As we tuck into our meal, Lizi narrates how she found a shop that sells ground cassava flour in Brixton near her new church.

"I will never understand why you would go all the way to London for church. Can you not find local churches here in Kent?"

"*Sindikufuna* these *azungu* churches. They do nothing for me because they don't perform miracles! Besides, when I go to London I have the opportunity to buy foods from Malawi and hair extensions."

"Ah, that makes sense! It's always nice to have a change of scene as well." I concur.

She goes on to tell me how lucky she is that meat is always abundant in her home because of Dereck. He brings loads of fish when he returns from his fishing trips.

Dereck has grown-up children whose photographs are scattered around the house. The pictures of his first three white wives are on the mantel over the outdated electric fireplace. Lizi has one grown-up son from childhood rape, Thomas, now in his late thirties, and is in and out of prison for various reasons. Lizi does not like to talk about him. There is only one tiny childhood photograph of Thomas, remotely tucked away behind the other family pictures. Lizi has only pulled it out once to show me, the one time I had perfunctorily asked if she had any children.

After our meal, we return to the guest bedroom and Lizi serves me more bizarre stories all afternoon, and before I know it, my task is complete.

Before I leave, Lizi feeds me again, this time with chicken curry served with fragrant Malawi white rice, *mtedza* and *kachumbari.* She seems to have saucepans of cooked food sitting on her cooker every time I visit to braid her hair. *Coming from a place of lack can breed unhealthy attachments with food when money becomes abundant*, I muse while I wait for Moses to come and pick me up. I'm grateful for the delectable meal, because it means I do not need to worry about food when I return to campus. Lizi pays me £70 for the microbraids, then hands me Tupperware filled with more food from her buffet. She sees me out and jokes that I must have a rich boyfriend who drives a nice car.

"Oh, he's not mine Lizi. I am waiting for the one back home and he is waiting for me too." I tell everyone that I have a boyfriend back home so that they do not give me a hard time for being single. I am uninterested in men and the heartbreaks affiliated with their presence in women's lives. Being single has helped me to focus on my studies and I rather like it that way.

"Eh! It's good to be hopeful my daughter." As she waves me goodbye, an expression of chronic loneliness quickly envelops her face. "*Zikomo achimwene,* thank you my friend," she continues to wave as Moses and I drive off.

When I return to my room on campus, it is 6pm and I feel exhausted. I enjoy a hot shower then nap for four hours before waking up to tackle a revision marathon.

**Monday**

My client, June, is a Zimbabwean woman in her mid-forties and is a student nurse at a local technical college. I braid her hair every other month and we have a short pre-booked appointment to touch up her braids. I have already texted her to confirm it will cost £25 and that I will arrive at her place at 8am sharp by bus. June does not live very far from my university campus.

"*Zviri sei* Tariro?" she asks me how I am as she lets me in.

"I'm ok, but exam pressure *sha*. I'm writing a paper this afternoon, *saka mahwani ega ega*. It's tough."

"You're nearly there my dear, so don't stress. Shall I make you a cup of tea?" I accept the offer and she turns the kettle on, which is in full view as is everything else in June's bedsit. A tiny CD player on the windowsill softly plays Brenda Fassie's greatest hits. As *Vulindlela, Nomakanjani* and *Black president* play in turn, I am overwhelmed with nostalgia. I begin organising the hair extensions in preparation for my task. When June hands over my tea, I take a sip to lubricate my dry throat, then quickly undo two rows of untidy looking braids dotted around the entire circumference of her hairline. As I do so, she tells me about the money she has been sending back home to build a property she will move into when she returns. June fishes out a Kodak envelope from her black faux leather handbag. It contains printed photographs of her project, which her mother manages. She narrates the journey of building her future home in Chitungwiza, taking her time to explain the obstacles she has faced along the way.

"Sometimes even if the money is there, the cement is scarce or even the bricks at times. And what tends to happen is when I've sent the money and we're looking for the materials, a crisis always arises and that money is spent to fire-fight the problem. Sometimes I feel stuck in this cycle, and it's worse for us singletons. *Nyaya yekushaya varume iyi vasikana!* This issue of not having a husband, my sister!" She lets out a cackle then proudly says, "But I think I wouldn't have it any other way, because men can be a nuisance."

June goes on to narrate the latest local scandals of cheating husbands.

"Did you hear that Jacob left his wife of 20 years for a kid at your university. I don't know what it is with these men and wanting to feel younger. We all saw how hard Susan worked when she arrived here, washing old people's bottoms until she brought Jacob and their four kids here. And you know when he arrived he refused to do any menial work, saying he was a headmaster in Zimbabwe, so she looked after them on her own. Until he finished his degrees. And now that he is lecturing there, he is just changing those little girls like underwear. Rumour has it that he's actually sick, but he sleeps with them anyway. There are rumours that he has a few children out there that he refuses to acknowledge. But *haaa*, this latest one is a real shocker. Moving out of the marital home for *chanana ichocho*, that small baby!" I express shock at the story, but deep down I am not surprised because these sort of stories are not new. They existed back home and they followed us overseas. June quickly turns to talk about her own sister's husband.

"*Fanika* that Patrick. Mmmmm *umuchenjerere!* Be careful of him. I heard you're going to braid July's hair tomorrow?"

"Yes I am."

June and July are identical twin sisters. I also braid July's hair on a regular basis. June loves to tell me a lot of personal things about her sister and husband, which I find uncomfortable but unsurprising, because most of my clients offload their issues onto me when I place my hands on their hair. It makes me wonder whether that could be my claim to miracles, albeit inadvertent; a unique superpower to make people open up through touch.

It takes me a little over three hours to complete the job and June pays me £30. I thank her profusely for the tip, "*Unondigonera veduve*, you're so good to me!" She walks me to the bus stop just outside her block of flats and wishes me good luck for my exams.

I arrive on campus around noon, buy a portion of chips and an energy drink from the students union, then head to my room swiftly to collect my stationery. I subsequently head off to the examination hall to write a three-hour paper on the law of Tort. My aching wrists manage to churn out numerous words, reason, analysis, with the aid of my mind which spits out memorised legal precedents and theories examining differing philosophies of justice for negligence. There is never a moment to breathe or stop to scratch my head, which feels fried by the time the invigilator calmly announces, "Time's up, put your pens down."

After the exam, I am too exhausted to think about food so I gale straight to my room, shower and sleep until the next morning.

**Tuesday**

When June told me about July, she said her sister was a lovely but "very angry black woman", because her husband had infected her with HIV. "She has rollercoaster moods, my poor sister. But once you get used to her, you will love her!"

I've been to July's house thrice, and I find her outspokenness intriguing. She is hefty and much taller than her husband, which I find interesting. She picks me up from the railway station in her BMW X5 each time and takes the coastal route to her new-built home in a concrete jungle. She loves to drive over the speed limit and tell me about her fascinating past. "*Vele* we were very well known in Bulawayo. We had things, *yho*! Everyone knew our house *nje*!" She says in a Shona accent. I wonder if her opening and closing Ndebele interpolations were an underhand way of convincing her Ndebele friends that she was not a tribalist.

"*Vele* my kids were going to Petra and that's why they go to private school here. Patrick earns so much money, at least I don't have to work." I respond to her baroque narrations with a "wow" each time.

"You should teach me isiNdebele sometime July. We never had the opportunity to learn it in Masvingo." I said to her one time.

"*Eish* I can't really speak it, *wena*!"

"How come? I thought you lived in Bulawayo?" She swiftly changed the subject without providing a convincing answer. I found her Ndebele insertions more amusing after that.

I am sitting on the train on my way to July's, enjoying a pot of strawberry compote corner yoghurt. An unusual treat. My intuition is trying to tell me something, but I cannot hear it. I am wondering what surprises July has in store for me. The last time I braided her hair, I had been wearing slim fitted chinos and a long-sleeved polo-neck. I tend to cover up well when I braid clients with husbands. Despite my effort to look boring, July shocked me with a confession when she drove me back to the railway station last time.

"You know what Tariro, I find you very intimidating, *haibo*."

"What? Why?"

"It's your hips and breasts *nje*. Your shape is too much and I think Patrick likes it."

"Oh!" Was all I managed to say.

"Next time you come to do my hair, just wear something looser than that, *wena*."

"Ok."

"Yeah, that's why I like you. *Vele*, you understand me." She chuckled then put the radio volume up. She knew all the words to the Bongo Maffin and Mafikizolo tracks playing.

When she picks me up, we discuss the hairstyle she wants this time.

"I think we should do cornrows in front and singles at the back, *vele*! Medium sized ones. How much will that be?"

"Just £50 for you."

"No problem!" She stops at a cash machine and withdraws some money.

We arrive at July's large home in the property development which sticks out like a sore thumb relative to the archaic Victorian landscape. Patrick is doing some DIY and gardening. He has been installing lavish modern garden lights at the front of the property. I smell fresh paint and notice he has been touching up the sage green Durawall paint. The work is done in good faith, but exacerbates the peculiarity of the modern residence in such a historic British tourist town. I suspect that it is Patrick's day off and he is doing these jobs to avoid being in the house with July. I greet Patrick as we walk past him and he offers a cursory response, avoiding eye contact. I understand his predicament and do not speak to him again.

I begin preparing the synthetic blonde hair extensions as July fixes a quick afternoon meal for her two overweight children. Two boys aged ten and eight. She places a pepperoni and Hawaiian pizza in the oven. Almost as an afterthought, she adds a tray of chicken kievs, garlic bread and oven chips as sides to the buffet. Her kids are instructed to finish their food and they do so with ease. I am offered to join the racket, but I politely decline as eating will only delay me. I also generally do not like eating at my clients' houses because they sometimes use that as a bargaining tool when it is time to settle their bill. July would not do that though, because she likes the world to know that she has money. She would never negotiate my prices down.

When the faffing about is done, I finally begin to braid her hair. July sits on a dining chair that she has moved into the lounge so that she can watch her favourite catch up television shows. It is a warm summer afternoon, and the large patio doors leading to her back garden are open, letting in just enough air to keep me from fainting. Wearing a polyester maxi skirt and an oversized dashiki top, I look like I have just come from a backward African funeral, *kunhamo*.

I occasionally catch a glimpse of laughing seagulls hovering in the cloudless turquoise sky. They remind me that the sea is not very far away, and I vicariously enjoy their freedom to roam the sky without a worry about what tomorrow holds. I begin to feel sticky between my legs and look forward to completing the task. I'm only halfway through when July asks to be excused. I assume she has gone to use the bathroom and I take the opportunity to sit on her chair and rest my legs.

July waltzes back downstairs and I descry her figure when she swings into the kitchen to pour us cold drinks. *Do my eyes deceive me, could I be dreaming, or is she actually naked?*

"Lemonade, Fanta or Coke? Ice or no ice?" She yells from the kitchen.

"Coke with ice!" Patrick responds before I do.

"Lemonade with ice please." I add after Patrick.

She enters the room and walks past me to serve Patrick his drink at the front door. With only a tank top on and no underwear, July calmly announces she's too hot. Her dimpled buttocks flip flop as she casually floats around her house, and I'm not sure how to react. Her husband and sons do not respond to the anomaly, perhaps it is a sight they have become accustomed to. When she returns to the lounge and walks towards me, I briefly notice her Brazilian wax and look away. I can smell cognac in her drink and sense a scene brewing up.

July cackles just like June, then comments on celebrity scandals on television. She acts as if there is nothing awkward about her performance and I wonder to myself how far she will take her liberalism today. July begins to flip between television channels until she arrives at one where she has to enter a pin number and make a payment. As soon as she does, a naked threesome emerges on the screen; a man with two women. One woman is heartily tickling the man's phallus while the other straddles his face. The man devours the second woman's vulva and cups her breasts. The women never seem to fight over him and appear to find each other more attractive. They occasionally abandon him to play with each other, like cute mischievous kittens. They look into each other's eyes lovingly and purr as they nibble each other's sacred bits. The man attempts to detangle them by smacking their buttocks with one hand, while brandishing his member with the other.

"Do you watch these types, *nje*?" July queries unreservedly.

"Not really." I mumble, unsure what she is expecting me to say. I suddenly feel another wave of moisture between my legs that I cannot control or account for. *Is it coming from the aching aperture I have been preserving for the love of my life? Or is it the summer temperature that has suddenly risen?*

In that moment, Patrick saunters in with his left hand resting on his waist and the right clenching his drink. For the first time in the time I have known him, he chortles uncontrollably like a child experiencing a sugar rush. In between swigs of his drink, he casually announces, "We should try that sometime!"

Too shocked to respond, I focus on July's head and avoid the television screen. July screams in delight and offers a running commentary of what is plain to see, to Patrick who is now perched on a sofa across from us. He squints his eyes and shoots a piercing gaze at me. The one time I make the mistake of looking in his direction, he winks and licks his upper lip. *Gross!* I begin to double the hair partings, *kubhanzura*, so that I finish the job and leave before things get out of control. Patrick takes large quaffs of his drink and returns to the kitchen several times to top up his glass. Like a German supercar, he goes from zero to sixty miles per hour in what feels like three seconds. I can see him pouring unmeasured amounts of cognac into his and her coke. When he returns, he comments on the size of the actor's penis.

"Ah, *kasondhla ako*! You can't compare that *mopane* worm to my *mandingo* warrior! You can't even fit mine in your mouth." Patrick growls in self-indulgent zeal. *Yuck!* Only a few moments later, he abruptly passes out on the sofa and I let out a sigh of relief. Patrick is short and stout, and his inflated stomach clumsily spills out of his t-shirt. His tight fit shorts show no sign of a warrior.

"*Nxa*, useless man, *bakithi*!" July mutters under her breath then turns off the television. I eventually finish the braiding, then gladly announce that I am done. After checking herself over in the large mirror hanging in the lounge, she decides she is too drunk to drive me back to the railway station. She calls a taxi then gives me £80. I offer her copious appreciation for the tip then leave shortly thereafter.

About an hour later, I sit on the train and play back the drama at July's house in my head. The whiff of desire diffuses slowly, leaving my warm body as it permeates the cooler atmosphere in the air-conditioned train carriage. As I settle on the train and drift into a snooze, I receive a text message.

Nokuthula: *Hey, Thandi needs her hair done ASAP.*
*Can you come over this week?*

*I'll pay for your train fare etc.*
*You could sleep over and we'll have wine and girly chat after.*
*Let me know x*

Nokuthula is a well-off, well-travelled South African expatriate who lives in Guildford, only one railway station stop away from Mhamha in Woking. She has everything any woman in her early 40s could ever wish for. A great career, mansion with several unnecessary rooms in an affluent neighbourhood, a wealthy Angolan husband and a super intelligent daughter. I admire her and sometimes she intrudes my thoughts, but I do not question it. I get flashbacks of her beautiful smile, gentle eyes and her concoction of accents when she patiently explains foreign concepts to me. My thoughts of her are accompanied by an earworm, a Zimbabwean classic song from the mid-1980s by The Four Brothers, *Vimbai*:

> "*Ndiye mwana uye wandaireva, ndiye mwana uye wandaitaura. Vimbai mwana akanaka. Mwanasikana chichekererwa seshereni. Chitora moyo pakaperera shungu dzaMwari. Ndiye akatora moyo kwete wangu ndega. Tiri vazhinji vanomurumbidza. Meso akapfekedzwa tsitsi nengoni.*
> She is the girl I meant, she is the one I was telling you about. Vimbai is a beautiful girl. Baby girl is finely shaped like a shilling coin. A heart snatcher and God's masterpiece. She stole my heart and not just mine. There are many of us who praise her. Her eyes reflect kindness and tenderness."

*Vimbai* is still playing in my head when I text her back.

Me: *Yes, I can do Thursday if that works for you.*
Nokuthula: *Fab! Let me know when to pick you up. X*

I text Mhamha to announce I'm arriving on Friday night to spend the weekend at hers. When I get to campus, I find a note in my room slipped under the door. It is from Deziri, my Nigerian friend who is on the same Law course as me.

"I need my hair done tomorrow, where are you? Text me and let me know *sha*." I decide against texting her because I need a break before I travel to Surrey. Plus I need to work on my outstanding Equity and Trusts assignment. *Dull!* Besides, Deziri is notorious for complaining that my braiding is either too tight or too loose. *Anything to dodge paying me in full or on time. She is so stingy she can't even text me.*

**Wednesday**
It's around 9am, and I am lying in after a long night of studying. The morning news channel is showing on my small television screen when I hear Deziri stomping her feet up the stairs and speaking pidgin on her mobile phone, headed towards my room.

"Oh for fucks' sake!" I murmur under my breath. She attempts to open my door without knocking, but thank heavens I remembered to lock it. *Who on earth does she think she is*, I cogitate as I wrap around my gown and undo the latch.

"Hey!" I exclaim in feigned excitement.

"*Ah ah*, what are you still doing in your pyjamas? Fine fine African girl, did your mother not teach you well o?"

"I'm tired *sha*. I had a client all day yesterday then had to complete the Tort assignment last night."

"I see now. *Eh eh*! Why do you still have this rubbish tv now?" Deziri is not the first person to mock my cube retro analogue television set, which my own people call *tv yegotsi*. In the wake of flat screen plasma televisions, I couldn't care less about the ever-progressing technology, and am content with my vintage looking basic necessity. Banging on it occasionally when it makes static sounds is a nostalgic exercise I do not mind partaking.

"I love my tv *sha*. Leave it alone."

"So do you have extensions?"

"Some. But I can only do cornrows because I need to study today. I'm writing my second last paper tomorrow."

"Ok, let's do it. Are the extensions black? Number 1B?" When I affirm her desired extensions are in stock, I begin working on her hair. Deziri is an Igbo woman whose age I cannot guess. We discuss tribalism between the Hausa and the Yoruba, and she claims the Igbo are not so bad.

"Have you eaten? I'm hungry *sha*. Do you have food?"

"No, I'm fasting. I have cereal though."

"*Chineke*! I don't eat those processed things full of sugar and God knows what else. Do you ever cook Tariro? You need to eat proper African food my sister. When you're so far away from home, it is the food from back home that will keep you grounded now. Next time you come to mine, I will make you pounded yam and *ofe owerri*. In fact, I'm going to London to buy fresh ingredients this weekend, so I will let you know when I've cooked it."

"I don't have the time or budget to do better Deziri. You're making me feel hungry now. I had *Amala* and *Ewedu* soup a couple of months ago. It was delicious! Unforgettable. A client of mine had cooked it when I went to braid her hair and I simply could not refuse it. "

"Oh, is she Yoruba?"

"I have no idea. I just love all Nigerian food. I miss *jollof* rice...*egusi* soup..."

"You need to try my *ofe owerri*. You'll never want to eat anything else."

"How do you make it?"

"I can't share my secret recipe now, but it's made with assorted meats and four different vegetable leaves, *ugu, uziza, okazi* and *oha*. The meats can be beef, goat meat, cow legs, snail..."

"Snails! Count me out!" We burst out laughing and Deziri assures me I would love the dish."

"We have a slightly similar dish in Zimbabwe which we call *High-firidzi*, although we just mix fried beef chunks with rape or covo greens. It's not as elaborate as your *ofe owerri*. We eat ours with *sadza*, ground mealie meal thick porridge. I'm going to visit my mother this weekend and I hope she cooks something from back home."

"Ah, it is well my sister. Tell me, what does your name mean?"

"Tariro. It means 'hope'."

"I like it! We must be hopeful and trust in God *o*!" She says as she whips out her bible from her handbag and reads Hebrews 11 vs 1, 'Now faith is assurance of things hoped for, a conviction not seen.' Very similar meaning to my name actually." She shuts her Bible in an animated manner and proudly returns it into her bag.

"What does yours mean?"

"Chideziri. It means 'God wrote my story well' *o*. Or 'God plans'."

"Oh, that's beautiful!" I exclaim as my mind momentarily wanders back to my hope for a miracle.

"So what will you do after graduation Tariro? Any big plans?"

"I think it depends on how well I do. If I get a first or upper second class, then I will try for the Legal Practice Course and a training contract. If I don't do so well, marriage and children is my alternative, I guess. How about you?"

"I'm definitely going back home. I'm not sure yet what I'll do when I get there, but a man is not part of the plan. My forty years in this world have been stress-free because they have not revolved around those animals with things dangling between their legs. I will die a virgin *o*!" She concludes her assertion with a single loud clap and kisses her teeth, *mschew*.

We lapse into a deeper discussion around societal expectations of women and how Deziri is considered a radical because she is a non-conformist. I secretly admire her and am shocked that a woman who is not a Catholic nun might voluntarily choose to "die a virgin."

"I certainly won't be returning home, because there just aren't career opportunities for me there right now. Although I'm conflicted, because the love of my life is there and he may never come to join me here. Sometimes I wonder whether I should let him go," I cogitate loudly without an ounce of guilt.

"What is meant for you is meant for you my *sisto*. If he is yours, time will tell o. For now, prepare yourself for life in corporate UK with these their old boys club." Deziri advises sceptically, with the corners of her mouth turned down.

"Yes, I hear you have to be someone's child to even dream of getting your foot in the door, unless you're super-brainy of course."

"Ah, you see them here in cliques on campus. Their grandparents went to private schools together, and so did their parents. Whether they do well or not, they already have jobs. They are just here to while up time with us o! That's why I would rather go back home to claim my portion. This problem is everywhere!"

Before we know it, Deziri's hair is done. We haggle on the price for a few minutes and she ends up paying £30 for just the cornrows. She does not like the brand of hair extensions I used, so she will not pay for them. Unsurprised by my friend's attitude and grateful for the money, I let it go and see her out.

"Don't forget to give me a shout when you cook *ofe owerri* soup!" I shout after her.

I go over my Tort assignment, again, then take a stroll to the Law school building to submit it before the 3pm cut-off. I spend the rest of the day revising for my European Law exam.

**Thursday**

I arrive at the examination hall at exactly 8.30am, feeling lively, energetic and hopeful. European Law is one of the few modules I enjoy and I know I will do well. When the invigilator asks us to "Turn our answer sheets over and begin" at 9am, my aching wrists pelt out words explaining the history of the European Union, its institutions and the constitutional issues arising from the supremacy of European law from a UK sovereignty perspective. Before I know it, and oblivious to my mental endurance, the invigilator offers the usual final announcement at 12noon, "Time is up. Put your pens down." I leave the exam room mind boggled but excited to travel to Surrey. I return to my room to pack my bags and immediately leave campus for the railway station. At 3pm, as I wait on the platform for the approaching train, I quickly text Noku.

| | |
|---|---|
| Me: | *My train arrives at 5.45pm* |
| Nokuthula: | *No worries honey. See you soon X* |

Once I get comfortable on the train I decide to hound Moses for my money, but I am not hopeful.

| | |
|---|---|
| Me: | *Ndeipi. How far nemari yangu sha?* |
| | *Hi. Do you have an update on my money please?* |
| Moses: | *Hey babes! Gimme your account details.* |

I am delightfully shocked by the response, but am annoyed that I have to give Moses my bank details again. *What is it with people who owe you money – they always make it extra difficult for you to get it back?* When I send him my bank details, he transfers £300 into my bank account immediately, which is a third of the money he owes me, but I am grateful for the respite.

When I arrive at the Guildford railway station, Noku ferries me to her mansion in a red Porsche 911.

"So how are you sweetie? It's been ages!"

"I'm okay Noku. The last few months have been really tough though."

"How so?" She asks, gently placing her hand on my thigh. It feels a little awkward, then I quickly blame the discomfort on my overactive imagination.

"You know my degree is coming to an end now, so I'm writing my finals. I wrote a paper this morning actually. And I have one more to go on Thursday next week, thank goodness for that!"

"And what are your plans after graduation?"

"I'm not sure. It would be great to get some work experience, but I don't really know how to go about it."

"Oh, I'm sure I can sort out a three-month gig for you in my office." Noku works for a large oil and gas corporation as a Director of Legal and Compliance. I don't really understand what her role entails, but it sounds extremely important when she narrates the drama in the Boardroom with the middle-aged white men she always manages to shut down.

"Oh my goodness, that would be amazing!" I scream unable to contain my excitement. "I would really, really love that!"

"Good, I'll text you my email address. Get your CV over to me asap and I'll get the ball rolling."

When we get to her home, it is early evening and her husband is already home, cooking. Adam is tall, dark, handsome and very humble and respectful. He seems thorough and purposeful in everything he does, including the way stirs the food he is cooking, and the way he blinks first before chewing it deliberately when he tastes it.

I am always mesmerised by Noku's palatial home. The high ceilings, French limestone flooring in the vast entrance hall where a colossal, aged-stone Moai head fountain sits in the centre, gently oozing crystal clear water in constant mesmerising trickles. The bamboo floors in the lounges, marble in the kitchen and bathrooms, and thick wool carpets in the individually designed bedrooms – all with underfloor heating. The gigantic oak framed cathedral bay windows and doors add to the charm and warmth of the atmosphere. Original abstract framed paintings and ornate carvings in varying dimensions, from all over the world, are dotted around in prominent positions, including Bhudda heads and others I do not recognise. It is all extremely far removed from what I am used to, but I like it and I take it all in like a child on their first day of school.

When Thandi sets the imposing carved French oak dining table, we sit together beneath a statement agate chandelier and enjoy a seafood pasta dish served with parmesan and rocket. Thandi and I praise Adam for his culinary skills and I am pleasantly surprised that a man can cook so well. I do not remember the last time I had such a delicious meal. Noku and I enjoy a glass of chardonnay with the food. Adam says he gave up drinking, so declines the wine. I cannot help but admire his graceful intent, in how he speaks and carries himself. Noku seems amused by Adam's mannerisms and suppresses a snort.

We discuss my degree, life on campus and how Noku and Adam would love their 14-year-old Thandi to do as well as I have done. Thandi attends a prestigious private school and has won numerous accolades. She does not speak much and when she does, she seems to have the intelligence of someone at least twenty years her senior. I rarely come across children like Thandi and cannot help admiring her.

"Daddy has just won a takeover bid of a big international company aunty! I'm so proud of him."

"Thanks honey, but that's not something aunty would be interested in." Adam blushes and humbly ends that conversation.

Noku suspends the bottle of chardonnay over my glass and I refuse a second helping in order to stay alert when I braid Thandi's hair. Adam bids us "goodnight" then disappears upstairs. We do not see him again the rest of the evening, and according to Thandi he is going to meditate then read the latest books from his spiritual guru. I begin braiding Thandi's hair and she does not seem particular about how I do it. A 60-inch flat screen television shows a news channel on very low volume, it seems pointless to have it on. Thandi is reading a serious-looking navy blue hardback. Noku is working on her laptop and occasionally clicks her tongue, shakes her head and swears about someone's unconscious incompetence, then peers over the machine and breaks the silence.

"How are you getting on ladies? Oh, Thandi you look so beautiful, you should see how amazing those braids look on you honey. Isn't aunty Tari just amazing?"

"I'm beautiful with or without the braids mum!"

"Yeah I know baby, but you hate keeping your hair tidy so..." Noku receives a call and abruptly leaves the room for a while.

"What are you reading, Thandi?" I resuscitate the conversation.

"It's The Bhagavad Gita."

"The what?"

"The Bhagavad Gita. Some say it's the eternal message of spiritual wisdom from ancient India. It's a Sanskrit epic in the Hindu tradition, in the form of dialogue between the warrior-prince Arjuna and the god Krishna. You should read it!" She loudly whispers in a wise intentional tone that reminds me of her father.

"I will! It sounds interesting!" I respond enthusiastically, wondering when I would ever find the time to read something so foreign and far-removed from my reality.

"So aunty, have you thought about where your life is headed after university?" Thandi's question comes as a surprise.

"Good question Thandi. I guess it depends on how well I do in my exams. I would like a great career like your mum's, that's for sure."

"Mmm. Perhaps you need to define who you are first. Once you figure that out, your life purpose becomes clearer, and everything else falls into place."

"Wow, that's interesting!" I respond, unsure where this conversation is going. "Have you figured out who you are and what your life purpose is?"

"Yup. I'm a soul going through a temporary earthly experience. My life in this body is finite and I intend to be authentic and happy in all I do. That can only happen when I leave this prison though." Thandi is clearly disgruntled. "Know yourself first before getting married and having kids aunty. That way you can never become an extension of somebody else. It is better to live your own destiny imperfectly than to live an imitation of somebody else's life with perfection."

Before I express my amazement and ask Thandi to qualify her statements, Noku bounces back into the room and cheers me on.

"My goodness you're so fast. And those braids are so neat!"

Thandi seems to loosen up only in her parents' absence and returns into her shell as soon as Noku reappears. *Teenagers! Been there and done that.* By the time I finish Thandi's braids a few hours later, Noku has decided she will have her hair done too, if I have the energy. *I can't say "no" to the money.* So, when Thandi bids us "farewell" only Noku and I stay up in their spare lounge, chatting. I am on the sofa with my legs apart and her shoulders between them. She is on the carpet and occasionally squeezes my aching feet which have begun to swell.

"Oh you poor thing, you've been working so hard."

When I am about halfway through, Noku opens another bottle of wine and she offers me a drink again. I decide to take it and nurse it; it will probably give me the extra energy I need to see the job through.

"Adam can be a real dick sometimes." Noku's revelation comes as a bombshell.

"But he seems so lovely?"

"As he does when there are people around. Our marriage ended a long time ago for us and it feels like we stay together for Thandi. I just wish I could have more children."

"So why don't you?" There is prolonged silence as she pours a full glass of wine down her throat. "I guess your work commitments wouldn't really allow it, would they?" I answer myself with another question.

"No, I've had seven miscarriages. And each one just made us grow further and further apart. I think my inability to give him more children makes him cheat on me. He used to do it openly, but after giving him an ultimatum, he's a bit more respectful about it now. But I don't love him anymore." Noku swallows a hard ball of pain, and for the first time in the time I've known her, she sounds vulnerable. She seems tired of being in a situation she can get out of, but won't. The expression on her face shouts, "there is too much at stake".

"What a shame," is all I manage to offer, stunned that what seems like a perfect life is not happy after all. I am disappointed, because all along I had hoped to have a life like hers.

When I eventually finish braiding Noku's hair, it's already 4am and we have had a few more glasses of chardonnay. She shows me to the guest bedroom and where all the essentials are. The en-suite guestroom looks pure, with cream furnishings throughout. A giant pendent candelabra hangs from the ceiling and makes me feel like I'm in 5-star hotel. The luxurious marble bathroom with gold-plated fittings is obscenely delightful and to an extent unfathomable, given the tiny shower room I share with 5 other students on campus. She asks if I want the electric blanket on, and when I nod, she turns it on before she disappears. Keen to try the lavish toiletries and cosmetics on display in the bathroom, I decide to enjoy a hot shower before I sleep. When I am done exploring the skin caviars and scented oils, I step back into my room, moist and naked. I find Noku waiting for me, standing next to the bed with her silk robe on the floor, her shimmering body moist and naked. Her wide hips, flat stomach and full breasts look perfect.

"You are the most beautiful soul..." a whisper escapes Noku's full lips as she walks gently towards me and presses her body against mine. Her erect nipples tickle mine and the scent on her glowing skin is shockingly sensual. When her lips merge with mine, my mind is muddled by how my body responds. I am overpowered by her energy, her dominance and promises she might withdraw. *How dare I push back? I think I might like this!* My reciprocal kisses are tainted by doubt, but we find ourselves in bed a few minutes later, at first facing each other, kissing, her hands exploring my curves and feeling each goosebump of shocking desire. As she appreciates me like a priceless piece of art, Noku whispers avowals into my ear that make me feel wanted, needed, loved. And I give her soft gasps of pleasure in return. She peels herself off the bed and hovers over me.

"I have never done this befo..."

"Shhhhh...I know. Don't worry..." Noku whispers back with her forefinger placed on my lips. She kisses my lips again, then nibbles all the inches of my throbbing body with care and precision. I feel the pressure I have felt for many weeks evaporating from my tense being. Like flotsam, all my worries float away gently with each breath I take. My body, feeling lighter with each smooch, responds affirmatively and longs for hers. Remembering what I saw on July's television just the other day, I return her kisses with more certainty and probe her steamy nether regions. She parts my thunder thighs slowly, then takes the southern route to tip the velvet with her warm moist tongue. *This is obscenely delicious!* Within seconds, after attempting with all my might to hold on - gripping the sheets, clenching my jaw, tightening my core and curling my toes - I explode into a thousand modicums of bliss then collapse into deep sleep.

**Friday**

When I wake up around noon, there is an envelope on the bedside cabinet. The note inside it reads:

"Help yourself to breakfast and call a taxi when you're ready to go. Won't be back till this evening. I miss you already. X"

The envelope contains £500 and I am not sure whether to be grateful or offended.

I arrive in Woking around 3pm. At the railway station, I insert my ticket into the machine that swallows it, which marks the end of my journey. I cross the traffic lights and begin walking down the high street towards Boundary Road, all the while fighting the flashbacks of my encounter with Noku. *What was that? What does it mean? I'd rather not think about this!*

Crispen is in Weatherspoon pub watching football with other men. He is a bald, short and overweight married Zimbabwean man who will not give up pursuing me. He is on the dole – everyone knows this. He is also a serial cheater who beats up his wife. Everyone also talks about this.

"Hey! Hey! Wait!" he calls out to me. I walk faster and hope he gives up calling.

"Tari! *Iwe* Tariro!"

I walk even faster, crossing the side roads without checking for oncoming traffic. A taxi nearly runs over me and the Pakistani man driving it hurls profanities towards me. I am immune to such insults. *The Asians hate us blacks and treat us like we're inferior to them, yet we are all foreigners in the UK. To the whites in this country, we are all inferior. What makes them think they are less inferior than we are?*

"Hey! Could you not hear me calling you?" shouts Crispen who has finally caught up with me.

"No. What do you want?"

"The number you gave me last time is wrong. Can you give me your number again?"

"No. Why do you need it?"

"You know what Tariro, I love you. I dream about…"

"Dream about what? While you're lying next to your wife, you dream about what?"

"Me and you babes!"

"Get away Crispen. Your wife is pregnant! How can you have the capacity to accommodate other women in your life when your wife is carrying your child? You should be ashamed, man!"

"I'm serious, I love you. The only way I am able to sleep with my wife is I think of you first. On the night I got her pregnant, all I had to do was imagine you dancing to *Gate le coin* in Club Afrique. *Mazakwatira ayo!* The way you move those hips. And that waist of yours, ha ha! And your legs…"

"Argh! Stop, you pervert! I'm going to tell your wife if you don't stop."

"Do you think I care? She knows she's not special." I shoot a chastising eye at him and crimp my lips downward in disgust. "Don't act like you don't know us men. We are hunters, that's what we do!"

Crispen lives across the road from Mhamha's two bedroomed house, but he follows me until I arrive at the door. I let myself in using Mhamha's spare key and shut the door in Crispen's face. I drop my bag on a threadbare floral fabric sofa Mhamha bought for next to nothing at a local garage sale, then head to the kitchen to put the kettle on.  I turn the small LCD television on, scroll for something to watch and begin to unwind. I check Mhamha's recordings for interesting soaps and decide to binge watch Eastenders until she gets home. As the first *doosh doosh* ensues and I prepare to watch the next episode, the doorbell rings. I open the door and find Crispen's wife, Venus, standing in front of me.

"Hi *Mai* Vongai. How can I help you?"

"I saw you walking with *Baba* Vongai." *Oh shit! Here we go. She better not think I'm messing with that douchebag of hers!* "He says you braid hair very well and must do our daughter's hair before you return to university. Are you free today or tomorrow?"

"It depends. Do you want cornrows or single braids?"

"I think it will have to be cornrows because I don't have much money at the moment. I just sent money back home and Crispen, who is not working, won't stop drinking. What are your prices anyway? For a child?"

"I usually charge £25 for cornrows and £50 for medium size box-braids. £70 for long microbraids. It costs a bit more if I'm using my own extensions."

"Ok, that's reasonable." Venus says, scratching her head and looking indecisive.

"I'll do cornrows for £20 for the child. And I can do lovely singles for £40."

"Ok. Can you do big singles for £30?" I wouldn't usually agree but I pity her and accept her offer. "Do you have extensions?" I involuntarily roll my eyes because I know she won't pay extra for them. "Are you free now?" She asks with an air of desperation.

I look at the time and it's only 4pm. Mhamha is working a double shift at the nursing home and will only arrive home after 9pm. I decide that I might as well be productive and kill some time while I wait for her.

"Ok, let me get my stuff and I'll come with you." I grab my mobile phone, handbag and a couple of synthetic hair extension packets that I always travel with. We arrive in a dingy council flat which looks like a hoarder's lair. Crispen is watching football and causing a racket of jeering interjections.

"Go *bhora*!... Ah *pena*!... *Ko* ref, aaaagh!... Corner!... Offside!..." His bellowing noise makes me vow to never marry a football fanatic. "Ah, *hesi* Tariro!" He greets me with an impish smile. "See I got you a customer. Make my girl look pretty, hey." I want to tell him he has no right to make such righteous demands because he is not paying, but my eyes do the talking.

Five-year-old Vongai is quiet and beautiful, like her mother. I caress her hair softly to judge her tolerance for discomfort.

"*Hauthli kugwadziwa*? Are you not afraid of the pain?"

"*Aiwa. Ndoda kuchena*. No, I want to look pretty." Her response makes me smile. It is the response of one who lacks. A response which reminds me of life back home, where the braiding of hair was a luxury for children when I was growing up. We never took it for granted and always appreciated the privilege. We tolerated all sorts in the name of looking beautiful, including the straightening of our afro hair with red hot granite rocks straight from the fire. The risk of those stones slipping out of handlers' hands and falling onto our bare necks never crossed our minds. *Taida kuchena*. We wanted to look pretty.

I begin to part Vongai's hair and attach artificial fibres, one after the other in a continuous repetitive sequence. I immediately get lost in thought as I usually do, until I reach my destination.

"Would you like some tea?" Venus interrupts my reverie.

"Yes please. Not too much milk. One sugar. Please leave the tea bag in." Within minutes, my tea arrives with no accompaniment and atypically I muse, *she could have offered some biscuits!*

Two hours into it, I can see an end in sight. Vongai's head is small and I will soon be done. At around 7pm, my mobile phone beeps. It is a text message notification and I suspect it is from Mhamha instructing me to begin cooking. I pick up my phone and I was right to think it was her. The message brings much-needed delight and anticipation.

Mhamha: *They bought pizzas at work for the patients tonight, so don't cook.*

*I'll bring you some. I have some great news too! Will tell you later. X*

Me: *Yum! See you later X*

We rarely have good news. Wondering what it could be, I smile and put my phone back into my bag. Just then, I catch Crispen staring at me.

"Is it your boyfriend?"

"No."

"So why are you smiling?"

"*Hezvo!* Am I only allowed to smile when I get messages from men?"

"*Mai* Vongai!" Crispen bellows to his wife who is cooking in the kitchen.

"*Baba!*" She yelps as she scrambles to kneel before him.

"Go and get the notebook where we keep our phone numbers. Tariro is an excellent hairdresser and from now on she is the one who will braid Vongai's hair."

"Yes, that's a good idea!" Venus responds, then awkwardly bounces off to get the said notebook, trying to keep her balance as her oversized pregnant belly seems to weigh her down. "Give me your number Tariro." Before I open my mouth, Crispen says "I'll put it in my phone first to dial and check it's correct. It's very easy to miss a digit."

My stomach churns as I parrot the number to both, and Venus adds it enthusiastically to the notebook, as does Crispen to his mobile phone. A few seconds later, I receive a missed call from Crispen. Despite the triumphant look on his face, I remain stone cold and expressionless. When I complete the task, Venus pays me £30 and walks me out. As I saunter back to Mhamha's house, my mobile phone vibrates and I open the text message.

Unsaved number: *Haikona kutamba ne boiz dzekuMbare!*
*Don't mess around with boys from Mbare.*

Me: *Who's this?*

Unsaved number: *Crispen. Save my number.*

Me: *Futsek! Zidhoti!*
*Get away! You piece of shit!*

*Unsaved number:* *Ndokuda sha!*
*I love you!*

I turn off my phone and hope this nuisance goes away. When I get home, Mhamha awaits with an enormous smile on her face, beaming with pride and relief.

"You know the lawyers you contacted about the abuse at work? They contacted my boss. I have no idea what they said to him, but this afternoon he gave me this." She says, handing over a cheque.

*£5000!* We hug and kiss on both cheeks, and dance around in joy. At the back of my mind, I cannot help wondering how much Mhamha would have been awarded had her case gone to court. I nip the thought in the bud as I force myself to remain present and celebrate our miracle. We feast on the free pizza with cheap store brand lemonade.

"So how is my *mukuwasha?* Are you two still together?" Mhamha's enquiry is unexpected, but I have a well-rehearsed response for her.

"Oh, John is fine. We have actually been discussing taking things further. But the problem is the distance, and a visa. How can I get him here?" I feel slight guilt lying to Mhamha, but even she can't handle the embarrassment of a single daughter in her early twenties. *I have to do this to protect her*, I console myself.

"Ya, it's tough. It would be nice to speak with him one of these days. I would love to hear his voice."

"Mha-mha! Where have you ever seen that happening? You'll talk to him when he confirms that the cows are ready!" We burst into mischievous giggles and go to bed shortly thereafter.

Before I fall asleep, I ruminate over my brief conversation with Thandi. *It is better to live your own destiny imperfectly than to live an imitation of somebody else's life with perfection.*

I turn my mobile phone back on and read only two of the several text messages.

| | | |
|---|---|---|
| 1. | Nokuthula: | nokuthula.dingane@efficientoilandgas.com see you soon honey X |
| 2. | Moses: | Got the rest of your money babes. Call me! |

**Saturday**

Mhamha has taken a day off to spend the day with me, a very rare thing to happen. We walk into town to bank the cheque, and I update Mhamha on Byron and the mobile phones. Her response is predictable, "*Hazvina mhaka,* it doesn't matter. God will sort him out. Besides, we have money now, so leave it." Mhamha immediately transfers my outstanding tuition fees to the university to clear the debt. "I will pay your rent too Tariro."

"Oh Mhamha, thank you! But what will I do with all the money I made this week?"

"Buy yourself a beautiful graduation outfit and start organising your party! Perhaps you could go home to visit John this summer?" I offer a smile in response and *Vimbai* begins to play in my head.

Together, Mhamha and I window shop for potential graduation outfits and accessories. I do not worry about my examination results because failure is not an option. Later that afternoon, we end up *kwa*Atif on Boundary Road, on our way home. It is an international grocery store run by a Pakistani family where we stock up on mealie-meal, a variety of dried beans, spices and fresh vegetables. At the back of the store, a Halaal butchery offers skinless chicken thighs and breasts, lamb and goat meat. We buy a bit of everything and make our own version of *High-firidzi* when we get home. Another corner shop further down the road, *kwa*Khan sells alcohol. Mhamha uncharacteristically suggests that we buy a bottle of red wine.

That evening, we celebrate our little miracles and the brilliance of hope.

***

THE END

Ingram Content Group UK Ltd.
Milton Keynes UK
UKHW012321140323
418546UK00004B/72